"Tell me, Miss Dinwoody, would you like to know what I see when I look at you?"

"Yes," Eve blurted, and then winced because she knew well enough what men thought when they looked at her: *ordinary*, if they were charitable.

Plain if they were not.

"I see," Asa Makepeace said, his deep voice musing, "a woman afraid, but fighting her fears. A woman who carries herself like a queen. A woman who could rule us all, I suspect. But I also see a woman who has a deep curiosity. Who wants to feel but is worried—of herself? Of others?" He shook his head. "I'm not sure."

He leaned forward slowly, destroying his pose, and she had to fight herself not to scoot her chair away from him. "But I think she has a fire banked within her. Maybe it's only embers now, glowing in the dark, but if tinder were to be put to those embers..."

He grinned slowly. Dangerously. "Oh, what a conflagration that would be."

⌒⌒

"Hoyt's writing is almost too good to be true."
   —Lisa Kleypas, *New York Times* **bestselling author**

"There's an enchantment to Hoyt's stories that makes you believe in the magic of love."
   —*RT Book Reviews*

"4½ stars! Top Pick! *Darling Beast* is wondrous, magical, and joyous—a read to remember."
—RT Book Reviews

"A lovely book that I very much enjoyed reading. I love the Maiden Lane series and can't wait until the next book comes out!"
—BookBinge.com

Duke of Midnight

"Top Pick! A sensual tale of forbidden love...Plenty of action and intriguing mystery make this a page-turner."
—BookPage

"Richly drawn characters fill the pages of this emotionally charged mix of mystery and romance."
—Publishers Weekly

"4½ stars! Top Pick! There is enchantment in the Maiden Lane series, not just the fairy tales Hoyt infuses into the memorable romances, but the wonder of love combined with passion, unique plotlines, and unforgettable characters."
—RT Book Reviews

"I *loved* it. I loved Artemis. I loved Max, and I loved their story. I have enjoyed every Elizabeth Hoyt book I have read (and I have read most of them)."
—All About Romance (LikesBooks.com)

Lord of Darkness

"*Lord of Darkness* illuminates Hoyt's boundless imagination...readers will adore this story."
—RT Book Reviews

"Hoyt's writing is imbued with great depth of emotion... heartbreaking...an edgy tension-filled plot."
—Publishers Weekly

"*Lord of Darkness* is classic Elizabeth Hoyt, meaning it's unique, engaging, and leaves readers on the edge of their seats...an incredible addition to the fantastic Maiden Lane series. I Joyfully Recommend Godric and Megs's tale, for it's an amazing, well-crafted story with an intriguing plot and a lovely, touching romance...simply enchanting!"
—JoyfullyReviewed.com

"I adore the Maiden Lane series, and this fifth book is a very welcome addition to the series...[It's] sexy and sweet all at the same time...This can be read as a stand-alone, but I adore each book in this series and encourage you to start from the beginning."
—USA Today's Happy Ever After blog

"Beautifully written...a truly fine piece of storytelling and a novel that deserves to be read and enjoyed."
—TheBookBinge.com

Thief of Shadows

"An expert blend of scintillating romance and mystery... The romance between the beautiful and quick-witted Isabel and the masked champion of the downtrodden propels this novel to the top of its genre."
—*Publishers Weekly* **(starred review)**

"Amazing sex scenes...a very intriguing hero...This one did not disappoint."
—*USA Today*

"Innovative, emotional, sensual...Hoyt's beautiful blending of the essential elements of a fairy tale into a stunning love story enhances this delicious 'keeper.'"
—*RT Book Reviews*

"All of Hoyt's signature literary ingredients—wickedly clever dialogue, superbly nuanced characters, danger, and scorching sexual chemistry—click neatly into place to create a breathtakingly romantic love story."
—*Booklist*

"When [they] finally come together, desire and long-denied sensuality explode upon the page."
—*Library Journal*

"With heart and heat rolled into one, *Thief of Shadows* is a definite must-read for historical romance fans! Hoyt really has outdone herself...yet again."
—**UndertheCoversBookblog.blogspot.com**

"A balanced mixture of action, adventure, and mystery and a beautifully crafted romance...The perfect historical romance."
—HeroesandHeartbreakers.com

Scandalous Desires

"Historical romance at its best...Series fans will be enthralled, while new readers will find this emotionally charged installment stands very well alone."
—*Publishers Weekly* (starred review)

"4½ stars! This is the Maiden Lane story readers have been waiting for. Hoyt delivers her hallmark fairy tale within a romance and takes readers into the depths of the heart and soul of her characters. Pure magic flows from her pen, lifting readers' spirits with joy."
—*RT Book Reviews*

"With its lush sensuality, lusciously wrought prose, and luxuriously dark plot, *Scandalous Desires*, the latest exquisitely crafted addition to Hoyt's Georgian-set Maiden Lane series, is a romance to treasure."
—*Booklist* (starred review)

"Ms. Hoyt writes some of the best love scenes out there. They are passionate, sexy, and blazing hot...I simply adore Ms. Hoyt's books for her sensuous prose, multifaceted characters, and intense, well-developed story lines. And she delivers every single time. It's no wonder all of her books are on my keeper shelves. Do yourself a favor and pick up *Scandalous Desires*."
—TheRomanceDish.com

"*Scandalous Desires* is the best book Elizabeth Hoyt has written so far, with endearing characters and an all-encompassing romance you'll want to hold close and never let go. If there's one must-read book, especially for historical romance fans, it's *Scandalous Desires*."

Notorious Pleasures

"Emotionally stunning…The sinfully sensual chemistry Hoyt creates between her shrewd, acid-tongued heroine and her scandalous, sexy hero is pure romance."

Wicked Intentions

"4½ stars! Top Pick! A magnificently rendered story that not only enchants but enthralls."

SWEETEST
SCOUNDREL

OTHER TITLES BY ELIZABETH HOYT

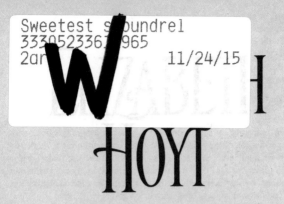

ELIZABETH

HOYT

SWEETEST SCOUNDREL

GRAND CENTRAL
PUBLISHING

NEW YORK   BOSTON

Grand Central Publishing
Hachette Book Group
1290 Avenue of the Americas
New York, NY 10104

www.HachetteBookGroup.com

Printed in the United States of America

OPM

First Edition: November 2015
10 9 8 7 6 5 4 3 2 1

Grand Central Publishing is a division of Hachette Book Group, Inc.
The Grand Central Publishing name and logo are trademarks of Hachette Book Group, Inc.

The Hachette Speakers Bureau provides a wide range of authors for speaking events. To find out more, go to www.hachettespeakersbureau.com or call (866) 376-6591.

The publisher is not responsible for websites (or their content) that are not owned by the publisher.

In loving memory of my mother,
Beverly Walton Kerr McKinnell
1940–2005

Acknowledgments

Thank you to my beta reader, Susannah Taylor, and my editor, Amy Pierpont, because, dudes, you would *not* have wanted to read this book without them. ;-)

And thank you to my Facebook friend Jaclyn R. for naming Henry.

SWEETEST
SCOUNDREL

Chapter One

*Once upon a time there lived a king so monstrous he
devoured his own children....*
—From *The Lion and the Dove*

It took an extreme provocation to rouse Eve Dinwoody.

For five years her life had been quiet. She had a nice
house in an unfashionable but respectable part of town.
She had her three servants—Jean-Marie Pépin, her bodyguard; his pretty, plump wife, Tess, her cook; and Ruth,
her rather scatterbrained young maid. She had a hobby—
painting miniatures—which also served to bring in extra
pin money. She even had a pet of sorts—a white dove she
had yet to name.

Eve *liked* her quiet life. On most days she quite enjoyed
staying inside, puttering around with her miniatures and
feeding the unnamed dove oat kernels. Truth be told, Eve
was rather shy.

But Eve could, in fact, rouse herself from her quiet life,
given enough provocation. And Lord knew Mr. Harte, the

owner and manager of Harte's Folly, was *very* provoking indeed. Harte's Folly was the preeminent pleasure garden in London—or at least it had been before it'd burned to the ground over a year ago. Now Mr. Harte was rebuilding his pleasure garden, and in the process spending quite scandalous amounts of money.

Which was why she stood on the third floor of a disreputable boarding house very early on a Monday morning, glaring at a stubbornly shut door.

A drop of rainwater dripped from the brim of her hat onto the worn floorboards beneath her feet. Really, it was an absolutely disgusting day outside.

"Do you wan' me to break the door down?" Jean-Marie asked cheerfully. He stood well over six feet tall and his ebony face beneath a snowy wig gleamed in the low light. He still had a faint Creole accent from his youth in the French West Indies.

Eve squared her shoulders. "No, thank you. I shall handle Mr. Harte myself."

Jean-Marie raised an eyebrow.

She glared. "I *shall*." She rapped at the door again. "Mr. Harte, I know you're within. Please answer your door at *once*."

Eve had performed this maneuver twice already without result, save for a crash from inside the room after the second knock.

She raised her fist for a fourth time, determined to make Mr. Harte acknowledge her, when the door swung open.

Eve blinked and involuntarily stepped back, bumping into Jean-Marie's broad chest. The man standing in the doorway was rather...intimidating.

He wasn't tall exactly—Jean-Marie had several inches on him and the man was only half a head or so taller than Eve herself—but what he might have lacked in height he more than made up in breadth of shoulder. The man's arms nearly touched the doorway on either side. He wore a white shirt, unlaced at the throat and revealing a V of tangled dark chest hair. Wild tawny hair fell to his shoulders. His face wasn't pretty. The exact opposite, in fact: it was strong, lined, and fierce, and everything that was masculine.

Everything that Eve most dreaded.

The man glanced at Jean-Marie, narrowed his eyes, leaned one shoulder against the doorjamb, and turned his attention to Eve. "What." His voice rasped deeply, like that of a man newly roused from sleep—a quite unseemly intimacy.

Eve straightened. "Mr. Harte?"

Instead of replying he yawned widely before running a hand over his face, pulling down the skin around his eyes and cheeks. "I'm sorry, luv, but I haven't any more parts available for the theater. Per'aps if you come again in another two months when we stage *As You Like It*. You might make a passable"—here he paused, eyes fixed *quite* rudely on Eve's nose—"maid, I suppose."

He turned his head and shouted over his shoulder, "*Are* there maids in *As You Like It*?"

"A shepherdess," came the reply. The speaker was feminine and had a beautifully accented voice.

Mr. Harte—*if* it was he—glanced back at Eve without any real apology in his haggard face. "There. Sorry. Although I have to say, at your age and with"—he actually *flapped* his hand at Eve's nose this time—"I'd look into something *behind* the stage, luv."

And he shut the door in her face.

Or at least he tried to, but Eve had had enough, thank you very much. She stuck her foot in the gap, pressed her shoulder against the door, and walked into Mr. Harte.

Who, unfortunately, didn't move back as he ought to have done.

He blinked, scowling down at Eve.

This close she could see the little red veins in his bloodshot eyes and smell some sort of stale spirits on his person. Also, he seemed not to have made use of a razor in several days.

His virility was nearly overwhelming.

She could feel the old panic rising in her chest, but she fought it. This man posed no threat to her—not in *that* way, in any case—and Jean-Marie was right behind her, besides. She was a woman grown and ought to have been over these terrors years ago.

Eve tilted up her chin. "Move, please."

"Look here, luv," he growled. "I don't know your name or who you are, and if you think this is how an actress gets a part at *my* pleasure garden, you're—"

"I'm not an actress," she enunciated clearly, in case he was hard of hearing as well as a drunken oaf. "And my name is Miss Eve Dinwoody."

"Dinwoody..." Instead of clearing his brow, her name made him scowl harder, which should've made him positively repugnant and yet somehow...didn't.

She took the opportunity of his distraction to slip triumphantly past him.

And then she skidded to a halt.

The room was an absolute shambles, crowded to overflowing with mismatched furniture and dusty *things*.

Stacks of papers and books slid off chairs and tables, falling to alluvial mounds on the floor. In one corner a huge heap of colorful fabric was piled, surmounted by a gilded crown; in another a life-size portrait of a bearded man was propped next to a four-foot-tall model of a ship, complete with sails and rigging. A stuffed raven eyed her beadily from the mantelpiece, and on the hearth itself a kettle steamed next to a teetering tower of dirty dishes and cups. Indeed, so filled was the room that it took Eve a moment to notice the nude woman in the bed.

The bed itself sat square in the center of the room, an overgrown, unwieldy thing, hung with gold and scarlet curtains like something from a Turk's harem, and in the middle reclined an odalisque, the golden coverlet barely concealing her curves. She was dark and sensual, her ebony hair spilling to olive-tinged shoulders, lips a deep natural carmine.

Eve's eyes widened abruptly as she realized what had been going on in this room perhaps only moments before. Her gaze darted to Mr. Harte before she could stop herself looking, for confirmation of . . . of . . . *well*.

But Mr. Harte merely looked big, male, and irritated.

Eve cocked her head. Shouldn't there be *some* way in which to tell—?

The woman sat up, the coverlet falling perilously to the very tips of her breasts. "Who are dees peoples?" she asked with a heavy Italian accent.

Mr. Harte crossed his arms on his chest, his legs spread wide. The stance emphasized the bulge of muscles in his upper arms. "I don't know, Violetta."

"I do apologize," Eve said stiffly to the woman, presumably Violetta. *Must* Mr. Harte take up so much space in the crowded room? "Had I known you were in disha-bille, I assure you—"

Mr. Harte barked a nasty laugh. "You came bursting in. When, exactly, would you have stopped to—"

"I *assure* you," Eve began, glaring at the awful man.

"It's-a no problem," the odalisque said at the same time, grinning and revealing an incongruous gap between her two front teeth. She shrugged again and the coverlet gave up the fight, falling to her waist.

Mr. Harte glanced at the woman, paused, his eyes fix-ated on her now-revealed bosom, and then visibly shook himself before dragging his gaze back to Eve. "Who *are* you anyway?"

"I already told you," Eve said through gritted teeth. "I am Eve Dinwoody and—"

"Dinwoody!" Harte exclaimed, pointing at her *quite* rudely. "That's the name of the Duke of Montgomery's man of business. Signs his letters 'E. Dinwoody' in the most affected hand I've ever seen..."

He frowned suddenly.

Jean-Marie and the odalisque looked at him.

Eve raised her eyebrows, waiting.

Mr. Harte's moss-green eyes widened. "Oh, the Devil damn me."

"Yes, no doubt," Eve said with a completely insincere smile. "But before that happens I've come to cut off your credit."

And this *was the inevitable reward for a night of too much drink*, Asa Makepeace—known to all but a select few as Mr. Harte—reflected sourly. For one, in his wine-fogged daze last night he'd thought it a fine idea to take

Violetta to bed again—when she was much too important an asset to the garden to risk an emotional entanglement. And for another, the aftereffects of a night of drinking—pounding temples and a generally weakened state—put him at a disadvantage in dealing with the termagant in front of him.

He glared at *Miss* Dinwoody through his throbbing eyes. She was tall for a woman, thin with a mannish chest, and had a face dominated by a large, long nose. She was as plain as a shovel—and he was glad of it, because the witch was trying to steal away his sweat, his dreams, and his blood. Long nights lying awake, making bargains with the Devil and devising desperate plans. Hope and glory and everything that he breathed for, God blast his miserable soul. All he'd lusted for, all he'd despaired over, all he'd lost and then fought with bloodied fists to regain.

She was trying to steal his goddamned *garden*.

He lifted his upper lip. "You haven't the right to cut me off."

"I assure you I have," she snipped back in accents that would've made the Queen jealous. She wasn't afraid of him, he'd give her that, though at the moment that fact irritated him.

"The Duke of Montgomery promised me a full line of credit," Asa said, slamming his hand down on the table and finding that the pose fortuitously helped to keep him from swaying. "We're scheduled to reopen in less than a month. The musicians have the score, the dancers are practicing, and a dozen seamstresses are working night and day to finish the costumes. You can't cut me off now, woman!"

"The duke didn't give you carte blanche to steal from

him," she said, her lips curling a bit on *steal*. Who was she to look down her overlong nose at him anyway? "I've sent you letter after letter asking to see your books, to examine your receipts of purchase, to be informed in *some* way of what you're spending thousands of pounds on, and you've ignored all my correspondence."

"Correspondence!" He stared, incredulous. "I haven't time for bloody *correspondence*. I have a theater to finish, gardens to plant, tenors, sopranos—and God help me, *castrati*—and mimers and musicians to order and collect and keep happy—or at least working *hard*—and an *opera* to put together. What do you think I am, a bloody mincing aristocrat?"

"I think you're a *businessman*," she shot back. "A businessman who ought, at the very least, to be able to account for his expenditures."

"My *expenditures* can be found at the garden," he roared. "In the buildings, the plantings, the people employed. Who are you to ask for my accounts?" He looked her up and down. "Why has the duke employed a female man of business in any case? What are you to him—his mistress? I'd think he could do better, frankly."

Behind him Violetta inhaled sharply, and the footman glared.

Miss Dinwoody's eyes widened—blue, he realized. Blue like the sky on a cloudless summer day—and he almost felt regret for his blunt words.

Almost.

"I," she said with awful clarity, "am the duke's *sister*."

He arched a skeptical eyebrow at her. She'd introduced herself as *Miss* Eve Dinwoody—the sister of a duke would be styled *Lady* Eve.

Her lips thinned at his expression. "We have different mothers. Obviously."

Ah, that explained it, then: she was a bastard by-blow of her father's, but no less an aristocrat for it. "And your blue blood makes you qualified to manage the garden's finances?"

"The fact that *my brother* entrusted the funds to me makes me qualified." She inhaled and threw back her shoulders, pushing that meager bosom at him. "And none of that is to the point in any case. I'm cutting off your credit and your funds as of this moment. Mr. Sherwood of the Royal theater has offered to buy out my brother's stake in Harte's Folly, and I warn you now that I am seriously considering his suggestion, since it appears to be the only way my brother will see his money again. I merely stopped by to tell you in person as a courtesy."

She turned and swept from the room, as grand as any royal princess. Her giant footman smirked at Asa before following her.

Courtesy? Asa mouthed the word incredulously at his closing door. What in the last five minutes did the woman think had been in any way *courteous*? He looked at Violetta, spreading wide his arms. "Bloody fucking *Sherwood*! She wants to sell my garden to my biggest rival. Never mind that Sherwood must be talking out of his ass—the man hasn't the money to buy Montgomery's stake out. God's balls! Have you ever met a more unreasonable woman?"

The soprano shrugged, jiggling what had to be the loveliest breasts in London, *not that it mattered at the moment.* "That is hardly the most important consideration for you right now, yes?"

"What?" He shook his head. God, it was much too early for him to be parsing feminine riddles.

She sighed. "Asa, *caro*—"

"Hush!" He scowled at the door and then back at her. "You know I don't like anyone overhearing that name."

"I doubt Miss Dinwoody and her footman lurk outside the door." She actually rolled her eyes at that. "Mr. *Harte*, do you need the money this woman controls?"

"Yes, of course I do!" he shouted, outraged.

Violetta made a moue at his temper. "Then you had best go after her."

"That woman is rude, condescending, and just plain *mean*." He waved wildly at the door behind him. "Are you insane?"

"No." She actually smiled at his bellow. "But *you* are if you think standing here and raging will change anything. Miss Dinwoody holds the strings to your purse and without her"—she shrugged again—"I will leave and so will everyone else who builds and works in your so-beautiful gardens. I love you, *caro*, you know this, but I must eat and drink and wear pretty gowns. Go now if you wish to save your garden."

"Oh, fucking *hell*." He knew she was right.

"And Asa, my love?"

"What?" he growled, already turning to the door.

"*Grovel.*"

He snorted as he bounded down the rickety wooden stairs of his boardinghouse, but Violetta was canny about people. If she said he had to grovel to that witch in order to get the money, he would.

Even if it gave him an apoplexy.

Asa burst out the door and into the street. Rain was

drizzling down in a halfhearted way, the sky cloudy and gray. A few paces away Miss Dinwoody and her footman were walking to a waiting hackney carriage.

"Oi!" Asa yelled, running after them. "Miss—"

He meant to lay a staying hand on her shoulder, but the footman was suddenly between him and the woman.

"Don' touch my mistress," the man intoned.

"I mean no harm," Asa said, hands palms out and at shoulder height. He tried for an ingratiating smile but had the feeling that it came off as more of an angry grimace. *Grovel.* "I wish to apologize to your mistress." He leaned to the side to see her, but the footman moved with him. "Apologize most abjectly. Can you hear me, luv?" This last he simply shouted over the man's shoulder. All he could see of her was the black hood of her cloak.

"I can hear you just fine, Mr. Harte," she returned, cool and composed.

The blackamoor moved aside finally, as if by some unspoken command, and Asa found himself staring into those blue eyes again.

They hadn't softened.

He swallowed a sharp retort and said through gritted teeth, "I'm so sorry, ma'am, I don't know what came over me to speak to a lady in that way, especially one so"—he caught himself before he praised her beauty, because that was a bit thick even for him—"*fine* as you. I hope you'll find it within your heart to forgive my offense, but I'll understand, I truly will, if you can't."

The footman snorted.

Asa ignored him and smiled.

Widely.

Apparently Miss Dinwoody was immune to his smile—

or maybe males in general. Those sky-blue eyes narrowed. "I accept your apology, Mr. Harte, but if you think such a blatant bunch of nonsense will make me change my mind about my brother's money, you're sadly mistaken."

And she turned to go—*again*.

Buggering hell.

"Wait!" This time his hand actually smacked against the footman's shoulder as the man moved between them. Asa glared at him. "Will you stand down? I'm hardly going to murder your mistress in the middle of *Southwark*."

"Mr. Harte, you've taken enough of my time," she began, infuriatingly aristocratic, as she stepped around her footman.

"Damn it, will you just let me think?" Asa said, rather louder than he'd meant to.

She blinked and opened her mouth, looking not a little outraged. Doubtless she wasn't used to commoners speaking to her so.

"No." He held out his palm. The last thing he needed was her sniping at him and making him angrier.

He took a breath. Anger hadn't worked. Insults hadn't worked. *Groveling* hadn't worked.

And then he had it.

He looked at her, leaning a little forward, ignoring the aborted movement of her footman. "Will you come?"

She frowned at that. "Come where?"

"To Harte's Folly."

She was already shaking her head. "Mr. Harte, I hardly see—"

"But that's just it," he said, holding her gaze—her *attention*—by sheer willpower alone. "You've not seen it, have you, Harte's Folly, since the work to rebuild was started? Come and *see* what I'm spending your brother's money on. See what I've accomplished so far. See what I could accomplish in the future—if only you'll let me."

She shook her head again, but her blue eyes had softened.

Almost.

"Please," he said, his voice lowering intimately. If there was one thing Asa Makepeace knew how to do it was seduce a female. Even one with a poker up her arse. "Please. Just give me—no, just give my *garden*—a chance."

And he must've found his infamous charm at last—either that or the lady had a gentler heart than he imagined—for she pursed her lips and nodded once.

EVE KNEW SHE'D made a mistake the moment she nodded. She wasn't entirely sure why she'd done it, either. Perhaps it was Mr. Harte's sheer presence, big and wide and muscular, the rain soaking his linen shirt until it clung transparently to his shoulders. Or perhaps it'd been his voice, softened in pleading. Or maybe even his eyes, still bloodshot, but a dark forest green, almost warm against the chill of the day.

Or maybe the man was a sorcerer, able to put otherwise level-headed ladies under some sort of spell that compelled them to act against their own best interests.

In any case she'd agreed and that was that and she must resign herself to *more* hours tramping about Southwark in the rain to strange places with a man she didn't even like.

And then the most extraordinary thing happened.

Mr. Harte *smiled*.

That shouldn't have been so very surprising. The man had smiled earlier that morning—nastily or in anger or in an attempt at persuasion—but *this* smile was different.

This smile was genuine.

His wide lips spread, revealing straight white teeth, and indents on either cheek, bracketing his mouth. His eyes crinkled at the corners and he looked rather appealing somehow. Charming. Almost handsome, standing in his shirt-sleeves there in the rain, his hair wet, a raindrop running down the side of one tanned cheek.

And what was terrible—quite *horrible*, really—was that Eve had the ridiculous notion that Mr. Harte's smile was especially for her.

Just her.

Ridiculous. She knew—absolutely *knew*, in that no-nonsense, sensible part of her—that he was smiling because he'd had his way. It had nothing at all to do with *her*, truly. But she couldn't entirely squash a tiny part that saw that smile and claimed it as her own. And it made her warm inside, somehow. Warm and a bit . . . excited.

He knew it, too, the awful man. She could tell by the way his smile widened, transforming into a grin, and by the way his green eyes looked at her knowingly.

She stiffened and opened her mouth to deny everything. To send the man on his way so she could go *home* and perhaps enjoy a soothing cup of tea.

He was wily, though, Mr. Harte. He immediately bowed and gestured to the hired conveyance behind her. "Shall we take your carriage?"

She had said she'd go. Or at least nodded. A gentle-woman shouldn't go back on her word—or nod.

Five minutes later Eve found herself sitting beside Jean-Marie as they rumbled through the streets of Southwark. Across from them Mr. Harte was looking quite self-satisfied.

"Normally, of course, my guests arrive from the river," Mr. Harte was saying. "We have a landing with stone steps and attendants arrayed in purple and yellow to give the feeling of entering another world. Once my guests have shown their tickets they proceed along a path lit by torches and fairy lights. Along the way are waterfalls of lights, jugglers, dancing fauns and dryads, and the guests may linger if they wish. Or they can explore the gardens further. Or they can continue on and attend the theater."

She *had* been to Harte's Folly before it'd burned— once, a year or two ago. She actually rather enjoyed a night at the theater, though she only ever went by herself—well, with Jean-Marie, of course, but not with a friend, because she really didn't *have* any friends.

She shook her head at her own irrelevant musings.

"It all sounds very expensive," Eve said, unable to keep the repressive note from her voice.

Irritation crossed Mr. Harte's face before he attempted a more benign expression. She wasn't sure why he bothered. The man's every emotion was transparent—and most of them were negative when it came to her.

Which troubled her not at all, naturally.

"It *is* expensive," he said, "but it needs to be. My guests come for a spectacle. To be amazed and awed. There is no other place like Harte's Folly in all of London. In all the *world*." Mr. Harte sat forward on the carriage seat, his elbows on his knees; his broad shoulders appeared to fill the entire carriage. Or maybe it was his personality that made the carriage so small. His big hands spread as if grasping possibilities. "To make money I must spend money. If my pleasure garden were like any other—if the costumes were worn, the theatrics tame and uninspiring, the plantings everyday—no one would come. No one would pay the price of admission."

Reluctantly she began to wonder if perhaps she had been overhasty. The man was proud and bombastic and very, *very* annoying, but maybe he was right. Maybe he could return her brother's investment with his wonderful garden.

Still, she'd always been cautious by nature. "I'm expecting you to prove all that you've told me, Mr. Harte."

He sat back as if satisfied he'd already won her approval. "And so I shall."

The carriage rounded a bend in the road and a tall stone wall came into view. It looked very... utilitarian.

Eve glanced at Mr. Harte.

He cleared his throat. "Naturally, this is the *back* entrance."

The carriage jerked to a halt.

Jean-Marie immediately rose, set the step, and held out his hand to help her down.

"Thank you," Eve murmured. "Please ask the carriage driver to wait for us."

Mr. Harte leaped from the carriage in one athletic bound and strode ahead of them to a wooden door in the wall. He opened it and gestured them through.

Beyond was a tangled growth of hedges and some muddy paths. Hardly the look of a pleasure garden, but he *had* said this was the back way.

Eve eyed the door as she entered. "Shouldn't this be locked?"

"Yes," Mr. Harte said. "And usually 'tis when we're open—it wouldn't do to have people walk into the gardens without paying—but right now we're still building. It's easier for deliveries just to come in."

"You have no problem with thieves?"

Mr. Harte frowned. "I—"

A young redheaded man came trotting briskly along one of the paths. Eve recognized him instantly as Mr. Malcolm MacLeish, the architect her brother had hired to rebuild the theater.

"Harte!" Mr. MacLeish exclaimed. "Thank God you're here. The damned slate's arrived for the roof and half are broken and still the driver's demanding payment before he unloads. I don't know whether to send the lot back or work with the usable stuff. We're already behind and the rain's leaking in the theater—the tarps won't hold it." The young man glanced up from his tirade, his eyes widening as he caught sight of Eve. "Oh! Miss Dinwoody. I hadn't thought to see you here."

And he flushed an unbecoming mottled red.

Eve felt a pang of sympathy. The last time she'd seen Mr. MacLeish he'd been begging for her help in escaping her brother's influence. The man was probably quite embarrassed to encounter her.

She gave him a small, reassuring smile. "Good day to you, Mr. MacLeish."

At that he remembered his manners and swept her a rather elegant bow. "And to you, Miss Dinwoody." He inhaled, obviously ordering himself. "You're a bright spot on this dreary morning, I declare."

And there was the sweet charm the architect usually displayed.

She nodded. "Shall we see to your shingle delivery?"

"I—" Mr. MacLeish glanced at Mr. Harte, his expression nonplussed.

The pleasure garden owner frowned. "I didn't bring you here to examine the dull behind-the-scenes stuff, Miss Dinwoody."

"But perhaps that's what I *ought* to be examining," she replied. "Please. Lead us on, Mr. MacLeish."

The architect waited for Mr. Harte's nod before turning back down the muddy path.

Eve picked up her skirts, stepping carefully. She regretted not wearing pattens on her shoes this morning, for she was beginning to worry that her slippers would be ruined by the wet and mud.

"I confess, I thought from your description that the gardens would be more..." Eve paused, trying to find a tactful word as they walked past a clump of sagging irises.

"Finished," Jean-Marie rumbled, supplying the word, if not the tact.

Mr. Harte's frown had turned to a scowl at her bodyguard's interjection. "Naturally the garden isn't at its best in the rain. Now here," he exclaimed as they rounded a tall tree and came within view of a pond, "*here* is where you can see what Harte's Folly will be."

The pond was very pretty. An island sat at its center, with an arched bridge connecting it to the shore. Another tree, young and straight, had been planted at the edge of the pond, framing the view. Even in the misty rain it held a sort of otherworldly allure.

Enchanted, Eve stepped closer... and right into a puddle, the cold, muddy water soaking her slipper and completely breaking the spell.

She turned to Mr. Harte.

His gaze met hers, rising from her dirtied feet. "We will, of course, be mending the paths before we open."

"I should hope so," she replied frostily, giving her foot a shake.

They continued along the path in silence, Eve's toes slowly turning numb with cold as she followed Mr. Harte's broad shoulders.

Another five minutes and they came within sight of a series of buildings, the central one obviously a theater. It had wide marble steps that led to a row of columns across the front, and a high pediment with classical bas-relief figures depicting acting and the theater. It was an impressive building, even with the tarps covering the roof.

Drawn up outside were an enormous cart and a team of horses. Three men stood by the cart, arguing loudly with a semicircle of people facing them. The crowd was a motley lot: a half dozen women wore matching bright-yellow dresses, their hems scandalously high—obviously for dancing. Another woman was in an extraordinary purple frock and still had paint on her face. Beside her was a plain woman in rather more ordinary clothing, holding a half-finished bodice. Several men were workers or gardeners—one had a rake over his shoulder—while others were better dressed and held various instruments under their arms.

"Pay up or we'll turn this 'ere cart around and take it back across th' river!" said one of the cartmen.

"Pay for vhat?" a slight man with a clever face and dark hair sneered. "A heap of broken shards? Bah!" He threw up his hands in disgust. "This theater, it vill never be finished. My musicians cannot practice vith vater dripping down their necks."

"What's this I hear about broken shingles?"

The crowd turned at Mr. Harte's deep voice, and several people started talking at once.

Mr. Harte held up his hands. "One at a time. Vogel?"

The dark-haired man stepped forward, his black eyes flashing. "Vonce again the theater is not done. MacLeish promised last month and was it done? No! He promised this veek—"

"It's hardly my fault the rain kept us from building," Mr. MacLeish said, his chin thrust forward. "And let me tell you, having to work around a crowd of musicians hasn't been easy."

Mr. Vogel's upper lip curled. "And vould you have us open vithout practice? Bah! You know nothing of opera or music, you English."

"I'm a *Scot*, you—"

Mr. Harte laid a hand on Mr. MacLeish's chest, stepping between him and Mr. Vogel. "What about my shingles?"

"Not my fault if they came that way," the leader of the shingle men said, suddenly sounding conciliatory. "This is the way I got 'em and this is the way I brought 'em."

"And this is the way I'll be sending 'em *back*," Mr. Harte said. "I paid for roofing tile, not broken shards."

"I can take it all back," the shingle man said, "but I won't be getting another shipment until December earliest."

Mr. Harte took a menacing step forward. "Goddamn it, man—"

The double doors to the theater burst open and a short, bandy-legged man dressed in a blazing orange coat came down the steps. Eve blinked in astonishment, for it was Mr. Sherwood, the proprietor of the Royal theater. Whatever was he—?

"Sherwood!" roared Mr. Harte, advancing menacingly on the smaller man. "What are you doing in my theater?"

"Harte," Sherwood returned, apparently unaware of the danger he stood in. "What a pleasant surprise. I didn't know you rose so early in the morning. And Miss Dinwoody!" he said, catching sight of Eve, peering around Mr. Harte's back. "A pleasure, ma'am, an absolute pleasure!"

"Mr. Sherwood." Eve nodded cautiously.

"Your exquisite grace brightens the day, ma'am." The theater manager beamed as if at his own wit and bobbed on his toes. He wore a white wig a bit the worse for wear and slightly askew. "Have you told Harte of my offer?"

"You haven't the funds to buy Montgomery's stake out," Harte sneered.

"*I* haven't," Mr. Sherwood replied blithely, "but my backer *has*."

Mr. Harte seemed to expand, his hands clenching into fists at his sides. Eve took a nervous step back into the comforting shadow of Jean-Marie.

"*What* backer?" Mr. Harte growled. "You can't possibly have—"

At the top of the stairs a tall man exited the theater. He wore a lavishly curled lavender wig and a flamboyant ruby coat with silver lace edging the cuffs and collar.

He glanced down and gave an exaggerated start on seeing Mr. Harte. "No," he cried, an arm outthrust as if to hold the pleasure garden owner back. "You shan't talk me out of it, Harte, not even with your silver tongue."

"What are you doing, Giovanni?" Mr. Harte's voice had lowered into ominous, gravelly depths.

Eve glanced around. Wasn't *anyone* else worried about Mr. Harte's simmering temper?

But all eyes were on the theater stairs as the tall man swept down them. Eve realized that he must be Giovanni Scaramella, the famous castrato.

"Leaving *you*," Mr. Sherwood trumpeted, confirming Eve's worst fears. "Giovanni's coming to the Royal. The most talented castrato in London shall be singing exclusively for *my* theater now."

"You can't do this, Gio," Mr. Harte said. "You agreed to sing for me this season. We shook on it."

"Did we?" the singer asked, eyes wide. "But Mr. Sherwood has a theater already built, a magnificent opera ready, and much money for me. You, Harte, have mud and a leaky roof." He shrugged. "Is it so strange I go to sing at the Royal theater?"

"Always get a performer to sign," Sherwood said merrily, shaking a piece of paper in one hand. "Thought you'd know that by now, Harte."

Harte's eyes narrowed and his voice lowered. Eve took an involuntary step back as he snarled, "Goddamn you—"

"Ha!" crowed Mr. Sherwood, skipping down the last of the steps. "You may've stolen Robin Goodfellow, you may've stolen La Veneziana, but see how far you get without a leading castrato, Harte!"

Mr. Harte didn't say a word. In a shockingly concise movement, he stepped forward and swung his enormous fist into the other man's face.

Mr. Sherwood fell with a shriek and a burst of blood from his nose.

Mr. Harte stood over him, still bareheaded and in his shirt-sleeves, the sputtering rain molding the fabric to the bulging muscles of his back and shoulders.

He looked like everything that was uncivilized and barbaric and *male*.

Eve inhaled and then had trouble exhaling. She didn't like violence. She never had.

This had been a mistake. A terrible mistake. The garden was a shambles, the opera didn't look like it would ever be staged, and Mr. Harte was a brutal animal.

"Take me away from this place, Jean-Marie," she whispered.

Chapter Two

Now, this king had consulted an oracle upon the birth of his first son. The oracle told him that should any of the king's children live to see midnight on their eighteenth birthday, the king would die.
If, however, the king ate the heart of every child he sired, he would live forever....
—From *The Lion and the Dove*

Bridget Crumb kept the house of the wickedest man in England.

Valentine Napier, the Duke of Montgomery, was handsome to the point of near-feminine beauty, powerful, wealthy, and completely—as far as she could see—without morals. She'd been hired only weeks before the duke's exile from the country. One of his many minions had discovered her reputation—as the best housekeeper in London—and had offered her double the wage she'd been earning as Lady Margaret St. John's housekeeper. Though truth be told the money had been only *one* of the reasons Bridget had promptly taken the job. In that short time before Montgomery had left for Europe he'd spoken directly to her exactly once—when he'd absently inquired what had happened to his butler. She'd told him politely that the man had decided to return to his birthplace in Wales. Which was, strictly speaking, true, although by no means the *entire* truth, since she'd certainly encouraged the butler in his dreams of retiring to become a shopkeeper.

She'd also omitted to explain that she hadn't hired a replacement butler. Why bring in another male servant who might challenge her authority?

Now Bridget had complete charge of Hermes House— the duke's London town house—which was quite convenient considering her *other* reasons for agreeing to come into the duke's employment.

However, the lack of a butler did mean that she often answered the front door herself when there was a caller.

Today when the knock came, Bridget glided across the ostentatious gray-veined pink marble floor—polished just this morning at exactly six of the clock. She paused at an ornately gilded mirror to check that her mobcap was straight, and the strings tied under her chin neatly. She was only six and twenty—a nearly unheard-of age at which to have already acquired the position she held— and she'd found it helped to bolster her authority to always be completely ordered.

Bridget opened the door to find the duke's sister on the doorstep, along with the woman's footman. Unlike the duke, Miss Dinwoody was a plain woman, though she and her brother shared the same guinea-gold hair. "Good morning, miss."

She stood aside to let them both in.

Miss Dinwoody looked a trifle flustered, which was unusual. "Good morning, Mrs. Crumb. I've come to look at my brother's account books."

"Of course," Bridget murmured. Miss Dinwoody had visited Hermes House once or twice a week since the duke had left the country, always to attend to the duke's investments in Harte's Folly. "Shall I send some tea and refreshments to the library, miss?"

"No need." Miss Dinwoody doffed a rain-soaked cloak and handed it to her. "I shan't be long."

"Very well, miss," Bridget replied. She gestured to one of the footmen stationed in the entry hall and handed over the cloak. "A letter for you from your brother arrived not an hour ago. I apologize for not sending it on to you at once."

"That's quite all right," Miss Dinwoody said. "I suppose it was delivered by that odd boy again?"

"Yes, miss. Alf brought it round to the kitchens."

Miss Dinwoody shook her head, absently muttering under her breath, "I don't see why my brother doesn't just use the mail coaches. Lord only knows how his letters travel across the Channel in the first place."

Bridget had an idea about that, but it wasn't her place to comment on the duke's unusual means of communication. Instead she led the way up the grand staircase and down a wide hallway to the library. The Hermes House staff was reduced, since the duke wasn't in residence, but Bridget ran a tight ship. The rooms on this floor were thoroughly aired and dusted every other week—that day falling today. She paused at an open door, catching the eye of one of the maids running a cloth over the woodwork in the room. "Stir the fire in the library, if you will, Alice."

Alice hesitated, still on her knees. She was a pretty girl of nineteen or so, a bit slow, but a hard worker nonetheless. Unfortunately she was also superstitious. "The library, ma'am?"

"Yes, Alice." Bridget let her voice sharpen. "At once, if you please."

"Yes, Mrs. Crumb." The girl bobbed and scurried out of the room and ahead of them.

When they got to the library Bridget held open the door for Miss Dinwoody and nodded toward the rosewood desk in the corner where the letter lay. "Is there anything else I might do for you, miss?" She noted that Alice was kneeling by the hearth, a lit candle in one hand, her face pale as she darted nervous glances around the room.

"No, nothing," Miss Dinwoody murmured as she pried open the seal on the letter. Her thin mouth crimped at the corners as she began to read, and Bridget reflected that it must be rather tiring being the Duke of Montgomery's bastard sister.

But then that wasn't any of her concern, was it?

She jerked her chin at Alice, who had the fire blazing, and the girl leaped to her feet, nearly running to the door.

Bridget sighed as she closed the door behind them. She'd already lectured the girl several times on the impossibility of ghosts in Hermes House, and there was simply no point in doing so again.

Especially since she wasn't entirely convinced herself.

IT WAS AFTER noon by the time Eve made her way back to her town house with Jean-Marie.

Her brother had found the town house for her, of course. Found it and paid for it. Paid for Jean-Marie and Tess and Ruth as well, come to that. Val saw to it that Eve lived very comfortably, but that wasn't the reason she'd agreed to manage his investment in Harte's Folly when he'd been forced to leave the country so suddenly.

She sometimes wondered if he had any idea at all why she'd done it. Val dealt so much in debt and money and silken threats that he might not recognize when a person did something purely for love.

The thought saddened her somehow.

Eve doffed her bonnet inside her hallway. "Ask Tess to bring me a luncheon tray, please, Jean-Marie. And some tea."

Jean-Marie shot her a look of concern but nodded before disappearing into the back of the house.

Eve wondered what he'd say to Tess about their morning's outing. About her fleeing the garden. About her trip to her brother's big, empty house and the letter she'd read there.

The letter in which Val expressly forbade her to cut off Mr. Harte or sell the stake.

Blast Val anyway. He'd put her in a very awkward position—managing a great deal of money, but having no real power over it if he wouldn't let her follow her instincts about how to deal with the garden and Mr. Harte. If he'd only let her sell the stake in Harte's Folly to Mr. Sherwood and his mysterious backer, she could invest the money. She knew she could make a profit for her brother. Over the last five years Eve had invested her own pin money in a shipping company and had seen a small but tidy increase in the capital.

Unfortunately, she wasn't at all sure that it was entirely the money Val was most concerned about when it came to Harte's Folly.

She sighed and climbed the stairs. Her sitting room

was at the top, and she crossed the room to her worktable. On it was her bronze magnifying glass. It was attached to an arm that swung from an upright stand so that she could comfortably look through it and keep both hands free. Beside the glass were several clean pieces of ivory and her paint box, all set out. Under the magnifying glass was the miniature she was working on now—a study of Hercules. She bent and peered through the glass. Hercules stood, one hip cocked, wearing his lion skin and sandals, a bit of cloth modestly covering his hips. It should've been a heroic pose, but somehow poor Hercules looked almost effeminate. His lips too pursed, his cheeks too pink, his face entirely too soft. It was the style, of course, to paint men as soft and gentle, and she excelled in that style, but somehow today she was suddenly dissatisfied.

She kept remembering Mr. Harte's face. His brows drawn together, his mouth in a grim line, his wet hair plastered to his cheeks and forehead as he'd borne down on Mr. Sherwood with his muscled arm raised. She hated—and feared—his violence, but she couldn't deny that there was something *alive* about Mr. Harte. Alive and vibrant and larger than life. Something exciting that made her heart beat faster, made *her* feel alive as well.

Eve sat at her desk, staring down blindly at poor, sweet Hercules.

Mr. Harte was a brute, anyone could see that. He wouldn't listen to reason, wouldn't abide by common decency or her very polite requests for information. He had actually *attacked* Mr. Sherwood right in front of her. How could Val expect her to work with a man such as he?

If she was entirely truthful with herself, she'd have to face the fact that she'd failed Val. She'd promised to look after his investment, but if the theater never opened again, and she wasn't allowed to sell the stake, he'd not see a return of his money.

He'd lose thousands of pounds.

Eve frowned, picking up one of the blank pieces of ivory and running her finger over the smooth surface. The sum already invested in Harte's Folly was probably a drop in the ocean of Val's wealth, but she'd *promised*.

She didn't like to forswear herself.

And then there was his letter, full of Val's usual flippancy and with that unusually to-the-point postscript, telling her to keep funding the awful man and his garden. She'd have to send a letter to Mr. Harte, apologizing and taking back everything she'd said this morning. The very thought was depressing.

Ruth came in the room, walking slowly as she carried the luncheon tray. The maid set the tray down next to Eve's elbow and stood back, beaming. "There, miss! Tess 'as fried a lovely 'erring with some stewed green beans beside it, and there's bread fresh-baked this morning as well."

"Thank you, Ruth," Eve replied, and the maid bobbed a curtsy and nearly skipped from the room.

Well, Ruth *was* very young—only fifteen and fresh from somewhere in the country. Everything was new to her. She had an appealing naïveté that Eve found both charming and alarming. The maid hadn't yet learned to be cautious of the world. No one had ever hurt her.

The dove, sitting in her square little cage on the table, cooed inquiringly. Eve took a few kernels of grain from a dish nearby and pushed them through the bars of the cage. Immediately the dove began pecking at her luncheon.

Eve picked up her fork and knife and then paused, staring at the herring. How quiet it was in her sitting room! Just the soft scrabbling of the dove and the clink of her silverware. She couldn't even hear the voices from the kitchen downstairs.

If she closed her eyes, she might imagine herself all alone in the world.

She shook herself, cutting into the herring, and a dreadful pounding suddenly started at the front door, belying her imagined solitude.

Eve set her knife and fork down again, sitting back, a feeling almost of joy overtaking her.

She could hear Jean-Marie's quick footsteps, the door opening, and then male voices raised in anger.

A smile flitted across her face. He really was the most obstinate man, wasn't he?

She wondered if she should go to the head of the stairs, but no. Footsteps were pounding up her stairwell. He must've gotten around Jean-Marie somehow.

Eve carefully composed her face and picked up her fork and knife again. Her appetite had suddenly revived.

When the door to her sitting room burst open, she was just taking a bite of the excellent fish.

"You have to listen to me!" Mr. Harte bellowed just as Jean-Marie got an arm around his neck.

Mr. Harte ducked out of the hold and whirled to face her bodyguard, his great fists ready.

"Mr. Harte!" Eve didn't like to raise her voice, but she wouldn't stand by and let Jean-Marie be hurt. "If you want me to listen to you, I suggest you *not* begin by staging a boxing match in my sitting room."

Mr. Harte's face took on a darker hue, but his arms fell to his sides.

Jean-Marie, however, hadn't dropped his protective stance. "Shall I escort 'im out?"

"I'd like to see you try," Mr. Harte growled.

Eve refrained with great effort from rolling her eyes. "Thank you, no, Jean-Marie. I'll speak with Mr. Harte if he'll take a seat."

The theater manager immediately dropped rather heavily onto the settee.

Eve cleared her throat. "Perhaps you can bring another teacup, Jean-Marie?"

The footman's brows drew together. "Best I stay 'ere, I think."

Normally he would, of course. Normally Jean-Marie never let her be alone with a man. But she couldn't bear the thought of seeming weak before Mr. Harte. Of needing a *nursemaid*—even if the truth was that sometimes she *did* need Jean-Marie.

She wanted to at least appear to be strong in the theater manager's presence.

Eve lifted her chin. "No doubt, but I think I'll manage on my own with Mr. Harte."

"Thank you for seeing me," Mr. Harte said quickly, before Jean-Marie could express any more disapproval.

She nodded. "Have you partaken of luncheon yet?"

"No, ma'am."

"Then please have Ruth bring up another tray as well," Eve told Jean-Marie.

The footman shot a dark look at the other man, but left the room without comment.

"Now then," Eve said, folding her hands in her lap. "What is it you wished to say to me, Mr. Harte?"

She expected him to immediately begin pleading his

case again. Instead he propped one ankle over the knee of the other leg and leaned back in her blue-gray settee, as comfortable as a lion lazing in the sun. "You left my garden very quickly."

She pursed her lips. "I dislike violence, and frankly, with the loss of Mr. Scaramella—and your composure—I didn't see any point in remaining."

"I can hire another castrato." He'd donned a coat and waistcoat since she'd seen him this morning, both a deep shade of scarlet, but his tawny hair remained unbound about his shoulders, giving him an uncivilized appearance. Wild. As if he might do anything—anything at all—in her proper sitting room. "As for the loss of my composure"—he curled his upper lip—"you have to admit Sherwood had it coming to him."

Eve forbore to retort that she didn't have to admit any such thing. Instead she looked at him curiously. "And do you always react so...physically to such situations?"

"I'm in the theater," he said, as if that explained his churlish actions. "We're a bit rougher perhaps than you're used to. A bit earthier, too."

Was that his way of delicately touching upon the subject of the woman in his bed this morning?

"I see." Eve pursed her lips, examining the backs of her hands. "You may be able to find another castrato, but can you find one with a voice like Giovanni Scaramella on such short notice? Mr. Scaramella's fame draws eager crowds. I can understand why Mr. Sherwood was determined to have him. Who else is so well known in London?"

"Perhaps no one," Mr. Harte conceded. "But I can send for a castrato on the Continent."

She glanced up. "And even if you do? Can you be ready to open in a month?"

He looked at her and she met his green gaze. They both knew that to open in less than a month would be nearly impossible.

"Look." He leaned forward, elbows on knees, his big hands clasped together. "You've been to a night at the opera; you know what's involved. I have the musicians and the dancers. I have Vogel's opera—a new one and I think one of his best. I have La Veneziana—Violetta, who you met this morning. She's the most famous soprano in London. All I need is the lead castrato."

She nodded. "You need a castrato, and without one you have nothing. It's the fame of the singers that will draw the attendees to your garden, and the castrato is key. He's the one with the most entrancing voice, the one people want to hear and see."

His mouth tightened. "I've already sent letters to the Continent and to the people I know here. I'll have a new castrato within a sennight."

"Which will give you barely over a fortnight to rehearse."

He set his jaw. "It can be done. I'll *make* it happen. All I need is your brother's money."

She smiled then, gently shaking her head. "I told you no, again and again, and yet you continued onward. Tell me, Mr. Harte, do you ever give up?"

"Never." His green eyes narrowed as his mouth firmed. He looked very much as he had when he'd struck Mr. Sherwood: savage, uncompromising, a force to be reckoned with.

She should be afraid of this man. Perhaps she was. Perhaps the hammering of her heart, the quickening of her breath were fear.

But if they were, she chose to disregard it. "Very well."

He sat back, a wide, lopsided grin spreading over his face, just as Ruth entered with another tray.

Eve indicated the low table before the settee where Mr. Harte sat, and Ruth hurried to place the tray there. She straightened, staring at the theater manager. Eve didn't often have visitors.

"Thank you, Ruth."

The maid started, shot her a guilty glance, and left the room.

"This looks delicious." Mr. Harte reached for the loaf of bread on the tray. Tess must've bought several herring from the fish market, for she'd sent up another luncheon identical to Eve's.

She eyed his fingers as he broke apart the bread. "I have one condition, however, to letting you have access to my brother's funds once more." She considered the matter a moment and then nodded, adding, "Actually *two* conditions."

He froze, those long, strong fingers still holding the torn bread. "And what are they?"

She inhaled silently, feeling her nerves spark. Feeling excitement.

Feeling *alive*.

"I'll be taking over the bookkeeping for Harte's Folly until it opens again."

His brows snapped together. "Now wait a—"

"And," she said firmly over his aborted objection, "I want you to sit for me—as a model for my painting."

FOR A MOMENT Asa Makepeace stared at the maddening woman.

Then he threw back his head and roared with laughter. It was that or weep. From the moment she'd woken him from a dreamless sleep next to a warm, naked Violetta, his day had gone from bad to worse. Miss Eve Dinwoody was like one of those harbingers of doom that were always lurking about some hapless hero in classical myths. A harpy or some such thing. Her nose was even a bit like a beak. Since he'd met Miss Dinwoody, he'd had a crashing headache, lost his castrato, gotten into a fight with bloody Sherwood—which he'd *won*, thank you very much—and now, *now* she wanted not only to worm her way into his business as the price of giving him back his letters of credit, but she also wanted him to *model* for her, as if he had the time to spend lounging about away from his garden.

Ah, but the garden was the only important thing, wasn't it? He'd dance in the middle of Bond Street, naked as the day he was born, if it meant money for his gardens. Naked in her sitting room was a paltry price to pay in comparison—and it wasn't as if he were a shy sort.

Asa looked up, drawing a deep breath, and saw that his harpy wasn't amused by his laughter.

"I can't think why you find the thought of me helping with your books so funny," she said in a stiff little voice. "Or, for that matter, letting me paint you." Her mouth—the only soft part of her, as far as he could tell—trembled just a bit.

Well, he hadn't meant to hurt her feelings.

"Don't worry about it, luv," he said, tearing off a bite of the bread with his teeth. "You'll find out soon enough when you see my books. As for the other"—he set down the piece of bread and shrugged off his coat—"do you want to start now?"

That got him a wide-eyed look, and he couldn't help but grin at her, mouth obnoxiously full, as he began unbuttoning his waistcoat. Had the lady bitten off more than she could chew?

"What are you doing?" she asked, her voice high and a bit panicked. He opened his eyes in mock innocence as he yanked his shirt from his breeches. "Stop that at once."

"Why?" he asked curiously, his fingers still on his lifted shirt. Her gaze darted to his bared navel and then away again like that of a sweet little canary frightened by an ugly alley cat. "You said you wanted me to *model* for you."

"I didn't mean unclothed!" she said, making *unclothed* sound a lot like *covered in shit.*

He scowled. "Then what did you mean?"

She inhaled, straightening her back further—which, had he been asked a minute before, he would've laid odds couldn't be done. "I *mean* I wish to paint you as you are. Entirely covered. And I should like to start tomorrow, not today."

He stared at her, and then glanced down at himself. His waistcoat was rumpled and his shirt still had water stains from this morning. Maybe she was painting one of those ghastly studied portraits of shepherds or field laborers. Maybe that was how she saw him: as a working-class lout, burly and unrefined, too rough to be painted nude.

The hell with it. At least he wouldn't be cold when he modeled.

"Fine." He jerked his shirt down and sat forward to pick up his bread again.

He could *feel* her relax, and snorted to himself at her obvious relief that he'd covered himself.

She cleared her throat. "As for the other," she began in

that stern tone of voice he was beginning to recognize. "If you think to keep your accounting books from me—"

"Oh, no." He waved aside her worry with the piece of bread. "You can see them first thing tomorrow if you want. Nine of the clock?" he asked innocently.

Most aristocrats wouldn't be caught dead out of bed before noon.

He should've known she wasn't like most aristocrats, though—she had, after all, shown up at his door only a little after ten.

She inclined her head. "Very well. Shall I come to your rooms again?"

"Better to come to the theater," he replied. "I've an office in the back. It's small and cramped, but we can find you a chair. And a box or something."

He grinned to himself as he took a bite of the herring— it was tastily cooked. She'd be fleeing again once she caught sight of his "office." No woman as primly upright as she would like the loud chaos that was often the theater.

"I'm sure I'll make do, Mr. Harte," she murmured. "And I'll bring my sketchbook as well so that we may start on the modeling."

For a moment he narrowed his eyes at the serenity of her voice. Did nothing shake her for long? Even when she'd run away from his garden, she'd done it quietly and without fuss. He hadn't known she was gone until he'd turned around from knocking Sherwood down and noticed she wasn't there. She had an almost mannish forthrightness about her. A hard, unemotional center nearly disguised by the elegant overlay of her aristocratic manners. The juxtaposition of the two—her iron core and her delicate exterior—was oddly fascinating.

And made for a formidable opponent.

At the thought he glanced around the room, curious as to her natural habitat. "So this is where you live, eh?"

Rows of books were neatly ordered on a corner bookcase. The windows were covered by thin curtains, letting in light, but shielding the room from the outside world. The settee he was lounging on was placed square in front of a low table holding his tray, and on the opposite side were two chairs in a pinkish red. Miss Dinwoody sat behind a long table, and he got up to closer examine the surface.

She stiffened at his movement and he suppressed a smirk as he bent to look. She had a beautiful polished brass magnifying glass on an arm, and a row of pots and paintbrushes laid out. He could smell the earthy scent of the paints, but there was something else as well—a ethereal, flowery scent. Maybe the perfume she wore? If so, it suited her.

He reached to pick one of the paintbrushes up and her chin jerked slightly. "Don't touch that, please."

He considered poking his finger at the paintbrush just to antagonize her, but her face had a pinched look. Instead he peered into a low little cage resting to the right of her elbow.

A beady black eye stared back, and the white dove inside the cage cocked its head before cooing.

"What's his name?" he asked.

"I believe it's a female," Miss Dinwoody replied, staring critically at the caged bird. "But I'm not entirely certain. And she hasn't a name."

He raised his eyebrows as he straightened. "You just got her?"

"My brother gave her to me several months ago," she replied, rearranging her spoon and bread knife beside her plate of fish. "Before he was forced to leave England, obviously."

"Forced?" Now that was interesting. The Duke of Montgomery had left London abruptly back in July, without a word of warning to Asa—or anyone else, as far as he knew. At the time Asa had been very put out—until he realized that his line of credit was still good. Then he'd simply put it down to the whims of the aristocracy. He looked at Miss Dinwoody expectantly. When she merely stared back at him, unperturbed, he prompted, "What d'you mean, *forced*?"

"It really isn't anything you need concern yourself with, Mr. Harte," she murmured. "Would you like some more fish?"

"No, thank you," he said a bit harshly. He'd be the judge of what bloody concerned him or not, thank you very much. "Is it creditors?"

She looked amused at that. "If my brother had problems with creditors, do you really think he'd be financing the rebuilding of your garden?"

"He might. Your brother is half insane, no offense meant."

"None taken," she replied. "Val might be a trifle... eccentric, but he's always been quite level-headed when it comes to his money and business. I've no doubt that he invested in your gardens because he meant to make a profit. Although..." Her brows drew together. "Knowing Val, I wouldn't be at all surprised if he had other reasons as well."

That was an alarming thought. "Such as?"

"Who knows? Perhaps he found an opera singer he wanted to sponsor? Or a play he wanted staged." She shrugged. "Really, it could be anything at all with Val."

He hitched a hip onto a corner of her table, ignoring a pointed glare. "Don't get on with him, then?"

"I'll thank you not to put words in my mouth." She glanced up. "I love Val more than any other person in this world."

He cocked his head at her vehemence. He realized, suddenly, that he might have it all wrong. Perhaps her core wasn't bloodless after all. Perhaps under that cold exterior, that polite, aristocratic facade, there boiled a passionate woman, hiding her emotion from all the world.

And he wondered what would happen if he stripped away her exterior, tore through her frozen, refined walls and dug his fingers into the molten heat at her center.

Chapter Three

This king lived in a vast palace with hundreds of concubines in his harem. He was a cruel, lusty man and every year dozens of his concubines were brought to bed with child. But whenever one of the king's offspring reached the age of seventeen, they would be summoned to eat a celebratory meal with their father. And after that they were never heard from again....
—From *The Lion and the Dove*

The next morning Eve arrived at Harte's Folly punctually at nine of the clock. She and Jean-Marie and the footmen she'd brought with her passed gardeners who doffed their caps to her. Workmen were on the roof of the theater, so they must've been able to use part of the shipment of roofing tiles. Inside the theater she passed a group of women who appeared to have only just arrived—they were still removing hats and shawls. They stopped chattering and stared as she approached. Eve bid them good day and got one shy smile from the youngest girl, who sported a beauty mark at the corner of her mouth. After she went by them, though, she heard a burst of hastily smothered giggles and couldn't help the humiliated flush that climbed her cheeks.

She was entirely out of her element here and apparently it showed.

Nearer the stage she could see Mr. Vogel waving his arms about as his musicians assembled.

He turned suddenly as she neared and stared at her. "Vhat?"

Eve cleared her throat. "Good morning. I am Miss Eve Dinwoody."

He cocked his head, eyes narrowing. "Yes?"

"I'm here to see Mr. Harte." She waited, and when he didn't respond, she said a little more softly, "Do you know where his office is?"

Abruptly he nodded. "I vill show you." Turning back to his musicians, he shouted, "Ve vill begin in five minutes. Be prepared."

And on that ominous note he jerked his head and led her behind the stage.

"You are the sister of the duke, yes?" he asked as they entered a warren of corridors behind the stage. "Harte says you vill continue his credit."

Did everyone know Mr. Harte's business?

Mr. Vogel must've caught her startled expression, for he suddenly grinned and looked quite ten years younger than she'd placed him—nearer thirty than forty. "Theater folk, yes? Ve gossip."

"Ah." She cleared her throat as they stopped beside a door. "Well, much depends on Mr. Harte's books."

"*Gott* save us all, then," muttered the composer, and opened the door for her without preamble. "Good luck, for I think you vill need it."

With that he turned and retraced his steps.

Eve blinked and stepped inside the little room.

Mr. Harte was lounging in a chair in front of a big table, his feet crossed and resting on the table edge.

He was twirling a brass letter opener in the shape of a dagger in his fingers, but he looked up at her entrance. "Morning."

With one arm he shoved an open shallow box at her. It slid across the table, shedding bits of paper as it went.

The box stopped at the edge of the table nearest her. Eve glanced at it and back at Mr. Harte. He had a suspiciously cheerful grin on his face. "What is this?"

"My accounts."

She'd prepared herself for nearly anything. She wasn't such a featherbrain that she hadn't noticed Mr. Harte's glee yesterday afternoon at the mention of his office. Obviously it wouldn't be nearly as orderly as she was used to.

Still. She hadn't quite been expecting *this*.

"What do you mean, these are your accounts?" She stared at the box he'd shoved at her. It contained a pile of receipts, scribbled notes, and what looked like a small bag of coins. She took out the bag and opened it, then poured the contents into her palm. No, her mistake. It contained walnuts.

She glanced up at the source of this mess, appalled.

"I'd wondered where those had got to." Mr. Harte seemed to be enjoying her horror. He wore the same suit as yesterday, and had it not been for his freshly shaven chin and still-damp hair, she would've thought that he'd slept in the clothes. He tossed the brass letter opener aside, stood, and leaned over the desk, reaching with one long arm to pluck two walnuts from her palm. He made a fist around the nuts.

Eve heard the distinct *crack*.

Mr. Harte opened his hand and held it out to her. "Walnut? Got 'em fresh just last week."

"Thank you, no," she replied severely as she replaced the remaining nuts back in the little bag. "You *must* have more records of your accounts somewhere."

He resumed his seat before plucking a nutmeat from the shell in his hand and tossing it in the air, to catch it in his mouth. "'Fraid not, luv. This's the lot."

And he smiled that blasted smile at her, dimples and all, as he chewed openmouthed.

Eve glanced away from him in exasperation. She wasn't going to make the mistake of softening for that smile and his roguish ways. She was much too intelligent for that.

Instead she examined Mr. Harte's so-called office. It was a wretched little room. One would think, if he was going to the trouble of having an entirely new building constructed, that he would make provisions for his own business space. Apparently not. The actors' dressing rooms she'd passed on the way were at least twice as large as his office.

He had a small fireplace against one wall and an enormous map of London pinned crookedly on the other. In the center of the room, taking up most of the floor space, was the table. Stacks of papers were piled right on the floor all around the table, making it nearly impossible to walk. In the corner was a moldering stuffed badger. Eve eyed it before taking a deep breath. Fortunately, she'd planned ahead.

She turned to Jean-Marie, who was leaning against the doorjamb. "You'd better bring in the footmen."

Jean-Marie flashed a white-toothed grin before exiting.

When she looked back at Mr. Harte, he'd stopped midchew, his eyes narrowing. "What footmen?"

She smiled sweetly. "The footmen I borrowed from my brother's house, just for today."

And in trooped George and Sam.

Eve gestured to the papers on the floor. "Remove these, please."

Mr. Harte's eyes widened in outrage. "Now wait just a damned—"

But the footmen were already crowding past him and picking up the stacks of papers.

"Oi!" Mr. Harte turned on her. "You can't take my bloody papers!"

"I'm just rearranging them," she said soothingly.

"But there's no need to rearrange them!"

"There is if I'm going to fit my desk in here," she pointed out serenely as George and Sam left with their burdens.

And Bob and Bill came in with her little cherrywood desk.

"Here, miss?" asked Bob, indicating the now-cleared space opposite Mr. Harte's table.

"Hm, yes, I think so," Eve said, cocking her head consideringly. "Perhaps if you just push the table over a bit, you can put my desk right up against it, so we both have room."

They did as she directed and in another moment Eve had dismissed the footmen for the day and was settling into the straight-backed chair they'd carried in before leaving. A basket was set beside her desk and her writing case was on it. Now she opened her case and took out an ink bottle, a quill, sand, and a new bound accounts book, setting them all neatly on her desk.

"There. I shall be quite comfortable, I think, as I go through your accounts." She eyed the box of untidy papers, her spirits faltering slightly. "Such as they are."

"And what about that chair?" Mr. Harte asked, pointing at an overstuffed chair the footmen had squeezed into the corner next to the badger.

"That's for Jean-Marie, naturally," she replied as Jean-Marie came back in and took the chair in question.

"Naturally." Mr. Harte exchanged an unfriendly look with her bodyguard before leaning a little forward and jerking his head at Jean-Marie. "Does he follow you everywhere?"

"Everywhere," she confirmed. "And his hearing has never been deficient, has it, Jean-Marie?"

"*Non,*" came her bodyguard's reply. "I can 'ear most perfectly."

Mr. Harte scowled and sat tapping his fingers against his table for a minute before saying, "There's no need to work here. You can take that box of papers to your town house and examine it in comfort."

She glanced up at him, a scrawled scrap of paper in one hand. "We did make a bargain, Mr. Harte. If you wish to renege, I can of course withdraw your letters of credit should you feel I cannot use your office space."

Mr. Harte muttered something quite foul beneath his breath before holding up his hands in grudging surrender. "Stay as long as you like."

"Thank you," she said drily, squinting at the scrap of paper in her hand. "What does this say? All I can make out is 'peas.' "

He reached across the table and took the paper from her, his fingers brushing against hers. She jerked back instinctively, her hand balling into a fist, but he didn't seem to notice, turning the paper to the side.

Mr. Harte frowned for a second and then said, " '*Trees,*' not 'peas.' This is a bill for three of the trees that 'Pollo—Apollo Greaves, Viscount Kilbourne, our garden designer—had planted in the gardens."

"Oh?" Eve uncapped her ink bottle and wet the quill,

turning to the first page in the blank accounts book. "And how much did you pay for these three trees?"

He named a sum.

Slowly she raised her head, her quill still hovering over the page. *"Pardon?"* Surely she hadn't heard correctly.

He repeated the same ridiculous number.

"Good Lord," she murmured. "Were the trees made of pearls and gold?"

"No, but they were—*are*—quite big." Mr. Harte thrust out his chin. "Kilbourne had the trees transported from Oxford and successfully transplanted them. Had we used younger saplings, we would have had to wait years for the trees to mature."

Eve reluctantly nodded. She could understand the need for a more mature tree—though she still thought the price scandalous. She made a neat notation in her accounts book, then took another of the papers from the box. "And this?"

Mr. Harte looked shifty. "Do you intend to go through all the receipts today?"

She lifted her eyebrows. "Naturally."

"Ah." Mr. Harte pushed back from his table, standing up. "Well, unfortunately, I've a meeting with…er… MacLeish this morning. The roof, you know."

"But—" she started as he strode to the door of the office.

"Sorry, luv. Can't stop. I'm late as it is." And he was gone.

Eve narrowed her eyes at the closed office door, then turned to Jean-Marie. "Doesn't it seem awfully early to have a meeting about the roof?"

"Oui, it does indeed," Jean-Marie said promptly. "Mr. 'Arte does not wish to 'elp you with this work, I think."

"I suppose I should've expected nothing else," she murmured, eyeing the bits of paper. She sighed and began sorting them.

It wasn't ten minutes later when she was interrupted. The door opened and the woman with the beauty mark poked her head in. She was dressed in a dancer's costume now.

"Oh," she said when she saw Eve.

Eve sanded her paper, frowning a bit over the figures. At the rate she was going it would take at least a week to write everything down. "Yes?"

"Erm..." The girl shifted, looking vaguely about the tiny room. "I thought Mr. Harte was here?"

"Not at the moment," Eve said, and added drily, "He rushed out for an important appointment."

"Oh," said the girl again, and began to chew upon her fingernail.

She didn't look as if she was in any hurry to leave.

Eve folded her hands on her desk and smiled encouragingly. "Can *I* help you?"

The girl's eyes widened. "*Can* you?"

"Certainly," Eve replied, rather optimistically. "What's your name?"

"Polly," the girl said promptly, and then in a gush of words, "Polly Potts. I'm a dancer at the theater but I don't see how I can come tomorrow because of little Bets. She cries and cries and Mother Brown who is supposed to take care of her for tuppence a day declares she'll not have her no more and I'd begun to think she wasn't feeding little Bets the porridge I'd left for her, so it's just as well, but there isn't anyone else."

Polly stopped to draw a deep breath and Eve took advantage to leap into the breach. "Little Bets is your child?"

Polly looked at her as if she might be a trifle slow. "Yes, that's just what I've been telling you."

"I see." Eve knit her brows. Really, this was a problem for Mr. Harte, but it seemed to have a quite straightforward answer. "Why don't you bring Little Bets with you to the theater until you can find another childminder?"

Polly's eyes widened. "Can I?"

"I don't see why not."

A smile bloomed across the girl's face. "Cor! You're not a bad sort at all, even if you are a duke's sister."

And with that rousing statement of approval, Polly ducked back out of the room.

Eve blinked and then glanced at Jean-Marie. "Do you think I did the right thing?"

"We shall see soon enough, *oui*?" Her footman shrugged. "And besides, that one 'ad to find someplace safe for her little *bébé*. It is well what you did."

Eve shook her head uncertainly, turning back to the pile of receipts still in front of her, and then she perked up, remembering. "I'm so glad I brought the tea things."

She bent to the basket of provisions beside the desk, and took out her teapot and a tin of tea. She glanced at the fireplace. "Oh, but there's no kettle in here."

"I will find one," Jean-Marie declared, standing. "If you do not mind my leaving you alone for a short while, *mon amie*?"

"No, no, go look," Eve muttered, bending once more to her stack of incomprehensible papers.

She heard Jean-Marie leave and then all was silent for several minutes, save for the scratch of her quill. Eve was lost in her task, deciphering the different scrawled hands on the bits of paper and turning them into neat columns in her accounts book.

It was a while, then, before she realized that she was not alone in the office.

She became aware of a panting breath and a smell— one that always brought back nightmares even in the light of day—and she looked up, her entire body freezing. A great slavering dog stood in the doorway, its jaws agape, sharp fangs bared.

Eve screamed.

AFTER HALF AN hour spent calming both MacLeish and Vogel—the architect and the music master were arguing over the theater boxes of all things—Asa had headed back toward his office. This was mostly out of belated guilt. He knew he should help Miss Dinwoody wade through the debris of his business, but the mere thought of numbers and accounting made him itch, so he wasn't moving especially fast when he heard a woman scream.

Somehow he knew at once who it was.

He broke into a run, pounding though the narrow corridors backstage of the theater. He made the office, panting, and flung open the door.

A mastiff dog, thin and hungry-looking, cowered at his abrupt entrance, but that wasn't what held Asa's attention.

Miss Dinwoody still sat at the desk, her eyes wide and fixed on the dog in absolute terror. As he watched he saw her draw breath and scream again, high, shrill, and mindless.

She didn't seem to even notice his presence.

He moved toward her, reaching out a hand instinctively as her scream ended. She looked at him then, her blue eyes shining with unshed tears, and the sight made something in him rebel. Miss Dinwoody was prim and precise and everything that was irritating, but she was above all things *courageous*. She should not look so lost and alone.

"Miss Dinwoody," Asa said. "*Eve.*"

But before he could touch her, he was shoved aside.

The blackamoor rushed past Asa and wrapped his arms about his mistress. "Shh, *ma petite*. Jean-Marie is 'ere now and nothing shall 'urt you, this I promise on my soul."

Over the footman's shoulder, Asa saw Miss Dinwoody blink and draw breath. Her face crumpled all at once, and she buried it in Jean-Marie's shoulder and sobbed.

He felt as if he was watching something too intimate, as if she'd lost all her clothes before him and stood there naked and exposed.

The footman glanced around, looking first at Asa and then pointedly at the dog, who had sunk to the floor, whining. The message was clear.

Asa stepped toward the animal. "Shoo! Go on, you."

The dog leaped up and scrambled from the room. It might have been big but it was scrawny and half starving. Hardly something to be afraid of.

Asa glanced back at the tableau by the desk. He knew she would hate him even more for witnessing her loss of control, and right now he didn't want her to hate him. He wanted...he blinked in surprise. He had an almost visceral urge to shove the blackamoor aside and take Miss Dinwoody into his own arms.

Madness, that.

He closed the door quietly behind him.

Outside his office the dog had disappeared and he was

confronted by a little crowd. MacLeish was at the front, his face worried. "What happened? Who screamed?"

Behind him Vogel had his mouth pursed, while two of the dancers gaped from one of the dressing rooms.

"It's nothing to worry about." Asa held up his hands in a calming gesture. "Miss Dinwoody has agreed to help with my accounts and she saw a...er...dog. It startled her, I'm afraid." He grinned and winked at the dancers, though he didn't feel very jovial after seeing the state Miss Dinwoody had been in. "Not used to stray curs running about the place in the part of London where she's from."

"Saw that mutt th' other day," one of the builders muttered, turning away. "Ought to catch and drown it. Might attack someone."

"Diseased animals." One of the dancers shuddered delicately before winking saucily back at Asa and withdrawing into her dressing room.

The crowd dispersed, people going back to the work they'd been doing before the alarm.

Everyone but Violetta.

She wore deep crimson today, the color highlighting her dark, exotic beauty. "Miss Dinwoody did not seem the sort to scream at the sight of a poor dog."

Asa glanced back at the door and then took her arm, drawing her away from his office. "She was scared out of her wits, I vow. I've never seen the like."

The soprano looked thoughtful as they walked toward the garden. "I knew a girl once. She had a terrible fear of dark rooms. She had been locked inside a root cellar, you see, when she had been but a child, by her mother—a terrible thing for a mother to do. She never screamed, this girl, but she would struggle like a wild thing if led toward a room without light."

As usual Violetta's "Italian" accent nearly disappeared now that she was alone with him and thinking intently on something. Asa had long wondered if she was from outside England at all.

Asa pushed open the door that led into the garden just as an odd deep scraping sound came from above them.

Instinctively he leaped, pulling Violetta with him away from the theater's walls.

A horrific crash boomed as a pile of roofing tiles smashed to the ground exactly where he'd stood only seconds before.

"Oh, my God!" Violetta exclaimed, her Italian drawl now suddenly a broad Newcastle accent.

"What the bloody hell!" Asa stared at the roofing tiles and then up at the roof. No one was to be seen on this side of the theater.

The door they'd just exited burst open and MacLeish and Vogel rushed out. "What happened?" the architect asked.

Vogel merely spun and stared up at the roof as well.

Violetta gestured to the tiles. "Someone tried to kill us!"

"Surely not?" MacLeish blinked, horrified. "A careless workman must not've secured the tiles properly."

He looked at Asa appealingly.

Asa glanced again at the pile of broken tiles. Had he been a trifle slower, both his and Violetta's brains would've been dashed out. The accident had been very . . . ominous.

"I do not like such accidents," Vogel muttered, voicing Asa's exact thoughts.

"Nor do I," Violetta said in a shaky voice. "I don't like them at *all*. A fright like this is bad for my health. Bad for my *voice*."

Asa placed a reassuring arm around the soprano's shoulders. "It won't happen again, luv." He looked at MacLeish. "Make sure all the roofers know to secure their tiles. Another accident like this and I'll fire the lot of them."

"Of course." The architect looked relieved to have instructions. He glanced back at the door, where the second crowd of the day had gathered. "Everyone back to work."

He and Vogel ushered the disappointed crowd back inside and shut the door behind them.

Asa frowned at the broken tiles, hands on hips. He had his enemies, true, but—

"Come, *caro*," Violetta said, Italian accent back in place and having evidently recovered from her shock. She pulled gently on his arm. "You were-a telling me of Miss Dinwoody's so morbid fear of dogs."

He shook his head, turning to walk with her in the garden. "She seems too sensible a woman to have such a baseless fear."

Violetta shrugged. "Even the most sensible of us have such weaknesses. Besides, I saw this-a dog. It was not small."

"No, but it looked near starving," Asa said, still frowning. "Hardly a threat, I'd say, and yet she was so terrified I'm not sure she even knew I was in the room."

She stopped, drawing him to a standstill as well. They were by the new musicians' gallery, an open space with a flagstone pavement and the columns from the previous, burnt gallery left standing in a semicircle on the outside. Apollo had assured Asa that the effect would be that of a classical ruin, and Asa had to admit it was very similar. At night, with fairy lights and torches set here and there, his guests would feel as if they walked through ancient Roman ruins.

Violetta smiled up at him, an amused light in her eyes. "You seem much worried about Miss Dinwoody."

Asa cocked an eyebrow at her, shaking his head. "I'm just worried about how all this will affect my garden."

"Of course," she murmured. "The garden is, naturally, the important thing."

"I've worked all my adult life for this garden," he growled.

"Yes, so you've told me before," Violetta said serenely. "Many times. Probably, then, it is vital that you see how Miss Dinwoody is. You would not like to lose her brother's credit once again—especially at this critical time."

"You're right," Asa muttered, already turning back to the theater. "Damn that dog anyway for scaring her. She's going to be harder than ever to work with after this." He remembered the look in her blue eyes. He wanted to erase it. To see again Miss Dinwoody's self-assured gaze, the crimp of her prim little mouth as she tried to take him down a peg.

"No doubt," Violetta said, falling behind his long strides. "Perhaps you ought to invite her to sup with you instead of me tonight."

Asa stopped short, wincing. "I hadn't forgotten that I meant to take you to dinner."

"I never doubted it." She smiled up at him good-naturedly. "But you see, I have a duke—a *royal* duke—

who has been sniffing about my skirts. As delightful as your company is, *caro*, he has more to offer me, I think. You do understand?"

Asa lifted the corner of his mouth wryly. He might have charm and he might have wit, but what he'd never have was a title and loads of money, so in fact he *did* understand.

He'd never be the permanent choice for any woman— that lesson he'd learned long ago.

He bent and bussed her gently on the cheek. "Make sure the bounder treats you as he should, Violetta, or he'll have me to answer to."

For a moment her eyes turned regretful, and she reached up and placed her palm on his cheek. "You are the best man I've ever known, *mio caro*, honest and masculine and good. I wish the way of the world could be otherwise…" Her voice trailed away as she stepped back and shrugged. "But it is not so, I fear. Go now and see to your Miss Dinwoody." A secret smile flickered across her face. "I do not think it would do for you to lose her."

Asa nodded and turned to stride to his office. She was such a prickly thing, Miss Dinwoody. Perhaps it would be best to pretend that he hadn't seen her fear at all. But the bodyguard knew he'd been there when she'd screamed that second time. Had he told his mistress? And should Asa find and capture that dog—not drown it, certainly, for he had a soft spot for animals, but perhaps let it loose farther away from the gardens so it wouldn't wander close again?

He shook his head, strangely anticipatory, as he pushed open the door to his office, but when he looked inside it was to find that Miss Dinwoody was gone.

*   *   *

EVE LAY ON her settee with a cloth dampened with lavender water over her eyes and wondered if she'd ever be able to face Mr. Harte again. He'd *seen* her. Seen her shameful lack of control. Seen her reduced to a little girl, crying witlessly at the sight of a dog.

Oh, if only she could go back and live this morning over! She'd never have let Jean-Marie leave the office. He would have prevented that animal from entering the room.

But that wasn't the real problem, was it? Eve took the cloth from her eyes and stared sightlessly at the darkened ceiling. She simply wasn't like other women, who could go about their days without the fear that they'd see a stray dog or accidentally brush against a man. They weren't plagued by those scents and odd sights, sometimes very small things, that would make her freeze and make her heart beat fast and hard with pure terror. Make her remember *that* night, so long ago now, when she'd run from the dogs.

Run and been caught by something—*someone*—far worse than the dogs.

Eve squeezed her eyes shut, *pushing* the memories, the sights, the sounds, and—oh, God!—the *smells* from her mind.

She was safe. She was safe.

She was safe, but she wasn't normal.

She heard murmured voices downstairs then, Ruth telling someone that she was indisposed. It wasn't until Cockney accents floated up the stairs that she realized that Val's messenger boy was in her house.

Eve got to her feet, patted her hair to make sure it was

still in place, and squared her shoulders. She might not be entirely like other women, but she refused to become an invalid.

She walked to the head of the stairs and called down, "Ruth? Please send up the boy."

Alf appeared silently at the turn of the stairs. Eve shivered. The boy moved with unnatural, quiet grace, despite his feral appearance. He wore a tattered wide-brimmed hat pulled low over a clever, watchful face, a too-large waistcoat and coat flapping about his narrow shoulders.

"Ma'am." Alf pulled off his hat, revealing long brown hair untidily clubbed back. "I 'as a package for you from 'Is Grace."

He dug into one of the square pockets in his coat and pulled forth a grubby package, wrapped in paper and tied with string.

"Thank you." Eve gingerly took the thing. She sat and began plucking at the string, and then became aware that Alf was still standing before her, gazing rather longingly at the remains of her tea. "Would you like some?"

"Ta." Alf promptly sat on a nearby chair and poured himself a cup of tea with one hand while reaching for a biscuit with the other.

Eve looked down as the string on the package came loose. Inside were a tiny velvet pouch and a folded letter. She opened the pouch and tilted the contents onto her palm—then gasped. An ornate opal ring lay in her hand, the center stone surrounded by brilliant multicolored gems.

Eve glanced at Alf, who was pushing most of the biscuit into his mouth, apparently oblivious to the expensive gift she'd received from her brother. She wondered if the boy had any idea what he'd been carrying about London in his pocket.

She pushed the ring onto the third finger of her left hand and was unsurprised to find that it fit perfectly. It was just like Val to know the size of her fingers.

The letter was sealed as usual, and she pried open the red wax embossed with a rooster crowing. She smiled crookedly at Val's seal—it had always puzzled her, since it had nothing to do with the Montgomery crest.

The parchment popped open and Eve read, hearing her brother's voice as she did:

Dearest Eve,

I found this ring in the oddest little market outside Venice and bought it because the girl selling it had a mole in the shape of a heart on her neck. If it amuses, keep it. If not, toss it in the Serpentine for all I care. I hope that the rebuilding of Harte's Folly is continuing apace. It occurs to me that you might have use of a boy, so I've instructed Alf to make himself available in whatever capacity you might need him. Don't take any lip off of him.

Your Ever Fond & etc. Brother,
V.

Eve stared at the letter a moment longer, bemused by Val's careless generosity. The ring was beautiful and naturally she'd keep it. What she was supposed to do with Alf's services was more confusing.

She looked up in time to meet the boy's gaze as he

wiped his mouth on the sleeve of his coat. "'Imself said as I was to do whatever you should be wantin' me to. Gave me a month's worf o' pay."

"Ah," Eve said cautiously. "That's quite generous of you—and of course my brother." She carefully folded the letter. "As it happens I don't have use of your services at the moment."

Alf shrugged. "Jus' leave a message for me at the One 'Orned Goat in St. Giles when you 'ave need o' me. Or"— he hastily added at the look of doubt on her face—"if it be easier, you can leave word wif Mrs. Crumb. I'm 'round at 'Ermes 'Ouse near every day."

Eve nodded, relieved. "I'll do that." Although she really couldn't imagine needing Alf for anything. Still, she had the feeling it might hurt the boy's pride to say that aloud.

Voices came from the stairs and Alf rose, smashing his hat onto his head. "I'd best go, then, miss, if you don't have work for me now?"

Eve shook her head absently. She thought she recognized the male voice nearing, and her heart had begun to pound as wildly as it had done at the sight of the dog.

Alf looked at her curiously, then nodded and slipped from the room.

Just as Mr. Harte entered . . . bearing a bunch of daisies.

Chapter Four

*Now amongst the multitude of the king's offspring there
was a girl. She was born of an unimportant concubine
and was neither particularly fair nor wonderfully witty,
but her nursemaid, who had raised many of the king's
children, loved her above all others.
Her name was Dove....*
—From *The Lion and the Dove*

Asa Makepeace eyed the lad, surprised somehow. The
boy didn't seem to fit into Eve Dinwoody's world.

Then he looked at the lady.

Miss Dinwoody was standing, hands clasped together
in front of her, not meeting his gaze. She wore the same
dove-gray dress she'd had on that morning, the color discreet and retiring, as if she wanted to fade into the back-
ground. Strange. She was forthright in her demands of
him, fearless even as she confronted him in his own gardens, and yet she was terrified of dogs.

And she was quiet and hidden in her own house.

Eve Dinwoody seemed to be made of two halves that
didn't completely fit together. She puzzled him.

When she continued to avoid his eyes, Asa cleared his

throat and held out his offering. "Brought these for you," he said, sounding gruff even to himself.

In his hand was a simple bouquet of daisies, bought on impulse from a flower girl as he'd walked to her house. It was a cheap present, childish even, and he began to feel like a bloody prize ass as he held it out to her.

She was the daughter of a duke. No doubt she was better used to hothouse roses and diamonds—gifts he couldn't afford. Gifts from a different life than his.

But when she looked up, her face lit with a small smile.

"Thank you," she said shyly as she took the small bunch of daisies.

Asa felt his chest expand. "You're welcome. I came to . . . er . . ." He gestured vaguely with one hand.

She touched one of the daisy petals. "Yes?"

If he brought up the dog, told her he'd come to make sure she was well and to see if she'd still back his garden, it'd just make her stiffen up.

So instead he lifted one of his eyebrows. "Came to model for you."

She blinked. "Now?"

"Why not?" He deliberately fingered the stock at his neck, watching her blue eyes widen in what looked like alarm. "Oh, that's right. I'm to stay properly clothed at all times."

He couldn't help his mouth's curving at her expression. She was so prim, so easily shocked.

"Yes, you are." She pressed her lips together. "Just let me give these to Ruth to put in water and have a word with Jean-Marie."

And she hurried out.

He was left to glance around the room. The dove was

still on the table, and he strolled over to feed her a few kernels before wandering to the bookshelf and glancing at the titles. His eyebrows rose when he realized that half the volumes were in French.

He turned when she came back in. "You read French?"

"Yes." She looked him up and down. "Please sit down."

He flung himself down on the settee, both arms spread across the back, legs canted in front of him, and raised an eyebrow. "Like this?"

"I suppose that will do." She crossed to her table and rummaged around the top with her back to him.

He found his gaze lingering on her slim waist, the sway of her skirts. If he tilted his head he could almost glimpse her ankles beneath them.

She turned and he straightened, widening his eyes innocently.

She shot him a suspicious glance before seating herself on a chair across from him. She held a large sketchbook and a pencil.

Asa jerked his chin at her sketchbook. "I thought you wanted to paint me."

"I do," she muttered absently. "But first I need some preliminary sketches. Turn your head to the left."

He turned.

She gave him a look. "Your *other* left."

He rolled his eyes and obeyed. "Why do you need—"

"And tilt your chin down."

He lowered his chin and gave her a look from under his brows. "—to make a sketch?"

"It gives me an idea of the painting I want to make," she said, and her pencil scratched across her book.

Her movements were graceful. Swift and decisive, in

the manner of a professional used to a particular job, and he realized that she knew exactly what she was doing.

"How long have you painted?" he asked.

"Don't move."

He huffed in exasperation. He had a sudden need to scratch his nose.

"I started when I was thirteen," she murmured, bending closer to her work. "When Val sent me to Geneva."

That bit of information made him curious. "*Montgomery* sent you, not your father?"

She froze for a fraction of a second, and he wondered what nerve he'd hit. Then she relaxed and resumed her drawing, saying casually, "Val always cared for me more than our father."

"Your father the *duke*," he drawled, watching.

"Yes." Her eyelashes fluttered, then stilled. "The old duke was a very cold sort of man. I lived in his house as a child, but I rarely saw him." Her eyes were lowered, intent on her drawing, and he couldn't read them. "That was just as well."

He had a gut feeling that there was more to it than that. "And your mother?"

She didn't answer for a moment, drawing in silence, then she said, "What of her?"

He smiled hard. "Who was she?"

She glanced up then, meeting his gaze with blue eyes so cold they might as well have been ice. "She was a nursemaid."

He waited, holding her gaze, but she said no more. After a moment she looked down and continued drawing.

He shrugged his shoulders, working out the tension from holding them still.

"Don't move," she murmured absently.

He narrowed his eyes. "Is that where you learned French? In Geneva?"

"And German." She held the sketchbook at arm's length, examined it, then turned her gaze to him, studying his face with a sort of abstract dispassion, disconcerting in its intensity. "I attended a small, exclusive school for girls. During the summers I lived with an elderly brother and sister—along with Jean-Marie, who came to me when I was fifteen. The brother was a quite well-known miniaturist. When he discovered I had some talent in portraiture, he took me on as a sort of apprentice."

"How long were you there?"

"I only returned to England five years ago," she said, bending to peer at something in her sketchbook. "By that time both the brother and sister had died of old age."

Her words were blunt, but he detected a trace of sorrow in them and pounced on it like a cat on an unwary mouse. "You miss them."

"Of course." She paused to stare at him, her brows drawn together over those sky-blue eyes. "They took me in, fed me, clothed me, and taught me."

"Because your brother paid them," he pointed out cynically.

"Maybe so." Two spots of color appeared high in her cheeks as she narrowed her eyes at him. He felt a spurt of satisfaction: finally he'd poked her in a tender spot. "But affection cannot be bought. Monsieur Laffitte did not need to teach me to paint, nor did Mademoiselle Laffitte need to bake me my favorite little rosewater cakes. They did it out of affection. They did it out of *love*."

That was important to her, was it? That people love her for herself rather than her brother's money?

"Stand down, stand down," Asa said, easily, palms raised. "I didn't mean to impugn your foster family."

"Didn't you?" Her eyes were still narrowed, and he couldn't help but think how regal she appeared as she looked at him as if he were a piece of shit in the gutter. "You seem to delight in bringing everything down to money."

He tilted his head, his jaw clenching even as he drawled, "Well, for some—those born *without* a golden tit in their mouths—much of life does come down to money. How to get money, how to keep money, how to have enough of it to live decently."

"I am aware—"

"*Are* you?" His voice was hard. How dare she bloody judge him? "But you've never wanted for money, have you? Your brother supplies whatever you need whenever you need it without a thought from you. What can you know, then, about how desperate the lack of money can make a man?"

She looked at him a moment before asking softly, "What do you know about it?"

"I know that I'm judged upon what money I have and what money I lack. I have no name, no title, no talent beside rousing people to work in a theater. What else, then, is there to judge me on than the weight of my purse?" He leaned forward, caring little that he'd destroyed the pose, and stared at her hard. "And I know there was a time when, had the Devil appeared before me, I would've sold my soul for a thousand pounds and a pair of diamond buckles for my shoes." His lip curled and he flung himself back on the settee, looking away from her. "Don't lecture me on my love of money. It's how *other* people find worth in me."

There was a pause and he clearly heard her swallow in the silence of the room. "Who judged you for your lack of money?"

For a moment a pretty, faithless face swam before his eyes. But that was ten years ago and he'd made himself forget the bitch's name in the interim. He turned back to her, his cynical grin firmly in place as he stared at her in challenge. "Who has not?"

She looked at him thoughtfully. "I don't."

"Don't you, luv?" he growled softly. Warningly. He tolerated polite lies in other people but for some reason he couldn't let hers go. "I wouldn't be sitting in this room with you had you no control over my funds."

But she didn't back down. "I control your funds. I don't control *you*. And I think, Mr. Harte, that had you all the money in the world, or sat penniless in a gutter, I still would not find you very likable."

He stared at her a moment before throwing back his head and shouting with laughter. There she was! That was the harpy he was beginning to know. It was several seconds before he could control himself again, and when he did, he wiped tears of mirth from his eyes as he said, "Damn me, Miss Dinwoody, I'd rather your acid tongue than any number of sweet lies from pretty lips."

He half expected her to be insulted by his blunt words, but when he looked, she had a small, satisfied smile.

It cleared soon enough, though. "Yes, well, perhaps you can assume your pose again?"

"With pleasure," he drawled, and tilted his chin down in the way he had before.

In this position he was gazing at her from beneath his eyebrows, and he watched as she lost herself in her drawing again. Her eyes flicked from his forehead to his nose to his chin, and then to his mouth. She bent to her work, sketching rapidly before she glanced up at him again, her gaze meeting his eyes almost challengingly. Her nostrils flared ever so slightly, her soft bottom lip caught between her teeth as she stared at him, blue eyes narrowed. It was a frank scrutiny, analyzing and bold, and it felt sexual.

Asa could feel his cock hardening and he spread his legs farther, holding her gaze. He felt his voice rumble softly in his chest as he asked, "What do you see when you look at me?"

WHAT DID SHE see when she looked at him?

Eve inhaled, trying and failing to tear her gaze from his.

Mr. Harte sprawled across her dainty settee like a Viking marauder in a pillaged Christian church. His broad shoulders took up more than half the width, his arms lazily draped over the back. His scarlet coat was spread open, contrasting with the sedate gray-blue of the cushions almost shockingly. One long leg was thrust straight before him, the other cocked open and resting on a booted heel. The pose made the apex of his thighs very . . . obvious . . . and even as she kept her eyes locked on his she could feel heat rising in her cheeks.

What did she see?

She saw violence and anger, kept under a control that was tenuous at best. She saw power and a strength that could hurt her—*kill* her—if he so chose. She saw the innate brutality that was, in larger or smaller part, in all men.

She saw her most terrible fears.

But—and this was the truly unprecedented part—she saw *more* in him. She saw temptation—*her* temptation—alluring and frightening at the same time, his virility so strong it was nearly a visible miasma in the space between them.

She wanted him. Wanted that brash gaze, those long, muscled thighs, that mocking, insulting mouth, and the shoulders that went on forever, big and brawny and so very, very *male*.

This was madness—she knew that intellectually. She'd never wanted a man before—was in fact *afraid* of almost all men, let alone one so obviously, blatantly sexual.

She took a breath, hoping that he couldn't read all this from her gaze—and knowing it was a lost cause already. His heavy-lidded green eyes were far, far too perceptive.

"I see..." She paused to lick suddenly dry lips. "I see that your hairline is nearly a perfect arc across the expanse of your forehead. That your eyebrows tilt ever so slightly up at the ends and that the right has a scar through it. I see that when you are solemn, the outer edges of your lips reach just to the midpoint of your eyes, but when you smile, they go beyond the corners. I see that your chin and jaw are almost in classical proportion and that a small white scar forms a comma on your chin just to the right of center." She finally glanced away from him, breathing heavily, certain that she'd not thrown him off the track with her artist's eye's impressions. She inhaled again and ended, "I see every line of your face, every line's intersection and how they relate. That is what I see when I look at you."

"And is that all you see? Lines?" His voice was deep and amused.

She chanced a peek.

He still watched her, his gaze utterly unperturbed by her observations about his countenance.

No, she'd not fooled him at all.

She licked her lips again, buying time. "I see," she said carefully, cautiously, "a very self-possessed man."

"Self-possessed," he drawled. "I'm not sure what that means, frankly. It sounds, just a bit, like a coward's answer."

Her gaze flew to his, outraged.

But before she could take him down a peg, he chuckled softly. "Tell me, Miss Dinwoody, would you like to know what I see when I look at you?"

She shouldn't. She really, really shouldn't.

"Yes," she blurted, and then winced because she knew well enough what men thought when they looked at her: *ordinary*, if they were charitable.

Plain if they were not.

She braced herself for mockery, but when she glanced again at him, his gaze was hot and hard. Certainly not gentle. Certainly not kind. But he wasn't dismissing her, either.

He looked at her as if they were equals. As if he really saw *her*, a woman to his man.

"I see," he said, his deep voice musing, "a woman afraid, but fighting her fears. A woman who carries herself like a queen. A woman who could rule us all, I suspect."

She gazed at him, her breath caught in her throat, afraid to exhale and break the spell.

A corner of that wicked mouth tilted up. "And I see a woman who has a deep curiosity. Who wants to feel but is worried—of herself? Of others?" He shook his head. "I'm not sure." He leaned forward slowly, destroying his pose, and she had to fight herself not to scoot her chair away from him. "But I think she has a fire banked within her. Maybe it's only embers now, glowing in the dark, but if tinder were to be put to those embers…" He grinned slowly. Dangerously. "Oh, what a conflagration that would be."

She'd stopped breathing altogether, watching him as a bird watches a tomcat just before it pounces. *Her*? A conflagration? The mere thought made her hot.

"I…" She glanced down at her drawing, realizing she had no idea where she was. "I…"

Jean-Marie walked into the room. "*Mon amie*? You said to tell you when it struck two of the clock." He stopped and glanced between her and Mr. Harte, his brows drawing together suspiciously.

"Yes, thank you, Jean-Marie," she said breathlessly. She felt a pang of disappointment. She'd given her footman the instructions earlier as a sort of safeguard in case the sketching session turned uncomfortable.

Well, it had at that, but not in the manner she'd anticipated.

Mr. Harte sighed. "I'd best go if it's already gone two. Have to make a trip to Bond Street."

"Oh?" She couldn't quite stifle her curiosity.

He nodded, standing. "Have to go buy a chandelier for the theater."

Eve came to a rather impulsive decision. "In that case I'll accompany you."

ASA BLINKED. "WHAT?"

Miss Dinwoody smiled serenely. Where was the woman

flushed from his mere *words*? Gone, it seemed, disappeared into the lady man of business. "Shall we take my brother's carriage? If I'm not mistaken, it's still in the mews from when I borrowed it this morning."

Of course she had the use of a carriage. He didn't even own a horse.

He scowled. He'd actually enjoyed the modeling session, odd as it was to admit, but he sure as hell didn't need her nursemaiding his errand to procure lighting for the theater. "It's just a chandelier. Bound to be boring."

She gazed at him with pity. "Mr. Harte, shopping on Bond Street is *never* boring."

Which was how he found himself in front of the house ten minutes later with Miss Dinwoody and her guard, watching a carriage round the corner.

The moment it stopped he grabbed for the door, then held it open for her.

That got him a scowl from Jean-Marie, which he returned behind Miss Dinwoody's back with an obscene pursing of his lips.

"Thank you," Miss Dinwoody said as she settled herself on the seat.

"My pleasure," Asa muttered as he took his own seat. He eyed the bodyguard a moment and then chose a safe conversational subject. "So, French and German. What else did you learn at that girls' school you went to?"

She shrugged. "Dancing, embroidery, a bit of maths and classical literature and a smattering of geography. Nothing very helpful, I'm afraid. The other girls who went there were mostly preparing to marry well."

He settled more comfortably in the seat. Might as well enjoy the carriage ride. "But not you?"

"I'm sorry?"

"You didn't expect to marry?"

There was a small pause, and Jean-Marie sent him an oblique glance that was hard to interpret.

She pursed her lips and looked down at her lap. "No."

Which was a bit odd. She might be a bastard, but the daughter of a duke was the daughter of a duke. She could've made quite a nice marriage had she wanted to, especially if Montgomery had been willing to dower her.

"And you?" Her voice cut into his thoughts.

"Beg pardon?"

She cocked her head. "How were you educated?"

"At home." He debated leaving it at that, but just because she'd decided to be damnably closed-mouthed didn't mean he had to be. He shrugged. "Along with my brothers and sisters."

She blinked at that. "You have family?"

He grinned. "Did you think I crawled out from under a rock three decades ago? I've three sisters and two brothers."

"Do you?" For some reason this information made her lean a little forward, her eyebrows winged up in interest. "I've always wondered what it would be like to have a large family."

He grimaced at that, thinking of the last time he'd seen Concord, his elder brother. *That* had ended in them shouting at each other, Con managing somehow to do it without blasphemy—which couldn't have been said for Asa. "On the whole, it's more trouble than it's worth."

She looked confused. "What do you mean?"

He sighed. "There are rules and expectations in a family—especially *my* family. And I've never been any good at rules *or* expectations, luv." He lifted a corner of his mouth in a mirthless smile. He'd never truly fit in with the rest of the Makepeaces—a cuckoo in a sparrow's nest. "So I've found it's easier just to avoid the lot of them."

She sucked in a breath. "*Avoid* them? You don't see them at all?"

He grinned hard. "Not if I can help it."

"Then you don't love them," she said, strangely intent.

"Didn't say that," he muttered, looking out the window. The carriage was moving at a bloody slow pace due to the London traffic.

She was silent a moment, and then, "I can imagine that you aren't very amenable to rules, but I would think that your family would consider you a great success."

He snorted at that. *Oh, if only she knew.* He glanced at her. Both she and the footman were looking at him. "My family isn't much…ah…interested in the theater."

"But you own Harte's Folly," she said, sounding almost outraged. "Until it burned down the garden was an enormous draw. I'd think your family would be very proud of you."

Pride hadn't been what his father had felt for him the last time Asa had seen him alive. He shook the thought aside. "It took years of constant work before Harte's Folly finally made money. Until then I put every ha'penny back into the garden. I expect my family still thinks I'm struggling—which, because of the fire, I am."

"Thinks?" She stared once more at him. "When was the last time you actually spoke to your parents?"

"They're dead," he said. "Mother when I was fifteen, Father five years ago."

"And that's when you inherited Harte's Folly?"

"What?" He smiled at the thought of his stern father's ever being involved with something as frivolous as the theater. Old Josiah Makepeace was probably rolling in his grave at the very notion. "No, I told you, my family frowned on the theater—and pleasure gardens, come to that."

"Then how did you become owner of Harte's Folly?"

"Ah, well," he said, scratching the back of his neck. "I don't usually tell people, but since you're an investor—or at least the sister of my main investor—as it happens I received the garden in a bequest left by Sir Stanley Gilpin, who was a great friend of my father's."

"Really?" She seemed truly interested in his answer. "He must've liked you very much to leave you the gardens."

"I suppose he did," Asa said. "Sir Stanley and my father had very little in common. My father worked as a beer brewer all his life, while Sir Stanley was moderately wealthy and liked to dabble in the theater. He bought Harte's Folly as a young man and worked to build it off and on over the years. When I was seventeen or so I started sneaking away from my family and hanging about the theater whenever I could. When he found out where I was going my father didn't approve." *A magnificent understatement.*

"But if Sir Stanley was his friend..." Her brows were drawn together as if she tried to understand.

He shook his head. "I think he genuinely loved Sir Stanley, but at the same time my father thought what he did was sinful. I was nineteen when he found out. I told my father then that I wanted to work at Sir Stanley's theater. He didn't take it well." He paused and swallowed, remembering the words his father had roared at him.

The words he'd screamed in return.

Asa shook his head and continued, "Sir Stanley took me in. He had no family of his own. He was kind to me, taught me all he knew about theater and opera and running a pleasure garden. Over the years I gradually took on more and more responsibility." Asa stared for a moment out the window, remembering Sir Stanley's childlike wonder and enthusiasm for the theater.

"You sound as if you were very fond of him," she said quietly.

"I loved him like a father," he said. "And when I realized that he'd left me Harte's Folly, I vowed to make it the most wonderful place on earth."

"So you've been laboring at the gardens ever since the age of seventeen." Her sky-blue eyes were narrowed thoughtfully on him. "That's over a decade, isn't it?"

"Yes," he said. "I'm four and thirty and I've worked all my adult life for the gardens."

She nodded slowly, her expression pensive. "There's just one thing I don't understand."

"What's that?"

"Well," she said as the carriage drew to a halt near Bond Street. "If Sir Stanley's last name was Gilpin, why did Harte's Folly bear your name *before* you inherited it?"

EVE WATCHED MR. HARTE curiously. He was a much more complex man than she'd initially thought, and she found she wanted to know more—more of what had made him the man he was today, more of what lay beneath that dangerously roguish exterior.

Mr. Harte's lips twisted as he glanced away from her. "Ah. Well, to be perfectly truthful…"

"Yes," she prompted drily. "I do like truthfulness."

Beside her Jean-Marie snorted under his breath, and Mr. Harte glared at him. "My name's not Harte."

She waited, her eyebrows arched, even as she felt her pulse jump. Discovering information about Mr. Harte—or whoever he was—was rather exciting.

"It's Asa Makepeace," he said, and she blinked.

Asa. The name suited him. She hadn't been aware of wanting to know what his Christian name was, but now that she knew it, she felt an undeniable gratification. *Asa.* Asa Makepeace. Pity addressing a man by his given name was simply not done.

Her eyes widened on a thought. "Makepeace. That's the last name of the manager of the Home for Unfortunate Infants and Foundling Children. I met him and his wife when I attended a meeting of the Ladies' Syndicate for the Benefit of the Home for Unfortunate Infants and Foundling Children there."

He nodded once. "Winter is my younger brother. So you've been to the orphanage?"

"Yes." She had, though under circumstances she wasn't particularly proud of.

Fortunately, the door to the carriage opened at that moment, providing a welcome distraction.

Eve rose and descended with the help of the carriage footman. She waited for the two men before she asked, "You took the name Harte from the garden, not the other way around?"

Mr. Makepeace held out his arm to her, not speaking for a moment.

She glanced at him curiously.

His face was grim. "When we had our . . . falling out, my

father made it clear that he didn't want me using the family name if I intended to continue in the theater business."

She inhaled sharply. She was beginning to think the "falling out" had been closer to his father's disowning him. Mr. Makepeace was a proud man—she'd seen that from the first. How must it have felt for his father to forbid him his own name? The thought sparked a feeling of... well, not *pity*, for Mr. Makepeace wasn't a man to be pitied, but perhaps sympathy.

"I see." She eyed his proffered arm a moment. Normally the only men she allowed to touch her were Val or Jean-Marie.

It felt daring to place the tips of her fingers on his sleeve.

He didn't seem to notice, though, as they set off down Bond Street. It was a lovely sunny day and her spirits lifted as she walked beside him. Jean-Marie was right behind, close enough to come to her aid should she need it.

"Where are we headed?" she asked.

One could buy nearly anything on Bond Street if one had the desire and the money for it. From stationery to furniture to lace and tobacco and everything in between. Goods from all the corners of the world streamed into the port of London and were offered for sale here. The street was lined with shops, each one with bulks in front— tables fixed to the shop's façade and used to display the wares. But Bond Street wasn't simply for commerce. Everyone who was anyone promenaded up and down the street, examining the displays, stopping to chat, and strutting for all to see.

"Thorpe's," he replied, solicitously steering her around a rather noxious puddle.

"The candelabra maker?"

"Yes. I need to outfit the stage with lighting. I'm thinking we'll want a large chandelier overhead, with many sconces and freestanding candelabra as well."

She nodded and then stiffened, instinctually stopping as she saw a small, fluffy dog on a lead coming toward them.

Mr. Makepeace glanced at the animal and then her before deftly turning her so that the dog passed behind and out of sight.

She blew out a relieved breath, feeling both foolish and irritated with herself. These fears were so silly! She knew this intellectually, but her body still responded without her consent to certain situations.

As if he knew her thoughts, Mr. Makepeace bent his head closer to hers. "Is it all dogs, then?"

She nodded jerkily, aware that she could smell some woody scent on him, perhaps his soap? "All canines, but especially large ones."

He straightened without comment, but he laid a hand over hers on his arm and gave a squeeze. The simple touch seemed to travel up her arm and straight to her center and she struggled to keep her face serene.

"Here it is," he said after another few paces.

Thorpe's sign swung overhead, the name of the shop in elaborate black script. Two wide bulks were laden with candlesticks of every description. There were no windows to the shop, but when Mr. Makepeace held the door open, Eve stepped into a large display room filled from floor to ceiling with thousands of candlesticks, candelabra, hanging chandeliers, and wall sconces, many of them lit, making the room blaze with light.

Eve stopped and stared, feeling the heat of the hundreds of candles beat against her cheeks, but Mr. Makepeace walked to the middle of the show room. He turned in a circle, examining the fittings overhead, and pointed to the largest chandelier in the shop. "There. That's the one I want."

"That looks very expensive." Eve squinted at the curlicues and swirls and the multitude of crystal drops hanging from them. The entire piece seemed to be gilded. "What about that one?" She pointed to a smaller brass chandelier with far fewer crystal drops.

"It won't do," he snapped, his face darkening with irritation.

She fought an instinctive urge to move away from masculine anger. Instead she made herself stand her ground. "Won't it? Explain." For a moment she thought he would simply argue. She touched his arm with a fingertip. "Please. I want to understand."

He actually closed his mouth, thought for a moment, and then indicated the chandelier she'd chosen. "Look at the number of candles it holds. I estimate it at only half the number of the bigger one." Mr. Makepeace turned to the chandelier he liked. "This one not only has more candle holders, but also more crystals to reflect the light of the candles." He looked at her. "The light in the theater is very important. If my guests can't see the stage and the actors, they'll not enjoy the show and they'll not return."

Eve glanced at him, reluctantly seeing his concerns.

He must've read her face, for he smiled wryly. "You thought I just picked it because it was the most expensive."

"Perhaps." She cleared her throat. "Then it's the light that most concerns you, not the gold?"

His eyes narrowed. "Naturally the appearance of the chandelier must be handsome as well."

"But it'll be high above your guests' heads." She looked shrewdly at the chandelier he liked. "I wonder if we can have one made like this, but in ungilded brass. From above, with all the crystals, I doubt most in your audience will know the difference." She glanced at him. "But the savings would be considerable. Do you see?"

"Yes," he replied slowly. "Yes, I think I do."

He was looking at her with admiration and she felt heat rise in her cheeks. Eve knew she was blushing as his smile grew wider. His green eyes were knowing, almost intimate, and she couldn't look away.

"May I help you make a selection, sir?"

She blinked, the spell broken by a shop assistant. The man was bowing before Mr. Makepeace, entirely ignoring her. She wondered what the man would say if he knew *she* was the one who held the purse strings.

She watched as Mr. Makepeace asked about having a chandelier made. He and the assistant began bargaining over the price and delivery times and she saw that same smile, the one he'd used on her, aimed at the other man.

Eve glanced away. She shouldn't feel disappointed—nearly hurt—that his smile wasn't just for her. She had to remember that Mr. Makepeace was a charmer—he made his living by convincing others to do things for him, whether they were singers or composers, a shop assistant, or *she*. It wasn't intimate or special when he smiled at her. She mustn't become confused and think that he had any particular interest in her.

She knew what she looked like, knew as well that she was too private, too odd for most gentlemen. Eve took a deep breath. And what did it matter anyway? If, in the unlikely event, a gentleman became interested in her, she would be unable to respond appropriately.

She'd long ago realized that such things were not for her.

"What do you think?" Mr. Makepeace said, his deep voice drawing her out of her morose thoughts.

She looked up and there was that smile again, warm and inviting. It was hard—so hard—to remind herself it wasn't hers, that smile. He gave it out freely to all comers.

"I think the chandelier still too expensive, even made with brass," she said slowly. "But if it is what you must have for the theater, then buy it."

His wide lips quirked, the dimples flashed, and his eyes were warm and lit. He wasn't a handsome man, Asa Makepeace—she'd realized that when trying to capture his essential allure this afternoon. It was frustratingly hard to put it on paper, for she'd discovered that it was in gesture and breath that he came alive. He was a being of action and vitality, and when he moved, when he smiled, he became almost impossible to resist.

But resist him she must.

Something must've shown in her face, perhaps her internal conflict, for his own sobered, that devastating smile faltering as he stepped closer to her. "Miss Dinwoody? Eve? Is something amiss?"

For the life of her she didn't know how to answer.

So it was almost a relief when she heard a familiar voice behind her. "Eve Dinwoody? Are you here?"

She turned, her heart plummeting for an entirely different reason as she saw Lady Phoebe, the youngest sister of the Duke of Wakefield.

The woman her brother had wronged so very horribly.

Eve felt her stomach roil. She glanced down at the opal ring gleaming on her finger and back up. "Lady Phoebe... I... forgive me, my lady. I did not know you would be on Bond Street today."

She felt Mr. Makepeace take her arm, and she was inordinately glad that he was there to steady her.

Lady Phoebe was short and plump and very pretty, and, if Eve wasn't mistaken, she had a small but significant bump at her waist. She had her hand on the arm of a taller, much sterner man, his dark hair pulled back into a severe braided queue. With his other hand he leaned on a cane.

Lady Phoebe had had a winsome smile upon her face, but it faltered at Eve's words and she looked a little hurt. "Are you avoiding me, Miss Dinwoody? I vow no matter what happened this last summer I don't think I have a need to forgive you."

"Don't you?" Eve knew she was speaking too bluntly, too plainly, but she couldn't stop herself. She'd felt horrible when she'd discovered what Val had done, and this was the first time she'd seen the other woman since that fateful night. "My brother tried to do you an unconscionable evil."

"Your *brother*, not you, Miss Dinwoody," Lady Phoebe said softly. "Why, were we all to be judged by our brothers, I'm not sure what we would do."

"I..." Eve felt tears prick at her eyes. She hadn't thought to find such simple kindness. "Thank you, my lady."

"Please." Lady Phoebe held out her hand. Eve took it— what other choice did she have? "Please, call me Phoebe."

"Oh, I—"

"And I hope I shall see you at the meeting of the Ladies' Syndicate for the Benefit of the Home for Unfortunate Infants and Foundling Children next week? I know Hero sent you an invitation, for she told me so most expressly. Apparently you've missed our other meetings."

Eve felt the blush climb her cheeks. "I...I don't know if—"

"But *I* do know," Phoebe said gently. "Please come."

Eve looked a little helplessly at Mr. Makepeace, who stirred and addressed the couple. "My lady, Captain Trevillion. I'd heard you make your home now in Cornwall."

"I do." Captain Trevillion glanced down at the woman beside him and Eve was amazed at the softening of his eyes. "*We* do. My wife and I have come up to London to assist my father in the sale of some horses. Phoebe, I think you remember Mr. Harte of Harte's Folly? He's accompanying Miss Dinwoody and Miss Dinwoody's footman, I believe."

Phoebe's blind eyes stared just past Eve's shoulder. "How nice to meet you again, Mr. Harte. Tell me, how is your garden renovation coming along? I do so miss the theater there."

Mr. Makepeace bowed, though the lady couldn't see his gallantry. "Steadily apace, my lady. I hope to reopen in less than a month. I trust you'll be there?"

She turned to her husband. "What do you think, James? Perhaps we can bring Agnes up for a fortnight or more?" Her head swiveled back to them. "My husband's niece has never been to the theater."

"Then she must come to our first night reopened," Asa said. "I'll send round a set of complimentary tickets to your brother's house."

"Oh, thank you!" Phoebe blushed quite becomingly. "That's very kind of you, Mr. Harte."

"It's my pleasure, my lady."

"Thank you, Harte." Captain Trevillion nodded at the other man. "Miss Dinwoody. If you'll excuse us, I believe my wife is meeting her sister for tea and cakes and I'll be in in trouble if she's late."

Mr. Makepeace bowed again while Eve dipped into a curtsy as they made their farewells. She watched as Phoebe and her new husband exited the candelabra shop. It was so wonderful to know the other woman didn't blame her for her brother's sin. She really liked Lady Phoebe.

So it was with a smile on her lips that she turned to Mr. Makepeace again.

Only to meet his suspicious gaze. "What exactly did the Duke of Montgomery do to Lady Phoebe?"

Chapter Five

On the day of her seventeenth birthday, the nursemaid took Dove's hand and said, "The king will command you to dine with him tonight. Do everything that he bids you, child, all but this: no matter what he does or says, never look away from his eyes." ...
—From *The Lion and the Dove*

Miss Dinwoody glanced about the shop nervously before whispering, "Lower your voice."

Asa arched an eyebrow, not bothering to do as he was told. "Are you going to answer me?"

She walked away toward the entrance to the shop.

Asa felt his ire rise.

In two strides he was beside her, though he didn't try to take her arm. Jean-Marie was right behind them, and no doubt keeping an eagle eye on his mistress. "I dislike being ignored, luv."

"And I dislike discussing my family's business," she snapped back as they walked outside. "What happened between my brother and Lady Phoebe isn't any of your concern."

He knew what she said was reasonable, perhaps even correct, but something inside him rebelled at being so

firmly shoved aside. At being told he had no right to discuss her family and her worries.

At being told to go away like a fucking bootblack boy.

"If the duke's actions impact upon my garden, it's
entirely my bloody concern," he said, sounding like a
pompous ass even to his own ears.

She blew out a breath. "This matter has absolutely
nothing to do with your precious garden. Why can't you
just let the matter drop?"

Why indeed? Because he'd made his interest known
and he wasn't about to back down now. More, he wasn't
going to be ignored by her, even if she was the daughter
of a bloody duke. Other ladies might tell him he was too
common, too fucking *poor*, but he wouldn't let her do it.

Not her.

He dodged around two ladies standing and gossiping by a shop display, and regained her side. "Did he
assault her?"

Miss Dinwoody stopped dead and turned to him.
"What?"

It was his turn to eye their surroundings. They stood
in broad daylight in Bond Street, the crowds streaming
by them. He lowered his head and looked at her intently.
"You heard me. Did your brother hurt the lady?"

"No!" Her look was pure aristocrat now, cold and
aloof, and it was driving him near insane. "I've already
told you that I won't speak on the matter."

For a moment he stared at her, his rage boiling beneath
his skin. Her eyes widened with something that might've
been comprehension, but he was already turning and
shoving his way through the crowd, leaving her behind.

"Wait!"

Her call jerked him to a stop, his chest rising and falling swiftly.

He heard the patter of her slippers and then she rounded his side, peering into his face. Her hand half rose, but she hesitated as if afraid and then let it fall.

She glanced away, biting her lip, and said softly, "Val didn't hurt her—at least not in the manner that you imply. Val would never hurt a lady so." She glared at him, her sky-blue eyes sparking as if she dared him to contradict her. "I can't believe you would think that of my brother."

"What else am I to think when you won't tell me the truth?" he growled.

"Not *that*. Never that," she whispered, and something in her voice made him want to take her into his arms and comfort her.

He shook his head, glancing around. "Damn it, where is your carriage?"

"This way," came Jean-Marie's deep rumble.

Asa jerked, having somehow forgotten the footman in the midst of their argument.

Jean-Marie was giving him a none-too-friendly look, but his face softened as he turned to his mistress. "Come, *ma chérie*, you are tired now. Let us go to your carriage."

She sighed. "Very well."

They set off, Asa prowling broodingly behind. At least the position gave him an excellent chance to try to catch a glimpse of her ankles again.

Five minutes later, when they were at last in the carriage and settled, he looked at Miss Dinwoody and demanded, "Well?"

She looked across at him, earnestly. "You mustn't tell

anyone, for the entire matter was made quiet by the Duke of Wakefield."

Asa placed a palm over his heart and cocked his head mockingly. "You have my word."

She pursed her lips at his sarcasm.

He stared at her, waiting.

Reluctantly, it seemed, she said, "You remember the kidnapping attempts against Lady Phoebe this last summer?"

Asa arched an eyebrow. "Yes."

The gossip had it that there had been several attempts to steal Lady Phoebe. Further, some said that at least one of the attempts had been successful and that the lady had been held against her will for days or even weeks—a huge scandal in the aristocracy. Lady Phoebe came from the bluest of blue blood and her elder brother was both powerful and wealthy. The gossip had abruptly died after Lady Phoebe's marriage to Captain Trevillion.

Happiness, it seemed, wasn't of any prurient interest.

Miss Dinwoody sat very straight, despite the swaying of the carriage. "Val was the kidnapper. He wanted to force her into marriage."

"What?" That didn't make any sense at all. "Montgomery is an aristocrat and rich to boot. If he wanted to court Lady Phoebe, why would he bother kidnapping her?"

"Because he didn't plan to marry her himself. He wanted to force her into marriage with—"

Here she stopped and pressed her lips together.

But Asa was still boggling over the idea that Montgomery had set upon such a harebrained scheme. *"Why?"*

Miss Dinwoody shrugged, looking miserable. "He was mad at the Duke of Wakefield and wanted revenge."

"By kidnapping his younger sister?" Asa stared, trying

to work out the Duke of Montgomery's thought process. "Your brother is insane."

"How dare you speak about Val that way," she said quietly.

He hadn't thought before he'd said the words aloud, but having said them he wasn't about to back down. Asa leaned forward, ignoring the jolt of the carriage, ignoring the footman's hard stare, ignoring the voice in the back of his head that said not to antagonize her. "Montgomery's amoral and crazy."

She stared at him, her lips stubbornly pressed together.

He narrowed his eyes. "Why are you helping him?"

"He's my *brother.*"

"And he doesn't care a whit for you or anyone else."

"You don't know that." Her voice had lowered instead of rising, but that only made her words more intense. "You don't know anything about me and my brother and what he's done for me in my life. *No one* does." She inhaled shakily. "Val might be without clear morals, he may be selfish and wicked and yes, perhaps even insane, but I *love* him. He's the only family I have in this world. The only person I can trust."

He stared at her. She was right: he didn't know her, didn't know her past or her relationship with her brother. That was the way it should be.

That was the way it *had* to be.

He spent the rest of the carriage drive staring out the window and trying to convince himself of that fact.

"LIKE THIS, ALICE," Bridget said gently—and ever so patiently—as she showed the maid how to polish the filigree on a silver cup.

"Yes, ma'am," Alice said, applying the rough side of her piece of leather to the cup. "But wouldn't it be easier to use sand?"

"Easier, perhaps," Bridget said. "But the sand would wear away the silver and the filigree over time. That's why we use a piece of leather and hard work."

"Oh." Alice knit her brows, apparently contemplating that as she bent to her task.

Bridget sighed silently as she watched Alice. Everything took just a bit longer with this maid—instruction, work, even getting ready in the morning. She knew she should've let Alice go from Hermes House at the start, but Bridget simply hadn't the heart to do so. A girl like Alice would have a hard time finding a decent job in London— she'd become a maid at Hermes House only because her cousin was one of the footmen. Left to her own devices in the city she might very well fall into a procurer's hands. No, Bridget decided, she wouldn't let Alice go.

Even if she did take a trifle more effort.

Bridget gave an approving nod to the maid—receiving a shy smile in return—and turned to leave the butler's pantry, closing the door behind her. She made her way down the narrow back passageway and into the huge kitchens. Mrs. Bram, the cook, was chopping vegetables while several scullery maids scoured the floor.

"Agatha," Bridget called to an upper maid just entering the kitchens. "Are you done dusting the music room?"

"Yes, ma'am," the maid said promptly. Agatha was a sturdy woman of forty years or so, stolid and dependable.

"Good," Bridget replied. "Please help Alice polish the silver in the butler's pantry. And Agatha?"

"Ma'am?"

Bridget looked her in the eye. "I've counted and recorded every piece of plate in the pantry. See that nothing goes missing."

Agatha swallowed audibly. "Yes, ma'am."

Bridget nodded and turned to walk to the front of the house. She might be too softhearted to let go a slow maid, but that didn't mean she was a fool. The silver plate in the butler's pantry was worth more money than any of the servants in this great house would ever see in a lifetime.

She was making her way along the dark servants' passage when a small shape suddenly appeared ahead.

Bridget stopped short, her hand involuntarily going to her heart.

"Afternoon, Mrs. Crumb," came Alf's cheery greeting as he moved closer.

Bridget eyed the boy through narrowed eyes. "Where did you come from?"

Alf shrugged. "St. Giles, if you be needin' to know."

Bridget ignored the cheek. "I was just in the kitchens and you certainly didn't come in the servants' entrance. I would've seen you."

"Maybe I felt like comin' in the front like proper folk," Alf said, his chin tilted cockily.

"Neither you nor I qualify as 'proper folk,'" Bridget retorted. "At least not when it comes to aristocratic homes like Hermes House. See to it in the future that you enter through the servants' door."

"Yes, ma'am," Alf replied, touching a finger to his wide-brimmed hat.

"And why *are* you in Hermes House, might I ask?"

"Doin' my job, ain't I?" Alf said. He leaned to the side,

pointedly looking behind Bridget. "Now can I get some tea or not?"

Bridget eyed the boy. He hadn't exactly answered her question. But then the duke had always been a secretive sort. Perhaps Alf really was about business he couldn't discuss. She sighed and moved aside. "Very well."

"Ta." Alf ducked past her, hurrying off to the kitchens.

Bridget watched him go. There was something about the boy that was just a little...strange.

She turned and glanced down the servant's passage. Alf had come from this direction, but there were no doors along the way, only the single entrance at the end that led into the front hall. He must've entered the passage without her noticing.

Thoughtfully Bridget fingered the wooden paneling on the wall. And then, on a whim, knocked.

The wall rang solid.

Well, of course it did. Shaking her head at her own foolishness, Bridget continued on her way.

EVE WAS SQUINTING at a receipt, trying to decide if a smear of ink was a seven or a nine, when the door to the theater office opened the next morning. Music drifted through the door—apparently the orchestra was rehearsing today.

"Oh, pardon me," came an accented voice, and Eve glanced up to see the outrageously beautiful creature who had been in Mr. Makepeace's bed that first day. What had he called her? Oh, yes: La Veneziana.

Eve straightened at her cherrywood desk, feeling especially drab in her sensible brown frock. "You don't happen to have a child as well, do you?"

So far this morning two of Polly Potts's dancing friends and one actress had stopped by to inquire if they too could bring their children to the theater while they worked. Apparently there was an epidemic of child care problems. Eve couldn't very well say no when she'd already granted Polly permission to bring little Bets, and so she'd said yes in each case.

She was beginning to wonder, however, how Mr. Makepeace might take it when he found a bevy of small children running about the theater.

Perhaps she should look into hiring a nanny for the theater.

"No, I don't have a child." The soprano glanced at Eve a little oddly. "I was just looking for Asa. You are Miss Dinwoody, yes? I think we met at Asa's rooms." She tilted her head, revealing the gap between her teeth as she smiled. "Though per'aps you do not recognize me clothed."

Eve felt heat climb her face. "I do recognize you, Miss...er..."

"Please, you must call me Violetta." She shrugged, dropping into Mr. Makepeace's empty chair. "Everyone does who does not call me La Veneziana." She wrinkled her nose. "*Signora* sounds so very old, do you not think so?"

"Erm..."

Violetta poked at a doorknob that Mr. Makepeace had inexplicably left amid the clutter on his desk. "Do you know where he is?"

Eve shook her head. "I'm sorry, no. Mr. Harte stepped out about an hour ago and I haven't seen him since." She glanced at Jean-Marie, sitting in the corner with a book. He'd put on his half-moon spectacles, which always made him look very scholarly.

Jean-Marie placed a finger in his book and pursed his lips. "I think he went to talk to Mr. MacLeish. I 'eard 'im say something about the tiles for the roof. Shall I go find 'im?"

Poor Jean-Marie had been sitting in the chair in the corner for several hours. No doubt he needed to stretch his legs. "Please."

The footman went out, but Violetta didn't seem in any hurry to leave. "You make the accounts, eh?" she said, watching with interest as Eve turned the paper in her hand. "I admire this, the so-orderly mind. Me, I do not have it, I am afraid." She shrugged elaborately, her smooth shoulders gleaming in a low-cut rose-colored gown.

"But then you don't need to keep books, I would think," Eve said tentatively.

Violetta's glance was suddenly sharp. "Books, no, but it doesn't do to forget about money and where it comes from. My voice is magnificent, but a singer only has a few years at best. I must consider my future when I can no longer sing."

Eve shivered, thinking how desperate such a life might become. "Mr. Harte has paid you a great deal to sing in the opera that will reopen his gardens."

"Yes, this is so," Violetta agreed. "But if he cannot find a castrato—and soon—I will have to leave for another house. Even I cannot sing an entire opera alone, and it would be death to go a whole season without singing in an opera."

Eve stared. That seemed very cold-blooded, especially considering how she'd first met the opera singer. "I thought you and Mr. Harte had an...er...understanding?"

Violetta cocked her head.

"I mean..." Eve cleared her throat, feeling very unworldly. "That is...well, you were in his bed the other day."

Violetta threw back her head and laughed, full-throated

and ebullient. "Yes, yes, Asa and I shared a passion that night, but it was not so serious, you understand."

Eve really didn't. Why would a woman give herself to a man unless she wanted to keep that man?

Violetta seemed to see her confusion. "He is so masculine, don't you think? I love his shoulders and his, how do you say? His heat, his vitality. He is so *alive*, darling Asa."

Eve lowered her eye. She was very aware of Mr. Makepeace's *heat* and she wondered for a moment what it would be like to be the focus of it.

Violetta shrugged, seemingly unaware of Eve's thoughts. "But alas, he hasn't the money. Now, I am friends with a duke, and he is not so young and vigorous as Asa, but he gifts me with lovely jewels and a carriage."

Eve blinked, a little shocked. Was Mr. Makepeace aware that he'd been thrown over for a richer man? She couldn't help a pang of sympathy. It would hurt his pride so! "I... I see."

"You do not approve?" Violetta raised her eyebrows in inquiry.

"No," Eve replied. "That is, it's not my place to approve or disapprove." She hesitated, then found herself blurting, "But I don't understand. Your duke gives you something for your... time. But you went to Mr. Harte's bed simply because..." She trailed away, honestly confused. "Because you wanted to?"

"But yes," Violetta said simply. "He is a very good lover, *caro* Asa."

"You enjoyed it," Eve said slowly. She studied the other woman intently, completely unable to understand.

Violetta looked at her a moment, her mobile face stilled, and then her eyes softened somehow.

"Yes," she said gently. "I enjoy a man's embrace very much."

Eve glanced down at the hands in her lap. Not for the first time she felt as if she were so different from other women she might as well be something else entirely. A mermaid or a walking statue, perhaps. Something sexless and apart. Something singular, destined to never find a companion, let alone a mate.

"You do not feel the same?" Violetta asked.

Eve inhaled, pasting a tiny smile upon her face. "I'm unmarried. Naturally I've never felt a man's embrace."

"But you enjoy men, yes?"

"I..." Eve frowned, thinking. "How do you mean?"

"Oh, men." Violetta smiled widely. "Do you like gazing upon the line of their shoulders, the strength of their hands, the hair on their arms? Sometimes it is simply a deep voice that makes me...mmm..." She smiled to herself, her eyes half closing. "It brings a warmth to me *here*." She placed her hands on her middle. "When I am near a man sometimes his scent, that musky, male smell, it makes me so weak. It is a lovely sensation, yes?"

She looked at Eve. And Eve simply stared back, bewildered.

"You don't feel this way?" Violetta's eyes were sad.

"I'm afraid." Eve bit her lip, horrified she'd said the words aloud. But having said them, she went on. "Mostly...when I see or hear or smell a man, I feel afraid."

"I am so sorry, *cara*."

Eve swallowed and looked away, not wanting to see Violetta's pity.

"It can be very, very nice," Violetta said kindly. "With

the right man, with a man who is good and knows how to touch a woman. It can be . . . so very beautiful."

Eve smiled—stiffly, she was aware—but there was nothing she could say. She knew that she would never feel "nice" with a man.

It would never be beautiful for her.

The door to the office opened and Mr. Makepeace came in, followed by Jean-Marie. "Damned shingles! They've found a second shipment—and half of those are broken as well. Perhaps between the two cartfuls we'll have enough shingles to roof the bloody theater."

He was like a summer storm, fast and hot and overwhelming in the tiny room. Eve felt her breath catch in her chest, unable to exhale, and she remembered Violetta's words: *He is very alive, darling Asa.* Jealousy and want, sudden and overwhelming, beat against her heart.

Eve glanced away. She simply had no right to feel jealous of Violetta and Mr. Makepeace. She knew that fact intellectually, but alas, jealousy was an emotion unaffected by her mind. She couldn't entirely shake it.

Mr. Makepeace had stopped suddenly, his eyes narrowed as he glanced at Eve and Violetta. "What?"

"Nothing, nothing, *caro.*" Violetta rose and bussed him on the cheek. "Come, I have questions to ask you about the opera we shall perform here soon. Shall we walk the gardens?"

"Oh, there's no cause to leave on my account," Eve said hastily. She needed to regain her composure. "Please stay. I'd like to take a turn about the gardens anyway."

Violetta beamed at her. "Thank you, my friend. I shan't be long."

Jean-Marie raised his eyebrows, but followed her

from the office without comment. They made their way through the maze of corridors behind the stage, the music from in front muffled, but slightly louder than it had been in the office.

Eve turned impulsively to Jean-Marie. "Let's see the rehearsal."

He threw a quick grin at her and they turned, coming out in one of the wings.

The musicians were indeed rehearsing, but they weren't the only ones. Polly and half a dozen other dancers leaped across the stage, their gossamer costumes floating rather scandalously around their legs. Because the stage had a half-moon apron that thrust out into the theater they were actually viewing the dancers from the back. When the dancers leaped into the air, they were backlit by the bright lights at the front, like fairies cavorting before a fire. Eve watched, enthralled by their grace, until the piece came to an end.

Mr. Vogel yelled something to the orchestra while the dancers milled for a moment, drawing nearer onto the main part of the stage. Polly caught sight of Eve in the wings and waved frantically at her.

"I think she wants to talk to you," Jean-Marie said beside her, amusement in his voice. "I shall stay 'ere in case it is an intimate discussion."

"She probably just wants to thank me for letting her bring little Bets today." Eve bit her lip in sudden worry. "Unless she has *another* friend with a child."

She heard Jean-Marie's bass chuckle behind her as she walked onto the stage. She paused a moment to look out into the theater, marveling at how the space seemed darker and somehow larger from this perspective.

"Miss Dinwoody!" Polly called, and Eve turned toward her. "Come meet my friends." Polly stood with two other dancers Eve hadn't been introduced to yet.

Eve smiled and started toward the center of the stage, and as she did so she heard the most startling sound, a loud abrupt CRACK!

For a moment nothing happened.

And then everything gave way beneath her.

ASA WAS RUNNING even before he heard the final *CRASH*.

The corridors behind the stage were narrow and dimly lit because they were the working part of the theater—the part never seen by his guests. He rounded a sharp turn and came out on a wing beside the stage. A half dozen or so dancers were huddled there and he pushed past them to look.

Where the stage had been was now a pile of jagged wood and still-falling dust. Bloody *fucking* hell. The stage had collapsed into the basement below.

The orchestra had been practicing in the pit. Some of the musicians were standing, while others were still sitting, holding their instruments in shock.

As Asa stared, Jean-Marie placed his bleeding palms on the still-standing floor in front of Asa and levered himself out of the ruins of the stage. "Eve." He inhaled and doubled over, coughing. *"Eve."*

Asa looked at the faces surrounding the stage, but even as he realized that Eve wasn't among them, his heart knew the truth:

Dear God, Eve was in the wreckage.

Chapter Six

*That night the king's guard came for Dove. They took her
deep, deep into the wild forest until they came upon a small
hut. Inside, candles flickered against blood-red walls.
The king sat beside a table, his enormous belly sagging
over his knees, and on the table were a bottle of wine and
a loaf of bread.
The guards departed, leaving the girl alone with her father.
Dove swallowed before dipping into a curtsy.
"Your Majesty."*...
—From *The Lion and the Dove*

The crash of the stage falling had drawn a crowd—gardeners,
roofers, musicians, and his theater folk.

"Help me clear the way!" Asa roared, taking a board
and wrenching it from the wreckage. The thought of Eve
trapped in the darkness below made his gut clench with
stark fear.

"Did you see her?" he demanded from Jean-Marie. "Is
she alive?"

"I do not know," the footman said grimly as he worked
beside Asa. "She was standing on the stage with two or
three dancers when it collapsed. I tried to find 'er, but
there are boards in the way and I could not see."

"Bring a light!" Asa bellowed as he tore off his coat for better maneuverability.

He clambered down into the small space they'd cleared. The basement floor was about eight feet below the part of the stage that still stood. Trapdoors in the stage had opened into the basement and the area was also used for storage. The dust was thick here, lingering in the air, and he coughed, squinting through the gloom. He could hear breathing and a low sob close by. He glanced back up to see Vogel thrusting a lit candlestick down to him.

Asa held the candlestick high. He was confronted by a wall of broken planks and debris.

Behind him he heard Jean-Marie drop into the small space.

Without a word Asa jammed the candlestick into a crevice and began heaving at the pieces of wood, passing them back to Jean-Marie as he pulled them free. A huge beam was revealed, lying diagonally across the space. Asa swore under his breath and set his shoulder to the beam. It shifted slightly under his weight, but so did the debris settled on it overhead. If he even managed to move the beam, he ran the risk of a further collapse. He turned sideways and began inching to the right, trying to find a way around the beam.

"Do you see 'er?" the footman asked.

Asa squinted, craning his neck. He could just make out a glimpse of yellow satin. The dancers had been wearing yellow costumes this morning.

"I see one of the dancers." Where the hell was Eve?

He moved another awkward step and then was stopped by a pile of planks. Asa took hold of a plank and wrenched it out. By tilting his hips, he was just able to move it past his own stomach and back to the footman.

He repeated the process twice more and was rewarded by the sight of a pale face. One of the dancers, Polly Potts.

She was biting her lip, looking frightened nearly out of her wits.

"We'll have you out in a trice, sweetheart," Asa said to her. "Do you know where Miss Dinwoody is?"

The dancer sobbed. "It's my fault. I called to Miss Dinwoody to come meet my friends. She wouldn't have been on the stage otherwise."

Asa set his jaw grimly. "Do you see her back there?"

"I can't see anything," was the reply. "I'm so sorry, Mr. Harte."

"Never mind, luv. Come, can you crawl toward me?"

She nodded.

With his help she crawled from the hollow she'd lain in until she was huddled beside him in the cramped space.

He patted her shoulder. "Behind me is Miss Dinwoody's man, Jean-Marie, who will help you out."

Polly nodded and crawled toward the light and Jean-Marie.

Asa got on his hands and knees and wedged himself into the space Polly had just been in. Instinctively his skin itched. Above him were the remains of the stage, balanced who knew how perilously. Should it collapse again he'd be buried alive.

But he could hear a low, continuous moaning, animal and hurt. His teeth gritted against the thought of Eve making that sound.

Mechanically he dug through the wreckage, trying not to think too hard when the moans suddenly stopped. She was all right. She *must* be all right. He couldn't fathom never arguing with her again.

He reached for the last plank, noting absently that fresh sawdust lay on the strangely even end. He pulled it toward himself and then froze for an instant.

The plank was half sawn through, the wood pale and fresh and ending on jagged splinters where it had broken the rest of the way.

Asa inhaled, tamping down rage, and pulled the board out, passing it without comment to Jean-Marie.

When he bent to look again he met Eve's wide blue eyes and went light-headed with relief. "Are you hurt?"

She half sat, half lay surrounded by debris and with a dark-haired dancer sprawled across her lap. Eve licked her lips and he saw that there was a smudged trail of blood at her temple. "You have to get her out, Asa. I...I don't know if she's breathing. She was moaning before but now she's stopped making any sounds."

He glanced at the girl across her lap and knew immediately that it was too late. "Eve, are you hurt?"

She lifted a hand, touching her golden hair, grimy with dust. "I...my head?"

He nodded. Either she'd been hit on the head or she was dazed from the collapse. "Hold on."

A great beam blocked his way to her. Asa braced his legs, wrapped his arms about the beam, and yanked.

For a moment nothing happened, save for his muscles trembling under the strain.

Then the beam gave with a creak and a shower of smaller debris.

Asa panted a moment, inhaled deeply, and, using his legs, shoved himself backward, hugging the bloody beam to his chest like a lover. Thrice more he did it until Jean-Marie's hands were helping to lift the damnable thing off him.

"Eve?" asked the bodyguard urgently.

Asa realized that he couldn't see her, only hear her voice. "She looks largely unhurt. Deborah, one of the dancers, is lying on her. I'm going to hand Deborah back to you."

"Is she—?" Jean-Marie started, but Asa gave him a sharp look and shook his head.

The footman winced before nodding. "Very well."

Asa crawled back into the space to find Eve with her hand on Deborah's cheek. She looked up, her eyes stricken. "She's very badly off."

"Let me take her, luv," Asa said.

He looped the dancer's slack arms around his neck and gently lifted her, pushing backward with his legs to half carry, half drag her out.

Jean-Marie took her without comment and Asa dived back in again, cautiously shoving aside planks of wood. Eve was nearly prone, a pile of broken boards lying directly on her right leg. Asa winced at the sight and started pulling the boards off her.

"Can you move, luv?"

"Yes, of course," Eve replied, and she even sounded a little insulted.

Asa felt a grin split his face. "That's my girl."

He pulled away the last plank, freeing the leg. He bent to examine it. To his relief there was no blood on her dress. He glanced up. Broken boards hovered overhead, ready to crash down at any moment.

He looked back at Eve, holding out his hand. "Come on, then."

She looked between him and his hand, pressing her lips together, but not moving.

He frowned. "Eve."

She inhaled and took his hand, awkwardly inching toward him without a sound.

"Brave lass," Asa purred.

He caught her other hand, ignoring her flinch, and pulled her into his arms. What a small thing she was! She might be tall, but Eve's body was as light as a bird's. He could feel the delicate bones of her shoulder, the slender span of her waist, and he thanked God that she'd not been crushed by the planks falling on her.

She trembled against him as he made his way back toward the light and those waiting for them. She held her body stiffly, almost away from him, and he would've made some sarcastic comment, but then they were in the light.

"Ah, *ma petite*," Jean-Marie rumbled when he saw them. "You 'ave been so courageous. A little more and this will be over."

The footman reached for Eve and for a moment Asa fought the urge to tighten his arms.

Then he was surrendering Eve to Jean-Marie, who lifted her up onto the solid floor of one of the wings beside the stage.

"She is the last," the footman said.

"What?" Asa wiped his sweating face on his sleeve. "I thought there were three dancers."

Jean-Marie nodded. "Vogel and some of the musicians were able to rescue the third dancer from the other side of the stage."

"Is she—?"

"Shaken but unhurt—or so Vogel has told me."

"Thank God," Asa replied.

"*Oui*." Jean-Marie was already climbing out of the wreckage.

Asa levered himself up and out, and then crouched down by Eve.

She sat, leaning against a wall, her eyes tightly closed. Asa frowned and then noticed MacLeish was there as well. He shot the architect a narrow-eyed glance.

"I've already sent for a doctor," MacLeish said. He glanced up as Vogel joined them and his brows drew together. "Hans! You're hurt."

"*Ja, ja,*" Vogel muttered, wiping a smear of blood from his neck. "Your theater has nearly killed us."

MacLeish flushed. "This wasn't my fault. My design was perfectly safe."

Vogel snorted as the scratch on his neck welled fresh blood. "Safe! *Gott im Himmel!* The stage fell in—"

Asa lifted his voice impatiently. "Where are Polly and the dancer you saved, Vogel?"

The composer turned to him. "Ve put both of them in one of the dressing rooms."

"Good." He'd have to consult with the doctor, send for supplies to rebuild the stage, and—

"What about the other girl?" Eve asked, interrupting his thoughts, her voice still weak.

Asa bent and picked her up, ignoring the way she immediately stiffened, and started striding toward his office.

"What are you doing?" Eve asked, pushing against his chest. "I can walk, and besides, I wanted to hear—"

"She's dead." He tried to make his voice gentle, but he wasn't a gentle man.

"Oh," Eve breathed. "Oh."

He waited for her questions, but there weren't any. Perhaps in her heart she'd known all along.

He tightened his arms as he strode through the corridors. He could feel the beat of her heart against his chest and he was fiercely unapologetically *glad* that she hadn't been the one to die.

She inhaled, one delicate hand coming to rest on his waistcoat. "How did this happen, do you know?"

"Oh, I know all right," Asa replied grimly. "Sabotage."

EVE STARED AT Mr. Makepeace. He'd just crawled into a space hardly large enough for a toddler, to save her—save her and Polly. She'd never seen such strength and courage, matter-of-factly displayed.

But that didn't mean she'd lost her senses. "Sabotage? You mean you think someone *deliberately* caused the stage to fall? But why?"

"To ruin me, of course." He halted before the door to his office, his arms strong bands around her body. Eve stiffened instinctually at the reminder that he was *holding* her. Asa Makepeace had one arm beneath her legs and the other under her shoulders. The position forced her entire side against his chest.

He was close—much too close.

He didn't seem to notice. He was already shouldering open the office door.

The moment they were inside, she pushed hard against his chest, wriggling until he let her down. Her feet touched the floor and she took a step back from him, leaning against a corner of his desk. Her legs were still wobbly and her head throbbed from being hit as she'd fallen through the stage, but she folded her arms and tried to compose herself. "Why do you think the stage fall wasn't an accident? Doesn't it make much more sense that it simply was badly constructed and fell?"

He scowled. "Because it didn't just bloody *fall*. I saw cut boards under that wreckage. Someone sawed through them and made the stage collapse."

She blinked at that. "Who?"

"What?"

"*Who* went to all the trouble of crawling under your stage and sawing through boards to make it fall?"

His head jerked back as he stared at her, incredulous. "You don't believe me."

"It's not that," she said, exasperated. "I'm just trying to understand."

"What needs understanding?" His voice was growing louder. "The goddamned stage was sabotaged."

"Fine. The stage was sabotaged." She inhaled, keeping her temper. "Now tell me *why* would anyone deliberately destroy the stage?"

"Bloody *Sherwood* has a reason to sabotage me and my theater."

She stared, incredulous. "You think Mr. Sherwood crawled under your stage with a *saw*—"

"He would've used a paid lackey, *obviously*," he interrupted.

"That doesn't make any sense," she objected. "Why would Sherwood go to all that trouble when only last week he was offering to buy out Val's share of Harte's Folly?"

He brought his fist down with a *bang* on the table. "That's exactly why he'd damn well do it—you didn't sell the buggering share to him. He's trying to ruin me—ruin my theater!"

She thought of the Mr. Sherwood she'd met only a few times: excitable, quick to smile, eager to make money, but not a violent man by any means. Whoever had sabotaged the stage must've known that someone might be hurt or killed. "That's ridiculous."

"Oh, I'm ridiculous now, am I, luv?" His eyes narrowed ominously. "I've spent over a decade in the theater, in this garden, and I think I might know a man like bloody Sherwood better than a frightened little mouse who's spent the better part of her life *hiding* from life."

She caught her breath in outrage, her hands balling into fists at her side. "How dare you? You're so obsessed with your garden it's all you see, all you care about. You're blind to anything else."

He leaned down into her face, his hot breath washing across her mouth. "Fucking right I am."

Tears of hurt pricked her eyes and she widened them to keep the drops from falling as she stared back at him. She didn't even know why she felt hurt—it made no sense. She knew who he was—what he was. Nothing he'd said—no matter how foully—was anything new.

She lifted her chin. "Then I suppose our discussion is done."

She turned to go, but he had a hard grip on her upper arm, pulling her back.

"Not yet it's not," he growled.

She fought down the old, nauseous fear. "Let go of me."

"Why?" He cocked his head, an ugly sneer on his beautiful lips. "Can't stand my touch?"

"Yes!" she tossed back, losing her patience, her self-control, and any upper hand she'd ever had in their argument.

Which was when he took her by the shoulders, pulled her roughly into his arms, and pressed his mouth to hers.

And Eve lost her sanity.

*   *   *

EVE DINWOODY'S LIPS were soft and sweet, entirely belying her sharp and tart personality. For all of a half second
Asa reveled in that yielding sweetness. He'd shut her up
in the most basic, the most primitive way a man could a
woman.

And then he realized something was very wrong.

He pulled back, his lip curled cynically. She was an
aristocrat. She probably thought him bestial, base, dirty,
and not worthy of her mouth.

No doubt she was disgusted by him.

But disgust wasn't what showed on her face.

It was fear.

White showed all around the blue irises of her eyes,
and there were pale indents on the sides of her nostrils.
Her expression reminded him of what she'd looked like
when he'd found her with the dog, but this was worse—
much worse. She wasn't making a sound.

"Eve."

Her brows creased and the most horrible sound came
from her lips.

She whimpered.

Before he could react, he was yanked away from her.

Asa stumbled over a chair and nearly fell, catching
himself at the last minute with a hand on the desk. "What
the hell?"

Jean-Marie had his arm around Eve. The footman
ignored him. *"Ma chérie*, it is safe. I am 'ere. You are safe."

She didn't respond, not even to whimper.

Asa straightened slowly, his eyes on her.

"What did you do to 'er?" Jean-Marie demanded, not
looking away from his mistress.

He sounded entirely unlike any manservant Asa had ever met. If Jean-Marie was a footman Asa was a grand duchess.

"Nothing." He stared at Eve, his chest constricting as if he were being squeezed in a great vise.

The other man shot him a black look. "Do not take me for a fool. You did something to put her into this state."

"I kissed her," Asa said, refusing to feel shame or embarrassment. He'd embraced her in a moment of anger, true, but he hadn't *hurt* her.

Jean-Marie made a sound of disgust. "Come, *ma petite.* Come, Jean-Marie will take you 'ome now."

Eve didn't speak, didn't move.

Asa felt a chill crawl up his spine. This was unnatural, as if her mind had left her body. "What's wrong with her?"

Jean-Marie ignored him, ushering her to a chair and gently helping her sit. "Stay here. I shall send for the carriage. We shall go 'ome and you can 'ave a nice cup of tea, *oui?*"

The footman moved toward the door, but Asa blocked his way, feeling a sort of helpless rage washing over him. *"Answer me.* What is wrong with your mistress?"

"You touched 'er." The blackamoor's face was stony with his own anger.

Asa didn't back down. "I told you, I never hurt her."

"You didn't 'ave to," Jean-Marie replied coldly. "Your touch—the touch of a man—is enough to do this to 'er."

"You're a goddamned man," Asa growled. "And *you* touch her."

Jean-Marie's lip curled. "I am 'er friend, I am married, and I 'ave spent years guarding 'er and winning 'er trust."

Asa shook his head, glancing again at Eve. She was

hunched now in the chair. At least she could move. But she wouldn't look in their direction, though there was no way she could not hear their argument.

Asa turned back to the other man. "Why? What made her like this?"

"This is not my story to tell," Jean-Marie said. He turned to the door, but hesitated, his hand on the knob, before saying in a near-whisper, "You need to ask 'er."

Then he opened the door and leaned into the hallway. There must've been someone there, for Asa could hear him giving directions. Jean-Marie returned to Miss Dinwoody and helped her up. "Come. A carriage is being brought round."

Asa fisted and un-fisted his hands, feeling powerless. "It'll take you over an hour to get to the Thames, cross it, and then hire another carriage to take her to her town house."

Jean-Marie lifted an eyebrow. "You 'ave a better idea, perhaps?"

Asa snorted. "Goddamn it, no."

He watched moodily as the footman helped her to the door. Eve had her head lowered now as if embarrassed, which, oddly, made him feel a little better: if she was aware enough to be embarrassed, surely it was a positive sign?

Any emotion was better than that horrible, utter blankness.

"I will take care of 'er," Jean-Marie said as they made the door.

Asa wanted to argue. Wanted to take her from the footman's arms and help her home himself. Wanted to find out what was wrong with her.

But he had a theater that had just been sabotaged.

He watched Jean-Marie and Eve go, then gritted his teeth determinedly and turned to make his way to the stage. *After.* After he saw to his theater, his garden, and his people, then he would go to Eve.

And find out once and for all what was wrong with her.

Chapter Seven

❧

The king gestured to the bread and wine. "Eat, girl."
So Dove sat on a stool and broke off a piece of the bread
and placed it in her mouth. She was very careful, though,
to not look away from the man who had sired her.
The king seemed irritated, but he pointed to the wine.
"Drink."
Dove poured herself a glass of wine, her gaze always on
her father, and now his face was enraged....
—From *The Lion and the Dove*

Later that afternoon Bridget Crumb opened the door of Hermes House to find a very disheveled Malcolm MacLeish on the doorstep.

She raised an eyebrow and stepped back. The architect was a regular visitor to Hermes House, so she was used to seeing him, though not usually with sweat stains on his coat and dust and grime in his hair.

"I need to write a letter to His Grace," Mr. MacLeish muttered, stumbling into the entryway. "The damned stage collapsed this afternoon. One of the dancers was killed."

Since this was a simple statement—rather than an inquiry or order—Bridget stood back without answering, then turned to lead the young man to the Duke of Montgomery's study.

She could hear the architect's stumbling footsteps behind her as she mounted the stairs, and a flash of pity went through her. The poor man seemed exhausted.

She opened the door to the study and said, "I shall bring up a pot of tea and refreshments as you write, sir."

She was rewarded with a quick smile. "God, thank you," Mr. MacLeish replied as he entered the room. "I haven't eaten since this morning."

Bridget nodded and left him to his letter writing.

Hermes House, like most grand residences, had a servants' staircase at the back of the house, cleverly disguised behind a door set into the wainscoting. She took this, descending rapidly to the kitchens.

Mrs. Bram was at the large kitchen table kneading some sort of pastry dough when she entered.

"I'd like a tray of food and tea for Mr. MacLeish, please," Bridget ordered.

"Yes, ma'am." Mrs. Bram was middle-aged, with wiry gray hair pulled into a tight knot at the back of her neck and covered by a white mobcap. She had quick small hands and thankfully seemed not at all bothered by being ordered about by a younger woman. "I'll have Betsy bring it up."

"No need," Bridget replied. "I can do it myself."

Mrs. Bram was also wonderful in that she never questioned what Bridget did. Indeed, she seemed to be entirely without curiosity, which, on the whole, Bridget was very grateful for.

The cook motioned to one of the scullery maids, who was elbow-deep in hot water. The girl dried off her hands and ran over to pull down a teapot and a caddy of tea. Mrs. Bram soon had a tray ready, and Bridget took it with a nod of thanks.

She mounted the stairs, glancing as she always did at one of the many gilt mirrors lining the walls. She noticed to her irritation that her cap was ever so slightly askew.

Mr. MacLeish was still furiously writing when she entered the study again.

She set the tray beside him and glanced at the letter, making out the words *possible deliberate damage* before glancing away.

"Bless you," Mr. MacLeish gasped, pouring himself a cup of tea. "I spent all afternoon helping to clear the damage."

"That sounds quite a chore," Bridget murmured sympathetically. "Do you know what caused the collapse, sir?"

Mr. MacLeish was busy buttering a scone. "No, but some of the boards holding the stage up seemed to be partially sawn through, Mr. Harte told me. He suspects sabotage."

Bridget lifted her eyebrows. It appeared that someone did not want Harte's Folly to reopen, which begged the question: were they after Mr. Harte?

Or the garden's investor—the Duke of Montgomery?

Mr. MacLeish bit into the scone and, chewing, scrawled his signature on the letter. He folded and sealed the letter and then handed it to Bridget, a small frown of irritation appearing between his brows. "I don't know why His Grace doesn't use the postal system."

"I couldn't say, sir," Bridget replied, taking the letter.

"Thank you, Mrs. Crumb. You are, as always, all that is efficient. Comes from being a Scot, I expect," he said with a wink.

She felt her face freeze. "I'm afraid you have it wrong, sir. I'm not from Scotland."

"No? I'm usually quite good at detecting my countrymen's accent." Mr. MacLeish stood and stretched, yawning widely. "I'd best get back to Harte's Folly. When I left we still hadn't finished clearing the room under the stage. It might take all night."

"Good luck, sir," Bridget said. She turned and led the way back to the stairs and then to the first floor.

Bridget saw Mr. MacLeish out, then bolted the door. Moving at an unhurried but swift pace, she walked to the back of the house, through the kitchen, and to her own little room off the pantry.

There she closed and locked the door and turned to the round mirror hanging over a sturdy chest of drawers. The mirror wasn't much bigger than her face, but it was adequate to reflect her motions as she untied her mobcap and took it off. Underneath, her hair was jet-black—all but one wide strand of pure white just over her left eye. The white snaked through the locks and disappeared into a tight knot at the back of her head.

Bridget made sure all the pins in her hair were still firmly in place before settling the mobcap back on her head, entirely covering the white streak in her hair.

Then she retied the strings, nodded at her reflection once, and returned to work.

IT WAS NEARLY evening by the time Asa made it to Miss Dinwoody's town house. He eyed the neatly swept front steps before mounting them and knocking.

Jean-Marie answered and raised his eyebrows silently.

"How is she?" Asa asked.

The footman hesitated, then said, "Unhurt, but tired. She is resting."

He started to close the door but Asa stuck his foot in the jamb, preventing him.

Asa suppressed a sigh. This was the third? fourth? time he'd confronted the man in the last several days. Jean-Marie was obviously more some sort of bodyguard than footman, and he appeared to take his duties to his mistress very, very seriously.

Jean-Marie looked at him stonily. "She will not see you."

"Of course not." Asa leaned wearily against the doorjamb. "But as it happens, I've come to see you instead."

The bodyguard tilted his head as if Asa's statement had caught him by surprise. "Is this so? And why would you want to see me, Mr. Harte?"

"Makepeace," Asa corrected absently. "I have to work with her and you seem to know her better than anyone else. I'd like to learn more about her."

"I'll not tell her secrets."

Asa shook his head. "I won't ask you to."

"A matter of business." Jean-Marie narrowed his eyes. "Is that all you've come about?"

Asa glanced away, hesitating. Harte's Folly was naturally the most important thing on his mind at the moment... well, *every* moment. It was his life's work, his soul and heart. But there was something about Eve Dinwoody. Her strict sense of order, her sharp retorts, the vulnerability she strove to hide.

The way she'd watched him when he'd modeled for her.

He wouldn't say that he'd become friends with the woman—how could he? She was from a different class,

SWEETEST SCOUNDREL   121

a different *life* from his, and they seemed to argue over nearly everything to boot—but they were certainly no longer enemies.

And if his purpose had been *entirely* business, would he even be here right now? On the evening after his bloody *stage* had collapsed?

He looked back at Jean-Marie and said truthfully, "No, I haven't come only because of business."

Those must've been the passwords for entrance to the house, for something cleared in Jean-Marie's face. He nodded and stepped back. "Come. You can speak to me in the kitchen."

Asa followed him into the house. Instead of going up the stairs, though, they made their way down a hallway to the back of the house.

A pretty red-haired woman looked up in surprise as they entered the kitchen. She was bent over the hearth, stirring a simmering pot.

"Tess," Jean-Marie said gravely. "We have a visitor. This is Mr. Asa Makepeace, the owner of Harte's Folly. Mr. Makepeace, Tess Pépin, Miss Dinwoody's cook—and my wife."

Jean-Marie said this last with his chin lifted proudly.

Asa had never heard of a black man's marrying an Englishwoman, but the theater held all manner of folk. His sense of shock at new things had long ago been dulled.

He bowed. "Mrs. Pépin."

The cook blushed a fiery red and dropped her spoon on the hearth. "Oh! A...a pleasure to meet you, sir. Would you like some tea?"

"I'd be most grateful," Asa said. He hadn't stopped for luncheon and his belly was beginning to feel hollow.

Mrs. Pépin nodded and ducked her head as she busied herself with a kettle.

Asa glanced at Jean-Marie.

The other man gestured to the battered kitchen table. "Will you sit?"

"Thank you." Asa took the seat, watching the cook as she poured hot water into a teapot. Was she as aware of her mistress's ills as Jean-Marie?

The bodyguard seemed to understand his hesitation. "Tess 'as been my wife for three years now. She came to Miss Dinwoody's service two years before that, but Tess is a cautious woman. It took me two years to woo 'er and make 'er mine."

The cook glanced at her husband, an expression of faint reproach on her still-pink cheeks.

Jean-Marie grinned at her, flashing white teeth in his ebony face. "Ah, but it was worth the wait, I assure you."

That made Tess blush again as she tutted under her breath and laid the tea things on the table.

Asa hid a smile before sobering and looking at the bodyguard. "And you? How long have you been in Miss Dinwoody's employ?"

"A little over ten years," Jean-Marie replied. "But you have it wrong. I am in the Duke of Montgomery's employ, as is my wife and Ruth, the maid. Miss Dinwoody is supported by 'er brother."

Tess banged a pot on her stove. "*That* man."

Jean-Marie frowned. "*Oui*, that man. I owe 'im—"

His wife whirled on him, her spoon held out. "You long ago repaid the debt you owed him. He keeps you from living the life you ought, the life you *want*."

She stopped, glanced at Asa, and bit her lip before turning back to her stove.

Asa's eyes narrowed. It always seemed to come back to the duke. He remembered first meeting the Duke of Montgomery. The man had found him and Apollo drinking wine among the ruins of the burnt theater. Asa had already downed a bottle of smoke-flavored wine, but he remembered the duke's guinea-gold hair, his mincing manners, and the extravagant falls of lace at his wrists. At the time Asa had been more interested in the money the duke had offered—a windfall, entirely unexpected, entirely beyond his dreams—than the man himself. He'd dismissed the duke as an aristocratic dandy, dabbling in the theater on a whim.

Now, a year later, he knew better. Montgomery had strong-armed MacLeish into designing and building the new theater for the garden, had insisted the garden open this autumn, and in general had wormed his overly manicured fingers into every aspect of Harte's Folly.

Asa no longer disregarded Montgomery. The man was powerful and strange, his motives known only to himself.

"How did Montgomery come to hire you?" Asa asked.

Jean-Marie pulled out a chair to sit down at the table. "Ah, but 'ere is a tale. You will 'ear it?"

Asa nodded.

The other man looked pleased. "Me, I was a slave, a slave on a sugar plantation on the island of Saint-Domingue in the West Indies. I was brought there as an *enfant* from Africa, or so *ma mère* told me when I was but a very small boy." Jean-Marie shrugged his shoulders expressively. "She died when I was only seven or eight years, so I know very little else of where I was born. I grew to manhood there on that plantation, one among many African slaves. The mistress took a liking to me and doted on me, keeping me in the 'ouse to do little chores for 'er." He sent Asa a sharp look that belied the smile that played around his mouth. "It is much better, you comprehend, for a slave to work in the 'ouse rather than in the fields?"

Asa didn't know, but he could imagine. To labor all one's life at the mercy of another man's whims without respite, surcease, or hope of anything better…That wasn't living.

That was existing in hell.

He looked the other man in the eye and nodded once, firmly.

Jean-Marie nodded in return and his smile grew cynical. "Yes, it is so. And I 'ad cause to understand this when my mistress died. I was fifteen. 'Er eldest son came 'ome and, seeing that I was young and strong, sent me to the fields. But I 'ad been spoiled. A year later when the overseer whipped an old woman for moving too slowly, I took the whip from his 'and. Then I was overpowered by many men and the overseer whipped me as well—for over an hour." Jean-Marie's smile was gone entirely now and he looked grim. "I have the scars still."

His wife quietly placed a bowl of stew before Jean-Marie and laid her palm on his shoulder.

Jean-Marie covered Tess's hand with his own. "They left me 'anging in the stocks that night as a lesson to any other slave who might dare to rebel. But I escaped and went running. I did not get very far." He looked over his shoulder finally at his wife's anxious face. "Come, *chérie*, come and sit and partake of your excellent stew."

She nodded and brought two bowls to the table, handing one to Asa before sitting with her own. Asa noticed she scooted her chair closer to her husband's as if to give him silent comfort.

Jean-Marie looked again at Asa. "So I was caught and of course beaten and then they decided to hang me by the neck. But what do you think? The Duke of Montgomery 'ad arrived in the port the night before. 'E saw the men gathered to 'ang me and 'e bought me from them. 'E sent for a doctor, paid to 'ave my wounds cared for, and, when I was recovered sufficiently, brought me with 'im on his travels. 'E taught me English, clothed and fed me, and waited patiently for months until I was strong and whole again."

Jean-Marie shrugged and took a spoonful of the stew.

"Why?" Asa demanded. "The duke doesn't strike me as a man with an ounce of pity for others."

Jean-Marie shot him a sly glance. "You do not think 'e saved my life and made me well again out of Christian charity?"

Asa snorted and took a bite of the stew himself. It was excellent, thick and meaty with big chunks of potatoes, carrots, and parsnips. "No."

"You are correct then," Jean-Marie said imperturbably. "The duke wanted a man who owed his life completely to 'im. As I do."

"Why?"

"Ah, that is the question." The footman nodded as if Asa had said something very wise. "'E needed a man 'e could trust perfectly to guard 'is sister."

"And that's you?" Asa narrowed his eyes. "You guard her safety?"

"*Oui*, for ten years now, but I guard more than just her safety. I am 'ired to make sure no man ever touches the mistress," Jean-Marie said.

"Montgomery's worried about his sister's virtue?"

"Non." Jean-Marie shook his head once. "'E is worried about 'er sanity."

Asa put down his spoon. "What do you mean?"

"You saw what she was like this afternoon," Jean-Marie said soberly. "She 'as demons, *ma petite*. Demons that come in the form of men and of dogs."

Asa clenched his fists on the table. It wasn't hard to guess why a woman might be afraid of men, but he wanted it stated. "Why?"

"Non," Jean-Marie said gently. "That question is not mine to answer."

Asa stood. "Then I'll ask her."

The other man stood as well. He'd doffed his coat on entering the kitchen and his shoulders in a white linen shirt were broad and powerful. "I cannot let you hurt 'er."

Asa set his jaw. He should leave. Forget about Miss Dinwoody and her overprotective brother and her so-called demons.

But he couldn't.

He couldn't.

Asa set his fists on the kitchen table and leaned toward the other man. "You think this is protecting her? Keeping her from ever touching a man? In constant fear whenever she leaves this damned house? This isn't a life, my friend. This is a bloody *grave* you've buried her in."

He expected anger, but strangely, Jean-Marie's lips curved, though he didn't look particularly amused. "You 'ave a better way of caring for 'er, then? You, who 'ave known 'er only days?"

Asa thrust out his chin. "Damn it, *yes*. I may not know what to do right now, but this"—he swept his hand across his chest, encompassing the kitchen and the house—"*this* isn't it."

The bodyguard stood staring at him for a full minute, his face expressionless. Then he cast his eyes upward, as if he could see through the ceiling to his mistress on the floor above. "*Bon*. Then you go to 'er."

EVE BENT OVER her magnifying glass, carefully peering through it at the miniature she was working on below. It was of a young lady, her head turned to the side, dark locks pulled back from her face.

Eve dipped her brush in carmine paint and carefully applied color to the lady's tiny smile. She looked happy, her painted lady, and Eve felt a small, sad pang of envy.

The door to her sitting room opened.

Eve didn't look up. "You can leave my supper on the table, Ruth."

"I'm not Ruth," came the answer in a deep voice.

She inhaled and froze. She'd heard the knocking at the front door earlier, of course, but when no pounding footsteps had sounded afterward, she'd assumed that Jean-Marie had successfully chased Mr. Makepeace away.

Apparently she'd been wrong.

She looked up to see Mr. Makepeace holding a tray of food like a badly trained footman.

He caught her eye and tilted up one corner of his wide mouth. "Your cook made coddled eggs for you and some sort of stewed fruit." He gave the tray a suspicious look.

She swallowed and nodded. "Prunes."

He glanced up. "What?"

She gestured to the tray. "Stewed prunes. My favorite."

He gave her a look of such patent, horrified disbelief that despite herself she nearly laughed. "Really."

"Yes, really." She smiled innocently. "Would you care for some? I'm sure Tess wouldn't mind making more."

"No!" He paused and cleared his throat, then began again more quietly. "That is, I'm sure the prunes are delicious, but I already ate in the kitchen."

His reply sobered her. "With Jean-Marie, I expect."

He watched her warily as he set down the tray on the low table before the settee. "Yes. He said you were unhurt from the stage collapse."

"He was correct."

No doubt their tête-à-tête had gone beyond that. They'd probably discussed her and her bizarre reaction to a simple kiss. She ought to feel betrayed by Jean-Marie, but all she felt was weariness.

She'd been living with this affliction for over a decade and sometimes she was simply tired of it all.

Eve rose and crossed to one of the chairs opposite the settee. Tess had given her a light supper, one she could easily eat and digest after the distress of the day, and Eve was grateful. Tess was not only a good cook, but a thoughtful woman.

She picked up the small plate of tender coddled eggs and sat back in the armchair.

Mr. Makepeace sat opposite her on the settee and watched her eat for a minute before he abruptly said, "I'm sorry."

She paused a moment, the fork lifted to her lips, then nodded mutely and ate.

He ran a hand through his wild hair. "I was angry—upset because of the stage collapse and our argument—and I should never have kissed you."

"Why did you do it, then?" she asked.

He shrugged and sat back, his legs spread in masculine ease. Why did men always take up so much *room* on a settee? "As I said, I was angry."

"And that made you want to kiss me," she said, intent on his reply.

He grimaced. "Yes."

"Why?"

He looked at her a moment, his eyebrows drawn together, and then suddenly sat forward. "I don't know, exactly. That's just how men are. Sometimes we confuse anger—aggression—with passion and we turn it on the women around us. Men are very primitive."

"Yes," she said quietly. "They are."

"That doesn't mean..." He reached out a hand toward her, apparently without thought, but then curled his fingers into a fist and withdrew it.

She watched, regretting that he couldn't simply *touch* her like any other woman.

He inhaled. "I would never hurt you, Eve. You or any other woman."

"I know," she whispered, staring at the hand he'd reached toward her. It lay on his knee now, large and masculine, several scabbing cuts marring the tanned skin. She had an unaccountable longing and had to blink back the moisture in her eyes. "I do, but it doesn't make any difference, not really. Whether you mean harm or not, whether you are a good man or a bad one, I cannot stand to be embraced by you or any other man." She raised her eyes to him. "I am broken in this way."

His expression didn't change, but she watched as the hand on his knee curled into a fist so tight that white showed around his knuckles. "I'll try not to touch you again and I'll certainly not embrace you again without your permission."

Her brows drew together. Didn't he understand? She'd thought she'd made herself more than clear. "My permission won't be forthcoming."

He nodded, oddly formal, as if he'd accepted a challenge to a duel. "As I said: I will not kiss you nor touch you in any other passionate way without your express word."

She frowned at him a moment longer, then mentally shrugged and bent to her small bowl of stewed prunes. Tess always used a dash of brandy, and the liquor burst against her tongue as she bit into one of the soft, sweet fruits.

Mr. Makepeace cleared his throat. "Jean-Marie told me I should ask you why you're this way."

She glanced up in alarm.

He shook his head immediately. "But I think it best that you tell me when you want to—*if* you want to. I'll not ask."

"Thank you." She blinked down at her prunes, feeling suddenly lighter. He was letting her hide still. Pretend to be normal. If it was up to her, then she would never tell him what had happened.

It wouldn't matter anyway. She was how she was. It had been this way for over a decade with very little change. She had resigned herself to being this way until she died.

She inhaled, setting her bowl back down on the tray and then folding her hands in her lap. "How are the dancers who were trapped in the wreckage?"

He, too, seemed to relax at the change of subject. "Polly and Sarah had little more than bumps on the head. The

doctor said they would recover with a few days' bed rest."
He hesitated. "I've made arrangements for Deborah's
body to be transported home, and sent enough money for
a proper burial."

She nodded. "I'm glad. And Polly and Sarah? Do they
have someone to look after them?"

"I've hired a nurse for them." A corner of his mouth
quirked, flashing a dimple. "Of course it was with Montgomery's money—Deborah's burial funds as well. Do
you think he'd want his money used thus?"

"I doubt it." She lifted her chin. "But he put me in
charge of the money and *I* think this a fair and just use of
it. Polly and Sarah wouldn't have been injured and poor
Deborah killed if they hadn't been dancing on that stage."

"That's my girl."

He smiled then, that wonderful smile, wide and intimate, and she blinked back at him, not a little dazzled.

Oh, he knew it, too, the terrible man. He tossed his
arms across the back of her settee, lounging back like a
lion newly fed. "Have you your sketchbook?"

"Yes, of course," she said cautiously. "Why?"

"I'm here." He shrugged broad shoulders. "I thought I
might model for you again."

She opened her mouth, ready with a half dozen
objections—and then shut it again. The truth was, she
liked sketching him.

And she had made it a part of their bargain, hadn't she?

Eve got up and went to her desk, picking up both
sketchbook and pencil before turning back to return to
her chair.

She halted, however, when she saw what Mr. Makepeace was doing: untying his stock.

His green eyes gleamed at her. "I know. You said you didn't want me undressed. But you've already drawn me dressed. I thought we could try something different this time."

She swallowed, completely unable to tear her gaze away from his fingers on the stock. "How different?"

He shrugged. "I'll stop when you tell me. Yes?"

She nodded jerkily.

"Eve."

Her name on his lips brought her eyes to his.

He had one eyebrow quirked. "Yes? You need to say it."

Was this what she wanted? He was big and male and in her sitting room, alone with her—but not touching her. Safely on the other side of the low table in front of the settee.

And, oh, she wanted to see what lay beneath that stock!

"Yes."

A corner of his mouth kicked up as he pulled at the stock, unraveling it from his strong tanned neck.

Eve exhaled and sat rather abruptly in her armchair, the sketchbook clutched to her chest.

He lifted his eyebrows and reached for the buttons of his waistcoat, flicking one open and then pausing to look at her.

Eve swallowed. "Please."

That smile flickered around his lips as he unbuttoned his long waistcoat. He hadn't bothered removing his coat, as if he knew that would be going too far with her. Now he spread the halves of his waistcoat to the sides. Underneath, of course, was his shirt, creased and stained from the day's exertions.

He looked at her a little challengingly then, his head tilted to the side, his face lined and grave.

She wasn't a coward. Not at her center. Not at the heart of her.

Eve lifted her chin and said clearly, "Unbutton it, please."

He grinned, quick and wide. His broad fingers seemed to work so slowly, pushing the small buttons through the tiny holes, gradually widening the gape of his shirt until he came to the last of them, midway down his torso.

He watched her as he pulled the edges wide, exposing a V of tanned skin, liberally scrolled with dark body hair. It wasn't much. She couldn't see his nipples, couldn't see below his chest, certainly couldn't see his belly. Oh, but it was enough for her. The dip at the base of his throat. The long tendons at the sides of his neck. The horizontal lines of his collarbones, disappearing into the sides of his shirt.

It was more than she'd ever seen of any man.

She should be afraid now. He was a huge, virile presence in the room, sitting so still on her settee, his shirt agape.

But she wasn't.

She inhaled on the thought.

She wasn't afraid of him—not a bit—and the realization brought a smile to her own lips.

He caught her eye and nodded, not bothering to speak, but his mouth was already twitching into his wide smile.

She opened her sketchbook, turning pages until she found a clean one. Then she drew, lost in the pleasure, the relief of her art. The only sound in the room was the scratch of her lead on the paper. Mr. Makepeace didn't even move—he seemed content to simply sit and let her gaze her fill of him.

Eve didn't pause until the china clock on her desk began chiming.

"Oh," she said. "It's gone ten."

Mr. Makepeace stood and stretched, yawning enormously, as if he'd just awakened from a nap. He began buttoning his shirt as he said, "I'd best be off, then."

She bit her lip regretfully, but closed her sketchbook and stood as well. "Thank you, Mr. Makepeace."

He paused, his fingers on his half-buttoned waistcoat, and cocked an amused eyebrow at her. "Might as well call me Asa, luv. You've had me half undressed."

Her eyes widened even as she bit her lip to suppress a smile. "Not nearly half."

"A quarter, then." He caught up his stock and stuffed it in his pocket.

She nodded solemnly. "A quarter."

He grinned at her before snapping his fingers. "I nearly forgot I had word this afternoon. Two castrati will come to the theater to sing—both Italian, naturally. Vogel and I will pick one for our opera. I assume, as Montgomery's money will pay the castrato I choose, you will want to hear them sing as well?"

She clasped her hands over her notebook, scrambling to put her mind to business. "Yes, of course."

"I'll see you tomorrow morning, then. Eleven of the clock is when they will come." He paused a slow wide smile spreading over his face. "Good night—*Eve*."

With that he strode from the room before she could comment on the use of her Christian name.

Eve watched him go thoughtfully.

Then she went to her desk, withdrew a small sheet of paper, and wrote a short letter.

She rang for Jean-Marie.

"Mon amie?" He was still dressed, for Jean-Marie didn't often retire before midnight.

She looked at him, seeing for the first time fine lines at the corners of his eyes.

It had been a very long day.

"Have I ever told you how very much I appreciate your friendship, Jean-Marie?"

"*Non*, but I 'ear it in your voice nonetheless every time you speak to me, *ma petite*." He arched an eyebrow. "And is that why you roused me from my warm fire? To ask this question of me?"

"No it isn't." Eve held out her missive. "Send a boy with this letter to the One Horned Goat as soon as it's light. I have need of Alf."

Chapter Eight

"Close your eyes, girl," the king ordered, and Dove saw the glint of a knife in his hand.
Her entire body trembled, but she kept her gaze on him.
"I cannot."
His upper lip lifted in a contemptuous snarl. "Do it now, I command you!"
Tears streamed from her eyes, but Dove refused to look away. "No."
At this the king screamed, "Avert your eyes so that I may carve the heart from your breast!"
But instead Dove jumped to her feet and dashed from the hut and into the black night....
—From The Lion and the Dove

The next morning Asa sat listening to one of the most beautiful arias, sung by a wonderfully voiced castrato... and tried to hide a yawn behind the hand propping up his chin. He'd been up until the early hours of the morning helping to clear the stage. The problem with castrati—well, all opera singers, really—was that they were incredibly touchy about their gift. The slightest hint of disregard and they were apt to go stomping off the stage. Asa had once seen a soprano walk out because a patron's *lapdog* had fallen asleep during her performance.

There was no stage to stomp off this morning—they'd decided to hear the castrati in the paved courtyard before the theater—but Asa wasn't taking any chances. Beside him Eve sat very straight in her chair, her expression intent, her eyes shining, and Asa couldn't repress a small smile. She was obviously enjoying the performance.

"Ach, vill you never hit that note?"

Unfortunately, the same could not be said for Vogel. Asa winced at the composer's sarcastic mutter.

The castrato, a tall man with long teeth and a yellow powdered wig, cut off his song with a very rude gesture. "I have sung in St. Peter's Basilica in Rome before the pope himself!"

"And yet you lumbered through that passage like a cowherd singing to his bovine love."

The castrato burst into Italian, which was probably just as well, considering the gestures he continued to aim at the composer. After spitting dramatically on the ground the man swept off.

"Well." Eve blinked for a moment before turning to Vogel. "The first singer, then?"

"He is young and not as famous as that one." Vogel shrugged pragmatically. "But a better singer, *ja*. Ve hire Ponticelli. I shall go tell him at once."

Asa nodded to indicate his consent to the choice.

The composer bowed and strode in the direction of the theater, where the other castrato had gone to wait after giving his performance.

"Oh, thank God," Asa said, rising and stretching out a kink in his back. "That's done and Ponticelli will cause me less grief, I think, than Gio ever did."

"In what way?" Eve asked as she rose. For once she

wasn't shadowed by Jean-Marie, as he'd asked to help clear the stage.

"Ah..." For a moment Asa stared at her blankly. The fact was that Gio was a terrible womanizer, which had resulted in weeping women showing up at the theater at all hours.

"He did seem very volatile when he left," Eve observed.

"Yes he did," Asa agreed, relieved.

"Of course I've noticed that many of the people in the theater are volatile," she mused and looked at him expectantly.

They were at the theater door and Asa widened his eyes in mock innocence before opening the door for her and bowing her inside with a flourish.

"Humph." She strolled inside.

He grinned, watching the sway of her hips ahead of him as he entered behind. Two small children ran past them and out into the courtyard.

Asa frowned. "What are—"

Eve cleared her throat and stopped to wait for him to catch up before continuing. "So now you have your castrato, the opera should be fine, shouldn't it?"

"Dear God, don't say that," Asa exclaimed, stopping abruptly to knock on the wood framing the door.

He turned back to find Eve watching him with raised eyebrows. "I'd never have taken you for a superstitious man."

"I'm in the theater," he growled. "We're *all* superstitious." Taking her arm, he led her toward their office. "My stage fell in just yesterday. We have a little more than three weeks until we open, and all manner of misfortune could befall us before then."

"And yet you've been the one urging me to believe in you and your garden," she said softly.

"That's because I don't intend to quit. *Ever*," he replied as he opened the door to their office. "Come hell or fire or floods, my gardens will open and we'll put on an opera if I have to sing the high notes myself."

"I doubt you'd approve of what you'd have to do in order to sing those high notes," she said drily. "But I do admire your perseverance."

She rounded his table and gracefully sat at her desk, apparently unaware that he'd stopped dead, staring at her.

"You do?"

She was feeding the dove, which for some reason she'd brought with her this morning, but she looked up at his words, her face curious. "Yes, of course. A man who sets a course and proceeds to sail it, no matter the barriers or odds, is very admirable in my opinion."

"Ah." He ran his fingers through his hair, feeling unaccountably ill at ease. No one had told him what he was doing was good—that *he* was good—since ... well, since the death of Sir Stanley, his old mentor. "Thank you."

"You're welcome." Her reply was entirely solemn, but then her lips twitched and she leaned a little forward. "Now will you tell me why Giovanni Scaramella caused you trouble?"

Damn, and he'd thought he'd gotten away with his vague answer earlier. Asa couldn't help a twinge of admiration, though, that she hadn't been so easily put off.

He sighed and sat at his table. "He likes the ladies, does Gio, and sadly they like him as well. He seemed to be particularly fond of setting his paramours one against the other and preening when they fought over him—usually at the theater." Asa shook his head, thumbing through a stack of letters he'd brought from his rooms. "He's a bit of a bastard, really."

"But…" He looked up to see that Eve had her brows knit, a puzzled look on her face. "That is…" Her cheeks pinkened—rather becomingly, really. "I thought a castrato sang with such a high voice because… well, because…"

"He's had his bits cut off," Asa finished her sentence for her kindly. "Before his voice had a chance to change to a man's."

"Then…?" Her voice trailed away in delicate question and for a moment he stared at her, trying to figure out what she was asking.

"Ah." The light dawned. "Er… not *all* his bits, actually. He's still got a…" For a split second all the names for the body part Asa was thinking of went through his brain.

None of them were fit to be uttered in a lady's presence by a gentleman.

Which, he supposed, made it a good thing he wasn't one.

"Cock," Asa said, rather louder than he'd first intended to. "A castrato still has a cock. It's just his bollocks that are cut off."

She tilted her head, strangely less self-conscious than he was at the moment. "And that's enough to let him, er…" She waved her hand vaguely. "*Entertain* ladies?"

He shrugged. "Seems to be? At least it is for Gio. Course for all I know he can't get it up at all and does everything by hand, so to speak." He grinned at his own wit.

She tilted her head slowly. "By hand."

"Yes, you know…" He started to make a gesture, realized it would be unforgivably crude, and diverted his hand to scratching his head, ending lamely, "By hand."

She shook her head decisively. "No, I do not know."

He swallowed, feeling his *cock* twitch at discussing this with her. *This*, this was a dangerous conversation and she *must* know it, no matter how innocent she was.

Yet she was staring at him, waiting for an answer.

Well, if she was brave enough to pursue the matter, then far be it from him to withhold the information.

"By hand," he said quietly, his voice deepening without conscious thought. "When a man slips his hand under a woman's skirts and touches her between her legs. Touches her slit."

Her blue eyes were wide, her lips slightly parted, and the pink still hadn't left her cheeks. He found himself breathing in unison with her, the room quiet save for the faint sounds of the work on the stage. He recalled how she'd looked last night as she'd watched him unbutton his shirt for her: naïvely, *sensuously* innocent.

They were all alone here, just he and she, and he was having trouble remembering that he'd ever thought her plain.

She licked her lips, the slip of her tongue wet and shockingly red. "What do you mean?"

ASA WAS WATCHING her, his green eyes glinting. "You've never touched yourself there?"

Eve should have been offended by such a question, but then she herself had started the topic. She was the one who'd kept pushing him.

She was the one who wanted to *know*.

She shook her head mutely.

His voice was deep and nearly gravelly as he said, "There's a bit of flesh, a little nubbin, at the top of a woman's slit. Some call it a pearl or a button or a clitoris, but it doesn't matter what it's called, for it holds the key to a woman's pleasure. If it's rubbed or"—he inhaled slowly—"*licked*, then the woman feels a wondrous feeling. She's transported, the very same as when a man spills his seed."

Eve could feel a warmth at the bottom of her belly at his words, but she wasn't sure whether to believe him or not. She had never felt a pearl in her slit. How could he know more about a woman's body—presumably *her* body—than she did?

"You've done this?" she whispered. "Rubbed and licked?"

"Yes." His eyes had gone half lidded, the green nearly hidden.

"Why?" she asked, truly bewildered. "How does it serve you?"

He smiled at her then, not in friendship or joy but as if he revealed a secret. "Because it brings me pleasure, too. To hear a woman's moans and gasps and whimpers, see her growing wet, to smell her spice rising in the air, and to know that *I* am the one driving her pleasure. *My* touch has made her lose her mind." He shook his head. "It's powerful, that feeling, that moment."

She was having trouble catching her breath, as if she'd run pell-mell across a field. His words, his *voice*, seemed to hold her in some kind of spell. "Do all women react this way?"

"No. Some hold themselves tight. I have to tease open their legs, their sex. They might lie still and quiet for some time while I kiss them and tell them how beautiful they are and play with their little pearl. My hand might be covered with their liquid, the air heavy with salt and sex by the time they come undone. Others are wanton, in the best sort of way. They hold up their skirts and spread their legs and giggle as I stroke, licking their lips, sighing, and enjoying their own pleasure."

She watched him intently, wanting to squirm at the forbidden things he was telling her, but keeping herself firmly in check. "Which do you like better?"

He laughed softly, almost a grunt, and she realized he was sprawled in his chair, his head tilted back. "I like them all. Highborn and low, sweet, giggling girls and ladies who have the knowledge of the ways of the world in their eyes. I like short lasses and tall, redhead and dark, big-bosomed women and ones with delicate little teacups. The type who flirt with just a dip of their eyelashes and those that let a man know right away what they want. I like women and I like making love to them. They're all beautiful to me."

"But…" Not all women were beautiful. *She* was not beautiful—he'd made that more than obvious the day they'd met. Did he not even consider her a woman, then? The thought made her unaccountably sad.

She meant to ask, to demand a further explanation, but the door to the office opened. Jean-Marie came in and Asa straightened in his chair.

The spell was broken.

But even as Eve turned to Jean-Marie, she caught a gleam in Asa's eye, and she wondered: what would it feel like if she let him touch her?

Jean-Marie looked from her to Asa, his eyes narrowed in suspicion, but he merely said, "Alf waits for you in the garden, *mon amie*."

Asa finally glanced away from her at this news. "Alf?"

"A boy who works for my brother," Eve said, rising. She was pleased to find that her legs held her. "And for me as well sometimes."

"What's he doing here?" Asa demanded.

Eve shrugged casually. "I thought he could help me with my work—perhaps do a few small chores and run errands for me."

She'd never been a particularly good liar, and he stared at her a moment longer before saying slowly, "Very well."

She nodded once and simply left the room. Really, what else could she do? There was no proper way to take leave of a gentleman one had been discussing . . . *that* with just minutes before. Eve shivered. What had possessed her to continue questioning him? It was as if she'd been bewitched—the quiet room, his blazing green eyes, her own quickened breathing. She should be appalled at herself. Ashamed and cowed.

And yet she wasn't. If anything, she wanted to return and ask him more about what he could do to a woman.

Eve shook the thought from her mind as she stepped into the sunshine, Jean-Marie behind her.

"What will you 'ave this boy do?" the bodyguard murmured at her elbow.

She inhaled, ordering her thoughts as they crossed the wide paved courtyard. "Mr. Makepeace thinks the stage might have been deliberately tampered with to make it fall. He says several of the beams bore marks of having been sawn partway through."

"Ah," Jean-Marie said. "I, too, saw this. But I still do not understand what that 'as to do with the boy."

"Show me where he is and you'll see," Eve replied.

Jean-Marie shot her a look and gestured ahead. "There, lurking about the pillars of the musicians' gallery. 'E is distrustful, that one."

"It's probably one of the reasons why Val employs him," Eve muttered as she strode briskly to the musicians' gallery.

Now that Jean-Marie had pointed out the boy's hiding place she could see him, blending into the shadows behind the pillars. Alf looked even more scrawny in broad daylight, and Eve had a pang. How often did the boy eat?

"Ma'am." Alf touched the brim of his battered hat as she stopped before him, but didn't remove it. "Yer wanted t' see me?"

"Yes, Alf," Eve replied. "I've a job for you, but it's a bit of a secret."

A smile flitted across his face. "Most o' my jobs are."

"Yes, well." Eve took a deep breath. "Mr. . . . er . . . *Harte*, the owner of Harte's Folly, thinks that someone may be trying to destroy his garden. Yesterday the stage collapsed in the theater, injuring two of the dancers—and killing one. Mr. Harte doesn't think it was an accident."

Alf cocked his head, arching his brows in question.

"I'd like you to be my agent in the matter and find out who might be behind the stage collapse," Eve said. "Jean-Marie and I will say that you're here to help me, but in reality you'll be on the watch for anything suspicious. Do you think you can do this for me?"

"Oh, aye, I can do the job," Alf said slowly, "but if'n I'll find a troublemaker or not, that I can't say."

"I understand," Eve said. "I just want you to look."

"I'll do it." Alf nodded. "What job d'you want me to do for you first?"

Eve hadn't thought that far ahead. She glanced around as if for inspiration, and a small movement in the nearby brush caught her eye.

She gripped Jean-Marie's arm in alarm. "I think we're being watched."

Jean-Marie followed the direction of her gaze and strode to the bushes, then parted the branches to look.

Eve saw when the taut line of his back relaxed. "It is nothing to worry over."

"What do you mean?" She went to where he was, Alf behind her, and looked in the bushes.

There lay the giant dog she'd seen in the office at the theater. This time, though, his eyes were shut and he made no movement at all, his gaunt frame lying still in the brush.

Eve felt guilt sweep through her. She'd been so fearful of the animal she'd never looked at him closely. Never realized he was starving. "Is he . . . is he dead?"

Jean-Marie bent and laid his palm on the animal's dirty side, waiting a moment before straightening and shaking his head. "He still lives, but not for long."

Eve stared at the dog. He had frightened her nearly out of her wits when she'd first seen him, but now he lay curled on his side, dirty and with ribs starkly revealed. No one could be afraid of such a creature.

Not even she.

Eve turned to Alf. "I have a job for you."

The boy looked between her and the dog, a brief expression of revulsion crossing his face before it blanked. "D'you want me to kill it?"

"No," Eve replied. "I want you to help me make him well again."

*   *   *

ASA WAS STARING morosely at a letter when the door to his office opened.

He looked up in time to see Eve enter. She turned without a glance to him and said, "Careful now."

Jean-Marie walked in, carrying a half-dead mangy mutt.

"What—?" Asa began.

"Put him there," Eve said to the footman—*still* not paying Asa any attention. "We can use some of those rags here."

And she gestured to a pile of crimson-and-gold cloth.

"Oi!" Asa rose, outraged. "Those *rags* are costumes."

Eve finally acknowledged him by lifting her eyebrow at him. "They look quite sooty."

Asa ran a hand through his hair. "They were salvaged when the theater burned."

Eve nodded. "And now they can be put to use, for I hardly think any actor or opera singer would want to wear them."

"But…" Actually he couldn't think of any retort to that, so he was forced to watch silently as Jean-Marie maneuvered the dog over behind her desk and laid the animal gently on the pile of costumes.

Eve was watching as well, a little worried frown between her brows.

He couldn't help but stare at her. She was afraid of dogs—he knew damned well she was—and yet here was seeing to the comfort of the same half-dead mutt that had sent her into a screaming fit not two days before. She was such a contradiction: the sister of a duke, proud and upright, but not half an hour ago she'd been wide-eyed and breathless as he'd described frigging a woman. It didn't make any sense. He could feel his cock stir just at the memory of *talking* to her—no touching, they'd had both the desk and his table between them. She wasn't pretty. He could see that even now. Her nose was too long, her face too plain. And yet he'd give nearly anything to see her body. To touch a slender hand or a pale shoulder, he who was used to doing so much more than that with his women.

Asa snorted under his breath. It must be the lure of the forbidden—the very fact that he *couldn't* touch her. If he were able to pull her into his arms, widen those prim lips under his mouth, why, he'd be tired of her immediately.

Wouldn't he?

The boy came in then with a basin of water and a sack slung over his arm.

"Oh, thank you, Alf," Eve said, motioning him nearer the dog.

Asa stalked to her to see what she was about. She was hovering over the dog, not quite touching him, but obviously wanting to do something.

"Here, let me," Asa said, taking off his coat. The dog stank to high heaven.

He rolled up his sleeves and bent to tear off a piece of the crimson material.

"What are you doing?" Miss Dinwoody asked anxiously.

Asa snorted, gently pushing her aside. "If you're going to keep him here, we might as well see if we can make him less odiferous." He jerked his chin at the boy, still standing with the basin. "Put it down and come help me."

The boy glanced at Eve and, at her nod, did as he commanded.

Asa squatted, examining the dog. The poor beast really was in bad shape, and Asa privately wondered if he would survive the night.

But he wasn't going to be the one to tell Eve that.

The animal had been massive when in health, with drooping jowls on a huge head, but now he was mostly skin and bones. His pelvis protruded painfully, carving deep hollows in the animal's hips. There were cuts and scratches all across the beast's hide, the badges of many a battle over scavenged scraps, no doubt. One ear was torn shorter than the other, and the animal's eyes and nose were crusted.

But when he laid a hand on the dog's head the animal opened his eyes and feebly thumped his tail against the material he lay on.

"That's a good lad," Asa murmured. He wetted his cloth in the water and gently wrung it over the animal's mouth.

The dog stuck out his tongue and lapped the dribble of water.

"Got it some cheese and meat," Alf said by his side. He opened his sack, showing a lump of cheese and a slice of beef.

Asa shook his head. "Might be too rich, the condition this dog is in. Go and ask around, see if anyone has brought bread for their luncheon today."

"Right," Alf said, and scrambled to his feet.

"You 'ave lost your 'elper," Jean-Marie observed. "What do you need now?"

"Let's sponge him clean as much as we can," Asa said, stroking the dog's filthy head. "Best we not get him too wet, though. He'll get cold easily with no fat on his bones."

The footman nodded and removed his coat before kneeling as well.

Asa gave the dog a little more water, then used his cloth

to stroke over the animal's hide. It must've hurt—several of the cuts and scrapes were fresh and began bleeding as he rubbed over them—but the dog never moved. He just lay quietly, watching his every movement. Asa noticed, too, that once in a while the animal's eyes swiveled to look at Eve, and that when they did, the dog thumped his tail again.

Asa felt his lips curve. "You've acquired an admirer."

"What?" She turned to look at him, her brows knitted rather adorably.

He nodded at the dog. "He likes you."

She frowned down at the animal. "But I screamed when I first saw him. It doesn't make any sense for him to like me."

Asa shrugged as he and Jean-Marie turned the animal gently to his other side. "Animals don't always have to have a reason to like a person."

"I see," she said soberly, still staring at the dog.

Asa felt his lips quirk at her seriousness.

The door opened again and he glanced over his shoulder to see Alf returning, holding a piece of bread triumphantly in his hand. "Got it."

"Good." Asa nodded as he threw the rag into the water and wiped his hands. They'd done as much as they could without submersing the dog in a tub—and that they couldn't do until the animal got better.

If he got better.

Asa frowned as he took the bread and broke a bite off for the dog. He held it out gingerly to the animal, wary of being bitten in the dog's eagerness. But the beast, despite his obvious hunger, took the bread delicately from his fingers.

"That's a gentleman, that is," said Alf admiringly as Asa fed the dog the rest of the bread. "Taking care not to bite the 'and what feeds 'im."

"Aye, he has very nice manners," Asa said softly, smoothing over the animal's brow. A pity the dog was in such bad shape—it seemed a friendly animal. "Well, that's the best we can do, I think."

Eve nodded. "Alf, will you take this dirty basin and bring back a fresh bowl of water for him?"

The boy nodded and took both the basin of dirty water and the soiled cloth.

Eve was still staring worriedly at the dog. "Do you think he'll recover?"

"I don't know," Asa said honestly. "But the rest will do him good."

She nodded reluctantly, then glanced at Jean-Marie. "This reminds me that I forgot to bring a luncheon of our own today. Will you see if you can find something?"

"There's a meat pie shop not half a mile from here," Asa volunteered. "Go out the back gate and then left down the lane. You can't miss it—the smell of baking pies will lead you. Mind bringing back one for me as well?"

He fished in his pocket and found a handful of coins to give the footman.

"Of course." Jean-Marie flashed his white teeth. "I shall return shortly."

And then he was gone.

Asa glanced at Eve as he sat at his table. If she felt any discomfort at being alone with him, she didn't show it.

Maybe she'd already forgotten the matter.

He glared down at his desk and saw the letter that he'd been reading when Eve and her dog had come in. "Damn."

Of course she heard him. "What is it?"

"Nothing, nothing," he muttered irritably, folding the letter and pushing it to the edge of his desk.

She raised an eyebrow. "I find that hard to believe. Come, if there is a further problem with the garden, it is within my right to know it."

"It has nothing to do with the bloody garden," he snarled irritably.

"Then—?"

He picked up the letter and waved it. "It's an invitation to the baptism dinner for my newest niece."

"Oh." She smiled, her sky-blue eyes lighting. "How lovely. How many nieces and nephews do you have?"

"Far too many, especially in my brother Concord's family. He must wear out his wife near every night, the randy old goat."

"Well." She cleared her throat, looking a little pink. "Congratulations. Will you be taking a present for the child?"

"No," he growled, flinging the letter away. "And I won't be going, either."

Her smile abruptly turned to a frown. "Whyever not?"

"Because," he said with as much patience as he could muster, "my *family* will be there."

She slowly raised her eyebrows.

He pointed his index finger at her forehead. "Don't give me that look. You haven't met my family, so you don't have any idea how ghastly this could be."

"I assure you I am fully aware how awful a family can be," she said with clipped accents. "But you've never given indication that your family are outright monsters."

He snorted. "Worse. They're *religious*."

"Even so," she said, "this child will someday grow and realize that hers was the only baptism of her family that you didn't come to, and it would be remiss—"

Asa muttered under his breath.

She stopped. "What did you say?"

"I said I've never been to any one of the damned baptisms," Asa said a little louder. Lord only knew why he was having trouble raising his voice—it wasn't a usual problem for him.

Miss Dinwoody froze for a moment and then sat a little forward and clasped her hands together on her desk. "Let me see if I have this correctly—"

"Oh, dear God," Asa muttered.

She continued over him. "You have five brothers and sisters and of these, how many have children?"

He flushed. "Well, Verity and Concord, certainly. I'm not sure about Silence—married a dodgy sort, y'know, and keeps rather to herself. Winter has the home, of course, and Temperance…" He screwed tight his eyes, thinking. Hadn't there been talk of a child sometime last year? "I think she has a girl?"

Miss Dinwoody inhaled sharply. "And how many children do Verity and Concord have?"

"Verity has three children," he replied promptly. That at least he knew. "And Concord has… oh, five or six?"

"Is that counting the new niece?"

He stared at her a moment. He had absolutely no idea. "Yes?"

She closed her eyes briefly, then opened them. "So, let me see if I understand. You have nine to possibly eleven nieces and nephews and *you've never been to a single baptism*?"

"I've been busy!" he shouted, having—thank God!—found his volume at last. "I've had a garden to run and a business to build!"

He stopped, glaring at her.

She crimped her lips, narrowed her eyes, and said very precisely, "You are going to that baptism, Asa Makepeace."

He laughed; he couldn't help it. "And how are you going to make me do that? Lift me and carry me clear across London?"

"No," she said. "I'm simply going to point out that they're your family, both young and old, and you can't keep running from them forever. Besides…" She smiled—not at all nicely, he noted. "You might enjoy it."

"I won't," he said, sounding uncommonly like a three-year-old child.

"Is your family so very terrible, then?" she asked seriously.

"Concord is an ill-tempered ass," he muttered.

She looked at him pointedly.

He could feel the heat climbing his neck and cast about desperately for a diversion. "What about you, then?"

"What about me?"

"I don't see you skipping off to attend family dinners," he said rather resentfully.

"I haven't much family," she replied drily.

He narrowed his eyes. "What about that Ladies' Syndicate?"

She glanced away. "That's a *social* assembly. It's hardly the same thing as family."

"Ha!" he said, pointing his finger at her again.

She batted at it. "I do wish you'd quit that. It's rather rude."

"You," he said with great glee, "are avoiding the subject."

"What subject?"

"The fact that while the Ladies' Syndicate might not be family, it *is* a social event that you don't wish to attend. Just as I"—he waved a hand at his chest—"have no desire to go to my niece's baptism dinner."

"It's not the same at all," she said, looking at him oddly. "One is a *family* obligation at which your attendance has been requested, and the other is a *social* event at which I'm not welcome."

"That's not true," he said. "Judging by Lady Phoebe's friendliness to you the other day, I'd lay wager that you'd be very welcome."

She scowled. "You don't know that."

"I do."

She wrinkled her nose. "Well, it would be most awkward in any case."

"Coward," he said fondly.

"Scoundrel," she retorted, and then looked surprised at herself. "Well, it's true—only a scoundrel would miss his baby niece's baptism."

He waved that away. "If I have to attend this wretched family event, then you must go to the next Ladies' Syndicate meetings. Agreed?"

She opened her eyes wide. "I never agreed—"

"And furthermore," he pronounced, "since it's your idea that I suffer through the dinner, I think you ought to attend as well."

"Me?" Her eyes widened. "But—"

He folded his arms on his chest. "You go or I don't."

She opened her lips and then simply gaped at him.

He was rather satisfied that he'd made her lose her train of thought.

He smiled to himself, picking up the letter and peering at it. "It's at seven of the evening three nights hence." He frowned for a moment, thinking, then grinned at her. "We'll take your brother's carriage."

Chapter Nine

*Dove ran and ran through the wild, dark forest. Branches
whipped against her face and she stumbled to her knees
more than once. But she got back up every time because
she could hear the king's guard close behind her.
She ran until her slippers were tatters; she ran until her
legs burned and trembled.
She ran until she heard a* horrible *roar....*
—From *The Lion and the Dove*

Late that evening Bridget Crumb moved through Hermes
House checking that all the doors were locked and
secured for the night. It was Bob the footman's job to lock
up at night, but Bridget liked to do the rounds as well to
double-check that he'd not forgotten anything.

She also liked to survey what she privately thought of
as her domain.

Bridget touched the lock on the grand front door of
Hermes House, nodded to Bill, whose turn it was to sit
guard by the front entrance, and turned to mount the
curving staircase. The light of her candelabra flickered
and jumped against the darkened walls as she climbed.
The stairs were hung with dozens of paintings, many of
them portraits, and the painted faces stared at her as she

passed. All the other servants were tucked in their beds—
or at least retired for the night—and the house was silent
save for the tap of her heels as she walked. On the upper
floor she checked each room as she passed until she came
to the duke's bedroom.

There she went inside.

Hermes House was an opulent mansion. Every surface
was carved, gilded, lined with imported marbles, or all
three. It was as if the duke had wanted to show the world
how much wealth he possessed—enough to build a house
a king would envy.

But even in such lavishness, the master bedroom
stood out.

Shell-pink walls were set with carved, gilded medal-
lions of twining vines and leaves. At one end a white marble fireplace took up half the wall. A thick red-and-blue
carpet lay on the floor, while overhead painted nude gods
and goddesses reveled in debauchery.

In the center of the room was the biggest bed Bridget
had ever seen—and she'd been working in aristocratic
households since the age of thirteen. It was carved of
some sort of golden wood, massive bowed posts holding
up a pleated, gold-tasseled, sky-blue canopy. More gold
tassels held back swaths of material around the posts, and
the bed itself held so many pillows they nearly obscured
the coverlet.

Bridget *humph*ed as she passed the bed. Dusting the
ridiculous thing took her maids half an hour each week.

Just past the bed was a delicate secretary inlaid with
ivory and gilt. It looked a bit like a rectangular box set on
legs. The top was hinged and could be folded back so that
a person could sit at the secretary and write letters.

In the center of the front of the secretary was a keyhole. The secretary was locked.

Bridget set her candelabra down on a side table and examined the lock. It was gold—*naturally*—and would scratch easily if care wasn't taken.

She sighed and straightened.

Over the secretary hung an enormous, life-size painting of the duke. Another portrait of the duke hung in the stairwell. It also was life-size. In *that* painting he stood, beautiful and arrogant, draped in ermine, velvet, and silk, and holding a book in his long fingers. In *this* portrait he was reclining.

And nude.

Well, not entirely, Bridget amended, staring critically at the painting. The duke did have a transparent wisp of fabric floating over his pelvis, but it merely served to highlight his genitals rather than conceal them.

Bridget had long suspected that the painter had flattered the duke with the size of his endowment.

But she had far more important matters to think about.

With a last glance at the self-satisfied smirk on the duke's painted lips, she turned back to the secretary. She withdrew a hairpin from her coiffure, bent it neatly, and, leaning down, inserted it gently in the keyhole.

Five minutes of patient manipulation later, Bridget heard a distinct *click*.

She smiled to herself and lifted the lid of the secretary. Inside were rows of pigeonholes. She methodically went through each one and found ink, pens—several nibbled down to nubs—paper, sand, two letters that were scandalously explicit in what the sender wanted the duke to do to her person, and not much else.

Bridget straightened and sighed. Well, at least she'd

ruled out the secretary. She spent a further few minutes testing for any hidden drawers, and, after finding none, set the secretary back in order and closed it, taking care to lock it again.

As she did so, she heard a faint sound, like a chuckle.

Bridget froze, then picked up her candelabra and held it high.

No one was in the room besides herself.

She strode to the door and yanked it open.

The hallway was deserted as well.

Behind her something moved.

She jerked around, peering into the far corners of the duke's room. A door on the wall opposite the fireplace led into a small dressing room. When the duke was in residence sometimes his valet slept there. Bridget went to that door and opened it as well.

The room was silent and empty.

Slowly she closed the door to the dressing room. Bridget Crumb had been raised in the country, but she considered herself a sophisticated woman.

She did not believe in ghosts.

Glancing once more around the duke's bedroom, she left the room and closed the door behind her.

And made a mental note to have the maid set mousetraps in the upper floors.

EVE WASN'T ENTIRELY sure how she'd come to be in a carriage with Asa—she'd certainly never agreed to such a thing—but that was where she found herself three nights later.

The carriage bumped over a rut in the street and Eve swayed with it as she examined Asa, sitting across from her. He wore a flaming red coat tonight, trimmed in gold lace. Underneath, his waistcoat was made of gold brocade, intricately over-embroidered in black, and his breeches were black as well. If his family was "religious," as Asa had indicated, she couldn't help but think that his attire was designed to provoke.

She herself had worn a simple gray silk with discreet white lace at elbow and neckline. A gauzy fichu was tucked into her bodice, for both warmth and modesty. She'd been persuaded to leave Jean-Marie behind for a much-deserved evening off tonight, but that didn't mean she was unprotected—besides Asa, she had the driver of the carriage and two of her brother's footmen.

More than sufficient for a drive through London.

Eve cleared her throat. "Did you decide on a present for the baby?"

She'd spent the last several days continuing to order the Harte's Folly books, but though he'd worked across from her for most of those days, Asa had been rather distant.

Now he stopped bouncing his knee and turned to her. "I'm not a savage, y'know."

She raised her eyebrows. "I was merely curious."

He grunted, moodily looking out the darkened window. "Got her a guinea."

"You're giving a baby money."

"It's practical," he growled. "Concord'll save it for her and she can use it later for…for…" He frowned, apparently unable to think what a young girl could buy with a guinea. Impatiently he waved a hand. "Anyway, I *did* bring a present."

"Of course you did," she replied soothingly. "I myself found a darling little bonnet that I hope her mother will like."

She'd actually spent far more time than needed searching

Bond Street for the perfect present. Shopping for baby gifts was rather enthralling.

He stared. "You didn't need to bring a present. It's *my* niece."

She felt an unaccountable spurt of hurt at his words. "I know that, but I wanted to give her something. A baby is a precious thing."

Eve glanced down at her hands. She'd never have a baby of her own, she knew. Could she be blamed then for wanting to dote on this one, though it was no relation of hers?

His face softened at her stiff words. "I'm sure Rose will like the bonnet."

Eve didn't have time for a reply, for they were drawing up before some sort of shop. She waited for the footman to set the step and then descended the carriage. They were on the outskirts of St. Giles—quite a terrible area of London, though this street seemed nice enough.

She peered up at the shop—a dressmaker's?—in confusion.

"My brother and his family live over the shop," Asa said in her ear, intimately close.

"Oh." Eve smoothed down her skirts, feeling suddenly nervous. The fact was that she wasn't very comfortable in company—especially with people she didn't know. Add to that the class differences and her fear that she'd make some sort of faux pas, and she had a sudden urge to get back in the carriage.

Asa must've sensed her unease. He held out his arm for her. "They're a loud and outspoken lot, but they hardly ever bite." His green eyes softened. "And I think you'll like my sisters."

"Well, then." She inhaled, trying to smile. "I suggest we go in so I can meet them."

He showed her to the little door at the side of the shop. Behind it was a steep staircase that led straight to the upper level. As they ascended, Eve could hear happy laughter and voices raised in talk.

Asa paused a moment at the landing, threw back his shoulders, and knocked loudly on the closed door at the top of the stairs.

The voices hushed a bit and then the door was opened.

A woman with strawberry-blond hair in a springy nimbus around her face stood there, her cheeks pink, her eyes a lovely green-blue.

She took one look at Mr. Makepeace and flung herself into his arms. *"Asa!"*

"Hullo, Rose," Mr. Makepeace muttered as he wrapped his arms around her slim shoulders.

"How wonderful you've come! Josiah will be thrilled—he still remembers when you took him to that puppet show, oh, *years* ago now, and Prudence, John, and George will be so excited—I think they believe you're a myth. Oh, and you've never met little Rebecca, let alone Rachel, our new baby." She pulled back, grinning, and caught sight of Eve, standing awkwardly to the side. Eve could almost see the inquisitive light fire behind the other woman's eyes. "But who is this?"

Rose's excitement had drawn interest from inside the flat. Several children crowded around her skirts, staring wide-eyed at the newcomers, while three women came to peer over Rose's shoulders.

One, an elegantly dressed woman with blue eyes and mahogany hair, smiled curiously at the sight of Eve. "Why, Miss Dinwoody, how lovely to meet you again."

Eve swallowed, for it was Isabel Makepeace—the wife of Winter Makepeace, manager of the Home for Unfortunate Infants and Foundling Children.

She held out her hand. "Mrs. Makepeace, good evening. And...Lady Caire?"

Eve blinked in confusion at the second lady. She had a grave face, brown hair, and quite extraordinary golden eyes. Both women were in the Ladies' Syndicate, but why would the younger Lady Caire, who was the wife of the quite notorious Lord Caire, attend this baptism?

But Lady Caire solved her confusion by taking her hand and saying, "My maiden name is Makepeace. I used to manage the home with our brother Winter." She shot a wry look at Asa. "I take it Asa didn't tell you I was his sister when he decided to bring you?"

"Erm..." Eve hedged, not wanting to embarrass Asa. She glanced at him, but he was glowering in the general direction of his sister and not helping one bit. She took a breath. "I hope it's not inconvenient, my coming?"

"Oh, not at all," Isabel drawled, linking her arm with Eve's. "In fact, I would call it very fortuitous indeed."

Asa looked a trifle alarmed. "Look here—"

"We'll introduce you to everyone." The last woman finally spoke. She had the Makepeace brown hair and an infectious grin. She curtsied to Eve. "I'm Silence Rivers, Asa's youngest sister. I'm so very glad you could come, Miss Dinwoody."

"Thank you," Eve said, smiling shyly. "And won't you call me Eve?"

"Eve, then. Come in, won't you?" Silence slipped her arm into Eve's and gave a gentle tug.

Eve stepped inside and caught her breath at once. Even

though Asa had told her how large his family was, she hadn't quite been anticipating the impact of them all gathered together in what was obviously a too-small room.

She could discern a row of windows across the back of the house, no doubt overlooking a courtyard. Underneath the windows a long table was laden with all sorts of meats and breads and puddings. As she watched, a small dark-haired girl stood on tiptoe and attempted to stick her finger in a shimmering pink confection. Before she could touch it, however, the child was scooped up by a man with long white hair clubbed back with a black ribbon. He looked rather intimidating, truth be told, but the child seemed to disagree with this assessment, laughing as he flung her into the air.

Silence must've seen the look on her face. "I suppose it's a bit daunting at first, but really, we're all quite friendly."

"The females, anyway," Asa muttered directly behind her.

A large man with brown hair streaked with gray turned at that moment, his eyes narrowing at the sight of them. "Asa! Little brother, I'm surprised you managed to tear yourself away from whatever you do and come to your niece's baptismal dinner."

Rose quietly detached herself from the ladies, walked to the man, linked her arm with his, and, while still smiling at him, firmly ground her heel into his instep.

The man didn't make a sound, but his eyes widened a bit.

"We're *very happy* Asa could come, aren't we, dear husband?" Rose said.

"Of course, darling wife." Concord Makepeace dislodged himself from his wife's hand and moved a prudent pace away. "Welcome, Brother."

"Con," Asa replied stiffly.

Eve fought not to roll her eyes.

Apparently Rose had no such qualms. "Concord, this is Miss Eve Dinwoody, Asa's friend."

Friend. It was an innocuous word, but Eve had to suppress a shiver at being linked to Asa even in such a little way. Were they friends? Well, they must be. He'd hardly make a mere acquaintance accompany him to his niece's baptismal dinner.

"Ma'am." Concord gave her a half bow. He was obviously years older than Asa, but there was a similarity in the stubbornness of the jaw and the frank gaze. That gaze darted to Asa, standing half a pace behind her, and the older man's eyes narrowed as he looked between them.

"Mr. Makepeace, it's a pleasure to meet you," Eve said quite truthfully, and she saw a softening in Asa's brother's gaze.

"Call me Concord," he said gruffly.

Rose patted her husband's hand. "Now, let me introduce you to the rest of the family."

What followed was, in Eve's opinion, a bit like running a gauntlet. Rose introduced her to the remaining Makepeace family, including the white-haired gentleman, who turned out to be the notorious Lord Caire, and Silence's overwhelmingly handsome husband, Mr. Rivers. Verity Brown, the eldest sibling, who had apparently raised all but Concord when their mother died, was a serene woman of middling years, her hair more silver than brown. The children were very confusing, as there were half a dozen running about, as well as several toddlers.

Eve met the baby being honored last. Rachel Makepeace was a pretty baby with a hand-knit bonnet tied under her chin. A tiny wisp of dark hair peeked from under the bonnet just at the center of her forehead. She lay in a basket, fast asleep despite the noisy crowd around her—not least her uncle and father. Concord had drawn Asa into a corner and their discussion was obviously heated, as their voices grew steadily louder.

"Don't mind them," Rose said, noticing her glance. "They do argue quite a lot, but they *are* brothers, and Concord wouldn't dare do anything too awful on Rachel's day."

"That reminds me," Eve murmured, tearing her gaze away from Asa and his brother. "I brought this for Rachel."

She held out the small parcel she'd tucked into her pocket.

"Oh!" Rose beamed at her. "You didn't have to."

Eve smiled shyly. "Who doesn't like buying presents for babies?"

Rose giggled and drew off the ribbon tying the present closed. She unfolded the light paper Eve had wrapped the present in and then gasped. "It's lovely."

She held up a white linen cap, delicately embroidered in palest pink around the edge, so that the other ladies might see. Temperance and Silence exclaimed over the fine embroidery while Isabel asked the name of the shop that Eve had found it in.

Rose looked at Eve, her eyes glinting. "Thank you. I'm so glad you came."

"We're all glad," Temperance said softly.

Eve glanced at her, puzzled.

"She doesn't know," Isabel said, a thread of amusement in her voice. She glanced at the other women as if asking permission.

Rose nodded.

Isabel turned back to Eve. "As long as I've been married to Winter, Asa hasn't brought a friend to visit his family."

Verity snorted under her breath. "Oh, it's more than that, Isabel dear. Asa's never brought a *lady* around." She smiled conspiratorially at Eve.

Oh, dear. Eve opened her mouth to explain that it wasn't like that between her and Asa. They were *business* acquaintances.

But she never got the chance, for at that moment Concord hit his brother Asa full in the face.

ASA STAGGERED BACK under Concord's fist. The blow to his cheek hurt like bloody hell. He growled as he lowered his head and charged, catching Concord around the waist and running them both into a chair behind him. The chair flattened with a crash beneath their combined weight and they both sprawled to the floor, Asa on top.

Fuck his brother and his sanctimonious ways!

Asa drew back his fist—only to find his arm restrained from behind.

He snarled, pulling against the hands holding him, but he was unable to break free. He glanced around and found his brothers-in-law, Lord Caire and "Mr. Rivers"—the former infamous river pirate known as Charming Mickey.

Rivers grinned and winked. "Got ye good, dear *brother.*"

"Let me go, you sodding ponce," Asa growled.

"I think not," Caire said from his other side.

His sisters had the *worst* taste in husbands—well, all except Verity, who had married John Brown. John and the youngest Makepeace brother, Winter, were holding Concord. John looked calm as a man twenty years his junior tried to escape his grasp.

"Concord Resilience Makepeace!" Rose was in front of her husband now, hands on hips. "Whyever should you strike your brother on our daughter's baptismal day?"

For a moment Con nearly looked sheepish. "Said he was too busy—that's why he never comes round. He didn't even know that Silence had Concordia in March!"

Rose widened her eyes at that, and Silence, standing a pace behind her, looked away, biting her lip.

"*Ass*," Mickey O'Connor hissed in his ear. "All this time she said you didn't come to see th' babe for fear of exposing me."

Asa felt a horrible twisting in his gut, but he refused to be distracted. He jerked his chin at Concord. "You're as rigid and unforgiving as our father ever was. Why the hell should I come to *any* family gathering when this is the reception I receive?"

"Don't you speak his name," Con yelled. "You haven't the right after the heartache you gave him."

"The *right*?" Asa felt his upper lip curl. "Oh, pardon me. I wasn't aware he'd made you with golden *spunk*."

Someone gasped loudly, but he wasn't paying attention. This had been a stupid idea from the start. As if any of his family, let alone Concord, would ever really welcome him again.

"Shut your mouth!" Concord bellowed, and now some of the children were crying. "How dare you? How dare you after he—" He stopped abruptly, his mouth closing with an audible snap of teeth.

Oh, but even Con knew better than to speak of *that*.

"What were you going to say, dear brother?" Asa purred. "How dare I after our wonderful sainted father *disowned* me?"

In the sudden silence even the toddler stopped crying.

"What?" It was Verity who spoke. "What are you talking about, Asa?"

He finally glanced away from Con and looked at her, his elder sister. Verity had been the heart of the family since their mother's death. He was surprised, though, at how gray her hair had grown. Was it that long since he'd last seen her?

Suddenly he was weary. He yanked his arms from his brothers-in-law's hands. "Father disowned me, Verity. When I was nineteen. Told me to go and never come again as long as he lived. That's why I left home."

"But..." Her warm brown eyes were wide and shocked as she looked between him and Concord. "Why didn't he say anything to us? Why didn't *you*?"

He shrugged. "Who knows why Father did anything? I didn't tell you because I didn't think there was any point. Father's word was law, wasn't it?"

She winced at that, but then glanced thoughtfully at their brother. "Con knew, though, that Father had forbid you the family."

"I don't know if Father told him before he died, but Con certainly knew when he read Father's will five years ago." Asa grinned without mirth. "There had to have been some explanation when I was cut from it."

Con grimaced, glancing away from his gaze.

And that confirmed every suspicion Asa had ever had. His mouth twisted as he looked at Verity. "Didn't you wonder when Con inherited the entire brewery after Father died?"

Verity shook her head slowly. "I didn't know. I thought—I assumed—that you simply didn't want anything to do with the business."

"He was a good man," Con said loudly, almost as if he were convincing himself. "Father was a godly man with a strong sense of righteousness."

"He was righteous all right," Asa sneered.

"But *why* did he disown you, Asa?" Temperance asked quietly.

He glanced at her and let his upper lip curl. "Because of my business."

He heard Eve inhale and knew she'd put together all the pieces. God, he hated this. Hated to be judged. Hated that *she* was seeing him laid bare like this.

"And what kind of business is it, I'd like to know?" Concord demanded. "Whatever it was, it shocked and appalled our father. You come dressed here like some lady's man, all in lace and velvet, obviously making fine money, and I can't see how unless you've been running a bawdy house these last ten years."

Asa threw back his head and guffawed. "A whore-house! Of course that's what your sanctimonious mind would immediately think. Tell me, Con, do you lie awake imagining me cavorting with ladies of the evening while you wear a hair shirt to bed?"

"Asa!" Verity exclaimed.

"Damned feckless fool!" Concord yelled.

"Bloody self-righteous prick!" Asa roared back.

"I don't understand." Eve's clear voice cut through the shouting.

"What don't you understand?" Verity asked.

But Eve was looking at him. "You mean all these years and you never told your family how you make your living?"

"No." Asa glared at her.

"But why?" she asked, sounding perplexed. She turned to Verity, who was standing beside her. "He's the manager of—"

"*Eve!*"

"Harte's Folly." She looked at him oddly, perhaps since he'd used her Christian name. "The owner, actually."

"But it burned down." Temperance looked worried. "A little over a year ago. We were there when it happened." She stared at him, her light-brown eyes hurt. "*Why* wouldn't you tell us?"

"I didn't think you'd care."

Temperance gasped as if he'd hit her and Lord Caire took her hand. "We're your family. Of course we *care.*"

Eve cleared her throat. "Asa's rebuilding the garden." She pinkened when they all turned to her, but stood her ground. "He really has been busy, actually. At least for the last year. My brother is the Duke of Montgomery. He's invested in Harte's Folly, and I manage his investment. We'll reopen in another fortnight."

There was a short silence.

Then Concord looked at Asa, his brow wrinkled. "A pleasure garden? Father disapproved of a pleasure garden?"

"And the theater in it," Asa replied, "which was bloody hypocritical of him, considering Sir Stanley Gilpin was his best friend."

Con had stiffened when Asa had called Father a hypocrite.

Asa pointed at his face while turning to Eve. "There, see? *That* is why I never told them."

"I'm so sorry your father didn't approve of Harte's Folly," Eve said simply. She looked at Verity earnestly.

"It's the loveliest garden in London, I think, and the theater is simply magnificent. We've just hired a new castrato for the opening opera, and of course La Veneziana will be singing." Her brows knit as she looked around doubtfully at his family. "You *have* heard of La Veneziana?"

"Oh, yes," Isabel said, and Temperance and Silence both nodded eagerly.

Eve smiled, her blue eyes lighting. "Then you know how wonderful the opera will be. Would you like tickets to the gardens when they open?"

"Oh, for—" But Asa's words were drowned out by the children's clamoring.

"Mama, can we?" cried either John or George—they were twins and Asa had a damnable time telling them apart.

"Of course," Rose said warmly. "How exciting!"

Asa blinked. He'd never thought Con or Rose to be as religiously strict as Father had been, but for Rose to be openly interested in Harte's Folly was a surprise.

"Then we'll be sure to send tickets," Eve said.

"For *everyone*?" either George or John asked. The boy had obviously inherited his tenacity from his father.

"Yes." Eve smiled down at him. "You're family, after all."

Asa groaned.

Caire slapped Asa on the shoulder—*hard*. "How *generous* of you, brother dear."

Asa would've glared if he hadn't heard the murmur from his other shoulder.

The bloody pirate was whispering in his ear, "Ye'll have to watch that one—she'll have given away yer entire business out o' the sweetness o' her heart if'n ye don't."

Sweet? Eve? Asa nearly scoffed—until he looked at

her. Eve was smiling down gently at a toddler who had one sticky hand tangled in her skirts. Was this the same woman who'd invaded his rooms and cut him off without hearing his side? The same woman who sat so straight as she entered line after line in her damned accounting book?

The same woman who had looked so scared when he kissed her?

It was, he realized. She was harpy and dove, sharp and soft, tightly laced, but with a curious gleam in her blue eyes when he'd described touching a woman.

He watched as she gingerly lifted the toddler into her arms, and thought, *Damn me, I'm in too deep this time.*

Chapter Ten

*Dove dropped to her knees in fright, blind in the darkness,
and something—something big and furry and strong—
rushed into her and pushed her over.
"Have pity!" cried the girl, but her only answer was
another deafening roar.
And after that she knew no more....*
—From *The Lion and the Dove*

Late that night Eve climbed wearily into her carriage. The
evening hadn't been a total failure, despite the argument
between Asa and his brother. She'd quite enjoyed meeting
his family, and even if Asa and Concord hadn't spoken
again after the argument at least they'd not fought.

It was a small positive note, but she thought on the
whole she ought to take it.

Across from her, Asa slumped against the squabs.
"Thank God that's over."

She frowned at him in disapproval. "It was very nice,
I thought."

He cocked an eyebrow. "Even the screaming babies?
Even the screaming *men*?" He reached up to knock on the
carriage roof to signal the driver that they were ready.

"It would've been better without the screaming men,"

she acknowledged, and hesitated a moment. The carriage lurched as it started forward. "They really didn't know about Harte's Folly?"

He shrugged, glancing out the window, though it was dark and she doubted he could see anything. "They didn't ask, I didn't volunteer the information. After Father..." He waved a hand, then dropped it into his lap, shaking his head.

"That..." She chose her words carefully. "It must've been hard when your father disowned you."

"Hard." He laughed, the sound sharp and pained. "He threw me out of the family. I was forbidden the house, couldn't come around when he was there." He shook his head, glancing out the window. "Father had long been friends with Sir Stanley—he was practically family. When I told Father that I wanted to work in the theater— Sir Stanley's theater—it never occurred to me that he would disapprove so severely. He said flatly that I could, but not as his son, and I, being young and hotheaded, took him up on his bloody offer. I was packed and out of the family home before sundown without a farthing to my name. Thank God Sir Stanley took me in, for I hadn't even thought of where I'd lay my head that night."

Her heart ached for him. To be so completely rejected by one's parent must be terrible. The old duke had never been a father to her, but she'd always known that Val, in his own mercurial way, would take care of her.

"I'm glad Sir Stanley was so kind," she said gently.

"He was. Kinder than my father, certainly." His upper lip curled.

There wasn't much she could say to that without condemning his father more, so Eve simply watched him.

Asa sat staring out the blackened window, his hand

fisted on one thigh. "I never spoke to my father again, did you know? For nine years I lived with Sir Stanley at Harte's Folly and never attempted to contact him, despite Sir Stanley's urging. Perhaps if I'd tried…" He shook his head and glanced at her. "Father's death was sudden. No illness, no warning. He just went to bed one night and never woke up the next morning—or so Con told me later. That was when I found out Father had cut me from his will as well. It was as if I'd never been born."

"I'm sorry," she whispered.

He thrust out his chin, his green eyes narrowed. "There's no need to pity me. I made damn sure that Harte's Folly was a brilliant success before—and I'll make damned sure that it's an even better success in the future. I'm not some feckless dilettante, no matter what my father thought or what Con thinks now. I don't need them, family or not."

Eve stirred uneasily, suddenly aware that Asa's drive to reopen the garden was about much more than money.

"I know you're not a dilettante," she said. "And that the garden is important to you, but you only have one family. Concord didn't seem to know *why* your father disinherited you—and I'm not at all sure he is as against the theater as your father was. After all this time, can't you talk to him?"

"Concord is as stubborn as our father ever was."

She smiled, tilting her head. "As stubborn as you?"

He half smiled. "Perhaps."

She folded her hands in her lap, smiling back. "Well, in any case I enjoyed meeting your family and seeing the babies today."

"You like babies, then?" His voice was a near-purr.

She looked down at her hands, as her mouth wobbled

just once. "Who doesn't like them? They're so soft and vulnerable and their fingers are so tiny."

She bit her lip, knowing she'd revealed too much.

He was silent, and finally she looked up to see that his green eyes had softened as he watched her.

She swallowed and pasted on a bright smile. "And there are so many babies in your family."

He snorted, spreading his legs wide. "We're obviously one of the most fertile families in London. Concord ought to be ashamed of himself."

"I thought he looked rather proud, actually," Eve murmured.

That got her a glare.

She smiled wistfully. "Perhaps you're jealous that you haven't started a family yet?"

"Oh, no." He shook his head emphatically. "I don't plan on any family."

"Whyever not?"

"Haven't you been paying attention?" He spread his hands, swaying easily with the movement of the carriage. "I have the garden to manage. Harte's Folly takes all of my time, and it comes first."

A trace of unease shivered through her, and Eve knit her brow. "Really? But there are many men who have businesses and yet are able to marry and beget children. Your brother runs a brewery, if I'm not mistaken, and yet we helped celebrate the birth of his sixth child tonight."

He shrugged. "That might work well enough for Concord—his neat little brewery and his batch of children—but I'm not in that sort of business. I work night and day on Harte's Folly. I haven't room in my life for anything else."

"Or any*one* else?" She tilted her head, studying him. "That sounds rather...lonely."

One corner of his mouth kicked up, his green eyes suddenly amused. "Not as lonely as all that, I assure you. I have needs like any other man and I make sure to fulfill them."

She pursed her lips to hide the fact that her heart had sped up at the thought of his *needs*. "I understand from Violetta that you are no longer...er...entertaining her."

"Ye-es," he drawled, his head laid back against the squabs. He was watching her from beneath lowered lids. The flickering lamplight reflected in his eyes. He'd sampled three or four pints of his brother's beer at the dinner, she'd noticed, and she wondered now if they were perhaps affecting him. "I suppose I'll have to find someone else to satisfy my desires."

She licked her lips nervously.

His gaze fixed on her mouth and his voice was deeper when he said, "Or I might have to satisfy myself."

His hand had drifted to his thigh and...was it her imagination or was there a bulge at his placket?

She swallowed. "What...what do you mean?"

He smirked at that, white teeth flashing, those wicked dimples appearing in his cheeks. "Oh, Eve, such an innocent." She should be insulted, she knew she should, but his gravelly purr promised information. "Didn't I tell you that a woman could be pleasured by a man's fingers or mouth without his ever entering her?"

"Y-yes."

"Well, a man might be pleasured in the same way," he rumbled, rubbing his thigh. "By a woman's hands...or mouth."

Her breath caught on the thought. Was he saying that a woman would put her hands—her *mouth*—there?

Her bodice felt suddenly too tight as her breaths became faster. She didn't know where to look: at those long fingers massaging his own leg or his glinting, knowing green eyes.

"And of course," he continued, "a woman can pleasure *herself*—with her hand—and a man..." His hand drifted up, straight to the top of his widely spread legs. He gripped himself frankly—lewdly—and looked at her.

She lost all sense of propriety. All sense of place and time and who he was and who *she* was.

She stared back into those sensuous green eyes and whispered, "Show me."

His eyes widened, whether in surprise or delight or something else entirely, she wasn't sure, and it didn't matter anyway because her own gaze was fixed on the juncture of his thighs. His hand flexed against *something* under the fabric and then his other hand joined the first.

Unhurriedly, deliberately, he flicked open the buttons to his placket.

Eve fisted her hands against the seat cushions on either side of her as the carriage rocked around a corner.

He spread apart the placket. "Ah, that's better."

Her eyes jumped to his face.

He was smiling, watching her. "Gets tight when I'm big."

She bit her lip, unable to keep her gaze from returning to his lap. His white undergarment showed there, a thick column outlined beneath.

"You want to see it, don't you," he murmured, squeezing himself. "Want to see *me*."

She licked her lips. *"Yes."*

"Then watch," he whispered, and pulled loose the string that kept his smallclothes closed. He braced his feet against the floor and lifted his hips a fraction, pulling down the front of his breeches and smallclothes.

It popped free, ruddy and thick, bigger than she'd imagined. He held it upright for her so that she could look her fill. It seemed to pulse against his fingers, the shaft wrapped with twining veins, the hood beginning to pull back from the swelling head. It looked wet there, as if he wept, and she swallowed heavily.

"Watch," he said again, tightening his fist, running it from the root to head, bunching the loose skin at the head when he reached the top.

Her chest felt constricted and her stomach in contrast was warm and somehow liquid. Something tingled between her thighs and she knew somewhere at the back of her mind that she should stop this. Make him put himself to rights. Close her eyes against this wanton, lewd display.

Oh, but she didn't want to.

She didn't want to.

Her eyes flicked to his face, reddened now, his eyes mere slits. He was watching her. As if her gaze was important to him as he worked himself.

As he touched his *cock*.

She inhaled on the thought of the word, looking back down. He'd pushed his shirt out of the way with his other hand and she could see the flat muscles of his belly flexing as he worked himself. A tangle of dark hair surrounded his navel, narrowing abruptly below to a thin line that disappeared into the thicket of curls around his cock. He sat, spread-legged, still dressed in white shirt and gold waistcoat, his scarlet coat spread wide around his thighs. His feet were braced against the floorboards and she could see his hips begin to move, thrusting up into the steady rhythm of his fist.

He looked like a debauched satyr, all sex and male desire, and she had a sudden wish that he'd taken *all* of his clothes off. She wanted to see his nipples and his buttocks, wanted to discover the broad sweep of his nude chest.

He'd laugh and let her, she knew. Somehow she knew. Asa Makepeace would do anything she asked. He had no shame.

No, more: he *reveled* in shamelessness.

And she was glad—so very glad—that he was such a man. At what other time would she ever have the chance to see this, a man lost to his own needs, gasping now, panting with his exertion? This would never happen again in her lifetime and she was suddenly fiercely happy that she'd had the courage to ask him to show her this.

Oh, but she couldn't think of that now. Now, at this moment, when this incredible thing was happening in front of her, she had to absorb it all. Had to commit the sights and sounds and, dear God, *smells*, to memory.

Her nostrils flared as she inhaled. There was a musky scent in the air, salty and animal, and it made her clench her legs together.

He grinned suddenly, his white teeth gritted together, as if he knew what he did to her. His fist was moving faster now, the deep red head of his cock appearing and disappearing between his fingers. It shone, fully revealed, and so big she bit her lip.

"Now," he grunted. "Now, Eve, watch me. Are you watching me?"

"Yes," she moaned.

The muscles stood out in his neck as a white liquid erupted from his cock, flowing and spurting, his legs shaking, his hand slowing.

And the entire time he watched her.

*   *   *

LETHARGY STOLE THROUGH Asa's limbs as he watched Eve through heavy-lidded eyes. Her face was flushed a soft pink; her bosom, veiled by a soft fichu, lifted and fell rapidly.

She was aroused.

He knew it even if she didn't, and *that*—more than his shockingly good orgasm—satisfied him.

Asa closed his eyes and hummed to himself, feeling the sway of the carriage as they traveled through darkened London. It was strange. He wasn't touching her—*couldn't* touch her—and yet he felt closer to her than he had to many women he'd fucked. Perhaps because the act he'd performed was an intimate one. Perhaps because she'd obviously never gone so far before.

Or perhaps it was simply because he'd done this for Eve. Just Eve.

"Is it…" Her soft voice roused him from drifting into sleep. "Is it always like that?"

He opened his eyes. She was still staring at his half-hard cock, lying naked and redolent on his thigh. He smiled. It was always nice to be admired by a woman. "Mostly. Sometimes better, more often not quite as good."

He sighed and sat up, then wiped his hands on a handkerchief before tucking his cock away and doing himself up.

"Thank you," she said.

He looked up. She was biting her lip, a small line between her eyes. Was she regretting what they'd done? Or worse—thinking that she'd done something wrong?

"You're welcome," he said gently. It was a pity that he couldn't show her more. He'd like to make her feel the wonder of an orgasm.

To go through life without ever experiencing that—

well, it was a tragedy, really. And that it was *Eve* who was so frozen…he frowned to himself. Something about its being *she* made it particularly wrong. Eve should be free to fall apart, to let herself go without hesitation or fear.

It was a fundamental wrong in the world that she could not.

The carriage jerked to a stop suddenly, nearly sending him flying into Eve's lap. At the same time a shot blasted the night and someone shouted, "Stand and deliver!"

What the hell? They were in the middle of London.

"Get down!" Asa hissed at Eve.

Only just in time, too. The door to the carriage was wrenched open. A masked man stood there, brandishing two pistols.

Behind him Eve whimpered in fear.

Rage, white-hot and purifying, burned through Asa's veins at the sound.

The masked man grinned.

"Fuck." Asa rose into the man's face. *"You."* He knocked one arm aside. *"Who."* The pistol shot blasted through the seat cushions as he grabbed the other arm. "The *fuck*." He wrenched the arm up toward the ceiling. "Do *you*." The second pistol shot through the roof. *"Think* you are." Asa took the pistol from the other man. "You *fucking*." He reversed it. *"Little."* And struck the man across the face with the embossed butt. *"Poxy."* Blood spurted from the highwayman's nose as he fell out of the carriage screaming. *"Prick?"*

Asa tossed aside the empty pistols and leaped after the man. Outside, a second masked man sat on a horse gaping at his partner, who was writhing on the ground.

"How *fucking* dare." Asa strode to the prone man and kicked him in the bollocks. "You *threaten*." The fallen man wheezed, his hands flying from his bloody face to between his legs. "*My* lady." Asa reached down, picked him up by the back of his coat, and shook him hard enough to make his head flop back and forth. "You sodding *fuck*?"

"Let him go." That was the second highwayman, his voice high and panicked.

"Gladly." Asa dropped the first highwayman, and prowled toward the mounted man, his hands lax by his side.

The second highwayman's eyes showed white behind his mask and the pistols he had trained on Asa trembled. "What . . . what are you doing?"

"I'm going to pull you from your *fucking* horse, take away your *bloody* pistols, shoot you in both *fucking* knees, and then I'm going to beat your *sodding* brains out against the cobblestones," Asa said.

One of the footmen squeaked.

The first highwayman made a sudden valiant move for freedom, scrambling onto the second highwayman's horse. The horse wheeled, and in seconds more the sound of its hoofbeats was receding into the distance.

Asa was actually rather disappointed.

He looked back at the driver and footmen. They appeared unhurt, although their eyes were unnaturally wide.

Asa remounted the carriage. "Get us out of here."

He ducked in and flung himself onto the seat just as the carriage rattled into motion.

Across from him Eve didn't seem to have moved since the attack had begun. She was still huddled in the corner, her face white, her eyes closed as if to block out the world.

His brows drew together in concern. "Eve?"

She shuddered and opened her eyes, looking at him dazedly.

Asa got up and moved to her side of the carriage, but when he reached for her she shrank back. "Don't touch me!"

He tightened his jaw, looking away from her. He was *not* hurt by her obvious fear of him. "So you hate me now?"

"No." She shook her head. "No, of course not."

"But you won't let me touch you."

She glanced away. "I don't let any man touch me."

"Am I any man, Eve?" he asked, hard and blunt. He shouldn't be pushing her now, not when she was in shock and still shaking, but he couldn't stop himself. He was tired of this.

He hated her fear of him.

"No...I..." She swallowed. "You were so violent."

"I was protecting you!" He winced at the loudness of his voice in the small confines of the carriage.

"You didn't need to—"

"Bullshit." He turned—not touching her, no, God, not *that*—but facing her on the seat. "I'll use any means necessary—any fucking violence I *want*—in order to keep you safe. Do you understand, Eve? This isn't bloody nego-tiable. I will fucking *kill* if it means it'll keep you safe."

Oddly, his harsh words seemed to steady her. "I under-stand," she said quietly. "I know intellectually that you needed to hurt that man." She twisted her hands together in her lap. "But emotionally...I just...I can't get over this fear."

She sounded angry at herself, and he wondered if she even knew how frustrated she was.

"Fine," he said. "Fine. You can pull away from me for now. You can keep your distance and shake. But Eve, I'll not let you do it forever."

She looked up at that, her blue eyes wide and startled. "What do you mean?"

"I mean," he said, a deep sense of rightness spreading through him even as he gathered the words, "that I won't let this stand. I *will* touch you. Sometime. Somewhere. I'm going to touch you all over, Eve, and what's more, you'll enjoy it."

His voice had deepened as he'd spoken until the last words left his mouth in a purring rumble. He could feel his cock stirring at just the thought of touching her.

Of her *permitting* his touch.

She watched him as if mesmerized, her pretty pink lips still trembling, and when she parted them to speak, he had to drag his gaze up to her blue eyes. "But... but you promised not to touch me without my invitation."

"And I won't," he vowed. "You'll be *asking* me to touch you, Eve Dinwoody, never fear that."

Her eyes widened as the carriage rocked to a halt, and he realized that they'd arrived at her house.

He stood, then opened the door and jumped down to set the step for her.

Asa turned back, automatically holding out his hand to help her down before remembering.

Fuck it.

He didn't withdraw his bare hand, but let it stay, an offering to her.

She was at the carriage door and he expected that she'd simply ignore his gesture. She clearly thought about it, contemplating his outstretched hand. But then she straightened a little as if bracing herself.

She met his eyes and placed her hand in his.

Bare skin met bare skin and he had to repress a shudder.

This was more intimate than a kiss.

He helped her down to the pavement.

"Thank you," she said huskily.

He bowed, clearing his throat. "It's I who should thank you for accompanying me to my family dinner."

"I enjoyed it," she said.

Her face glowed pale in the lamplight, and he wanted... he wanted more than she could give him right now.

He backed up a step, withdrawing his hand, as Jean-Marie opened the door to her town house, flooding the step with light. "I'd best be home."

She looked suddenly worried. "Take the carriage. I wouldn't want you to be attacked again this night."

He scoffed. "I was more than able to take care of those highwaymen, and I assure you that if another such a one wants to try for my life..." He stopped, realizing abruptly that this was the *second* time in less than a fortnight that his life had been imperiled. Those falling roof tiles had nearly brained him and Violetta.

First the roof tiles fell, then the stage collapsed, and now highwaymen had attacked them. The chain of events was suspicious.

"What is this you say about 'ighwaymen?" Jean-Marie had descended the front steps.

Eve turned to him. "We were stopped just outside St. Giles by two men on horses. Asa—Mr. Makepeace—fought them off."

"Mon Dieu!" Jean-Marie frowned ferociously. "Are you unhurt, *ma petite*?"

"I'm perfectly fine," Eve said, her cheeks pinkening as she glanced at Asa. "As I said, it was Mr. Makepeace who confronted them."

"Then I must thank you," Jean-Marie said solemnly, "for doing my job."

Asa nodded.

Jean-Marie shook his head. "So many things to have 'appened in only three days. The stage and now this . . ."

"Not to mention a load of shingles falling from the theater roof and nearly crushing Violetta and me the other day," Asa said drily.

Eve's eyes widened. "What?"

"You are under attack," Jean-Marie said simply.

Asa looked at the other man, meeting his serious gaze. "Yes, I think I am."

"What will you do?" Eve whispered. "You don't . . ." She bit her lip. "You don't still think it's Mr. Sherwood behind this, do you?"

"Maybe." She opened her mouth and he held up a hand, forestalling her no doubt impassioned defense of bloody fucking Sherwood. "I don't *know.* Murder seems a bit much for Sherwood."

Her shoulders sagged, seemingly in relief. "Then you'll not confront him."

"Oh, I didn't promise that, luv," Asa drawled, watching as her shoulders tensed again. "But I'll wait a bit until my man at the Royal has news."

Her mouth dropped open. "You planted a *spy* at Mr. Sherwood's theater?"

"Of course." He winked at her. "Over two years ago."

"Oh, my God."

He laughed at her outraged face. "I'm thinking it's time I took that carriage home. Good night."

He turned as her voice floated on the night air behind him. ". . . Night."

Asa climbed in, the vision of her face, shocked and indignant, firmly at the front of his mind. She was special to him, his little harpy. And he'd not lied when he'd told her earlier that he'd do anything to keep her safe—up to and including murder. If that part of him, that violence that simmered beneath his skin, ultimately drove her away, he wasn't sure what he'd do.

But he knew he wouldn't change. That part of him had saved Eve.

TWO ACTRESSES, AN opera singer, and three dancers crowded around Eve's desk at the theater the next morning, all of their attention on her. Behind her the dog was gently dozing, looking much better after several days' rest with proper food, and the dove in the cage on her desk was pecking at seeds.

Eve made a notation in her notebook and then straightened. "Now let me see if I have this correct. Daisy, Theresa, and Mary will share the little dressing room on the east side on most days, but when Daisy brings in her son, Bernard, she'll dress with Polly and Charlotte, who also have small children. Martha will dress most of the time with Margaret, except when Margaret is practicing her singing, when Martha will then move to the east side dressing room with Daisy, Theresa, and Mary."

She studied the chart she'd drawn and then glanced up at the women. "Won't that make the east dressing room very crowded, though, on the days Margaret practices?"

Martha, a willowy redhead, shrugged. "It's not so bad, and a body can't even think when there's that shrieking going on."

Margaret, who was compact and rather sturdy, narrowed her eyes. "I don't shriek."

"Would anyone like some tea?" Eve hastily asked, just as the door to the office opened.

Asa took one step in, his shoulders filling the doorway, and stopped dead. "What," he asked softly, "is going on?"

Eve felt a shock shiver through her at the sight of him. It was the first time she'd seen him since last night.

Since that carriage ride.

She'd thought about him last night as she'd lain in bed alone. Remembered how his voice had deepened as he told her to watch him, and as she did so, she'd tentatively slid her fingers into the curls at the junction of her thighs.

She felt heat creep up her face and wondered rather wildly if there was any way he could tell what she'd done all alone in her bed last night just by looking at her.

Asa shot her a searing glance that made her press her legs together. Oh, dear. Perhaps he could read her thoughts.

The corner of his mouth curled as if he could and then he turned to the theater ladies.

Unfortunately, they'd all tried to answer him at once, resulting in a cacophony of sound without any meaning.

Asa raised his hands and the room fell silent. He pivoted and pointed at Theresa. "Explain, luv."

Theresa was one of the actresses who specialized in matronly roles. She folded her arms over her bosom and said, "Miss Dinwoody's been seeing to the dressing rooms."

Asa blinked slowly. "What?"

"Well, some were not respecting others' space, Mr. Harte," Polly said, shooting a look at Mary before fluttering her eyelashes at Asa. "And now that we've been allowed to bring our wee ones..."

"What?" Asa turned to Eve.

She couldn't help the spread of warmth through her middle at his gaze. Just last night he'd stared at her with those same dark-green eyes as he'd—

She cleared her throat and stood. "Several of the ladies have found that they have no one to take care of their children.

Naturally they cannot practice in such a situation, so today I hired quite a nice woman to come and watch the children."

Asa's brows drew together. "Why wasn't I consulted on the matter?"

"Well, you are quite busy, as you keep telling me," Eve pointed out.

"And Miss Dinwoody's ever so easy to talk to," Polly said.

"Oh." Eve felt a shy smile spread across her face. "That's a lovely thing to say."

"It's true," Mary said, which was quite remarkable, because as far as Eve could see Mary and Polly rarely agreed on anything.

"And *you* aren't," Theresa said bluntly to Asa. "Easy to talk to, that is."

Polly shrugged apologetically. "Sorry, Mr. Harte, but it's true."

Asa frowned, opened his mouth, shut it, and then said, "I see. Sounds like I should've brought in Miss Dinwoody much earlier."

And he gave her a warm look.

Eve could feel herself blushing as she met his gaze, for Asa's warm look was very close to the look that had been in his eyes last night in the carriage—*before* they'd been attacked by highwaymen.

One of the women cleared her throat and then there was a general exodus as they all decided they had things they must do.

When Eve tore her gaze from Asa and glanced over, they were all gone. She frowned for a moment, puzzled, before turning back to Asa. "I do hope you don't mind that I settled their arguments?"

"No, not at all." He thrust his fingers through his hair.

"Fact is, arguments between the actors and dancers and singers are the bane of my life."

"Then I'm glad to help," she said softly.

"Eve," he began, but at that moment a very large man appeared at the office doorway. "Asa, I thought we were to discuss the gardens today—oh, I beg your pardon." The man's voice was slightly off—strained and raspy. His eyebrows had shot up at the sight of her.

Asa straightened. "'Pollo, this is Miss Eve Dinwoody, the Duke of Montgomery's sister and his man of affairs in regard to his investment in Harte's Folly. Miss Dinwoody, Apollo Greaves, Lord Kilbourne, the designer of the gardens."

"A pleasure to meet you, Miss Dinwoody," Lord Kilbourne said, bowing. He wasn't a handsome man—in fact, rather the opposite—but he had a gentle manner.

Eve curtsied. "If I'm not mistaken, my lord, you're also husband to the former Robin Goodfellow?"

A smile lit the big man's face at the mention of his wife. "Indeed."

"I've always admired her work upon the stage." Eve smiled in return. "I fear you've stolen a great talent from London theater."

"And yet I'll not give her up," Lord Kilbourne replied good-naturedly. "Though she does still pen plays. I'm afraid London theater will have to be satisfied with her writing instead."

"Oh, we will, I feel," Eve said. "I truly look forward to her next play."

Asa cleared his throat rather obnoxiously.

They both looked at him.

He jerked his head in the direction of the door. "The garden?"

Lord Kilbourne looked amused. He bowed to Eve again, gesturing toward the door. "After you, Miss Dinwoody."

"Thank you, my lord," she said, pointedly ignoring Asa.

She swept from the room and nearly ran into Jean-Marie, holding a dish of water for the dog in his hands. Her footman lifted an eyebrow.

"I'll be touring the gardens, Jean-Marie," she said. "Can you see to the dog?"

He eyed both Asa and Lord Kilbourne and then nodded. "Of course. I'll see if 'e can go out to do 'is business."

"Thank you," she said gratefully.

She turned to find Asa holding out his arm pointedly. "Shall we?"

She swallowed and nodded, laying her hand gingerly on his sleeve. She almost expected an electric shock. This wasn't the same as their touch last night—there was no skin-to-skin contact—but even so she was very aware of the human warmth of his arm through the fabric.

She turned to Lord Kilbourne. "Mr. Makepeace told me that you were able to successfully transplant several mature trees into the garden."

"Yes, indeed," the garden designer replied, and Eve was treated to a fascinating dissertation on how he'd managed to do just that. This took them into the garden, where Lord Kilbourne pointed out the maze, which was apparently what he'd wanted to discuss with Asa.

"The evergreen hedges will take years to grow," Lord Kilbourne explained, gesturing to the new plantings. "So I thought in the meantime to construct a sort of faux wall. It'll be out of wood, but I have a man who can paint it to look like marble. It's not permanent, of course, but your guests will be able to enjoy the maze until the hedges grow tall enough to disassemble the wooden wall."

"But won't the elements destroy the paint on the wall?" Eve asked.

Lord Kilbourne shrugged. "Yes, after several years, but as I say, by then the planted hedge should be big enough to use."

Asa nodded beside Eve. "I like the idea." He glanced at her pointedly. "And a wooden wall should be fairly cheap as well. I'm sure you'll like that, Miss Dinwoody."

"A monetary savings is always welcome," she said primly.

Asa laughed, and the sound made her feel warm, as if they shared a secret joke between the two of them.

They began to stroll, Lord Kilbourne pointing out other planned projects. They'd almost made it back to the theater when they were met by a gentleman walking toward them. He was of middle age, with a sloping belly and arms so long they didn't seem to quite fit the rest of his body. His face was reddened and dominated by a great lumpy nose. At the sight of him, Eve began to slow, feeling strange.

"Mr. Harte," the gentleman called. "Just the man I wanted to see."

Eve stopped dead. That *voice*.

She'd heard that voice before.

He extended his hand to Asa. The gesture caused his coat sleeve to pull back. On the inside of his wrist was a strange little design—a *tattoo*—of a dolphin.

Horror coursed through her.

She looked up to see that he was watching her. A genial smile broadened his lips. "Why, if it isn't little Eve!"

And Eve remembered where she'd heard the voice before:

In nightmares.

Chapter Eleven

When Dove opened her eyes again, it was daylight and
a man was glaring down at her. His hair was tawny, his
shoulders broad, and his eyes as green as the forest leaves
that surrounded them.
"You should not be here," the man growled, looking quite
put out. "Who are you?"
"My name is Dove. Who are you?"
"I am Eric." With that he stalked away.
Which would've been the end of the matter—and my tale—
had not Dove jumped up and followed Eric....
—From *The Lion and the Dove*

Asa felt Eve's fingers dig into his arm. He glanced at her
sharply before looking back at the gentleman who stood
before them. The man's smile was friendly, his dress not
of the first style, but certainly expensively made, and yet
Asa found him just the smallest bit...oily.

He pasted on his business smile. "You have me at a
disadvantage, sir."

The other man bowed—very briefly—still smiling.
"I am George Hampston, Viscount Hampston, and I'm
interested in investing in your gardens."

Asa straightened. An investor was never to be disregarded, oily or not. A pleasure garden could always use

more money. Still, Eve's fingers were, if anything, clutching his arm even tighter, so he proceeded with caution. "And how do you know Miss Dinwoody?"

"Oh, Eve and I have been acquaintances for a very long time." Lord Hampston smiled fondly at her. "I was friends with His Grace, the late Duke of Montgomery, her father. Why, I've known Eve since she was but knee-high."

"But..." Eve's word was croaked and she stopped to clear her voice. "But I don't have recollection of you, my lord."

"Don't you?" He inclined his head, looking at her intently from under rather bushy gray eyebrows. Asa fought down an unaccountable urge to growl. The man put his back up, though he couldn't put his finger on why. "You were but a young thing and it was years ago, of course."

"And yet you recognized Miss Dinwoody." Apollo spoke up from behind Asa.

Lord Hampston looked at him. "And you are, sir?"

"Forgive my lack of manners," Asa said. "Lord Hampston, Apollo Greaves, Viscount Kilbourne."

"Ah, of course," Lord Hampston exclaimed. "You're designing the gardens, if I'm not mistaken. A pleasure to meet you indeed, my lord."

Apollo nodded as he shook the other man's hand, but his expression was wary. "Sir."

Beside Asa, Eve shuddered.

He laid his palm over the hand on his sleeve without looking away from Hampston. Her fingers were slim beneath his, small and delicate, and as cold as ice. He ought to discuss business at once with Lord Hampston, strike while the iron was hot—or the investor eager, in this instance. But Eve was afraid.

Something primal and protective made him say, "I'd

be most pleased to discuss my gardens with you at a later date. I fear that I have several appointments today."

"Of course, of course," Hampston replied. He inhaled, looking around the garden—they were nearly back at the musicians' gallery. "You've done an excellent job rebuilding. I remember when Sir Stanley Gilpin first bought the place, nothing but a few buildings and a bit of marshland." He grinned at Asa, revealing overlarge square incisors. "Tomorrow, then, shall we say, in the afternoon?"

"I look forward to it."

Hampston nodded and strode away.

Asa immediately turned to Eve and lowered his voice. "Are you all right, luv?"

Her cheeks, which had gone pale, flushed a little at his words. "Yes, yes, of course. I don't know what came over me. It's so strange. His voice..."

She knit her brows as her words died away.

Asa watched her. He wanted to comfort her and at the same time he wanted to run after Hampston and confront him over... what, exactly?

"Perhaps some tea might help," Apollo said.

Asa shot him a grateful look. "I've got a kettle in my office."

"Thank you," Eve murmured. "I'd like a cup very much."

Apollo bowed. "Let me say again what a pleasure it was to meet you, Miss Dinwoody." He sent Asa an amused glance. "I'm not used to Makepeace keeping such reputable company."

"Oi!" Asa shot back good-naturedly.

Apollo turned to go with a last bow and Asa drew Eve toward the theater. He could feel tremors still racking her body every now and again, and he made a grim mental note:

Find out who bloody George Hampston was.

Fortunately, the corridors were mainly empty as he led Eve toward their office. The sounds of the orchestra drifted from the theater, while feminine voices murmured behind the doors of several dressing rooms. The corner of his mouth curled up as he recalled how he'd found Eve earlier, surrounded by the women of the theater. He'd been reluctantly impressed with her skill at solving the squabbling over dressing rooms. It was the sort of petty bickering that he found particularly maddening to deal with. In the past, more often than not, he'd been reduced to flinging up his arms and stomping away when one of the actors or musicians or singers complained to him about another performer.

He glanced at her as he opened the door to his office. Odd to think that he might miss her presence here when it was time for her to leave.

Odd to think that he'd once discounted her as stiff and prim.

He felt now as if an invisible wire linked his body to hers, making him aware of her at all times.

"Come sit down and I can make you some tea," he began, and realized that she'd stopped just inside the door.

He half turned back. "What—?"

"Oh," she sobbed, covering her mouth with her hand. "Oh, the dove."

He looked at her desk. The cage was where it had been this morning, but the door was now ajar.

And a single feather lay on the desk.

Damn.

The dog had its bed directly behind her desk, and it had been half starved.

"Don't look," he said, spreading his arms to try to keep

her away from the desk and whatever lay behind it. "Eve, please..."

But she was swift, ducking under his arms. "I have to see. Oh, Asa, I have to see."

She halted.

He turned, placing his hands on her upper arms in case she collapsed. "The dog was very hungry, luv. I know it's hard to understand now, but I don't think we can hold him responsible for what he's done. I'll take him out and—"

But his comforting words were interrupted.

By a giggle.

He stared at her, concerned. Had the death of her pet turned her mind?

But her blue, blue eyes glanced up at him now, sparkling through the tears that still lingered. "Oh, Asa, *look*."

He turned and peered behind the desk.

The mastiff lay on his side on the pile of discarded costumes, apparently asleep. On his back the dove was strutting confidently, apparently without a care in the world. As Asa watched, the dog opened his eye, glanced at the humans, closed his eye again, and sighed gustily.

The dove just cooed.

EVE HAD NOT had the nightmare for years, but despite the time between, she recognized it immediately.

It was the baying of the dogs that gave it away.

They panted behind her, their breath stinking of raw meat and hunger, and she ran blindly. Wildly.

Desperately.

Up an endless flight of stairs that suddenly turned back down again. Through doorways that grew progressively smaller. And now she could hear *them* as well. The men.

They were laughing and they were masked, the dolphin tattoo swimming over their skins.

Something nipped at her heels and she knew with instinctive dread what would happen next. *Let me die*, she thought desperately. *Let me pass beyond this life before I feel the pain.*

She was always a coward in the dream.

But it happened anyway, despite her pleas, her attempt at bargaining with an uncaring fate. She crawled around a corner and met a wall.

A dead end.

They were on her immediately. Men or dogs, she couldn't tell, and perhaps it didn't matter anyway. They were both ravenous.

And then came the wash of blood.

Eve started awake, her eyes staring in the darkness of her own bedroom. Her muscles were locked tight and she lay unmoving, as if by her very stillness she could remain unseen.

Hidden safe.

But eventually her breath evened, her muscles unlocked, and she realized rather prosaically that her bladder was full. Slowly, painfully, she rolled to the edge of her bed and got up. There was a little moonlight coming from the window and she used its guidance to find the necessary and relieve herself.

After that she should've returned to bed, but really it was no use.

So Eve donned a robe and made her way in the darkness to her sitting room.

There she knelt by the fireplace and stirred the banked coals. In another couple of hours Ruth would rise to do the job, but it seemed a shame to wake the girl now.

Let her sleep and dream of things other than blood.

Eve sighed and placed coals on the embers, using the tongs so she wouldn't dirty her hands. It was rather soothing, doing such a mundane task. She watched as the coals took, as tiny orange flames licked along their sides.

When the fire was well established she rose, lit a candle, and went to her desk. Dove was in her cage, her head tucked beneath a downy wing. Eve smiled slightly at the sight. She'd been so horror-struck when she'd seen the empty cage yesterday afternoon, so sure that the worst had happened.

And yet it hadn't.

The dog she'd been so afraid of had proven as gentle as a lamb, letting Dove explore his back all afternoon. He hadn't seemed to mind even when Dove had taken it into her head to clean the dog by pecking for bits of crumbs in his fur.

Eve had spent a good fifteen minutes watching the two friends, enchanted by the unlikeliness of it all.

Such simple happiness shouldn't have been followed by the nightmare she'd had tonight.

And yet it had.

Eve sighed and turned to her work. She'd been painting a cupid, based on Rebecca Makepeace's fat little cheeks. The second youngest of Concord and Rose's children had seemed the perfect model for what was essentially a fat toddler. She sat and peered through the magnifying glass. The cupid's curls were only half painted in.

Uncovering her watercolors, she wet a brush and carefully dabbed it in an ocher-brown.

And then she set to work.

The light was beginning to show through the curtains when Eve next looked up. She blinked, noticing that Dove was pecking at a few seeds at the bottom of her cage, and then she turned and saw Jean-Marie at the door.

Her bodyguard's face was watchful and solemn. "Are you all right, *ma petite*?"

"Yes, of course." She dipped her paintbrush in a lovely sky blue, but then saw that her hand trembled. She wiped the brush carefully on a cloth.

"Eve," Jean-Marie murmured, and it had been a very long time since she'd last heard him so sad.

"I . . . I dreamed last night," she said, still not looking at him.

She heard him walk farther into the sitting room. "Is it the pleasure garden manager? 'As 'e done something 'e shouldn't'?"

"No." She looked up in surprise. "Asa Makepeace has been perfectly gentlemanly." Well, not exactly *gentlemanly*, but he'd certainly done nothing to hurt her, and that was what Jean-Marie meant.

"Then what is it, cherie?" he asked. "You 'ave not dreamt for three years at least."

Her eyes widened. "You've been keeping track of my nightmares?"

"It is my job, *ma petite*."

A sudden thought struck. She glanced down at the opal ring on her finger. "Have you told Val? About my nightmares?"

He shrugged, but his eyes were hard. "That, too, is my job."

She looked away, feeling a bit bitter. "To let him know that his sister is insane."

"To let the duke know when she feels unwell or unsafe." Jean-Marie sighed. "'E shows it very oddly, but make no mistake: the duke cares for you very much. 'E wants you to be 'appy."

Happy. Was that even possible?

Eve closed her eyes. She was so very, very tired of being afraid.

With sudden energy she stood from her worktable. "Come, let's go to Harte's Folly. I've still not finished those books and Violetta said she would be practicing today. An aria from La Veneziana is really not to be missed."

A slow smile spread across Jean-Marie's face. "Me, I would not miss it for the world."

Eve grinned. "I'd best get myself bathed and dressed, then."

Which was how Eve and Jean-Marie arrived at the theater nearly before anyone else. They met a guard at the back entrance and two more at the doors to the theater—both new since the stage collapse. Once inside, Eve was startled to see Mr. Vogel in a whispered conference with Mr. MacLeish, both men looking serious.

They broke apart as she neared, and Mr. MacLeish smiled a cheery "Good morning," while Mr. Vogel merely nodded curtly.

A few minutes later Eve found to her disapproval that Asa didn't keep his office locked. "Why," she muttered to herself, glancing at the shiny new lock, installed the day before, "go to the trouble of putting a lock on the door if he's not going to use it?"

Behind her, Jean-Marie snorted and put Dove's cage on her table.

"Shall I fetch water for tea?" he asked.

"Oh, please," Eve said, sitting behind her desk. She remembered the new guards. "And can you find out if Alf is about? I'd like to hear if he has anything to report."

She heard the door close as she examined the dog.

"You're looking much better," she told the animal. "Good enough that Jean-Marie might be able to take you outside to wash you. Oh, don't get up."

This last was said nervously as the dog climbed laboriously to his feet.

"You really shouldn't."

Eve watched wide-eyed as the animal staggered toward her.

"Sit back down, *please*," she said, arms raised, but the animal either didn't know what an order was or ignored hers. He walked unsteadily right to her as Eve glanced wildly toward the closed door, hoping that Jean-Marie would make a sudden, early reappearance.

And then the animal laid his big head on her knees.

"Oh," she said, for she had no idea what else to do. The dog was *looking* at her with huge brown eyes, his forehead wrinkled up as though he was worried. His enormous drooping jowls were spread like a messy black skirt upon her lap, and the animal's triangular ears were back.

Actually it was rather adorable.

Hesitantly Eve laid her palm very gently on the beast's head.

Slowly the dog's tail swayed back and forth, and he gave a great sigh.

WHEN ASA WALKED into his office that morning he nearly did a double take.

Eve Dinwoody sat behind her desk, the mastiff's huge head on her knees, and she was *stroking* him with slim fingers as she whispered to him.

The dog was looking up at her as if she were his personal goddess, which, Asa supposed, she was.

Dear God, he hoped he didn't have the same expression on his own face.

Jean-Marie entered behind him, holding a kettle.

Asa tilted his head toward the other man. "What happened?"

The footman said slowly, "What do you mean?"

Asa looked at him askance and then gestured a little wildly to the scene in front of them. "What do I mean? I leave last night with Miss Dinwoody still absolutely terrified by dogs—she refused to touch the animal even when the *dove* showed herself unafraid of it—and arrive this morning with her *petting* that beast. *Something* must have happened in the interval."

"Henry walked over and put his head in my lap," Eve said softly. "Isn't he clever?"

For a moment Asa merely boggled. "Henry?"

"I've always liked the name Henry," Eve said thoughtfully. "It seems a very kind name, don't you think?"

"Ah...," Asa began, because the only Henry he'd known in his life had been a small boy who'd enjoyed throwing stones at sparrows and picking his nose, but then Jean-Marie elbowed him rather hard in the side. "Oof."

"Oui, ma petite," Jean-Marie said loudly. "'Enry is a most lovely name."

"It's a nice name, I suppose," Asa muttered, rubbing his bruised ribs.

She looked up then, a smile spreading across her face, and Asa stilled, his blood heating, and he realized something. Eve Dinwoody would never be called pretty, but there was something alluring about her nonetheless. She had the sort of plainness that surpassed mere symmetry of feature, transcended simple beauty, and became quietly compelling.

And when she smiled at him like that? With joy and happiness and a sort of peace?

She was radiant.

Asa coughed, turning away, because the thought had shaken him somehow. How could he have been so completely wrong about something? About some*one*?

A knock came on the door and Alf, the strange urchin boy, popped his head in. "Yer wanted to see me, miss?"

Eve looked up. "Oh, yes, but do you have anything to report?"

Asa's head jerked up. "What's this?"

Eve shrugged. "I set Alf to looking into the stage collapse to see if he could discover if anyone was behind it."

Asa's eyebrows rose and he made a mental note to never underestimate Eve's intelligence. "That was smart—the more eyes looking the better."

Eve cleared her throat, a blush rising up her throat becomingly. "Yes, well, Alf?"

"I 'as a bit o' news, ma'am, but it ain't much," the boy said. "Word is one o' the gardeners—man by th' name o' Ives—never came back to work th' day after th' stage fell. I asked about and found that no one knew 'im well—or at least none wanted to tell me so."

Eve looked skeptical. "That doesn't sound terribly damning."

Alf grinned slyly. "Aye, it don't—until I 'eard tell that one of the dancers caught this same Ives fellow in th' theater last week. Ives said as 'ow 'e just liked to listen to the music. Seemed innocent enough—save for th' fact that th' musicians weren't playing at th' time."

"Why didn't the dancer report the matter?" Asa growled.

Alf shrugged, looking wary. "'Tisn't too uncommon

for people to wander in and out of th' theater, as I understands it. Don't think the dancer thought the matter that important."

"And you haven't wanted to tell people that the stage was sabotaged," Eve reminded him. "There would've been no reason to report the gardener to you."

"Blast," Asa muttered. "You're right. I'll send one of my men to see if he can find anything on this Ives."

Eve nodded. "Thank you, Alf. I'd like you to continue watching for me and Mr. Harte, please."

"Yes, miss." And the boy disappeared into the corridor.

"Damnation!" Asa slammed his hand down on his table, making Eve jump and the dog lay back its ears. "We're so close to opening the garden again and now this—gardeners sneaking about the place sabotaging the theater, and attacks on you and me."

"Have you no news from your spy at Mr. Sherwood's theater?"

"No." Asa shook his head, frustrated. "Sherwood has apparently fallen in love with one of his singers and has been mooning about the woman. Other than that, my man has nothing to report."

Eve gently pushed Henry's head off her lap and rose, coming closer to him. "But we know now to be alert and we have people watching." Hesitantly she laid her hand on his, warm and so light, like a butterfly alighting. He didn't dare move lest he frighten her away. She looked at him, her sky-blue eyes earnest. "Harte's Folly will open again, I promise."

He stared at her and felt his chest warm as her fingers fluttered uncertainly on his hand. There was a connection between them, a sort of rapport that he'd never had before with any other woman.

From outside the room came the sound of the orchestra tuning up.

"Oh, are they readying for La Veneziana?" Eve's eyes lit. "I've so been looking forward to hearing her sing again."

Asa raised his eyebrows. "Again? You've heard her before?"

"Hasn't everyone?" Eve answered absently, withdrawing her hand and brushing at her skirts. "I mean everyone who likes opera, of course."

"Of course," Asa parroted, faintly. *So very wrong . . .*

"Come, Henry," Eve said to the dog, and set out as if she fully expected the mongrel to understand and follow.

And the odd thing was that he did.

Though as they passed close to him, Jean-Marie stiffened.

"Perhaps," he said carefully, "I will take 'Enry to bathe 'im, for 'e stinks most dreadfully."

Eve's brows drew together anxiously. "Do you think he's well enough to bathe?"

"I think so," Asa said. He had a bit of a vested interest in the matter, since his office had smelled ever so slightly of shit for the last few days.

"Well, if you consider him well enough," Eve said. "Oh, but you wanted to hear La Veneziana, Jean-Marie."

"I shall hear 'er from the gardens, for she 'as a legendary voice. Come, 'Enry," the footman said, bending to scoop the dog into his arms. He staggered a bit as he straightened. Henry wasn't a small dog by anyone's standards, even half starved. "We will see about 'eating some water for you. You shall 'ave a bath fit for a king."

The footman strode out and Asa turned to Eve. "Shall we?"

She smiled at him, taking his arm without hesitation, and Asa couldn't help a small swell of pride.

This woman had come to trust him, and that was no small thing.

Asa led Eve outside to the musicians' gallery. The stage was still in the process of being rebuilt, so chairs had been set out here for both musicians and the few people in the audience—Asa, Eve, and some of the dancers and other opera singers. Eve smiled at Polly and nodded to MacLeish, who was lounging on the sidelines.

Asa found two chairs side by side and seated her. He didn't look at her as he sat beside her, but this close he could smell that flowery scent she wore.

The same one she'd worn two nights before in the carriage when he'd taken out his cock and—

Violetta came out in costume. She wore a bright-red dress with gold spangles sewn on the underskirt and bodice. Gold lace framed the deep neckline and cascaded from the sleeves.

She stood in the center of the round courtyard, as composed as any queen, and like a queen she nodded to Vogel to signal she was ready.

Vogel stared sternly at his musicians and raised his arms.

And then the music began, beguiling and beautiful.

Asa caught his breath. Years now he'd owned Harte's Folly. He had sat through innumerable performances and rehearsals, and still he felt a thrill each and every time.

God, he *loved* the theater.

The music, so grand, so bold. The costumes, gaudy in the light of day, but somehow sublime under the candlelight in the theater. And the people—the actors and singers and dancers. Individually they rarely looked extraordinary during the day. One saw the spots, the too-small eyes, the nasty personality. But under the lights, with the music and the costumes, they were deified. Gods and goddesses, more graceful, more quick, more beautiful than any mere mortal. And when one sat in the theater, saw the play, listened to the music, experienced the wonder, why then one felt for a time close to Olympus. To the kingdom of the gods and goddesses themselves.

He'd given up his name and his family for this. Had turned his back on his father's wrath and Con's continual disappointment, and in this moment, here, surrounded by his people in his garden, he didn't regret a damn thing.

La Veneziana—for here she was no longer merely Violetta—parted her mouth, and sweet ambrosia fell from her lips.

Asa felt the clutch of Eve's fingers and he turned. He saw at once that her reason for gripping his arm was very different than it had been yesterday.

"She's beautiful, isn't she?" Eve whispered, never taking her eyes from the singer.

A corner of his mouth cocked up to see in her blue eyes the same enthusiasm that he felt. "Yes," Asa murmured in her ear. "Yes, she is."

This was his world. His family. He'd created it with his own blood and sweat.

And by God, he'd protect it with his blood and sweat, too.

Chapter Twelve

Eric frowned. "You must not follow me."
"Why not?" asked Dove. "I haven't anywhere else to go."
"Because I am busy," Eric said, "I am in thrall to a
powerful sorceress and she has set me a task to do."
"Well, perhaps I can help you," Dove replied hopefully.
At that Eric snorted, but he didn't chase Dove away,
so she was content....
—From *The Lion and the Dove*

Eve hummed as Asa escorted her back to the office, her senses still alight from La Veneziana's magnificent performance. If they could rebuild the stage in time, finish the theater roof, complete the garden plantings—oh, and all the *other* myriad things that needed to be done before they opened... *if* they could do all that, then Harte's Folly would be a guaranteed success, she *knew* it, for she'd never heard such wonderful music, such sublime singing, in all her life.

All they had to do was get people in to *hear* it.

They were almost at the office door when Eve saw Jean-Marie. He was standing, holding a very sad Henry and dripping from head to toe.

Eve's eyes widened. "What—?"

"'Enry, 'e does not like to be clean," Jean-Marie said

with great dignity. "If you do not mind, I shall return 'ome so that I may obtain dry clothing."

"I'm so sorry, Jean-Marie," Eve said, feeling rather guilty, especially when Henry took the opportunity to sidle away from the footman and over to her side. Apparently the dog felt she was above sneak baths. "Of course you may return home and change your clothes."

"You will feel secure?" Jean-Marie asked very seriously.

"Yes," she said stoutly.

She might've started the day with nightmares, but now it was broad daylight—and she was in the company of Asa. She glanced at him. He was right: he was no longer "any other man."

She looked back at Jean-Marie. "I'll stay here in the office with Mr. Makepeace. I'll be just fine."

Jean-Marie exchanged a glance with Asa that seemed to impart some male information, and then he nodded. "*Bien.* I shall return as swiftly as I can."

He shivered and walked away.

Asa turned to the office and held open the door for her and Henry. The dog made a beeline for his colorful bed, turned completely around, and collapsed into it with a long-suffering sigh.

"It couldn't have been as bad as all that," Eve chided, touching one ear gently. "You needn't have drenched Jean-Marie."

The dog merely thumped his tail against the floor once and closed his eyes.

Eve glanced up to see Asa watching her intently, and she suddenly realized that this was the first time they'd been alone since the carriage ride when he'd . . .

She couldn't help it. He was leaning against his table

in his usual wide-legged stance, and her eyes went to the juncture of his thighs.

Oh, what she'd give for just one more look!

She hastily averted her eyes, but it was too late. She saw him watching her and knew he'd caught her.

Eve felt her cheeks heat. "It was very good. The music, I mean."

"Yes," he said absently. He straightened, his hips thrusting away from the table.

A small movement, but very evocative.

"I think..." Her voice emerged a croak and Eve was forced to stop and swallow. "I think that La Veneziana's voice has improved since last I heard her sing."

"Do you?" He came around the table, slowly stalking to her side of her desk.

Eve backed a step and sat abruptly in her chair.

He stopped and propped himself against the corner of her desk, facing her. It was a very cramped space and her knees nearly touched his.

Nearly. Not quite.

Her eyes dropped, because really, his hips were *right* at eye level, and she thought the bulge beneath his breeches had grown.

Slowly she raised her gaze to meet his eyes. She hadn't even pretended this time that she hadn't looked.

He knew.

He knew.

His hands dropped to frame the placket of his breeches. "I can't stop thinking about it," he said, his voice low and intense. "The way you looked at me. The desire in your eyes." He inhaled. "The scent in the carriage that night. I think about it and I grow hard."

She stared at him, entirely unable to look away. Her heart beating fast.

"I think about it," he said again, his voice deeper now. "And I wish I could've seen you."

"Seen me," she said, very precisely. Very cautiously. And yet with an edge of excitement.

There was no use denying it to herself.

"Seen you." He was watching her carefully. "Seen your legs, your thighs, your cunt."

She inhaled at the word. So plain. So crude. There was no doubting it, and even she knew what he meant.

She wasn't such a fearless woman.

Was she?

"Can I?" he whispered. "Can I see you?"

Her lips parted, but no sound came.

"I'll not touch," he said, a male siren. "I'll stay right here and keep my hands to myself. I just want to see you. Please, Eve. Show me your cunny."

She couldn't. It was wrong, surely? Except she couldn't think why, and at that moment she wanted to give this to him.

Wanted to give it to herself after years of living in the dark.

Of living in fear.

She didn't want to live in fear anymore.

Her hands were moving before she'd made a conscious decision, inching toward her skirts. Inching toward her hem.

His gaze was fixed on her fingers, as if she were going to show him the wonders of the world.

Maybe she was.

Slowly she bent and grasped the hem of her skirts, then drew them upward. She didn't look down—*she* was more interested in his face—but she felt the cool air through her stockings. First at her ankles and then at her calves.

"More," he whispered, and she saw him begin to unbutton his falls.

She felt a warmth between her legs at the thought that this was arousing him—*she* was arousing him—and she pulled her skirts higher. She felt the air on her knees and then her thighs, naked above her garters.

He groaned, flipping open the remainder of his breeches buttons. "Eve, darling, I'd give my right hand for another couple of inches."

"You don't have to," she whispered, pulling her skirts above her hips. She closed her eyes then, too shy to see him look, but the silence was too much for her.

She opened her eyes and saw that he'd unfastened his smallclothes and had taken out his cock. He was stroking himself, his eyes fixed on the juncture of her thighs.

"Will you spread your legs for me?"

She caught her breath.

Slowly she spread her knees, feeling cool air on that most intimate part of her.

He groaned, fisting himself faster. He was thick and standing tall and something within Eve whispered it was because of her.

"Can you feel it?" he asked, his voice a rumbling purr. "Have you touched yourself there before, Eve?"

"I…" She couldn't say it, she couldn't. "Only the night before last. After the carriage. Just a little."

"Good girl." He chuckled, low and dark. "Did you think of me?"

Oh. She closed her eyes, for she couldn't look at him and tell him. *"Yes."*

"Did you make yourself come, thinking of me, fingering your pretty pussy, darling Eve? Tell me."

"I..." She opened her eyes again, looking into his knowing gaze. He was so carnal, so completely the master of this moment, as if he lived to tell her about her deepest, darkest desires. She wanted to meet that command, to somehow become his equal in this. She licked her lips, holding his green eyes. "I don't know what you mean?"

"Then you didn't," he said decisively, pausing in his stroking to squeeze himself. His voice had roughened, and for a moment he closed his eyes, not moving at all, almost as if he were trying to control himself. "*God.* You'd know if you had."

She panted, watching him helplessly as he stared at her flesh. Waiting...*wanting* for him to show her what came next.

"Can you feel that part of yourself, Eve?" His hand was moving again—slower now, as if he wanted to draw this out—and his eyes flicked suddenly up. They were green like emeralds. "Touch yourself."

She gasped and skimmed her right hand over the bunched fabric of her skirts. She felt the wiry curls and below...she gasped at the first touch.

"Oh, yes," he crooned, his hand stilling suddenly. He closed his eyes, his head falling back, and she could see his Adam's apple bob as he swallowed. "I nearly went there, Eve, when you put your fingers on your pretty cunny. Did you know?"

"No," she whispered. "Tell me."

"Ah, God," he muttered under his breath. "Just the thought of you touching yourself...and then to see it." He opened his eyes, tilting his head to look again. "Run your fingers down, will you? Let me see your fingers get wet."

This was so shocking. She wasn't even sure exactly what he meant. But she pushed her fingers between the folds of her sex and he was right—she was wet there. She might've been embarrassed, save for the fact that he had apparently expected her to be thus.

She licked her lips as she felt the soft flesh. "What shall I do now?"

He glanced up, meeting her gaze. "D'you remember what I told you before? About that bit at the top of your slit? Your clitoris?"

"Yes."

"Find it."

She drew her fingers up slowly, feeling the slickness. It was a strangely lovely feeling. She'd explored here once before—tentatively, furtively, and in the dark—but now, in front of him in the light, she was bold. She brushed something that made her jerk.

"There," he moaned. "Oh, there, Eve. That's my girl. That's my darling. Touch yourself there for me."

She closed her eyes and slid her fingers over that spot again, feeling that same jolt. A sort of spark, sudden and unexpected, that seemed to be attached to something deep inside her.

Her skin felt prickly, the soles of her feet tingled.

It was so very odd... and so very wonderful.

She opened her eyes to find that he'd begun stroking himself again, leaning back against her desk, his cock pointed at his navel. The head was shining and red and she wished she could touch it.

Maybe lick it.

The thought sent another jolt through her, this one quite frankly attached to the place she was rubbing.

He caught her shudder, grinning, his eyes happy and green. "That's it, sweetheart, oh, you're nearly there, my girl. D'you know how pretty you are down there? So pink and plump, your maiden hair a lovely reddish blond. If I were a painter like you I'd paint that. I'd paint it and hang it over my bed so I might look at it every night, your beautiful cunt."

She gasped and lost her breath and the most extraordinary thing happened.

She burst, plain and simple, heat radiating out from her body, warmth invading her limbs and racing toward her toes. It was so sweet, so wonderful, and for a moment she lost her sight.

Everything just went white as she trembled with the aftershocks.

But she hadn't lost her hearing, for she could hear him, Asa Makepeace, roaring with laughter as his seed splattered her knees.

ASA FELT JOY race through him, more potent than any wine, as he watched Eve's face as her orgasm shook her. Her mouth opened, her cheeks flushed, and her eyes closed in bliss as her fingers worked faster and faster.

This was her first time experiencing this and he felt strangely tender toward her, this strict woman who had let herself go in the most basic of ways for him. He wanted to hold her and kiss her gently. Feel her body tremble and relax as she recovered. He wanted . . .

Asa looked away, oddly frustrated. He wanted something from her, something *with* her, and it simply made no sense. He'd just coached her through her first orgasm, had gone further with her than he suspected any man had. Still held his softening cock in his fist, his come cooling on his fingers. And he wanted *more*.

The damnable thing was that he suspected—rather worryingly—that the *more* he wanted wasn't physical.

"Oh," Eve breathed, opening her eyes.

She looked dazed. She looked *fucked*, and Asa's cock twitched at the thought. He might want more than the physical, but he was a man. He'd certainly not turn away anything physical she might offer.

Except she wasn't offering anything. He'd talked her into this, hadn't he? Even now she was pulling down her skirts, hiding her pretty, pretty cunny, and he almost stayed her hand for just one more glimpse.

Just one.

But he'd already persuaded her to do more than she'd probably ever dreamed of, and he really ought to feel guilty for that. Except he didn't.

She was looking at her fingers. They gleamed from her wetness and she wrinkled her nose like a displeased cat.

He couldn't help but smile as he withdrew a handkerchief from his pocket and handed it to her. "Here."

"Thank you," she said primly, as if she weren't wiping her come from her hand.

She held the handkerchief between thumb and forefinger, obviously uncertain what to do with it.

He took it from her without a word and deliberately swiped the cloth over his prick, mingling her come with his.

She watched him, wide-eyed and silent, and when her gaze met his, he smirked.

She looked away, clearing her throat as he put himself to rights. "I . . . that is. I want to thank you."

"*Thank* me?" His grin widened.

"For showing me..." She waved a vague hand. *"That."*

"Anytime, luv," he said. The urge to pull her into his arms was stronger than ever.

He stood before he could do anything he'd regret. "I s'pose I should go find if Hampston is here yet."

She made an aborted movement, almost as if she wanted to grab his arm.

He looked at her. "What?"

"Don't see him," she said in a rush. "Please."

He sat back down on the desk. "Why?"

He thought he knew, but something cruel inside him wanted to make her say it.

She waved a hand rather helplessly, and shook her head.

"Is it because he's offering me money you have no control over?" he drawled.

Her face snapped around. "You know that isn't it."

Yes, he did.

"Then what is?" he asked, suddenly frustrated. He'd been extremely patient for a not-very-patient man, but she'd not told him *anything.* All his information had come from guesses and Jean-Marie. If the man posed a danger to her—if he'd *hurt her* in the past—she needed to *tell* him, damn it.

"I..." She inhaled, sitting a little straighter. "I had a nightmare last night."

Oh, the hell with it.

"Let me hold you."

"What?" Her blue eyes were startled and wide.

He held out his arms, waiting. If she turned him down now, he wasn't sure what he'd do.

But she didn't. She eyed his arms a second and then nodded tentatively.

He didn't wait for her to complete the gesture. Asa leaned forward, scooped Eve up into his arms, ignoring her squeak, and turned to sit in the chair where she'd been.

She sat very still and stiff.

Goddamn it, he wasn't about to let go of her.

He ignored the fact that she felt like a wooden doll and curved his arms about her, pulling her close. Her golden hair smelled faintly of flowers and he inhaled, stroking her arms slowly, almost in the same way he might a frightened animal. It was in no way sexual.

But it was warm, and though it might not give her comfort, it did give him some.

"Tell me," he crooned in her ear. "Tell me what happened in your nightmare."

She sighed and very slowly her neck bent until her head came to rest on his shoulder, a sweet burden.

He'd take that as a victory any day.

"It's a dream I've had ever since I can remember," she said so softly he had to lower his head to hers to hear. "It always begins the same: with dogs."

Asa glanced over to where Henry was snoring in the corner. Now that he was washed he was a fawn color with black markings at muzzle and ears. He was beginning to fill out, and although Asa had never been afraid of the animal, he could see how Eve might be.

"What do the dogs do?" he asked.

"They hunt me," she said flatly, as if she'd long ago come to terms with the fear, the horror, and now simply endured it. "I'm in a large house and they chase me from room to room, through the hallways and up and down the stairs, baying all the while."

He swallowed, for he wanted to growl. To shout his out-rage. But he knew that would not help Eve. "And then?"

"They catch me," she said simply. "They catch me and tear me limb from limb and behind the dogs are men in masks, laughing."

Dear God. He blinked, for though he'd seen and heard terrible things in his life, he wasn't sure he'd ever witnessed anything as terrible as Eve recounting her own slaughter.

He hugged her tighter, feeling the fine bones, the warmth of her skin. She was delicate, his Eve, but so strong underneath that.

"Why do you dream this?" he asked carefully.

"I don't know," she replied in that same dead voice. He was beginning to hate it, truth be told. And what was more, he was sure somehow that she lied.

"But..." He hesitated, choosing his words very care-fully. "This never happened, did it? You bear no scars from dogfights." Did she, though? He'd not seen her upper half unclothed.

So he blew out a silent breath of relief when she said, "No. I'm unscarred."

"Thank God," he said, stroking her downy cheek. "Thank God."

She turned her face into his chest, and for the first time her hand crept up to lie against his waistcoat.

He sighed, wishing she'd tell him more. "Do you know where you are in the dream? What house it is?"

"Yes," she whispered into his chest. "I'm in my father's house."

He was silent a moment, waiting for more, but of

course it never came. He should be happy, he supposed, that he'd gotten her to admit that much.

Finally he said, "And what has this to do with Hampston?"

"I don't know," she admitted. "But I hadn't dreamed the nightmare for years before I saw him yesterday."

"Perhaps—" He winced before he even uttered the words, but they had to be said. "Perhaps one thing has nothing to do with the other. It may be only coincidence that on the same day you encountered a long-ago friend of your father's you dreamed that particular nightmare."

"Maybe you're right," she said, her voice a little stronger. She lifted her head and looked him in the eye. "But there's one other thing. Lord Hampston has a tattoo on his wrist"—she pointed to her inner arm to show the spot—"I saw it yesterday. It's of a dolphin. In my dream the laughing masked men have dolphin tattoos as well."

He stared down at her tender inner wrist and then up at her blue eyes. "Eve."

"I don't want you to see him today—or any day."

A knock sounded at the office door, and Asa just had time to rather unceremoniously dump Eve into the chair by herself and scramble around to his side of his table before it opened.

Lord Hampston stood in the doorway, grinning. "Good morning, Harte."

"My lord." Asa moved so that he stood between Hampston and Eve. She might not want him meeting the man, but if Hampston was a threat to Eve, Asa needed to find out more about him. "Shall we walk the gardens as we talk?"

But his movement only seemed to draw Hampston's attention to Eve. "Why, little Eve, I almost didn't notice you there." His smile widened. "Tell me, have you remembered me since yesterday?"

That was quite enough. Asa moved forward, forcing Hampston to take a step back. He pasted a genial smile on his face and gestured to the door. "Shall we? I'd like you to see the maze that Lord Kilbourne is constructing."

Either his diversion worked or Lord Hampston hadn't been much interested in Eve to begin with, for the older man nodded. "There are rumors as to Kilbourne's innovative designs. I would indeed like to see them for myself."

Asa risked a glance over his shoulder to Eve. "I shan't be long, Miss Dinwoody, for I know you wanted to discuss those books." She hadn't said any such thing, of course, but he wanted somehow to signal to her that he wasn't abandoning her. "If you wish to work undisturbed, perhaps you should lock the door." He pointed to the bolt.

Eve cleared her throat. "Thank you, Mr. Harte."

He couldn't tell from her voice or her manner if she'd gotten his message—or even if she was angry at him for going with Hampston after she'd begged him not to.

But this was the most expedient way of getting the man away from Eve.

Asa ushered Hampston into the corridor. "Had you been to Harte's Folly before it burned, my lord?"

"Yes indeed," Hampston chuckled. "I brought both my wife and her daughters here, and she insisted—verily insisted, Mr. Harte!—that I bring her back again, she loved the pleasure gardens so much. Well, I don't mind telling you that my wife is a little younger than I—for it's a second marriage for both of us—and I'm apt to indulge her. I meant to bring her once again, but then the tragedy of the fire struck." He shrugged and sent a cheerful smile Asa's way. "She's been in mourning ever since."

"I shall send tickets round to your house at once for

both you and your wife and also her daughters," Asa said. "So you can all attend the grand reopening."

"Thank you, Harte," Hampston said as they walked out into the gardens. "You don't know how pleased that'll make her. My stepdaughters as well. There are three of them, Flora, Grace, and Marie, and three of the loveliest girls you've ever seen." Hampston winked. "Verily, I married their mother as much for their beauty as hers, for it cheers a man's heart to have so much feminine beauty about his house."

Asa smiled vaguely. They came within sight of the maze and he stopped. "Ah, here we are, you can see the maze and how Lord Kilbourne means for it to grow. Later it will be painted to look like marble."

For the next half hour Asa kept his mind on business, showing Lord Hampston the theater and gardens as he would any other potential investor. Hampston was properly impressed, exclaiming enthusiastically over the transplanted trees and the island folly Apollo had constructed. He was everything Asa would normally look for in an investor, actually: keen, intelligent, and, most important of all, rich. One didn't have to *like* a man to take his money. Hampston was a little strange, true. He grinned too much, made odd comments now and again, and generally rubbed Asa the wrong way, but there didn't seem to be anything actively *bad* about the man. He offered letters from his bankers to show that he was fully capable of giving money to the garden. He seemed, in fact, to be entirely normal for an aristocrat: casually arrogant, assured of both his superior rank and Asa's need of him, a bit contemptuous of those who made their living with their hands.

Asa had held his nose and taken the money of far greasier men then Hampston.

In fact, had it not been for Eve's dread of the man, Asa had no doubt he would've gladly made a deal with Hampston.

"No?" For a moment Lord Hampston stared at Asa as if dumbfounded. "I confess, sir, that I'm astounded. Rarely have I offered funds and been turned down."

"I understand, my lord, and I truly appreciate your offer," Asa replied easily. "But I already have enough backers for my needs at present."

Lord Hampston grunted. "Many men would take the money anyway."

"Many men become hopelessly entangled in debt," Asa responded with a smile.

A smile Lord Hampston returned. "You have a good business head on your shoulders, sir."

The viscount was obviously disappointed, but he took his leave cordially enough a few minutes later.

Asa made his way back to his office, his head down-bent in thought. What, exactly, did Eve have against the aristocrat? Did he merely remind her of her father? Of something far worse?

Had Hampston hurt her?

He pushed open the door to his office, determined to find the answer, only to discover it empty.

Eve was gone.

BRIDGET CRUMB WAS supervising the polishing of the grand marble staircase—a laborious job that had to be done monthly—when the pounding came at the front door.

That was interesting. Most people knocked sedately at a duke's door.

Bridget gave a last sharp glance to one of the maids—

Fanny had a tendency to stop work if an eagle eye wasn't kept on her—and walked to the front door.

She'd only just pulled it open when Miss Dinwoody pushed past her.

"I must write a letter to my brother," she said, rushing toward the stairs.

"Of course, miss," Bridget said, though the other woman didn't seem to be listening.

The footman who always accompanied Miss Dinwoody stepped inside after her. He had a worried frown as he watched his mistress run up the stairs.

"Shall I send for some tea?" Bridget asked.

The footman gave her a grateful glance. "Thank you."

And then he followed Miss Dinwoody.

Bridget murmured an order to one of the maids, who rose immediately and dashed to the kitchens. The housekeeper followed more slowly, a slight frown between her eyes.

The tea tray was ready by the time she made it to the kitchens—an advantage of always having a kettle of water on the hob. Fanny was just lifting it when Bridget forestalled her.

"I'll take it," she said. "Continue polishing the stairs, please. I expect the banister to be done by the time I return from upstairs."

"Yes, ma'am," Fanny said, resentment seeping into her voice.

Bridget sighed to herself as she climbed the stairs. Fanny wouldn't be much longer at Hermes House. A lazy, surly maid was more bother than she was worth. Bridget often had to organize the staff when she took a new position: she kept those who were industrious, teachable, or smart—hopefully all three—and the rest she let go. Anyone too lazy, too indifferent, or, God forbid, too light-fingered was gone immediately.

A housekeeper was only as good as the servants she commanded.

As she made the upper hall, Bridget could hear the murmur of voices from His Grace's library, and indeed, when she entered, Miss Dinwoody was speaking rapidly to her footman. "This must go at once to my brother. I need to know, Jean-Marie, or I shall go mad."

She turned as Bridget entered with the tea tray. "Oh, thank you, Mrs. Crumb. Can you send at once for Alf? I need to get this letter to Val as soon as possible." Miss Dinwoody had a letter clutched in one hand, but she froze suddenly. "Oh. Oh, damn."

Bridget paused an infinitesimal second in setting out the tea things. Miss Dinwoody did not strike her as the type of lady who swore.

Something must truly be amiss.

"Is there anything I can do, miss?" she murmured. She daren't make any more of an offer.

She was a servant, after all.

"No, thank you, Mrs. Crumb. It's my own stupidity." Miss Dinwoody closed her eyes tightly. "Alf is at Harte's Folly. I set him to work there. Oh, how could I have forgotten?"

She looked suddenly defeated.

"You are much excited, *ma petite*," the footman murmured, "and not thinking clearly. Come, I will send for Alf. It will not take 'im long to arrive and then 'e will send your letter on to 'Is Grace."

"You make it sound so easy, Jean-Marie," Miss Dinwoody murmured, and Bridget was horrified to see that her eyes shone as if from tears.

The sight so discombobulated her that she pressed a cup of tea into the other woman's hands.

Miss Dinwoody took a sip as Bridget exchanged a worried look with Jean-Marie.

"It is easy, *chérie*, truly," Jean-Marie said. "Come. Finish your tea while I make the arrangements to send for Alf, and when I return we shall go 'ome, *oui*? You did not sleep well last night. I think perhaps it would be good to rest."

"You're right, Jean-Marie," Miss Dinwoody sighed. "You're always right." She sat and cradled her cup of tea in her lap like a small girl while the footman went to run his errand.

Bridget ought to depart the room as well, but she didn't like to leave Miss Dinwoody alone.

She looked so fragile.

So she busied herself quietly, ordering the already ordered desk. Miss Dinwoody didn't seem to notice her presence, so lost in her own thoughts was she.

In another moment the footman returned. "Everything is good. I 'ave sent for Alf and when 'e comes Mrs. Crumb will show 'im the letter."

"At once," Bridget murmured.

Jean-Marie nodded at her. "So there is no reason to linger here. We shall return 'ome and find what delicious thing Tess has made for our supper."

He held out his hand and Miss Dinwoody took it, rising. Bridget followed them from the room and saw them down the stairs and out the front door.

The moment the door closed, however, she turned and strode swiftly back to the duke's library, locking the door behind her.

The letter sat on his desk, ready for Alf.

Bridget picked it up and turned it over to look at the seal. She set it down and took a letter opener shaped like a small, sharp dagger from the desk drawer. She walked to the fireplace and held the blade of the letter-opener in the flames until it was hot.

Then she swiftly and efficiently slid the hot blade under the wax seal, melting it enough to pop it off the letter without destroying the embossed figure or tearing the paper.

She opened the letter and read:

Val:

Do you know the name of the man that night?

> *Your loving sister,*
> *E.*

Bridget stared at the simple letter a moment longer, her brows knit. Then she reheated the knife and held it to the reverse of the seal, melting the wax. She turned the seal over and carefully pressed it back onto the letter.

She placed the letter on the desk, exactly where it had been, and said clearly and out loud, "I hope the duke receives this soon."

And then she left the room and quietly closed the door behind her.

Chapter Thirteen

Eric and Dove walked for what seemed miles until they came to a clear, bubbling stream. Beside the stream grew a luxurious bed of watercress. Dove smiled at the sight—for she was rather hungry—until she noticed Eric scowling down at the green leaves.
"My mistress bid me bring her a bag of this watercress, but it's enchanted," he explained. "It shrinks from my hands every time I try to pick it." And to demonstrate he reached down to grab a bunch, only to have the leaves retreat into the ground....
—From The Lion and the Dove

Jean-Marie took one long look at Asa when he answered Eve's door that night, and let him in.

"Where is she?" Asa asked tiredly. It took over an hour to travel from Harte's Folly on the south bank of the Thames to Eve's town house on the north bank, and he was bloody weary.

"Upstairs," Jean-Marie said. "'Er mind is much agitated."

Asa paused, his foot on the bottom step of the stairs. "I know."

Then he mounted the stairs.

She was in her sitting room, but instead of working on

her miniature, she sat on the settee, her hands folded in her lap.

She glanced up as he entered. "I heard your knock."

"Did you?" He watched her, this woman who irritated him, amused him, engaged him, and aroused him. He'd come armed with explanations and reassurances. Reasons why she shouldn't fear Hampston and questions about what had happened to make her so fearful in the first place.

But he was tired and she looked so alone sitting there, her blue eyes sad.

"The hell with it," he muttered, and, taking two long steps, he sank to the cushions beside Eve. He held his hands, palms up, between them. "May I?"

It was a risk after he'd walked away with a man she so obviously feared. She had every right to reject him.

Every right not to trust him.

But she looked at him and simply said, "Yes."

And he kissed her.

EVE FROZE AS Asa's lips touched hers. She wanted this—wanted to at least *try* to do this with Asa. She'd reached a breaking point this afternoon, running to Val's house, trembling with fear and horror, not knowing if she was remembering Lord Hampston or if it was all just a terrible coincidence. In some ways it didn't matter. She couldn't go on like this, a half woman, crouching alone and afraid inside a glass cage made of memories and nightmares.

She wanted to live.

And she wanted Asa with an unfurling passion that trembled with possibility. So she kissed him, but she froze because she was waiting for the old fear. The revulsion.

Except it never came.

His lips were soft on hers, the scrape of his stubble an exotic juxtaposition.

She shivered and realized to her surprise that the only thing she felt was excitement.

He drew back on a regretful sigh.

Eve opened her eyes and found Asa looking at her with his brows drawn together. "Eve? Do you want me to stop?"

"No." She wasn't going to lose this opportunity because of a misunderstanding. She hadn't frozen from disgust but from caution.

His expression sharpened. "Then *kiss me*."

Eve clutched his coat and leaned into him, crushing her mouth against his, clumsily chasing that excitement she'd felt before. She couldn't lose it now.

She *couldn't.*

Oh! *There* it was. She shivered as he tilted his face, sweetly fitting their lips together. He brushed his mouth back and forth over hers until she relaxed from her anxious searching, until her lips softened.

Until her lips parted under his.

Even then he was slow, as if he waited for some signal from her. He pressed tender kisses to her mouth. Sharing his breath with her.

And then she felt a moist touch.

His tongue swept over her bottom lip, teasing, flirting, so softly that she couldn't help but chase it, her own tongue venturing out to meet his, a little frustrated now by how gentle he was being with her.

Asa wasn't a gentle man by any means. In some ways that was what she loved about him—*more*, it was what she wanted from him.

She nipped at the corner of his mouth.

He laughed under his breath then, seeming to understand her unspoken plea, as he widened his mouth. He bit at her lips, groaned against her mouth. He drew her into his arms, into his embrace, his wide shoulders surrounding her as he tilted her head back over his arm. He was all around her, holding her, strong and big, and she ought to be afraid.

Ought to be struggling to escape.

Instead she pressed closer to him, feeling the beat of his heart under her fingertips, striving to meet that wild animal within him.

His palm pressed lightly against her jaw as he slipped his tongue into her mouth, sliding it against hers. She closed her lips, instinctively wanting to keep him inside her. Tentatively she suckled at his tongue, and that must've been the right thing to do, for he groaned.

He pulled back, laying his forehead against hers, his eyes closed, his breath coming in pants.

She was astonished to see that his big body was trembling.

Was that her doing? Did she arouse him so much? It made her proud, that thought: that she, a plain, rather ordinary woman, should make Asa Makepeace, the most masculine man she'd ever known, *tremble* with passion.

He opened his eyes and the green was the darkest jade. "Will you show me your bedroom, Eve Dinwoody?"

She replied without hesitation. Without doubt. "Yes."

She stood and held out her hand to him, her heart beating in her bosom so fast she thought he must hear it.

He rose, broad and alive—so alive—and all hers for this small moment in time.

Eve had always been a sensible woman, and a sensible woman would be a fool to pass up what Asa Makepeace had to offer.

So she led him without speaking down the hall and to her bedroom.

This was her inner sanctuary and she looked at it anew, wondering what he thought of it. Her sitting room was comfortable. Prettily put together with practical pieces.

But in her bedroom Eve let a little indulgence show.

The walls were painted palest blue, with white pilasters, wainscoting, and woodwork. A dainty desk sat in a bay window, gray-blue damask drapes pulled to the side so that she might look over her back garden when she sat to write letters.

A gilt marble-and-rosewood chest of drawers sat against one wall. On the opposite was a white marble fireplace, the tile surrounding the hearth in blue and white. And in the corner sat her bed. It was piled with gray-blue damask cushions, and drapes of the same color were held back by cords of midnight blue velvet.

Eve turned to Asa and found him watching her. He was smiling.

"Come," he said, "will you lie with me?"

"Oh, yes," she said, and walked to the bed. She stopped there and found she wasn't sure what to do next.

What exactly did he want of her?

She almost fled then, but he came behind her, his heat surrounding her. If any other man had stood so close to her she might've panicked.

But this was Asa and he was the man she wanted.

He laid his palms on her waist and she felt his breath on her bare nape. Then his lips as he kissed her.

"May I take your hair down?" he whispered in her ear.

She nodded jerkily, then held her breath.

His hands drifted upward from her waist, over her sides, up her shoulders, and into her hair. He'd deliberately kept away from her breasts, and she wasn't sure whether to be grateful or resentful.

Then he began plucking the pins from her hair, carefully, without touching her anywhere else, and Eve began to wonder if *hair* could possibly be erotic.

She found herself holding her breath, listening to his deep, even exhalations as he worked, her hair loosening and beginning to slide.

It fell all at once, uncoiling heavily over her shoulders. She turned her head to look at him, suddenly shy.

He was staring at her hair.

"It's beautiful," he murmured, burying his fingers in the long tresses, gently working apart the strands, lifting and spreading them. "Like liquid gold." He suddenly lifted the mass to his face. "And perfumed. Like flowers."

"Lily of the valley." He made her feel exotic, still dressed in her sensible gray frock, only her hair loose about her shoulders.

"Lily of the valley," he murmured. "I'll remember that scent forever now, and whenever I smell it again I'll think of you, Eve Dinwoody. You'll be haunting my tomorrows evermore."

She gasped and turned, looking up at him. She'd thought that he'd be smiling teasingly at his words, but he looked quite serious and she stared at him in wonder. Had he always carried this part of himself inside? This wild poetic lover? If so, he'd hidden it well underneath the aggressive, foulmouthed theater manager. She had a secret fondness for the crass theater manager, but the poet...

She swallowed, suddenly nervous.

She might come to love a wild poet.

He framed her face with his palms and leaned down to kiss her. On her forehead, drifting down to her cheeks, brushing like silk over her mouth.

"Let me undress you, Eve?" His words whispered against her lips, a kiss in and of themselves.

She nodded, afraid to speak.

He straightened, looking at her, then reached slowly for the gauze fichu tucked into her bodice. "May I?"

"Yes," she whispered.

He tugged, drawing the ends out from underneath the laces of her bodice. He looked down as he did, examining the tops of her breasts, revealed by her square-necked bodice.

"Your skin is like white velvet." He touched the laces of her bodice. "May I?"

"Yes." She swallowed, wondering if he would ask her for each article of clothing she wore. Should she tell him he had no need? But they gave her control of the moment, his inquiries.

She liked that.

Eve looked down and watched as his blunt, tanned fingers deftly unlaced her bodice.

He caught the edges, then glanced up, meeting her eyes. "May I?"

"Yes."

"Then lift your arms for me."

She raised her arms and he drew the tight sleeves off her, carefully placing the bodice over a chair.

She stood in stays, skirts, chemise, stockings, and shoes.

He placed his hands on the strings that tied her skirts to her waist. "May I?"

She nodded.

He unknotted the strings as she tried to steady her breathing.

Then her skirt slipped to the floor.

She looked up expectantly, and a smile flickered across his lips as he tapped the laces of her stays. "May I?"

"Yes."

He started on the laces and she watched him. His green eyes were intent on his task. They bore slight wrinkles at the corners, and she could see more lines around his wide mouth. He glanced up and met her gaze, his lips twitching before he looked back down again.

She was glad—so glad—that he'd come here—that he'd come to her. No man had ever sought her out before, pursued her—so carefully—yet so persistently.

It was lovely to be wanted.

Her stays loosened and she inhaled as they did, her lungs and ribs and breasts free. Without waiting for his order, she raised her arms.

He drew off her stays.

Her chemise was lawn, fine and delicate.

Nearly transparent.

She daren't look down. She kept her eyes on him, even as she began to tremble. She'd only been this exposed to a man once before—

She pushed the intruding thought from her mind, but couldn't help the small shake of her head.

He looked at her, hesitated, then knelt before her.

He touched her slipper, holding her eyes. "May I?"

She nodded jerkily. She wanted this—*needed* this. She wouldn't let the past control her future. "Ye-es."

He pulled off first one, then the other of her slippers.

She was nearly shaking now.

He looked worried, a line imprinting itself between his brows. "Eve," he said. "We can stop here. We needn't go any further."

"No." She inhaled sharply. *"Please."*

He nodded.

He slid his hand slowly up over her ankle, letting his fingers rest on her calf. "May I?"

"Yes."

He reached up under the chemise and untied her garter.

She could feel his fingers, warm and reassuring, fumbling with the stocking, and she closed her eyes, concentrating on *that*.

Not on panting dogs or the wash of blood.

It was easier with the second stocking, and then he was rising.

She opened her eyes to find him standing before her, not touching her at all. "May I?"

She swallowed, grateful, *relieved*.

Heated. "Yes."

He kept his gaze on hers, as if to steady her, as he took the chemise skirt in his hands and drew it over her head.

She was naked. Entirely naked.

Her hands immediately flew to her breasts, covering them, as she looked at him wildly. His lips twitched and he laid his hands over hers on her chest. "May I?"

Her mouth opened, but no sound came. She nodded instead.

He curled his fingers over hers, interlocking, and drew her hands away from her breasts, holding them wide.

She was too thin, too tall, too bony, her breasts too small—

He bent and kissed one nipple, the slight brush of his lips making it contract. Then he kissed the other.

She stopped breathing, watching him, astonished.

He opened his mouth, stuck out his tongue, and licked.

All thought fled her mind. This, *this* wasn't at all what she'd expected. It was strange and foreign and...

Delightful.

He glanced up at her through thick eyelashes, his mouth still hovering over the nipple he'd licked.

"Do that again," she said.

He chuckled, leaned forward, and took her nipple into his mouth.

"Oh," she breathed. A tension was pulling, from her nipple through her body and somehow ending up between her legs and it was tart and sweet and... *"Oh."*

He popped off her nipple and bent, suddenly lifting her into his arms like a baby. She stared at him, her arms raised, not sure exactly what to do with them, and this seemed to cause him some amusement, for he chuckled again. "Eve. May I?"

"Yes," she replied, having no idea at all what she was agreeing to.

He turned and deposited her in her bed and then climbed in after.

She tensed as for a moment he was over her, but then he settled beside her and she relaxed again, watching him curiously.

He grinned and bent his head to her breast again, sucking her tender nipple back into his mouth. It felt...oh, it felt so lovely, like sparks lighting and flickering under her skin as he sucked and sucked again. Her legs felt restless.

She curled her toes into the mattress as he lifted his head and moved to the other nipple.

When he sucked, she arched a little under him, feeling like a banquet, like an offering to a pagan god.

He grazed the tip of her breast gently with his teeth and then looked at her, his hair falling across his brow. "May I?"

His voice had lowered, gone into those gravelly depths.

"Yes," she said.

And he licked from her nipple to the flat plane between her breasts. Swiftly he kissed down to her belly, tonguing around her navel, making her fist her hands into the sheets, and then he was just above her bush.

She looked down, wide-eyed. His tawny hair fell about his face, obscuring his mouth, but she could feel the tiny kisses, the sharp, thrilling nips as he edged her maiden hair.

He lifted his head and she recognized him then, as he stared with green eyes through the strands of his hair: he was Pan, god of all wild things.

God of male virility.

"May I?" he rasped.

"Please," she whispered.

Watching her, he lifted his body, shifting apart her legs, and hesitated as if he waited for some objection from her. And when there was none, he settled between her thighs, big and male, dark and sensuous, a stranger and the man she'd come to know intimately in the last few days.

A dream, not a nightmare.

He lowered his head slowly until he hovered over her mons, his breath stirring her damp curls. "May I?"

She nodded wordlessly.

But it wasn't enough anymore.

He shook his head sternly, still looking into her eyes. "Say it."

She licked her lips. "Yes."

"Good girl."

And he bent and kissed her clitoris.

She froze because she'd had no idea what he was going to do and if she had—

He opened his mouth, licking her.

Oh, God!

One hand flew to her mouth. She bit down on her knuckles, trying to keep any sound from escaping. The other hand clutched at his hair, that tawny mane, as he ravished her with his mouth, licking, kissing, *sucking.*

She gasped, unable to fill her lungs. What he was doing to her was diabolical, something supernatural, an act so extraordinary she wanted to squirm away.

Wanted to hold him there forever.

How was it possible that he could give her such pleasure?

He tongued her and she arched into his face, wanting, wanting, rubbing herself against him, noises from her throat escaping around her knuckles. She was hot, trembling, shaking, waiting for a transformation.

He opened his mouth wide over her, thrusting his tongue again and again against her clitoris.

She fell apart, exploding from her center, moaning mindlessly, her hands filled with his thick hair as he licked her relentlessly.

She was scattered, her mind blanking, her body racked with undiluted pleasure for some long, unmeasurable time. She simply existed, a creature of wonderment.

And when all her parts finally resettled, when she

unclenched her fingers from his hair, and gasped for breath, her body dewed with moisture, she knew:

She'd been born anew.

ASA LICKED HIS lips, tasting Eve.

He watched her eyelids flutter open. She sprawled before him, a sybarite, replete in her satisfaction, and he couldn't help but feel proud that he'd shown her such pleasure.

Even if his cock was hard as marble.

He stroked her legs, her belly as she recovered. He still lay between her legs, so close to her cunt, open and wet like a blown flower. He could smell her salty sex, taste her still on his tongue, and he wanted—wanted with a deep twist of his gut—to lever himself over her and shove his cock into that warm, wet, welcoming center.

But he couldn't. Not now. Perhaps not ever.

The thought grieved him, tearing at a part of his soul he hadn't even known he had.

Asa sighed and pushed himself up, slowly—and rather painfully—crawling from between Eve's legs and to her side. He propped himself on one elbow and, wincing, adjusted himself in his breeches.

Eve opened dazed blue eyes. "Asa."

"Aye, luv," he murmured, leaning over her to kiss her gently on the mouth.

"That was wonderful," she murmured, her words nearly slurred.

He couldn't help the smirk, though it turned to a wince as he straightened.

She was more alert than he'd thought. "What's the matter? Are you hurt?" Her gaze drifted down his body and then widened when she saw the tent his cock was making in his breeches. "Oh. You didn't...doesn't that hurt?"

"A little."

She arched those imperious eyebrows. "Then why don't you do something about it?"

He arched his brows back. Before her he'd never touched himself in front of a woman—in front of anyone. It was a solitary activity, after all, one done out of boredom or desperation or because he didn't have a woman to serve his needs at that moment.

Or at least he'd always thought of it thus.

That masturbation might be an erotic act between two people had never occurred to him before the carriage ride with Eve.

Now he felt his cock jump at the thought.

He lay back and, reaching down, unbuttoned his falls.

Her gaze dropped to his hands and he had to close his eyes a moment for fear that he'd spill in his breeches.

Gingerly he opened his falls and his smallclothes and pushed them down his hips. His cock bobbed blessedly free and he groaned at the liberation.

He was about to take himself in hand when he felt a hesitant touch.

He opened his eyes to see Eve tracing a finger down his throbbing shaft. Jesus! Her hand was so cool, so soft against his flesh.

"It's hard." She looked up at him, her blue eyes alight with curiosity. "I hadn't expected it to be so hard. Can I—?"

He swallowed, nodding, clutching the bedclothes in one fist. He could endure this if it kept that happy expression on her face.

She bent over him, her glorious blond hair drifting over her white shoulders, and ran her finger over his balls.

Then she giggled.

He could only glare at her—he'd lost the power of speech many moments ago.

"They're so hairy," she said in explanation. "And wrinkly. Like prunes in a bag."

She bit her lip as if to still further giggles as she peered at him.

Her gaze flicked to his. "Do you mind?"

How could he protest? She was unafraid in this moment and she was *touching* him.

He shook his head and spread his legs. "Be my guest, luv." His voice sounded like charred gravel.

It didn't seem to deter her curiosity, though. The tip of her tongue peeked between her lips as she leaned over him and rolled his balls in her slim fingers. Her gold hair fell over her shoulders in gentle waves, brushing the clear, delineated bow of her collarbone. Her breasts were delicate, pretty things, with just the barest curve underneath. They came to a sweet point as she hung over him, her nipples palest pink. And her fingers...

He swallowed and looked away for a moment, gritting his teeth.

Dear God. Her fingers, those prim, soft lady's fingers, were wrapped around the crude, ruddy flesh of his cock.

He'd been handled far more expertly in his time—been handled by experts, come to that. But the very fact that she didn't quite know what she was doing. That this must be the first time she'd touched a cock.

God.

He couldn't remember *ever* having been so hard for a woman.

Her fingers trailed over his burning skin, so lightly they nearly tickled. He wanted to tell her to grip him, to make a fist over his damned cock and *pull*, and at the same time he wanted to endure this. To merely lie here, undone and aching, letting this virgin *play* with him.

He sneaked a glance, just in time to see her bend closer, tracing the foreskin drawn back tight around the head of his swollen cock, and *bloody hell*, he felt the brush of her breath on his weeping flesh.

"You're going to give me apoplexy," he rasped.

She looked up, her blue eyes wide.

He couldn't take it anymore.

He wrapped his hand around the back of her head and pulled her up, pulled her across his chest, pulled her into a kiss so filthily explicit his tongue might as well have been fucking her mouth.

They groaned in unison and he wrapped his hand over hers, forcing her fingers tight around his erection, showing her how to pull up, the loose skin sliding over his hot core—oh, sweet, sweet *God*—and down, fisting tight, moving faster, his hips pumping up into their shared grasp.

She moaned and his hips jerked at the sound.

And then she sucked his tongue and hot pleasure speared him. He convulsed, spunk spewing over his fingers, over hers. He smeared them both in it as he yanked himself through it, shuddering.

Groaning as if he were dying. Maybe he had. Maybe this was sweet death.

He released his flesh then, but he still clasped her hand,

twining their fingers together, sticky with his release. A wild idea came to him, of rubbing his seed into her skin. Of marking her with his scent.

She sagged against him, sprawled over him, as he lazily explored her mouth.

Mine, a primitive part of himself whispered inside. *Mine*.

He had to push the thought down and away, for that was impossible. Eve deserved to be the most important thing in some man's life and that place was already taken in his.

By his garden.

Always his garden.

Plain and simple, she deserved someone more giving than he. More open, more gentle, more *gentlemanly*.

Someone who didn't eat, drink, and breathe the theater, day in and day out.

He frowned at the thought and then pushed it away. For the moment—*this* moment—he had Eve Dinwoody in his bed.

Asa tucked her head against his chest and lay back on her perfumed pillows, closing his eyes.

If this was all he'd ever have of her, it was more than enough.

Chapter Fourteen

*Dove laughed softly. "No wonder the leaves flee from
you. Your touch is too rough."
She knelt by the stream and slowly stretched out her
hand, petting the shining leaves before gently plucking
them. In no time at all she had filled a bag with the
watercress.
"Huh." Eric took the bag from her and tied it
to his belt.
And then he turned and set off through the
forest again....*
—From *The Lion and the Dove*

The dogs were at her heels, snapping with dripping fangs,
when Eve woke that night.

They didn't catch me this time, was the only thing she
could think as she lay staring into the darkness. *They
didn't tear me limb from limb.*

She sobbed on an indrawn breath, and then realized
she wasn't alone.

Asa Makepeace held her to his chest, gently rocking
her as if she were a child.

"Hush, sweetheart," he crooned into her hair. "Hush,
luv."

She could feel the brocade of his waistcoat under her cheek, the warmth of his hands in her hair, on her arms, and she was glad—so very glad—that she'd not waked alone from her dream.

She curled her fingers into the collar of his shirt. He must've removed his coat at some point during the night, for he wasn't wearing it. She could feel the warmth of his throat, the rasp of his chest hair.

He held her like that, rocking slowly, not speaking, for some long, interminable time—impossible to count seconds or minutes in the dead of night. She could hear the soft sigh of his breath, the slight creak of the bed, and nothing else.

They might as well be the only people alive in the world.

WHEN NEXT EVE woke, the sun was shining through the windows. She blinked and realized a large male arm was thrown across her stomach, pinning her in place.

Oddly, she didn't panic.

Instead she gingerly removed the arm and slowly, carefully levered herself up to peer at her sleeping bedmate.

Asa Makepeace was on his back, his arms and legs spread wide and taking up most of the bed. A sunbeam struck his hair, making gold and red strands glint in the brown. Dark reddish brown hair stubbled his jaw. His lips were slightly parted and on each exhalation was the faintest suggestion of a snore.

Eve smiled at the sound and reached for the small sketchbook and pencil that always sat on the table beside her bed.

She settled back against the pillows and began drawing him: the slightly overlarge nose, the eyes unlined in sleep, the slack, beautiful mouth. How was it possible that this man she'd at first found merely irritating, overwhelmingly male—*frightening*—should turn out to have so many sides to him? A lover of opera. A fighter of highwaymen. A shouter of arguments. A savior of stray dogs.

Stubborn, cynical, violent, and sometimes mean.

And yet a man who had tenderly shown her how to love.

No one had ever cared so much for her.

The pencil trembled in her hand at the thought and she carefully laid both pencil and sketchbook down.

Asa had made no promises. Indeed, he'd told her that he devoted his time to the garden and had never looked for either wife or family. Whatever they had between them, therefore, must perforce be temporary.

To allow herself to become…emotionally invested in him would be a very unwise thing.

Eve bit her lip. Still. Right now, right here, she could watch her lover sleep. She bent to her sketchbook again and for the next several moments the only sound in her bedroom was the scratch of her pencil.

The door to her bedroom opened and Ruth dropped her ash bucket on the floor.

Eve blushed as the maid stared at the very large male in her bed.

Asa opened his eyes, grimaced, and slammed them closed again. *"What."*

Eve cleared her throat. "Good morning."

He opened one eye again, squinting up at her. "Thought I heard a gunshot."

"Erm, no," Eve murmured. "That was Ruth, my maid, with her bucket."

"M...morning, sir." Ruth spoke up. "Would you like some tea?"

"God, yes," Asa said, rubbing vigorously at his face.

Eve nodded at the maid. "Leave the fire for now, Ruth, and fetch a tray of tea, please."

"Yes, ma'am." Ruth bobbed a curtsy and hurried from the room, regrettably leaving her bucket behind on the floor.

Eve slipped from the bed and found her chemise, then pulled it over her head before crossing to her chest of drawers for a wrapper.

When she turned, Asa was watching her don the article of clothing with a mournful frown. "Have you considered doing away with servants?"

"No," she replied briskly. "And if I did, there would be no one to bring you your breakfast."

"Ah." He stretched, his fists nearly reaching the canopy of the bed. "I suppose that's a good point."

"'Tis," she said. She cleared her throat delicately. "There's a washbasin and necessary in my dressing room." She indicated a small door.

He nodded and stood, buttoning the falls of his breeches.

Eve hastily looked away. Ruth would be back in minutes.

And indeed, five minutes later Asa and she were sitting down to tea and gammon steak.

Eve poured Asa a cup and handed it to him, watching as he added both milk and sugar. "Will you be going to the garden today?"

"Yes." He took a sip of the tea and hummed under his breath. "Today and every day until we open."

She nodded. Of course he would. "We might as well go together, then."

"Oh, no." He shook his fork obnoxiously in her face. "I haven't forgotten the day, even if you have."

Her heart sank a little and she knew she had a guilty expression on her face. "I don't know what you mean."

He gave her an old-fashioned look. She'd never been very good at lying. "The Ladies' Syndicate, luv. It meets today if I'm not mistaken."

She winced. "I didn't think I should go."

He arched an eyebrow.

She turned her teacup around and around in her hands, watching as her opal ring winked in the light. "It's just that they can't really want me there. Lady Caire..." She swallowed, not finishing the sentence. Val had blackmailed the elder Lady Caire to make the aristocrat bring Eve to the last meeting. She wasn't sure how—or over what—but Lady Caire would hardly welcome her back.

Fortunately Asa didn't seem to notice that she'd not finished her thought. He nodded, cutting his gammon steak. "I didn't want to go to Rachel's baptism, and yet you made me." He popped a piece of the gammon into his mouth and chewed, openmouthed. "Fair's fair."

"But the garden—"

"You can come afterward."

"And Dove—"

"The dove can stay home for one day."

She pouted.

"Or"—he rolled his eyes—"I'll bring her to the theater for you while you're at your meeting. You can join us later."

She sighed. "Oh, very well."

He grinned. "That's my girl."

She scowled morosely down at her tea.

"Eve...," Asa said.

She looked up warily.

"Last night," he said carefully. "Your nightmare. Was it because of Hampston?"

"I don't..." She inhaled, steadying herself. "I don't truly know. He makes me nervous. And then there's the dolphin tattoo he has."

He watched her as if waiting for more, but she took a hasty sip of tea instead.

He placed his hand on hers where it rested on the table. "I want you to know that I turned Hampston away yesterday. I merely went with him to find out something about the man"—he shrugged—"though in the end I learned little besides his being a pompous ass. In any case I turned him away. For you."

She smiled. "Thank you."

And this time she knew: the smile he gave her *was* entirely for her.

BRIDGET CRUMB HURRIED down a narrow lane in St. Giles, a hood pulled over her head. Around her the buildings seemed to lean in over the street, nearly blocking the sun. Bridget shivered and pulled her cloak more firmly about her person. It always seemed colder in St. Giles.

There was an open channel running down the middle of the lane, wet with noxious substances. She skirted a small child squatting and poking at something in the channel with a stick. The child wore a too-large waistcoat and nothing else.

But then in St. Giles he was lucky to have even the waistcoat.

A beggar sat in a doorway, his scarlet coat marking

him as a former soldier. He was missing both legs and held a filthy hand palm up in his lap.

The beggar didn't make a sound as she neared, but Bridget paused for a moment to fish a coin from her pocket and drop it in his palm.

Then she hurried on without a backward glance.

It didn't do for a respectable woman by herself to linger in St. Giles, even in the middle of the day.

She turned a corner and saw her destination. The Home for Unfortunate Infants and Foundling Children was newly built of practical brick. It stood in the middle of Maiden Lane, a beacon of hope in an otherwise cheerless district.

Bridget mounted the wide steps and rapped smartly on the door.

It was answered in less than a minute by a middle-aged butler with a sloping belly. "Good morning, Mrs. Crumb."

Bridget nodded as she stepped inside the home. "Mr. Butterman."

She doffed her cloak as a small white dog came racing around the corner, barking madly.

"Dodo." She bent and politely offered her fingers to be sniffed before petting the little dog.

"If you'll follow me, ma'am," Mr. Butterman said, leading the way into the house.

Bridget was always grateful at the butler's grave courtesy. As a fellow servant, he didn't have to treat her as a guest of the home, and yet he always did.

That quiet courtesy made him more of a gentleman than many an aristocrat in her book.

"Most of the ladies have already arrived," Mr. Butterman murmured as he opened the door to the downstairs sitting room.

Inside, the scene was cozy. A fire crackled in a small grate while a half dozen or so ladies sat and drank tea. Three little girls—orphans of the home—carefully passed plates of haphazardly buttered bread.

"Oh, Mrs. Crumb." A cheerful-looking woman with light-brown curling hair looked up at her entrance. She shifted a sleeping baby from one shoulder to the other. "It's so nice to see you again, though I confess I fear my house will never be as ordered as it was under your management."

"My lady." Bridget made a very correct curtsy to Lady Margaret St. John. She'd had the honor of serving as Lady Margaret's housekeeper before she'd taken the position at the Duke of Montgomery's house.

"Please sit down, Mrs. Crumb," Miss Hippolyta Royle, an olive-complexioned woman with fine dark eyes, said in a low contralto. She sat next to Mrs. Isabel Makepeace, who wore a rather dashing pink-and-black sack gown. "We're all most anxious to hear what you've learned."

"I'm afraid, ma'am—" Bridget began.

"I don't understand." A lady who had been sitting at the far end of the room stood, and Bridget realized with a bit of a shock that it was Miss Eve Dinwoody.

Oh, dear, this was awkward.

Bridget usually had no trouble keeping the expressionless facade of a very good servant, but she couldn't help her eyes widening—just a tiny bit.

"It's quite all right," Lady Phoebe said soothingly. The lady might be blind, but she was very good at picking up on the atmosphere of a room. She sat beside her elder sister, Lady Hero Reading, who, in contrast to Lady Phoebe's short, plump form, was tall and slender—and had gorgeous flaming-red hair to boot. "You do remember when I said none of us judge each other on our brothers' actions?"

Miss Dinwoody looked torn between fleeing and sitting back down. "Yes, I do."

"Well, it's quite true." Lady Phoebe smiled sweetly and beside her Lady Hero nodded.

Miss Dinwoody wavered, glancing at Bridget. "But what is my brother's housekeeper doing here?"

And at that the last lady in the room spoke. "Please. Sit down, Miss Dinwoody, and we'll explain." The elder Lady Caire, a woman in her sixth decade and with pure white hair, glanced at Bridget and nodded slightly.

Bridget straightened to attention under Lady Caire's gaze before turning to Miss Dinwoody. She took a deep breath and met the other woman's eyes. "I've been endeavoring since I entered your brother's employment to discover the whereabouts of some compromising letters as well as another artifact used by His Grace for the purpose of blackmail."

"Oh, dear God." Miss Dinwoody covered her mouth with one hand as she abruptly sat down on a settee. She looked at Lady Caire. "The letters are yours, aren't they?"

Lady Caire inclined her head.

Miss Dinwoody closed her eyes. "You must know that I have nothing to do with Val's schemes. I've attempted to dissuade him from his more outrageous actions in the past"—she glanced guiltily at Lady Phoebe—"but it's been impossible. Val listens to no one."

Bridget's lips tightened at Miss Dinwoody's obvious distress. How awful to feel guilty for the actions of a brother who simply had no shame.

"We truly don't blame you." Lady Margaret moved

to sit beside Miss Dinwoody, her baby still asleep on her shoulder. "You wouldn't believe some of the things my own brothers have done..." She winced as if at a memory. "Or possibly you *would*, but in any case, I'm very glad that I don't have to answer for their actions."

Miss Dinwoody pressed her lips together and then straightened her back. "Thank you." She glanced around the group of ladies. "Thank you all."

Lady Margaret laid her free hand gently on Eve's knee.

Lady Hero stirred. "Then we're agreed?" She looked at each member of the Ladies' Syndicate in turn and received a nod or a smile from every one. Lastly she turned to Miss Dinwoody with a small smile on her face.

Miss Dinwoody frowned as if in puzzlement. "Agreed on what?"

"On your membership to the Ladies' Syndicate, of course," Lady Caire drawled. "That was why you came today, wasn't it?"

"Oh." Miss Dinwoody looked uncertain.

Bridget couldn't blame her. Lady Caire had long been a lioness of society, elegant and cold and very imposing when she wanted to be. She stared at Miss Dinwoody without so much as a smile on her face. It was very hard to tell if she welcomed the younger lady or not.

But Miss Dinwoody rallied. She lifted her chin and said firmly, "Yes. Yes, I do want to join the Ladies' Syndicate."

"Congratulations." Lady Caire inclined her head. "You're our newest member, Miss Dinwoody."

"Oh!" Miss Dinwoody blinked and two spots of bright pink shone in her cheeks. "In that case, do call me Eve."

"To Eve!" Lady Phoebe cried, holding up her teacup.

"Hear! Hear!" Miss Royle said, and all the ladies toasted

Miss Dinwoody with their tea, which, unfortunately, woke up Lady Margaret's baby.

Bridget cast her eyes down and waited patiently in the resulting commotion. How lovely it must be to be welcomed into such a group of friends. Miss Dinwoody had glowed as the other members had held up their teacups. Bridget could almost be envious of her, save for the fact that the Ladies' Syndicate was so very far out of her league it might as well be like reaching for a star in the sky.

Better to know her place and take pride in being a good servant.

It was quite a little while before the meeting resumed.

When it did, Lady Caire nodded at Bridget.

Bridget folded her hands in front of her and said clearly and precisely, "I'm afraid I have to report that I haven't been able to find the letters." She cleared her throat. "Or the other item."

For a second there was dead silence, and then the information seemed to sink in.

Miss Dinwoody frowned. "Val's blackmailing someone else from the Ladies' Syndicate as well, isn't he?"

Bridget made sure this time that her eyes didn't stray to any one member in the room. She inclined her head.

Miss Dinwoody set down her teacup with a determined clink. "How can I help?"

Chapter Fifteen

Next they came to a great oak, the tallest in the forest. Eric tilted back his head and pointed up. "My mistress bade me pluck the acorns from this tree, but I cannot reach them." Dove smiled and shook her head at him. "And did you never learn to climb trees as a child?" So saying, she pulled herself up from branch to branch, and soon brought down a bag full of green acorns....
—From *The Lion and the Dove*

It hadn't been all that bad in the end, Eve reflected a few hours later. Even with her brother playing the evil villain of the piece, she'd enjoyed herself at the Ladies' Syndicate meeting, not least because the ladies had been so very welcoming. Eve smiled to herself at the memory of being toasted with tea.

And she'd been able to offer a little help as well for Mrs. Crumb's search—or at least she hoped so.

Eve frowned at the reminder of Val's iniquities. *Why* did he feel a need to hurt so many people—people who were her friends? She shook her head, glancing out the window of her carriage as it pulled to a stop outside the back gates of Harte's Folly.

"We are 'ere, *ma chérie*," Jean-Marie rumbled in his deep voice.

Eve glanced a little guiltily at her footman as he helped her down from the carriage. What must Jean-Marie think of her? He must know—Tess, too—that Asa had shared her bed last night.

But Jean-Marie only gave her his white-toothed grin, his eyes perhaps a little more warm this morning.

If she didn't know better, she'd think he approved of her scandalous liaison with Asa.

They walked through the garden on the way to the theater, and Eve noticed all the small changes that had taken place in the last weeks. The gardens looked neater, the paths properly edged and graveled. The plantings had been filled in and Lord Kilbourne's maze was up and looking much more impressive than his description had given her to hope.

Harte's Folly was nearly ready to be opened.

She felt a thrill that she'd been a small—very small—part of helping to put the theater and gardens back in order.

She turned to Jean-Marie to tell him her thoughts, and then she smelled it:

Smoke.

They'd made it as far as the courtyard, and she looked up in shock to see a tendril of smoke drift over the gabled roof of the theater.

Dear God, surely not.

"Where is Asa?" She looked frantically at Jean-Marie. "He must be inside."

She started forward, but the footman stopped her with a hand on her arm. "Wait, Eve." He jogged to where several gardeners had brought buckets and a lander and spoke hurriedly to the men.

Jean-Marie ran back. "'E was seen going into the gardens with Lord Kilbourne."

Eve looked at him, dread in her heart. "We have to find him."

"Non." The footman shook his head vehemently. "Stay 'ere, Eve, do you comprehend? I will find Mr. Makepeace, *oui?"*

He waited only long enough for her nod, and then he was running into the garden.

More workmen and gardeners were rushing to the courtyard to help. Several had full buckets of water, but the ornamental pond was dozens of yards away. A bucket line would take minutes to set up.

And there were people in the theater.

Eve ran inside.

The orchestra was still playing, Mr. Vogel waving his arms, oblivious to the tendrils of smoke curling around the rafters overhead.

"Mr. Vogel!" she shouted as she hastened down the center aisle. "Mr. Vogel!"

He turned, startled.

She made his side, panting. "The roof's on fire!"

She didn't have to say anything else. Comprehension lit in the composer's dark eyes. He turned to his musicians and clapped his hands. "Out! Now. Ve must leave at once."

He started shooing his orchestra as she turned toward the stage. "Miss Dinwoody! Vhere are you going?"

"The dancers!" she shouted back, not bothering to stop.

Behind the stage the alarm had already been given. Half-dressed dancers and actors raced toward the doors.

Eve caught sight of Polly, her hair down about her shoulders as she carried a crying toddler. "Polly! The children—"

"Already outside, ma'am," Polly called back. "Everyone has heard that the theater is on fire. We're all getting out of the theater. Go yourself, ma'am!"

Eve was turning to do just that when she remembered.

Henry—and Dove, if Asa had done as promised and brought the bird in to her desk. Both were still in the office.

Eve whirled and, picking up her skirts, ran to the office. She burst inside, relieved to see Henry already on his feet.

"Come on, boy," she called, crossing to the desk. She picked up Dove's cage. "Come, Henry."

Behind her the door slammed.

Eve started and turned. Something pounded on the door. *What—?*

She carried Dove's cage across the small office and tried to open the door.

Tried and failed.

The handle twisted easily enough, but the door was jammed or blocked.

Smoke began curling under the door...

ASA STOOD SQUINTING at the newly painted wooden maze. "Damn me, you were right—it does look just like marble."

"And it'll hold," Apollo said in his rasping voice. "At least until the hedge grows up around it properly."

"Well done." Asa slapped his friend on the shoulder. "I think you've done the near-impossible and restored the garden in only one season."

"As much as can be done." Apollo shrugged broad shoulders. "I shall have to work on it next summer as well, you understand."

Asa grinned. "At least we'll *have* a next summer."

He meant to say more, but a shout came from behind them.

He turned to see Jean-Marie dashing toward them, and behind him...smoke coming from the roof of the theater.

Asa had heard of people's blood freezing in their veins, but until now he'd thought it hyperbole.

Now, though, for a split second, his limbs were entirely turned to ice. He couldn't move.

His fucking theater was on fire.

They'd formed a bucket brigade last time. They'd muscled in water from the Thames, bucket by bucket, man to man, all by hand, Asa standing between a yellow-and-lavender-beribboned footman and a wherryman, heaving for all he was worth until he'd felt as if his arms had been torn from his body and *it all had been for naught.* His theater, the courtyard, the musicians' gallery, the plantings, every fucking thing had burned right down to the ground.

He'd lost it all.

Not again.

"Water!" Asa roared, his throat shredded, and then he ran for the theater. "Get water on the roof!"

Nearby three gardeners threw down their rakes and started running toward the courtyard.

"Move your bloody arses! The theater roof is burning."

He ran toward the courtyard, aware that Apollo and Jean-Marie matched his pace. "Where's Eve?"

"I left 'er 'ere." The footman looked around the courtyard wildly.

It was flooded with shouting men, screaming women, workmen with buckets, dancers running out with costumes in their arms...and no sign of Eve at all.

"Eve!" Asa bellowed. "Eve!"

"She's in the theater!" Polly the dancer shouted, a

screaming child in her arms. "She was right behind me. I told her to get out—"

But Asa was no longer listening. He glanced once at Apollo.

"Go," Apollo said. "I'll take care of the buckets. *Go!*"

And Asa was dashing up the steps of the smoke-filled theater, Jean-Marie on his heels.

Inside the theater the smoke was, thankfully, rising to the rafters. Asa and Jean-Marie barreled down the main aisle. Asa vaulted to the partially rebuilt stage, not waiting to see if the footman was still with him. The corridors behind the stage were filled with billowing smoke.

Asa ducked, thrusting his arm over his face as the best barrier he had. "Eve!"

He listened and suddenly heard a pounding.

"Eve!" He raced toward the office they shared. What was the bloody woman doing? "Eve!"

The door was shut and Asa rushed to open it . . . but the damned thing wouldn't budge.

"Asa!" Eve's voice came from within the room.

He placed his mouth close to the wood. "Unlock the door, luv!"

"I didn't lock it. It's stuck."

Asa could feel sweat sliding down his spine. The smoke was thickening. He had the key and he took it from his pocket, jamming it in the lock.

It turned easily, but when he pulled, the door still stuck.

"It's been nailed shut," Jean-Marie shouted behind him, pointing to a series of nails along the upper edge of the door.

Asa swore and, after backing a step, ran his shoulder into the door, feeling the shock of impact down to his bones.

The door shook but didn't open.

Christ! Asa coughed as sweat ran in his eyes, stinging them. "Together."

They backed a step and then both he and Jean-Marie rammed against the door in unison, making the entire frame shake again. The door held firm.

Beside him Jean-Marie grunted, and Asa glanced over to see him holding his right arm with his left hand.

Shit.

The damned thing looked dislocated.

Asa was stepping back again, determined to break the fucking door down *alone* if need be, when he heard a shout and turned and stared.

Malcolm MacLeish was there in the corridor with a wet cloth over his mouth and nose. He removed it only to say, "This way!"

Asa gave him an incredulous look.

The architect scowled. "Do you want to save Miss Dinwoody or not? Come with me!"

MacLeish disappeared around the corner.

"God's balls!" What was the architect up to? Asa rounded the same corner to find MacLeish opening... Asa blinked. MacLeish was opening a door in the corridor paneling that simply hadn't been there before.

The architect ducked through the door.

"What the buggering hell?" Asa growled.

He followed and found himself in a second corridor *inside* the wall. It was so tight he had to sidle through.

"Asa!" He could still hear Eve's frantic shouts, and the sound put him on edge.

They crept perhaps ten feet down the strange passageway until Asa saw a pinprick of light at eye height coming from the inner wall.

"Here." In the dim light he saw MacLeish place his palm on the wall. "Your office is behind here. I just need to—" The architect bent and did something and suddenly a square panel popped out of the wall at knee height.

Asa shoved MacLeish aside. "Eve!" She was on her knees, already crawling through the space, the bloody dove cage in one hand.

"Come, Henry," she said as she rose, and suddenly the too-small passage was made even more cramped by the entrance of a huge mastiff.

Asa took Eve's hand—slim and warm and *alive*—in his and led her back out the way they'd come, Henry and MacLeish following.

Jean-Marie was waiting in the corridor when they emerged. "*Bon*. We must leave."

Was it his imagination or had the smoke gotten worse?

He gripped Eve's hand tight and ran through the smoke-filled theater, dog and dove and all. He shoved open the outer door and dragged her into the fresh air.

"Oh!" Eve exclaimed, and he turned to find that she'd dropped the dove cage. It smashed on the stone steps of the theater and the white dove fluttered free, flying up high above the roof. "Oh, no," Eve whispered.

"I'm sorry, luv," Asa gasped.

The sun shone brightly and he halted, drawing deep, soothing breaths of cool air into sore lungs.

He turned to squint at his roof.

Water was running off it in sheets from the buckets being passed up. Two ladders had been set against the building and several of the workmen clung to them, handing buckets up to other workmen standing on the roof.

"Asa."

Was it enough? He couldn't see the smoke, but fire was a cunning thing, smoldering unnoticed and then blazing suddenly, impossibly anew. If—

"Asa."

He looked finally and found that Eve had her hands wrapped around his arm. She was tugging gently to get his attention.

He scowled. "What are you doing?"

"It's all right, Asa," she said gently, as if speaking to a senile old man. "Lord Kilbourne thinks the fire is out."

Apollo was on his other side now. "It was a small fire, in one of the chimneys. I've sent some of the men up on the roof to inspect it." He shook his head and lowered his voice. "It might've been set."

Asa narrowed his eyes and turned to look at the roof again. The workmen were thoroughly sloshing the water about, but Apollo was right: there wasn't any more smoke.

Eve cleared her throat. "We should go. Jean-Marie's been hurt and I have to get him to a doctor."

He blinked down at her. Eve, *his* Eve—though he had no right to that claim—safe and sound. Someone had locked her in the office.

Someone had tried to *kill* his Eve.

"Not yet." Asa took two strides toward the architect and grasped him by his neckcloth, jerking him close enough to hiss in his face, "Why the *fuck* are there peepholes and hidden passages in my bloody theater?"

EVE HAD NEVER seen Asa so coldly angry. Instead of shouting and violent gestures, Asa was still and very, very quiet. He merely leaned forward to whisper in Mr. MacLeish's ear, "Tell me *now*."

That whisper sent a chill down Eve's spine, and apparently it was enough to frighten Mr. MacLeish into confessing.

"It was Montgomery," he gasped, and Eve closed her eyes.

Of course it had been Val. It seemed every time she turned around her brother was involved in something else nefarious.

Something else she felt shame for, even if he did not.

"Vhat do you mean?"

Eve opened her eyes to see that Mr. Vogel had joined the little circle around Asa and Mr. MacLeish.

Some of the theater folk were lingering, but Lord Kilbourne turned and waved to them. "Let's make sure the fire's out." He strode away, shooing people before him like a giant sheepdog.

"Malcolm?" Mr. Vogel's voice was low but sharp.

Mr. MacLeish closed his eyes and seemed to wilt in Asa's hands. His red hair was darkened and flattened by sweat in contrast to the white of his face and suddenly Eve felt impossible pity for him. "Montgomery insisted on the changed plans. Insisted that they be kept secret from you. I had no choice."

Asa shook him once, hard. "The theater's *mine*. You work for *me*."

"No," Mr. MacLeish snapped back, suddenly brave for a man being held in Asa Makepeace's fist. "I've never worked for you. Montgomery made that very plain when he forced me to work for him. *He's* my master, no one else, and when he told me to build secret tunnels, secret peepholes, I *had no choice*."

He stopped, pale and panting.

"Fuck." Asa let him go suddenly and the architect staggered back. "You're telling me my theater is riddled with peepholes?"

It was Mr. Vogel who said, "Forced you?"

Eve cleared her throat and said in a small voice, "My brother has been blackmailing Mr. MacLeish."

"What?" Asa's head snapped around toward her.

Mr. MacLeish's face paled even more, if that was possible, and he looked absolutely wretched as he stared at the composer. He licked his lips. "Montgomery has letters..."

Mr. Vogel's eyes narrowed. "You let yourself be *blackmailed*?"

"You don't understand." Mr. MacLeish took two steps to stand in front of Mr. Vogel and Eve felt suddenly like a voyeur. "There was another involved. I couldn't let him be—"

"So you became a slave instead."

Mr. MacLeish's head reared back as if the composer had slapped him across the face. "I'm no slave. *Hans...*"

Mr. Vogel lifted a contemptuous hand and turned without waiting for the other man to finish his sentence.

Eve felt very, very sorry for Mr. MacLeish.

"Why the bloody fuck would Montgomery want to put peepholes in my theater?" Asa asked quietly.

Mr. MacLeish actually backed a step. "I...I don't know."

"Blackmail," Eve said.

Asa whirled on her. "What?"

She lifted her chin, holding her ground. "That's what Val deals in, what he always wants. Information that he can use to make people do as he wishes." She looked at the theater, big and beautiful, a lovely enticement. "Think of the people who go to your theater—the affairs, the politicians making deals in their boxes, the society ladies whispering gossip." She shrugged sadly. "To Val it would be like a dish of bonbons."

"Jesus. I want them blocked up." Asa turned to MacLeish,

his hands on his hips. "The peepholes plugged, the passageways bricked, do you understand me?"

Mr. MacLeish gulped. "But Montgomery..."

"Leave Montgomery to me," Asa said grimly. "And MacLeish?"

"Y ... yes?"

"I want my theater fixed." Asa glanced over his shoulder. Water still streamed off the theater tiles and everything smelled faintly of smoke. He looked back at Mr. MacLeish. "We open in less than a fortnight. I want it fucking *pristine*."

He took Eve's arm and started striding away.

Eve glanced worriedly at Jean-Marie. He cradled his arm against his chest. Someone had found a bit of cloth to make a sling around his neck, but there were pale indents in the dark skin on either side of his mouth and he was quite obviously in pain. Henry walked with him, the mastiff pressed against her footman's side, and Eve couldn't help a small smile at the dog.

He was so sweet to comfort Jean-Marie.

Asa stopped suddenly, and Eve's attention was jerked around to find a quite extraordinary sight:

Alf was coming toward them, a small pistol held in one hand and pointed at the back of Mr. Sherwood.

Oh, dear, this couldn't be good.

ASA FELT A growl start in his chest at the sight of Sherwood, disheveled and soot-streaked, being marched at gunpoint and quite obviously against his will toward the theater.

"Found 'im trying to leave by the back gate," Alf said, gesturing with his pistol. "Seemed a bit suspicious."

Asa dropped Eve's arm and took two steps toward Sherwood.

Sherwood made a sound like a frightened mouse right before Asa struck him on the chin. The theater manager collapsed in a sprawl of limbs.

Slim fingers caught his arm and Asa looked down to see Eve holding him quite determinedly. *"Stop."*

"He tried to *burn down my fucking theater*," Asa roared.

She didn't even blink, this girl who only a little over a week before had turned tail and run from his violence. "You don't *know* that."

Asa waved one sweeping arm, encompassing the theater and gardens and all. "Then what's he doing here?"

She actually looked exasperated. "Maybe we should ask him."

"Oh, aye, I'll *ask* him," Asa said, standing over the man. He raised his fist.

"Don't hit me again!" Sherwood screeched, hands over his face. "For God's sake, don't hit me."

Asa lifted his upper lip. "Why the hell shouldn't I?"

"You broke my nose last time," Sherwood whined. His nose did look swollen and his eyes were rimmed with faded green bruises.

"And so I'll break it again," Asa said, cocking his arm.

"I wasn't doing anything!"

"You were trespassing," Asa growled. "Right after a fire started in my theater."

"It wasn't me!" Sherwood gasped. "I came to see if I could lure La Veneziana back, nothing more, I swear."

Asa snorted. "And what about my stage? Where were you when it was sabotaged?"

"What?" Sherwood looked honestly bewildered. "I

never did anything to your blasted stage. I wasn't anywhere near your garden when it collapsed. It fell on its own."

"And how do you know about it, then?" Asa roared.

"All of London knows your stage fell in," Sherwood screamed. "It's no reason to hit me again, though!"

Asa stared, disgusted and enraged, down at the little worm. He bent to thrust his face into Sherwood's face. "I. Don't. Fucking. *Believe*. You."

Sherwood went greenish pale. "Wait." He licked his lips. "What if... what if I can tell you who might've done this?"

"I won't believe *that*, either," Asa sneered. "The hell with it. I'm going to beat you to a bloody pulp and then maybe you'll stay away from my garden."

But Eve grasped his arm. *Again.* "Wait." She met his glare with a steady gaze. "Can we at least find out whom he means?"

Asa turned his head slowly back to Sherwood.

"Hampston!" the little man shrieked.

"What?" Eve whispered.

She'd dropped her fingers from Asa's arm, but he caught her hand and held it in his own, giving comfort.

"My... my backer is Hampston." Sherwood licked his lips. "I thought he was going to help me build my own theater here, but that's not what he's after at all."

"What's he after, then?" Asa growled.

"The land." Sherwood nodded rapidly as Asa's eyebrows went up. "I figured it out after I saw a letter from a builder. He wants to construct houses here. He's not interested in the theater at all."

Asa narrowed his eyes.

"And... and if he's not interested in Harte's Folly or

the gardens, well…" Sherwood shrugged jerkily. "Makes sense he might just try to burn you out."

It did make sense—a horrible twisted sense. But for the saboteur to be an aristocrat…damn it. Asa didn't have much recourse against a rich, titled man. Hell, he didn't even have any evidence, save for the babbling of a theater rival.

There wasn't much he could do—legally, anyway.

Suddenly Asa was bone-weary.

"Just get up," he said in disgust.

Sherwood looked at him suspiciously. "You're not going to hit me?"

"Not if you get up and leave my bloody garden *right now*," Asa growled. "I am beginning to reconsider, however…"

Sherwood lunged to his feet rather athletically and, with a last frightened glance at Asa, turned and fled.

"Arsehole," Asa muttered.

He felt Eve squeeze his hand.

Beside them Jean-Marie groaned under his breath.

Asa shoved a hand through his hair. "Come on, we need to get you to a bed, Jean-Marie."

Not to mention he needed to find out if Eve was withholding any more secrets about her sweet, darling brother.

Chapter Sixteen

❧

*Eric took the bag without comment—though Dove thought
she saw him smile—and set out again. Before long they
came to a large rock with a hole in the ground beneath it.
"Enchanted mushrooms grow in that hole," Eric said,
"But I cannot reach them, for it is too narrow for my
shoulders."
"Oh, that is easily done!" said Dove, and she wriggled her
way into the hole. When she emerged it was with a bag full
of colorless mushroom caps....*
—From *The Lion and the Dove*

The minute they entered Eve's carriage, Jean-Marie laid his head back against the squabs and set his lips. He made no sound, just silently suffered as the carriage rocked and bumped into motion.

It must be paining him terribly, but without a doctor, Eve wasn't certain what she could do.

Asa sat beside her, staring out the window, and Eve couldn't help wondering if he was brooding.

She cleared her throat. "Do you think Mr. Sherwood was right? That Lord Hampston has been wrecking the garden in order to make you sell?"

"I don't know that I should trust anything that little

prick says," Asa said, but then he shrugged. "It makes as much sense as anything, though."

Eve stared at him. He had a smudge of soot across his cheek and he looked both exhausted and very dangerous. "What will you do?"

He glanced at her, his green eyes gleaming. "If it is Hampston, I'll make him regret the day he was born."

"But..." She licked her lips. "He's a viscount."

His mouth kicked up and he turned back to the window. "And I'm just the disowned son of a beer brewer?"

It was the truth, wasn't it?

His smile wasn't pleasant at all. "There are ways for even plebeian men such as I to find revenge, luv."

Eve swallowed at that and turned her attention to Henry, who was attempting to climb onto the seat cushions, presumably to look out the carriage window. She wondered, a little sadly, if he missed Dove.

She did.

Eve couldn't help a relieved sigh when she stepped down from the carriage in front of her own little house. At last she could get Jean-Marie some help.

Behind her Asa was silent, though his big broad shoulders were beginning to droop.

Eve nodded to herself, making up her mind. She turned to the carriage driver. "Please fetch the doctor who lives around the corner." She gave an address only streets away. "Tell him he must come at once." She looked at Bob, one of the footmen riding the carriage today. "Bob, I'd like you to help Jean-Marie to his bed."

Beside her Jean-Marie made a protest that was so feeble, Eve was even more alarmed.

"At once, if you please," she said to Bob.

He jumped down with alacrity.

"And Bill, please tell Ruth to fill the bathtub in my dressing room."

Bill nodded. "Yes, ma'am." He trotted up the front steps.

He had been gone only moments when the front door flew open again and Tess came running down the steps, her face so white the freckles on her cheeks stood out like spots of blood.

Jean-Marie held out his good arm. "Do not fret, *ma chérie.*"

Eve watched as Tess and Bob helped Jean-Marie up the steps.

Then she turned to Asa.

"Come," she said, and led him, big and prowling, to her sitting room. Henry trotted after them cheerfully.

They ate a simple dinner of fish and potatoes—the supper Tess had already had warming in the kitchens—as Ruth filled the bathtub and reported on the progress of the doctor.

Afterward Eve went down and consulted with the doctor, a young man in a white bobbed wig.

He darted sharp dark eyes at her as he washed his hands in the kitchen. "The shoulder was dislocated and I set it. It's bound now, but your man must rest or it may fall out of the socket again. A week in bed at the very least."

Eve's eyes had widened in horror when he'd mentioned the bone falling back out of the socket, and she fervently assured the doctor that she and Tess would be sure to keep Jean-Marie bedbound.

She paid him and climbed the stairs back to her rooms.

When she entered she found Asa eyeing the steaming tub as he took off his shoes. "Damn me, that looks good."

She nodded and then hesitated. She should leave him to it, give him some privacy, but this was the man who had held her so tenderly the night before.

Was it so wrong to want to tend to him in return?

Matter-of-factly she went to him and helped him out of his coat, then laid it neatly on a chair.

She bent to unbutton his waistcoat, aware of the warm body beneath the gaudy silver brocade. He stood silently, his chest rising and falling with his breaths as she worked, and she felt herself begin to heat. He shrugged out of the waistcoat and tossed it to the chair.

She untied and unwound his cravat, pulling it from his neck. His white linen shirt was laced and her fingers trembled as she picked at the laces. How much more time would she have with him? She wanted—oh, she wanted much more than she thought he might want to give.

She wanted forever, really, with him.

He looked at her and then stepped back to pull the shirt off over his head. Swiftly he took off stockings, breeches and smallclothes, and then . . .

And then he stood before her entirely nude.

He watched her, silent, an amused gleam in his eye, as she stared at him, and then he gracefully stepped into her hip bath.

It was nearly too small for him. He had to fold his knees almost to his chin to sit, and some of the water slopped over the edge, soaked up by the linens lining the tub.

He let his head fall against the high back, his tanned neck elongated, his small brown nipples just at the waterline. His shoulders more than spanned the tub's width, and he let one arm hang over the edge. She looked at him and wished suddenly that she had her sketchbook. That she could draw him like this and keep the sketch forever as a memento of this intimate moment.

Years from now she knew she would look back at this time and wonder if it had all been a dream.

Without speaking Eve picked up a small cloth and, after dipping it in the hot water, laid it over his shoulders, slowly rubbing back and forth.

He groaned quietly deep in his throat. "God, that feels good."

She wetted the cloth in the hot water again and ran it down his arm, marveling at the vein that trailed along the muscle of his upper arm. She rubbed the cloth over his forearm and to his hand—so much larger than hers. Carefully she turned his hand over to wash his calloused palm and between each finger.

When she went to wet her cloth again she saw that he was watching her with half-lidded eyes, green gleaming slits, and she shivered in anticipation. She walked to his other side and rubbed the hot wet cloth over his neck and shoulder and down his arm, stopping to take his hand in hers, measuring her palm against his for a moment before she washed it.

When she was finished she leaned to dip the cloth in the tub again, but never got the chance to do so.

He grabbed her shoulders and pulled her against his wet naked chest before kissing her full on the mouth.

ASA PULLED EVE into his arms, uncaring if he drenched her dress with his bathwater. She tasted of the wine they'd drunk at dinner and herself—pure Eve. Sweet and tart, the most complicated woman he'd ever known in his life.

The most fascinating.

She'd frightened him this afternoon, locked in his

office, the prospect of fire destroying her scowls and smiles, her quick retorts, her prim looks of reproach. The mere thought had nearly made him panic. He'd been ready to use his body to knock down that door, to batter himself into unconsciousness to free her.

Now the memory of that visceral fear made him clutch her much too tightly. He couldn't lose his Eve, his sweet harpy. Even when she left him, he'd sleep at night knowing she was somewhere in the world, alive and petting a mangy mastiff with delicate lady's fingers.

Eve. *His* Eve.

She was here with him now, all prim and proper, as he ran wet hands over the bodice of her dress, leaving lewd handprints.

He needed to ask her questions. Needed to find out what her brother planned for his garden. But for once he needed something more urgently than his business.

He needed Eve.

"Eve." He broke their kiss, his wet mouth sliding down her neck, the water splashing as he moved to grip her waist. "Eve, let me make love to you."

And she smiled at him, secret and bittersweet, and said, "Yes, please."

YEARS FROM NOW, when Eve lay in a lonely spinster's bed, she would think of this moment and weep for all she had lost. But now, right now, her sleeves growing wet from the bathwater, her breath caught behind her stays, she would live and enjoy this man.

This wonderful man.

She looked down at him, nude and wet in her bath, and felt a kind of feminine power. Then she straightened, pulling away from his clutching hands. She stood and yanked free her fichu, unlaced her bodice, kicked off her slippers. She looked at him frankly as she pulled off her bodice and untied her skirts, letting them drop. He reached out an arm when she stood in only stays and chemise, but she shook her head and backed up a step. She slowly unlaced her stays, feeling her breasts expand. She pulled the stays off over her head and then held out a hand to him.

He took it and stepped from the bathtub, the water sliding in a stream down his body. Oh, he was glorious! He was everything she'd suspected—and feared—that first morning. His shoulders so wide, his chest swirled with wet, dark hair, his hips slim, and his sex framed by the V of muscle that ran from the sides of his belly to his groin. His cock bobbed wetly, the foreskin already pulled taut under the head. His thighs were long and bulged with muscle, and even his feet were large and hairy.

This man wanted *her*, and that would be the thing that surprised her to her dying day.

She went to him and wrapped her arms over his broad, slippery shoulders, pulling his head down to hers. She kissed him like a woman, fearless and frank, letting him know how very much she wanted him.

Her chemise was immediately soaked, plastered against both him and her, and her nipples peaked. She could feel the hair of his chest rasping against her breasts even through the wet fabric.

His knee pressed between her thighs, bunching the linen against her woman's place, spreading her and rubbing into her folds.

She found herself undulating against that knee, pleasuring herself with his hard, hot, wet body.

"Eve." He bent and picked her up suddenly, holding her easily as he walked naked from her dressing room to her bedroom like a conqueror with a prize. "Eve."

He tumbled them both onto her bed, lying beneath her. She sprawled on him, straddling him, her legs wide as she found that she could press her open cunny against him.

"Eve," he rasped. "Have you any idea—any idea at all? I've dreamed of these nipples, longed for your naked belly, your arse in my hands." He squeezed her buttocks in his big palms.

"Have you?" she whispered, honestly curious.

She shifted until his cock was under her. She rubbed herself against him, using his hard flesh to pleasure herself.

He arched under her, this big strong man. The tendons of his neck stood out; he flung wide his arms and clutched at the bedclothes. "Eve, what you do to me."

She watched him and slowly reached down to pull her sodden chemise up, up over her belly, over her breasts, over her head, undulating on him all the while.

"Let me," he gasped, his green eyes nearly black. "Let me come inside you."

She lifted herself in silent invitation and he grasped his cock, holding it upright, pushing the head through her wet folds.

She gasped as she found the right placement, as she began to push down.

"Slow, darling," he whispered. "Slow. Don't hurt yourself. Ah, Eve, I couldn't bear it if you hurt yourself on me."

She felt the pressure of his head against her entrance and it seemed an impossible act to fit him inside her, but she wanted it.

She wanted it with all her soul.

So she pressed, squirming, and he widened her slowly, slowly squeezing in. She threw back her head, half impaled, yearning, wanting, waiting to be made complete.

He held his hands on her hips, but made no move to urge her on. He simply lay there and accepted her. Let her move at her own pace. Made himself the sacrifice for her virginity.

She gasped, pivoting her hips, and looked down at him.

Sweat beaded his upper lip, but he smiled tightly up at her. "You're doing it, sweetheart. It's all up to you."

She took a breath, lifting herself a little.

And shoved down as hard as she could, embedding his cock deep inside her.

He threw back his head, his teeth bared and gritted. "Damn me, Eve, did you hurt yourself?"

"No." She shook her head and reached up to unpin her hair.

He watched her under half-closed eyes, his chest heaving. "You're killing me, luv. Slaying me cut by beautiful cut. I'll bleed away and die happy under you, Eve, my darling."

She flung aside the pins and spread her hair on her shoulders. Then she placed her palms on his chest, right over his nipples, and rose up. Oh, the slide of his cock inside her! It was a pleasure so deep it was nearly pain and she ground back down again, closing her eyes, savoring this purely physical joy.

Except it wasn't purely physical, was it? The thought that it was Asa inside her, Asa driving his hips up into her now, Asa begging her to go faster...oh, that was the addicting thought. She wanted to ride him, wanted to hide him away in her bedroom, to use only for herself.

She was jealous of every woman who had come before her. Had used this wonderful penis. Had heard his groan.

She opened her eyes. But it was the women who would come after that she truly wanted to kill.

He was hers. He should never share this part of himself with anyone else.

She threw back her head, riding him hard, the sweat sliding down between her breasts. He lurched up, half sitting, his arm propping him up, and licked the sweat from her body.

She cried out, gasping, holding his head to her even as he sucked one nipple into his mouth. She felt the pull, felt the answering gush, and knew she was falling apart, spreading outward, a star exploding.

He gasped and let go of her breast, bowing his head to her chest, his hair wild and tangled against her as he groaned and shook.

She felt heat inside her and rose one last time, spreading wide her thighs, shoving him as deep inside her as she could.

Trying to keep him forever.

It was late that night when Bridget held high her candle and walked the halls of Hermes House, checking the rooms.

She shivered. She'd worked in many houses, both great and small, since becoming a housekeeper. She specialized in finding a place of employment, discovering how it might best be run, fixing it so that the household ran like finely tuned clockwork, and then moving to her next situation.

Some of the houses she'd served had been in ill repair,

having been run badly by previous housekeepers and butlers. Some were unused, empty and echoing, the family not in residence as she did her work, making the house run smoothly and efficiently.

In no other home had Bridget felt such a coldness as she did in Hermes House. It was more than a lack of warmth. It was as if cold had settled in and taken up residence in this place. Making such a home homey was a daunting task indeed. Bridget could make sure Hermes House was shined and polished. That the maids rose promptly at five of the clock to black the grates and lay the fires. That the footmen's livery was clean and immaculate.

What she found harder was imparting *warmth*—the feel of comfort and home—to a place that had never had it.

She sighed and turned to retrace her steps.

And nearly shrieked when she found Alf standing behind her.

Alf grinned at her and Bridget was sorely pressed not to snap at her.

Oh, yes, she wouldn't have minded telling the *girl* that some were not so easily deceived by her disguise.

But that would have been needlessly cruel, and Bridget was familiar with the urge to hide one's true self in order to be safe.

So she contented herself with a disapproving stare. "Yes?"

"Got 'Imself's letter," Alf replied cheerfully, waving a scrap of paper about.

Bridget raised her eyebrows. Miss Dinwoody had only sent her letter to her brother the day before.

But perhaps this one was not in reply but instead had

been sent earlier. "You'd best take it to Miss Dinwoody, then, hadn't you?"

Alf stopped waving the letter. She glanced around the darkened hall. "*Now?* Kind o' late, innit?"

"Late it might be, but Miss Dinwoody should have the letter as soon as is possible."

Alf sobered. "All right."

And she was off, clattering down the stairs to the lower level.

Bridget stared after her thoughtfully and then continued on her way to the duke's bedroom. She entered it and went straight to the portrait of Montgomery, holding high her candle to examine it.

She wasn't sure why, but this portrait in which he was almost entirely nude seemed more true to the man's personality than the one in the stairwell, in which he was wearing silks, fur, and velvet. It was as if, stripped of the trappings of his wealth and rank, he revealed the savage animal beneath.

He lounged in the painting, his white skin nearly pearly, watching the viewer with amused blue eyes, his golden hair loose upon his shoulders. His gaze seemed to taunt the viewer, as if to say, *Here I am, cock bared, nipples tight. I'm laid bare for your eyes, but* I'm *the one who rules, not you.*

The arrogance of his nudity merely enforced his power.

Bridget cocked her head, slowly and deliberately examining the duke's naked beauty.

Then she whispered, "What are you up to, I wonder?"

Chapter Seventeen

At midday Eric stopped and, sitting on a fallen log, took
out a packet of bread and cheese. "I suppose you'll be
wanting some of my luncheon as well?"
"If you don't mind," Dove said apologetically.
He merely grunted and broke both the bread and cheese in
two, and Dove thought it possibly the most delicious meal
she'd ever eaten.
Afterward they continued their journey until at last they
came upon a ruined cottage.
Eric stopped and looked grim. "Best you be silent and let
me do the talking."
And then they went in. . . .
—From *The Lion and the Dove*

Eve lay quietly, tiredly on Asa's chest, his penis still within her, and felt peace.

Beneath her cheek his chest shuddered from his release and his hot breath stirred her hair.

She felt his cock soften and slip from her body and for a moment she remembered that he'd spent in her. That he might've planted the seed of a child within her.

She should've felt fear at the possibility. Instead all she felt was a wild joy. Oh, let him have given her a child! If he had, then she would have someone of her own when at last they parted. She was a bastard of one of the most notorious aristocrats England had ever produced. She had no reputation to destroy.

But she was lonely—she could admit it now. She needed something—*someone*—more than a stray dog and three servants.

Eve propped her arms on his chest and watched him, his thick lashes resting on his cheeks. He looked so tired. He'd been working nonstop since she'd met him, always worried about his gardens.

He, too, had no one of his own. Did he want someone?

If he did, he hid it well beneath declarations that the garden was the only important thing in his life. Eve wondered if he knew himself if he needed someone.

Perhaps he didn't.

At that moment Asa opened his eyes, green and glazed with weariness, and she said, unable to stop herself, "Your garden is everything to you."

He didn't even look surprised at her words. Perhaps it was always on his mind, Harte's Folly, even when he lay in bed with a woman.

"Yes," he said. "It's my food, my drink, my air."

The words were said simply, stated like a fact: the sky is blue; Harte's Folly is Asa Makepeace's air.

She rolled to lie beside him. "I'm sorry."

He turned his head to look at her, puzzled, maybe a little affronted. "*Sorry*? Why? It's beautiful, the most wonderful place in—"

"London, I know." She shrugged. "And it is, a truly magnificent place. But I and every other person in London can go and see the gardens and then go home again. You can't."

He didn't say anything to that, simply watching her

with wary green eyes. Perhaps he already knew what thrall the gardens held him in.

She hesitated, then said low, "I saw what the fire today did to you. I was afraid that you wouldn't survive if the gardens burned again and the theater was destroyed."

There was silence in the bedroom, and then he said, "You're being melodramatic."

"Am I?" She traced the edge of his nipple. "I've come to know you, Asa Makepeace, over the last weeks. You're hotheaded, stubborn, willful, not always correct, but entirely certain of your course. Sometimes you frighten your theater folk with your roaring, but they adore you anyway. You're kind to animals and small children, and you're intelligent, brave, and driven." She paused, looking at him. "I like you; I might even, given the chance, love you." She was watching him, so she saw the flicker of alarm in his green eyes. She shook her head. "But I won't let myself, since that's not what you want. But *you*, Asa, you deserve more than a *business* in your life."

"Deserve?" he scoffed. "You make it sound like I'm a martyr to the garden."

She smiled a little sadly then. "Aren't you?"

"*No.*" His eyes narrowed then. "What about you, then?"

She blinked. "What do you mean?"

He waved a hand around her bedroom. "Perhaps you should worry more for yourself than me."

She pulled back, feeling hurt.

But he'd hit his mark and wasn't afraid to stab deeper. "What do you have besides your house, your servants, and a brother you're insanely devoted to?"

She gasped. "I love Val—"

"Why?" He sat up, uncaring of his nudity. "Montgomery uses you as he uses every other person in his life. Does he even love you?"

"Yes." Why was he doing this? Digging into her life, her secrets?

"Because he gives you money and a house?" Asa sat in her bed, big and male and entirely out of place here in her feminine room, and made these nasty accusations as if he had every right.

"No." Her voice was raised, but she couldn't stop herself. "No. He loves me. He's the *only* one who has ever loved me. He was there when—"

She stopped, the words swelling, blocking her throat.

For a moment there was silence as he stared at her as if assessing her.

Then he abruptly pulled her into his warm, strong arms.

He stroked the hair back from her face, and said, *"Tell* me."

It was time.

She inhaled. Where could she start? How could she make him understand? "My father had an estate in the country. Well, several estates, of course, but I grew up at only one—Ainsdale Castle. My mother was nursemaid to Val when he was small. My mother..." She hesitated, for she'd never said it aloud.

She'd never said *any* of this aloud. The secrets she'd grown up with had penetrated her skin, growing within like a bloody, parasitic vine.

"My mother was not entirely right in the head," she said carefully. "She liked to pretend that distasteful things simply didn't exist. I don't know if she consented to the duke's advances or if it was rape, but he kept her for some time. Certainly until I was conceived and then after for a while. I think...no." She took a deep breath. "I *know* that he kept me and my mother in Ainsdale Castle purely to spite his wife, the duchess. Val's mother. She hated the duke and loathed me and my mother. We kept to ourselves mostly, in the nursery wing. Val was there when I was very young, before he was deemed too old for the nursery. Then I saw him only once in a while. I think the duchess tried to keep me from him. I was fed and clothed and educated a bit—the duke even hired a tutor for me for a year or so—but it was cold in that house. So very *cold*."

She was panting now and stopped to catch her breath. This—saying these things—was making her hot. Making her sweat. They said poison could be sweated from a body, and perhaps that was what she was doing:

Sweating the poison of her childhood, her conception, her *life*, from her body.

"He was an evil man, the Duke of Montgomery," Eve whispered, and she was glad that Asa held her, for she wasn't sure she would've been able to say the words out loud otherwise. "He beat servants, raped women. Hurt children."

The hand in her hair stilled for a split second, and then resumed stroking. "Hurt in what way?"

She swallowed. Her throat was closing, cutting off her breath. No one ever talked about it. She wasn't supposed to talk about it.

"Eve," Asa said, his voice deep and calm and *right there*. "Tell me."

She dug her fingers into the muscle of his chest, holding on, making sure she couldn't be flung loose from him. "He belonged to a secret society. They called themselves the Lords of Chaos. I think...I think they identify themselves with the tattoo—of a dolphin. Once a year, in spring, they would meet at Ainsdale Castle. The duchess always made sure to absent herself during that time, and they would...would..." She inhaled and said it, like vomiting bile, "They would drink wine and revel for days and days and there would be women and..." She swallowed. "And children."

There was silence in the bedroom. He'd even stopped breathing, and Eve knew suddenly that she'd disgusted him with her revelation of what she'd sprung from.

Of the filth she'd been conceived in.

She pushed, trying to leave his arms, trying to get away from what she was.

What she'd been.

But he only tightened his arms around her, holding her fast, and she realized he was speaking almost sternly. "Hush. Hush now. I'm not leaving you until you tell me everything this time, Eve."

She relaxed all at once then, almost as if his matter-of-factness had calmed her. "There's more."

"Tell me," he ordered.

She licked her lips, bracing herself. "Every spring when the duke's club met, my mother would hide me in Ainsdale Castle. Not, you understand, in a secret passage or room. She just locked us away in the nursery and we would pretend we didn't hear the sounds coming from without." She shivered. "Sometimes the sounds were horrible."

He stroked the hair back from her face, saying nothing.

She inhaled. "But one spring he came for me. The duke. He said I should be part of his...festivities. So I was dressed in a new frock, my hair put up, and I went down-stairs to dine with them all, lords and ladies and women from the street, and children too scared to cry. All the men were wearing masks. Terrible masks, in the shapes of horrid animals—strange dogs and leopards and baboons—all except the duke. He wore a plain mask, of a beautiful man with grapes in his hair. The food was exquisite but I couldn't eat. I was afraid I would vomit it back up."

He pulled her closer, his big chest a warm, safe haven.

"But the duke said I should drink wine so I had a glass and sipped from it. Later there was dancing and music and... it was very loud and some of the ladies took off their clothes. Some of the lords as well—all but their awful masks. And then the duke let loose his hunting dogs in the hall."

"Jesus."

She swallowed, her breaths fast and shallow. She had to finish this and then perhaps she would forget it finally. Never think of it again.

Never dream of it anymore.

"The dogs leaped toward me and the children and we ran, for we could do nothing else. Behind I could hear someone sounding a hunting horn and one of the children fell. The dogs attacked her and there was blood—so much blood that I don't know if..." She gulped air. "I kept running. I thought perhaps if I could get to the nursery I could lock the door behind me. I ran and ran, up the stairs, holding my heavy skirts away from my feet. But the hall was dark—all the candles put out by the duke's order—and I became turned around. I ran into a hall and realized I was cornered. When I turned the dogs were already on me. I thought they would tear me limb from limb. They were barking madly, foam dripping from their jaws, and I could smell their breath. But one of the masked men laughed and called them away. He was wearing a hound's head. He said that I was his now. That he'd caught me like a hare and now he would feast. He..."

Her breath caught on a sob. Asa framed her face with his big palms and brought his forehead to hers, as if he was trying to give her his own strength.

"He ripped my new dress," she whispered, her breath mingling with Asa's. "He threw up my skirts and put his hands on me, forced my legs apart, and put his fingers in me. It burned. It hurt so much and I screamed. He slapped me, and my head spun and I saw blood. The man had blood on his mask, on his clothes, in his hair. I thought that he was the devil and that he would kill me. But then a miracle happened. Val was there. My brother took hold of the man's shirt and threw him from me. He chased the bloody masked man away and then Val picked me up and took me. I don't remember where, but I was safe. Val saved me. The next day he sent me to Geneva."

"Thank *God*," Asa whispered, kissing her face, holding her cheeks with his big palms. "Thank God for your vain, crazy, loyal brother."

"You see," Eve gasped. "You see why I love him? Why I owe him everything?"

"Yes," Asa said. "I think I might love the bastard myself."

She almost laughed at that, but then he was kissing her and the memories fled as she opened her mouth beneath his. He kissed her as if he were giving her back life and love and happiness. As if he were all that was right in the world and he meant to share it with her.

There was a rap at her bedroom door and Ruth's voice called, "Pardon me, miss, but Alf is 'ere with a letter from your brother."

"Oh." Eve tumbled from the bed, searching for her wrap. "Tell Alf I'll see him in my sitting room."

"Yes, ma'am."

She whispered to Asa, "I won't be long," as she pulled her wrapper about herself.

Then she slipped into the hallway.

Alf was locked in a staring contest with Henry when she entered the sitting room.

"Is it true?" Eve asked. "You have a letter from my brother?"

"Yes, ma'am," Alf said gruffly, holding out the letter.

Eve took it and opened it with a letter opener, then held it close to a candle so she could read it.

The letter was short and to the point:

Viscount Hampston was the man that night.

There was no signature, but Eve knew Val's handwriting well enough. She drew in a breath, and as she did, behind her Asa's voice suddenly growled,

"I'll kill him."

EVE STARTED AND turned to look at him, but Asa was examining the letter. "When did you send a query to your brother?"

Eve frowned. "Yesterday."

"How did this arrive so soon? I thought Montgomery was on the Continent?" He glanced at the boy.

Who shrugged. "I just delivers 'em."

Asa grunted and threw the letter down. "Hampston's a danger to you. I'm going after him."

"He's a viscount," Eve said, her voice very small. "You can't attack him. You *can't*, Asa."

That remained to be seen, Asa thought grimly, but he

didn't want to distress her any more tonight. "Hush. He'll not be allowed anywhere near you in any case."

"I really don't think he's planning on hurting me," Eve said slowly. Her brows were knit as she stared at the letter. "He didn't make any move against me when he saw me in the garden."

"He kept asking if you *remembered* him," Asa growled. The mere memory made him want to hit something. "*Bloody hell.* I need to dress."

He turned to stride back down the hall to her bedroom and the rest of his clothes—he'd thrown on only shirt and breeches to come to the sitting room.

"You can't go." Eve had followed and she stared at him from the bedroom doorway, looking betrayed. "Now? It's the middle of the night. We were *attacked* last time we traveled at night." She held out her hands, palms uppermost. "Stay. Just for the night. Stay, Asa."

He couldn't help it, he looked toward the door. He felt torn. He wanted to stay with her, wanted to protect her. He turned to her. "Damn it, Eve."

She looked at him—just looked at him. "Don't leave me."

He closed his eyes and felt the sweat on his back. What if Hampston fled in the night? What if the bastard got away and continued to haunt Eve?

But she was looking at him with wounded blue eyes and he couldn't turn away from her. "I'll stay."

"Thank you," she said simply. She inhaled and waved to the door. "Let me write back to my brother—a short note only—and I'll send Alf on his way."

Asa followed her back into her sitting room, reluctant to let her out of his sight now.

The boy was still lounging against the wall as if he was used to waiting on lover's tiffs.

Eve went to her table as they both watched her, and swiftly penned a letter before sanding and sealing it.

She handed the sealed letter to Alf. "Be careful in the streets."

Alf looked contemptuous. "Nobody bothers me, ma'am— 'specially if they don't see me."

And he left.

Eve shook her head. "He's very self-reliant, but he's also very young. I worry about Alf sometimes."

Then she looked at Asa and smiled, though the smile was tinged with sadness. She held out her hand to him. "Come to bed."

"I HAVE HIM," Alf announced three days later from the doorway to the Harte's Folly office.

Eve started and glanced up from her desk. She had been rather deeply immersed in the accounts.

"Have who?" Asa asked sharply, across from her.

He'd been as surly as a lion with a thorn in its paw for the last several days, all because he couldn't find Hampston. The viscount seemed to have disappeared or at least left London, which Eve was secretly and rather shamefully relieved by.

She didn't want Asa arrested, or, worse, killed by the aristocrat.

Alf gave him an impatient look. "The agent."

Eve frowned, confused.

But Asa stood from his table. "Hampston's agent?"

Alf grinned. "The same."

He leaned out into the hall and jerked his chin at someone. Mr. Vogel and Mr. MacLeish frog-marched a man into the room. He was quite an ordinary man—slight, but not small, dressed in a workman's clothes—but his eyes were angry and scared.

"This is Oldman," Alf said. "Least that's the name 'e gave. I found 'im this morning underneath the new stage tryin' to light a barrel of gunpowder."

Without saying a word, Asa took two strides and struck Oldman in the face so violently, the man was torn out of Mr. Vogel's and Mr. MacLeish's hands and thrown against the wall.

Eve sighed. "I'm not sure how that helped."

"It helped *me*," Asa said, shaking his hand. "I feel better now." He bent, addressing the fallen man. "When did bloody Hampston hire you?"

"Dunno what yer talkin' 'bout," the man on the ground said.

"Viscount 'Ampston," Alf drawled. "You told me not five minutes ago that's 'oo paid you. Are you changing your tune now?"

Asa raised his fist.

"No!" Oldman sighed. " 'Twas 'Ampston who paid me true enough."

Asa straightened and slowly smiled at her. "We have a fucking witness."

Eve smiled in return. "You'll take the viscount to court?"

Asa shook his head decisively. "Me against an aristocrat? Not bloody likely. The court probably won't even see me. But I have a few friends." He glanced at Eve. " 'Pollo for one. His brother-in-law is the Duke of Wakefield. With a witness to what Hampston planned—what he *did*—against my gardens, perhaps he'll hear my case."

Eve frowned. "But what can the Duke of Wakefield do?"

Asa grinned, quick and sly. "What can't he do? He's near the most powerful man in England." He shrugged. "And if the duke won't help me, well. As I've said, I'm not averse to punishing the viscount myself."

Her heart constricted at the thought of him putting himself at risk. "Try the duke first."

He cocked a wry eyebrow at her as if he knew her thoughts. "As you wish." Asa grabbed the man's collar and hauled him up. He glanced at Alf, Mr. MacLeish, and Mr. Vogel. "You three come with me. You can serve as witnesses as well— you heard him confess." He frowned then as he looked at Eve. "Damn it, I forgot you haven't Jean-Marie with you."

"I have Henry," Eve replied impatiently.

The mastiff thumped his tail at the sound of his name.

Asa looked doubtfully at Henry. "I don't like leaving you alone."

Eve rolled her eyes. "It's the middle of the day and I'm hardly alone—there're people everywhere."

Asa hesitated and then, when Oldman wriggled, seemed to make up his mind. He shook the saboteur hard. "We won't be long. Stay here with Henry. Don't leave the theater, and—"

See touched her fingers to his warm lips. "Go on. I've got the books to finish here."

And then they were gone.

Eve slowly sank back into her chair, worrying her lip. Hampston was a titled aristocrat—a much more power-ful man than Asa—and possibly more underhanded. Even with the Duke of Wakefield's help he might not prevail. She sighed and looked down at Henry.

The big dog got up and came over to put his huge head in her lap, echoing her sigh.

Eve scratched him behind his ear. "Do you miss your friend Dove, too, Henry? I know I do."

Henry gave her a long mournful look before snorting and returning to his bed.

She shook her head and bent to her accounts books again, though it was many minutes before she could concentrate enough to read her figures.

When Eve first heard the growling an hour later, she didn't know what it was.

Henry had never growled before.

She looked up and stared at Henry.

The mastiff was standing beside her desk, the short fur along his spine on end. And he was making the most awful rumbling sound in his throat.

Eve might've been frightened of Henry save for the fact that he was facing the door.

She swallowed, watching as the door handle turned, and she wasn't entirely surprised to see that it wasn't Asa standing there when the door opened.

It was Viscount Hampston.

"Oh, dear," Lord Hampston said mildly. "I think I no longer need to ask if you remember me, sweet Eve. Your expression tells all."

Eve stood, placing her hand on Henry's head. "I do remember you, my lord, and I think you had better go. Mr. Harte knows it was you who was behind the sabotage at Harte's Folly and the highwaymen who attacked us the other night. He's gone to get help from the Duke of Wakefield and will be back at any moment with soldiers to arrest you." A small lie, but she felt it was justified, considering the circumstances.

"Will he?" Lord Hampston asked almost carelessly.

He shut and locked the door behind him. "I must confess that works perfectly with my plans. But I think we have a little time together before that happens." He cocked his head, smiling at her loathsomely. "Now tell me. How did you recognize me? I'm quite curious, for I wore a mask that night."

Eve opened her mouth and then closed it, dread flooding her limbs. What was he about? "Your voice. And you have a tattoo."

"This?" He pulled back his sleeve and turned his wrist to reveal the little dolphin. "We all have one, you know." He winked. "Even your father." He pulled down his sleeve again. "Though not all wear the tattoo on their wrist. It's the mark of the Order of the Lords of Chaos and we're all powerful, my dear."

"But *why*?" She was in danger, she knew, but she had to ask the question. Why had they taken such delight in inflicting pain? It seemed almost inhuman. "Why did you—why did all of them—do those things?"

He cocked his head and, disconcertingly, grinned. "Why not? We're the Lords. We do as we wish at our annual revelry." He shrugged. "You were merely one of many sacrifices. You ought to take it as an honor, really."

An *honor*? That horror? Eve physically recoiled, clutching at the ruff of Henry's neck to steady herself.

Henry barked, sharp and loud.

Lord Hampston laughed. "Oh, dear, I can see I've shocked you. Well, it's time, anyway." He tapped his covered wrist roguishly. "I'm supposed to kill you merely for telling you about this, but that's not the main reason I'll do it."

Eve licked her lips, glancing at the locked door. "What do you mean?"

The smile fell from his face so suddenly it might never have been there. "I mean that I want Harte's Folly, and since my men have been utterly incompetent in trying to burn the theater, wreck the stage, blow the place up, or kill you and Harte, I've decided to do the thing myself. When Harte and these soldiers return they'll find you murdered by Harte's own hand. He might be uncommonly lucky, but even he won't be able to escape the hangman's noose for the murder of a duke's sister."

She stared at him a moment before scoffing, "Are you mad? Why would anyone believe that Mr. Harte had killed me?"

"Well, for one I'll be using his letter opener," Lord Hampston said, picking up the item in question from Asa's desk. Eve swallowed as he twirled the brass letter opener. It was in the shape of a dagger and quite sharp. "And for another my spies have informed me that he's spent at least two nights at your house." His eyes widened mockingly. "Once that's known I think it'll be easy enough to believe that he killed you in a lover's quarrel, don't you?"

Chapter Eighteen

Though the outside of the cottage was mean and decrepit,
the inside was a grand and glorious hall with marble floors
and walls of gold. And standing in the hall was the most
beautiful woman Dove had ever seen.
Eric presented her with the bags, but when the sorceress
opened them, the watercress was fine silk, the acorns
were sparkling emeralds, and the mushrooms were
rich perfumes.
The sorceress smiled her approval, but then she
noticed Dove.
"Who is this girl you bring before me, Eric, my pet?" ...
—From *The Lion and the Dove*

Asa heard Eve's scream as he entered the theater with
Vogel and MacLeish on his heels. Halfway to the Duke
of Wakefield's house Oldman had made a further confes-
sion: Lord Hampston had never left London. Not only
was he in town, but he had plans to meet Oldman at the
theater.

Asa had immediately ordered the carriage back.

Now he broke into a run without thinking, feeling a
dreadful sense of déjà vu as he raced through the theater's
back corridors. He found two of the dancers at the office,
pounding on the door.

One of them, Polly, looked up. "It's locked."

Eve screamed again.

Asa didn't bother with the door. He rounded the corner and ran to where MacLeish had shown him the hidden door—the weak spot in the wall.

He backed a step, raised his right leg, and kicked the fucking wall down.

Plaster and wood splinters showered his shoulders as Asa broke into the office. Eve was behind her desk, bent double next to Henry, her cheek covered with blood, and a terrible growling was coming from the dog.

Asa's heart stopped in his chest.

He rushed toward the dog, wrapping his arms around the beast's chest and bodily lifting it away from Eve. He swung to throw the bloody beast on the floor, but Eve's hands were on his arms, staying him.

"No, no!" she shouted in his face. "No, it's not Henry!"

He stopped and stared. Hadn't the dog savaged her?

Then he looked to where she pointed.

Hampston lay moaning on the floor.

"He stabbed Henry," Eve panted, tears tracing through the gore on her cheek. "He was going to attack me and Henry got between us."

Asa looked and saw that the dog was bleeding from the side. Indeed, the animal yelped as he gently set him down.

Hampston made a snakelike move toward the letter opener on the floor, and Eve—quiet, serious Eve—stomped on his hand.

Hampston howled.

Asa sneered and kicked him hard in the head.

The viscount slumped to the floor.

"Oh." Eve's hands flew to her cheeks and Asa saw now

that her fingers were bloody as well—presumably from Henry's wound. "Oh, have you killed him? You'll have to leave the country." Suddenly she burst into tears.

"Hush." Asa took her into his arms. "I'm not going anywhere. Besides," he said more pragmatically, staring down at Hampston, "the viscount's still alive, more's the pity."

"Oh, but what about Henry?" Eve said, turning to her dog.

Henry, brave lad, thumped his tail at the sound of his name.

"I think," Asa said, examining the dog's side, "That the blade hit his shoulder only. It's a shallow cut and he should recover."

"Oh, thank goodness," Eve said. "Oh, thank God he's all right."

"I'd rather thank God *you're* all right," Asa replied, and kissed her fiercely.

A LITTLE OVER a week later Eve watched Jean-Marie gingerly stretch his arm over his head, the movement easy and obviously without pain.

She beamed at him. "I'm so glad that your shoulder has completely healed."

"As am I, *mon amie*," the footman rumbled. He flashed her a white-toothed grin.

They were in her sitting room after a day at the gardens, Jean-Marie on the settee and Eve in the armchair. Asa hadn't returned with her, because the grand reopening of Harte's Folly was tomorrow. When last Eve had seen him he had still been roaring orders to gardeners, workmen, and singers alike. She had no doubt, though, that he would come to her after he considered the work sufficiently done for the night.

He'd slept in her bed every night since the attack on her by Lord Hampston, after all. Nights filled with passion. Nights filled with love—but no declaration of love.

Eve looked down at her hands at the thought, the opal ring Val had given her winking in the candlelight. "I've been thinking..."

"And what is that, *ma petite*?" Jean-Marie cocked his head to the side.

She inhaled and straightened. "I've decided to go to the Continent. To find Val." She nodded at Jean-Marie's arched eyebrows. "Someone has to confront him over what he's been doing. Over blackmailing so many people. I was too much of a coward before. He may not listen to me—he may never listen to me—but I have to at least try."

Jean-Marie nodded gravely. "A wise and honorable decision, *mon amie*. I am very proud of you."

She felt heat climb her neck. Jean-Marie's opinion was very important to her. "Thank you."

He smiled a little sadly. "But I am afraid I will not be accompanying you on this journey."

Eve's mouth fell open. "What? But why?"

"It is time, I think," her bodyguard—her *friend*—said simply. "I 'ave been with you many, many years, *oui*?"

"Over ten years," Eve whispered.

He nodded. "This is so. Remember when I first came to you? How you 'ad so many nights in which you dreamed of terrors?"

She shuddered. The nightmares had plagued her for years. "Yes."

He shrugged. "And now you do not."

"I had three recently," she murmured.

"And that was all." He smiled, broad and wide. "But there is more: you 'ave let a man touch you. You 'ave taken a lover. Even if you should have another terror in the night, I think, *mon amie*, that you will be able to withstand it. Without me. You no longer 'ave need of me."

Her first instinct was to argue—she'd had Jean-Marie by her side for so very long, protecting and supporting her—but then she realized he was right.

She no longer needed him.

Eve looked at her old friend. "I may not *need* you any longer, Jean-Marie, but I *want* you by my side."

"Ah, *ma petite*, it makes me very 'appy, that we should be such good friends as this. But I 'ave another to consider, one—you should forgive me—who holds a more important place in my 'eart. My Tess."

Of course Tess came first for Jean-Marie—Eve had known that must be the case when he'd married her, for Jean-Marie was not a man to take such a step lightly. Still she couldn't prevent a pang of jealousy.

She wished that *she* were first in another's heart.

In Asa's heart.

But that was neither here nor there at the moment. She looked at Jean-Marie. "And what does Tess want?"

"A tavern in the village where she grew up," he said promptly. *"Oui."* He nodded at her startled look. "This is so. 'Er elder brother knows of such a place for sale and she wishes that we go into business with 'im and buy it. She says that she shall cook meat pies and we will call the tavern the Creole." He shrugged. "It will no doubt be quite exotic in a little English village, *non?*"

Eve laughed, for she could see Jean-Marie presiding

over a tavern, handing out ale and gossiping cheerfully with the local villagers. "I think it a wonderful idea, though I will miss you, my friend."

"As I will you, *mon amie*," Jean-Marie replied. "When do you plan to make this trip in search of your brother?"

"I don't know, but soon. I'll stay for the grand reopening of Harte's Folly, and then I'll find a ship to book passage on and leave."

"Ah." Jean-Marie frowned. "You will not be accompanied by Mr. Makepeace?"

"I..." She had to pause and clear her throat, for it had inexplicably closed. She would not weep—not when she had so recently triumphed over her fears. "No, I don't think so."

For a moment he simply looked at her.

And then he leaned forward, his expression urgent. "*Ask* him, *ma petite*. You are a strong woman—a brave woman. Do not let this opportunity slip away because of doubts and fears."

She swallowed, blinking at the tears that had come whether she wanted them or not. "But his garden."

Jean-Marie slapped at the air. "A garden is a wonderful place, but it is not the same as a woman—and the man who does not know this is an *imbécile*."

Eve shook her head, opening her mouth to say more, but then they both heard the knocking at the front door.

Her gaze flew to his.

Jean-Marie nodded, rising from the settee. "Remember what I've said."

And he left to let Asa in.

Eve rose, for she felt at a disadvantage sitting down. She turned to the door, feeling as if she prepared to face an adversary.

Asa opened it and walked in, stopping dead when he saw her face. "What."

She lifted her chin. He looked worn and weary from the long day at the pleasure garden, but at the same time there was a kind of restless energy about him, perhaps a residue of the excitement of the garden's being ready to open tomorrow.

Could she really compete with his life's work?

"I've decided to go to the Continent and find Val. To confront him with the wrongs he's done—the wrongs he's *doing*—in blackmailing others."

His face blanked. "When?"

She took a deep breath. "As soon as I'm able after Harte's Folly reopens."

A scowl immediately convulsed his features. "Why so soon? The garden will only be just opened. You can't leave me—"

"I want you to come with me." Her heart was beating, alive and vulnerable, in her hands when she said it.

He turned away and she felt as if he'd cleaved her in two. "I can't. You know that. I can't."

She took her bleeding heart in her palms and presented it anew. "I don't. The garden is alive again. After tomorrow night you can find another to manage it for a little time while you're gone. I—"

He whirled and slammed his hand down on the back of the settee. "Damn it, Eve, don't ask me to choose between you and my garden!"

"Why not?" she shouted back, uncaring that the rest of the house might hear their argument. Her heart was a bloody mess on the carpet between their feet now. "I have a right, don't I, to mean more than a garden? To be the first in someone's eyes—in *your* eyes?"

"You have every right." He grimaced as if in pain. "*Every* fucking right, Eve. I'm just not that man."

"Then who is?" She stared, incredulous. "Do you want me to go away and find another lover?"

"No!" he roared. "Stay here, damn it." He thrust a hand into his hair and then held it out to her. "*Why*? Why can't we go on as we have been? I with my garden, you in this house."

"Because I deserve more," she said. "I deserve a man who loves me above all else. I deserve a family and happiness."

"Then go!" he growled. "Go off and find this mythical man and spread your legs for *him* if it'll give you what you want."

She took two strides toward him and slapped him, quick and hard, and then her eyes widened as she realized what she'd done. "Oh, I'm sorry."

He turned his face back to her slowly, almost lazily. "I'm not."

And then she was in his arms, his mouth on hers, wild and hot and dangerously close to out of control. He thrust his hand into her hair, holding her head immobile, and ravished her mouth, biting, tonguing, thrusting.

She could feel her center melt, and she wrapped her arms around his shoulders, holding him close as she dragged her mouth away from his. "I want *you*, only you."

"And I want only you," he snarled.

He picked her up and strode to her bedroom, let her fall on her bed, and then straddled her prone body, on all fours like a predator over its kill.

She froze for a moment, staring up at him. His wild tawny hair was hanging over his brow and cheeks, his mouth red and wet from their kiss, his eyes glittering between slitted lids.

He paused. "Too much?"

She shook her head against her pillows. "No. Not enough."

He didn't smile, just looked at her and slowly lowered himself, his big body covering hers. He opened his mouth over hers as he grasped fistfuls of her skirts and yanked them up.

She twined her fingers in his hair, feeling the cool air brush her calves and then her thighs. Her breasts, trapped behind her stays, were pressed into his broad chest.

He thrust his tongue into her mouth as his hand found her center.

"Wet," he rasped into her mouth. "Wet for me."

She moaned and widened her legs, offering herself to him.

One broad finger slid through her slick folds, touching, claiming.

He bit her bottom lip. "You're not leaving London."

She squeezed her eyes shut and slipped a hand between their bodies, fumbling at his falls.

The tip of his finger nudged into her. "Eve."

Two buttons. Three.

"Eve."

She almost had it open.

"Look at me."

She opened her eyes, glaring, and saw his green eyes gaze triumphantly at her as he pushed his thumb against her clitoris.

She moaned, arching up under him, his falls forgotten, her fingers crushed between them.

"Eve, stay with me."

She remembered her hand and how to work it, tearing open his falls and the smallclothes beneath. Her breaths were coming in hot little pants now and she stared up at him as she took him into her fist. She would remember this. She'd remember this until her dying day, she promised herself.

"Ah, Eve," he groaned, his head falling back, his Adam's apple bobbing as he swallowed. He thrust once, convulsively, into her hand, and then he was lifting and spreading her legs, taking his cock out of her hand, thrusting into her.

She gasped, it was so fast. A complete possession.

He rose up over her, his arms straight on either side of her shoulders, and slowly withdrew, his flesh dragging against hers.

He was hot and hard.

She spread her thighs, reveling in this lush feeling, his thrusts blunt and hard now, pounding into her body.

And still he watched her, the green of his eyes slivers of want, demanding something of her. Something she was no longer willing to give, it was just too much.

When at last she came, her breaths hitching and halting, her legs trembling, her sex pulsing with every push of his cock, she watched him. She saw when he gritted his teeth, his lips drawn back in need and pleasure.

He shouted her name, loud in her quiet bedroom, as his big body jerked and plunged and emptied itself in her.

She hadn't answered his demand and she wasn't sure if that meant she'd emerged the victor or he.

Or perhaps, in the end, they'd both lost.

Chapter Nineteen

Eric knelt before the sorceress. "Mistress, she is but a girl
I found wandering the forest."
"In my domain?" asked the sorceress ominously. "Why did
you not slay her at once?"
She placed her bare foot on Eric's neck, bearing him to the
ground with unnatural strength.
But Dove jumped up. "No, do not hurt him!"
And with her shout still ringing in the glittering hall, she
slapped the sorceress full across the face....
—From *The Lion and the Dove*

The next night Harte's Folly reopened, and even if Asa was biased—which he was—it was a fucking grand success.

He stood in one of the boxes—at the back, not the front, for all the boxes on the stage were sold out, thank God. Violetta was on the stage, bedecked in purple and gold and singing like an angel.

"She's wonderful," Eve murmured beside him, her eyes on the stage.

"That she is," Asa replied, though his eyes were on her, not Violetta.

Eve was wearing a new gown tonight, a bright saffron yellow that made her shoulders gleam like pearls in the candlelight. He'd never seen her in anything but gray or brown, and the color—the intense brilliant color—was like the setting for a jewel. She was beautiful tonight, his sweet harpy, a golden goddess bent on leaving him.

He refused to think about that now.

Violetta ended on a shatteringly high note and the entire audience surged to its feet to clap.

Everyone in the box as well, for of course he and Eve weren't alone. First of all there was his family: Silence and her awful pirate husband, Temperance and her murderous-looking aristocrat of a husband, Verity and gentle John Brown, and Winter and elegant Isabel. They were all squeezed into the biggest box he had. Con of course hadn't bothered to sit with him—he'd *said* it was too crowded—and instead had settled on the pit with Rose and the eldest of their children. They seemed to be enjoying the opera well enough, though, even from their inferior seats. John—or possibly George—was cracking walnuts and when his mother wasn't looking, throwing the shells at his twin. A corner of Asa's mouth cocked up. That was a boy to keep an eye on.

Eve's Ladies' Syndicate was here as well, in the next box over, the members crowding into the hallway as the audience got up to leave the theater.

Asa held his arm out to Eve as he escorted her from the box. They were all swept along on a river of the richest and most beautiful people in London—Asa's customers. He looked on in satisfaction as he spotted Violetta's royal duke and several grande dames of society. Tomorrow anyone who had missed tonight would be bitterly regretting it—and clamoring for tickets for the next night.

Asa grinned to himself. A success indeed.

Outside, the moon had risen and the cooler night air was refreshing. Stringed instruments played in the shadows of the pillars surrounding the musicians' gallery. Those who wished to dine claimed tables and curtained alcoves where much more than food would be enjoyed tonight. Others drifted into the gardens along paths lit with strung fairy lights.

Asa pulled Eve aside, into the dimness of the musicians' gallery, and stood with her, watching his family, watching his guests. Overhead a firecracker boomed and then sparkling lights rained down on the crowd as ladies squealed.

"It's beautiful," Eve said, her face tilted toward the stars.

Something grabbed at Asa's gut, low and hard, as he watched her. The fireworks were reflected in her eyes, sparkling and enticing.

Over her shoulder a movement caught his eye as a couple slipped behind a pillar. They bowed together in embrace.

Asa's eyes widened. "Damn me, what the—"

Eve turned to see what he stared at. Malcolm MacLeish and Hans Vogel were wrapped together in a kiss that made Asa consider blushing for the first time in twenty years. "Oh, how nice. I was wondering if Malcolm would ever say anything."

He turned to stare at her in astonishment. "You knew that—?"

"Didn't you?" She arched her eyebrows pointedly. "I think it's wonderful that *they* aren't afraid to show their love—despite the far greater consequences for them should it be known."

No one had ever accused him of being a coward. He frowned. "Eve..."

He didn't have time to reply, though, for Apollo and a pretty dark-haired lady approached.

"Miss Dinwoody, I'd like you to meet my wife, Lily Greaves, Viscountess Kilbourne," Apollo said. "Lily, this is Miss Dinwoody, who has been making sure Asa's books are all in order these last weeks."

Lily Greaves, the former Robin Goodfellow, flashed a vivacious grin as Eve curtsied to her. "And I hear you've set up a child minder for the dancers and singers as well, Miss Dinwoody. How very thoughtful of you."

"Thank you, my lady," Eve replied, her cheeks turning pink. "But it was a practical decision as well—the ladies of the theater can't work if they have no one to mind their children."

"That only makes you all the smarter in my opinion," Lily replied, linking arms with Eve and drawing her aside. "Now tell me what else you plan to change at Harte's Folly."

"Hampston's dead." The rasping voice of Apollo sounded beside him. "Have you heard?"

Asa stared at him. "What?"

Apollo shrugged. "Stabbed in his prison cell, or so it's said."

"Thank God." Asa felt nothing but relief that the man was dead.

The viscount had been in Newgate in the first place only through Wakefield's influence. Hampston had had influential friends, it seemed, and even with the charges against him, it had looked likely that it would be just a matter of time before he was free again.

Asa had resigned himself to having to enact justice by his own hand.

That at least he would no longer have to do.

"I doubt many will mourn him," Apollo agreed. He lifted his head as his wife waved at him. Rose and Temperance had joined her and Eve. "Looks like Lily wants me." He glanced at Asa and suddenly grinned. "Wanted to say congratulations, though. You did it."

"*We* did it." Asa returned the grin, though his felt pallid. "Go to your wife, man."

Apollo nodded and strode away.

"You're a fool," a male voice rumbled in his ear, and Asa turned to see Concord.

Of course.

"So glad you're enjoying your free tickets," he bit out.

Concord shook his graying head. "Not that. *That.*" And he tilted his head to where Eve was smiling sweetly at Rose.

Asa scowled and turned away. "I don't know what you mean."

"Fool."

"Look," Asa said, "no one made you come to my garden, eat my food, and enjoy my theater."

"It's a good theater." Concord looked thoughtful. "And the gardens are nice."

Asa blinked. "What."

His brother looked at him. "I liked it. Rose *loved* it. And the children are already asking to return again. You've done a good job here."

Asa opened his mouth and then shut it.

"Father was sometimes..." Concord scrunched up his face, evidently trying to think of a word, and Asa wondered just how much wine his brother had had to drink. "Conservative."

"Yes?" Asa stared at him incredulously. Calling their father conservative was like calling the ocean wet.

Concord nodded. "A good man, but he didn't like new things." He glanced at Asa. "He should've given you a chance to prove yourself with the theater."

"I..." Asa wasn't sure exactly how to reply to that.

"But," Concord went on, because he'd never learned when to stop, *"you* are a fool if you let Miss Dinwoody get away. Rose says that she means to travel to the Continent soon and you're not going. What kind of man lets his woman run off alone? Have you any idea the sort of fops that inhabit France alone?"

Con had never been anywhere near France, but that wasn't the main issue. "She's not my woman," Asa snarled.

Concord pointed a finger in his face. "You want her to be."

"What if I do?" Asa hissed. "She's leaving me and I can't stay her."

"Then go with her!"

"I'll not leave my garden!"

"Then maybe you deserve to lose her to some frog-eater." Con looked at him. "Brother, don't be a drooling idiot. That woman is worth more than any number of gardens, no matter how magnificent. Take what you want."

Asa sighed, suddenly tired. "What I want and what I can have are two entirely different things. Most men learn that somewhere along the way."

He pushed past Concord and went to Eve.

She was laughing with Rose, but she sobered as he neared. "Asa." She glanced at Rose and almost smiled, but it died on her face. "Do you mind if I have a moment with your brother-in-law so that we might say our farewells before we leave?"

Eve had brought both Rose and Concord in her carriage tonight and naturally would be taking them home as well—without Asa. He meant to spend the night at Harte's Folly, overseeing the garden until daybreak, when the last of his guests left wearily for home.

It was his life's work, after all.

Rose patted her hand. "Of course." She turned a single, searing look on Asa and then turned to walk to her husband.

Eve looked at him gravely. "I'm so happy for you. For your garden. You've done a wonderful thing here, Asa."

"Thanks." The word came out gruffly. He looked away from her. She hadn't said when she'd leave and it might be days yet, but this felt like a farewell. "Have you bought that ticket yet?"

He didn't have to explain what ticket he was talking about.

"Not yet," she said. "Tomorrow, I think."

He stared at her, scowling. "So soon?"

"Yes," she said simply. She looked down. "I'll take Henry, of course, but Jean-Marie and Tess are returning to the small village where she grew up. Jean-Marie says they'll have a tavern there along with Tess's brother."

"You'll have no footman at all on your travels?"

She shrugged. "I'm bringing Ruth—she's quite excited—and I'm thinking of bringing Bob the footman from my brother's house."

"You should," he said, frowning. "You need a bodyguard."

"Do I?" She tilted her head. "I'm not sure that I do anymore."

"Just…" He squinted; the fireworks were shining in his eyes. "Just keep yourself safe when you go."

"I will." Lightly she touched her fingers to his cheek. "Good night, Asa Makepeace."

He bent and brushed his lips over her cheek.

320 ELIZABETH HOYT

Then he turned away.

Asa took one last look at success, at his guests laughing and merry, at Eve with fireworks in her eyes, at his garden packed with revelers, and turned and walked inside the theater.

A few dancers and actresses were still in the back, dressing and shouting happily at each other. Success meant money for everyone.

His theater and his garden—hell, *he*—was a grand *fucking* success.

Asa pushed open the door to his office, settled himself at the table, and then heard an odd sound. He got up again and peered over the table. There in the nest of old costumes that Henry had made was Dove, sitting and blinking beadily at him.

"How the hell did you get in?" Asa snorted, and sat back down. "Not that it matters. She's going away, Dove, old girl, though I suppose once she finds that you're back she'll take you as well. She'll leave just me behind."

He kept several bottles of wine under his table and he took one out, drawing the cork with his teeth as he threw his legs up on the table.

He raised his bottle to bloody success and took a drink.

A door slammed in the theater and then it was oddly quiet. He could hear the revelry from without, the sounds of laughter and chatter and the BOOM of the firecrackers, but it was all a bit muffled.

He took another drink, long and sour. It wasn't very good wine.

It occurred to him that his brother Concord, whom he usually regarded as a self-important windbag, might, in this case, actually be right.

He was indeed a fool.

"Fuck it."

Asa tossed the bottle to a corner and was out the door before it shattered. He ran through the theater, ignoring exclamations from musicians and singers as he flew past. He'd only left her moments before. She couldn't have gone far.

Outside the fireworks were exploding in a whistling, shrieking grand finale, all heads turned to the colorfully lit sky.

All except Asa's. He shoved through the crowd, cursing and looking for her. She must still be here. Who would leave before the final big fireworks display?

But he'd given her no hope. He'd practically kissed her good-bye.

Something very like panic tightened Asa's chest.

And then he saw her.

She was standing nearly in the center of the courtyard, his family and her friends surrounding her and with her sweet, solemn face tilted toward the exploding stars.

One last firework went up with a concussive BOOM!

And then there was abrupt silence as lights like fireflies drifted toward the ground.

He walked through the shower toward her and she must've sensed him for she turned her head to look at him. The torches around the courtyard lit her widening eyes.

He reached her side and fell to his knees.

"Marry me," he said, looking up at her. "I fucking love you, Eve Dinwoody, more than my garden, more than my life. I want to spend the rest of my days being managed by you, bickering with you, and falling asleep holding you in my arms. Leave or stay in London, I don't give a bloody goddamn, just as long as you let me be by your side. So will you marry me, Eve?"

For a long moment—the longest moment of his life—she stared at him, her eyes wide.

And then her plush lips parted. "Oh, Asa. *Yes.*"

Around them a cheer went up from family and friends and strangers—all the gathered crowd, both theater folk and guests of Harte's Folly.

But Asa Makepeace didn't care. He was kissing Eve, his sweet, wonderful, beautiful harpy.

Chapter Twenty

*Now here is a thing you may scarcely credit, for with that
single slap Dove slew the sorceress. The sorceress, you see,
had but one weakness, and that, as it turns out, was the
touch of a mortal.*
Dove looked at Eric and said, "Oh, I am so sorry!"
And at her words he threw back his head and laughed.
*"Never apologize, for you've freed me from slavery,
gentle Dove." ...*
—From *The Lion and the Dove*

The clock in the hall was chiming the midnight hour as
Bridget Crumb made her way to the duke's bedroom. It had
occurred to her earlier that day, while instructing the maids
on how to make a polishing cream of beeswax and lemon
oil, that the bed in His Grace's room was uncommonly big,
with an uncommonly thick headboard. The kind that might
very well conceal a secret compartment or two.

Which was why she was letting herself into his rooms
so very late at night.

The nude portrait of the duke watched as Bridget set
down her candlestick on the desk. The flame flickered and
bent as if from a draft.

Bridget frowned, hesitated, and then turned toward the

bed. First she felt over every inch of the big melon-shaped posters, finding nothing besides the fact that they needed to be dusted.

She stood back and stared at the headboard for a moment, but there really was no other choice. She kicked off her slippers and crawled onto the monstrosity of a bed. Once at the headboard, she began a careful, tedious probe of the ornate carvings, running her fingers over curlicues and hollows. Her fingers slid into a small hole and suddenly a panel the size of her palm popped open.

Bridget stilled, almost unable to believe her luck. She stuck her fingers into the little opening and retrieved a miniature painting: a man, his wife, and a baby.

The woman was dressed in the costume of a lady from India.

For a moment all was silence, save for her breathing. Triumph raced through Bridget's chest. At last!

Then she heard a masculine chuckle behind her.

Bridget froze, ice sliding down her spine. The sound could be nothing else, not the wind or a creaky house or even a mouse in the walls.

She turned, pushing the panel shut with her shoulder, and palming the portrait as she did so.

The Duke of Montgomery, all golden hair and sharp blue eyes, and wearing a purple velvet suit, smiled at her from the armchair in the far corner of the room.

"A lovely woman in my bed, what a fetching surprise." He cocked his head, a corner of his beautiful mouth curving cruelly. "Tell me, Mrs. Crumb, what are you looking for?"

"I HAVE SOMETHING to discuss with you," Asa told Eve late that night.

"Do you?" she asked absently. He was sprawled entirely nude over her bed and she'd made him *promise* not to move for at least five minutes.

"Yes," he said, his voice sounding a little strained, possibly because she was tracing up the veins of his cock. "If you still wish to go to the Continent to find your brother, I want to go with you."

"Hmm," she replied, because penises were truly fascinating things.

He lifted his head to peer at her.

"No moving," she snapped.

He obediently let his head fall to the pillows. "I'll need to find a manager to take my place while I'm gone."

"Yes?"

"And we'll need to marry first," he rasped. "I think my sisters and sister-in-law are already planning the wedding. I told them to keep it small, but I have a feeling it won't be."

Her heart beat a little faster as she trailed a finger around the head of his cock. "I'd rather like a big wedding."

He frowned ferociously. "Then you'll have one. I'll give you anything you want; you have to know that, Eve."

She arched an eyebrow. "Anything?"

He glared at her. "Yes!"

She leaned forward and touched her tongue to the moisture seeping from the slit at the top.

"Fucking God!"

She pulled back, a little shocked. "You swear too much, you know."

"Goddamn it, Eve, I just want to make you happy."

"I am," she said softly. "You make me very happy indeed and I can't wait to be married to you."

He rolled his eyes. "Then come here and kiss me properly."

She cast a forlorn look at his penis.

"You can play with my prick later."

"Promise?"

"Yes."

He pulled her into his arms and kissed her very lewdly and thoroughly.

"I love you, Eve Dinwoody," he said softly, his voice so low it was nearly a purr, when at last he pulled away. "I love you more than wine and my right hand and my garden. I think I loved you the day you burst into my rooms."

She pulled back at that, because there were only so many ridiculous statements she could take. "You did not! You told me I had an enormous nose."

He kissed her on the nose. "Well, maybe not then, but I was fascinated by you in any case. And I was a little in love with you by the time you made me touch myself in your carriage."

"I didn't *make* you," she retorted. "You seemed very happy to do it indeed."

"Hush," he said, "I'm trying to declare my love for you and you're ruining it."

"Not really," she whispered. "It seems quite perfect to me."

"Does it?" he asked, suddenly serious. "Because I would do anything for you, Eve, anything. If it means telling you I love you every day of my sorry life I'll do it, just to make up for my idiocy."

"Good," she whispered. "Because I love you, too."

He smiled then, that wide, confident, dangerous smile— that smile that was *all* hers now—and kissed her.

Epilogue

*"Now I can take you home," Eric said.
But at his words Dove grew sad. "I have no home,"
she said, and told him her sorrowful tale and that
her father and his soldiers no doubt still hunted her
through the forest.
"Well, that's easily answered," said Eric, and, taking
the bags of silk, emeralds, and perfumes, they set off
for her father's palace.
The moment they stepped foot inside the king's
courtyard, he came rushing out. "I'll have your heart!"
he cried to Dove.
But Eric turned into an enormous lion and, with a
terrible roar, he tore into the king's great belly. Out of
the dead king's belly spilled all the hearts of his children,
still beating, and as they did so, the children rose from
where they had been buried in the courtyard. The hearts
flew to the children they belonged to and entered their
chests and this is how the king's children were reborn,
whole and alive again.
"Sister!" called the cohort of reborn princes
and princesses. "You have saved us and thus
must be our queen."
Then the king's soldiers knelt and pledged
allegiance to Dove.
The lion turned and came to Dove as well, but when
he went to kneel, she tangled her fingers in his thick mane.
"Not you, dear Eric. You have no need to kneel before me."*

At that he became a man again and asked, "What then shall I be?"
"Why, my husband and king of this land," said she, "to rule beside me all the days of our lives, happily and in peace."
And so they did.
—From *The Lion and the Dove*

DISCOVER HOW THE
SIZZLING MAIDEN LANE
SERIES STARTED!

PLEASE SEE THE NEXT
PAGE FOR AN EXCERPT FROM

Wicked Intentions

Chapter One

*Once upon a time, in a land long forgotten now, there
lived a mighty king, feared by all and loved by none.
His name was King Lockedheart....*
—from *King Lockedheart*

LONDON
FEBRUARY 1737

A woman abroad in St. Giles at midnight was either very
foolish or very desperate. Or, as in her own case, Temperance Dews reflected wryly, a combination of both.

"'Tis said the Ghost of St. Giles haunts on nights like
this," Nell Jones, Temperance's maidservant, said chattily
as she skirted a noxious puddle in the narrow alley.

Temperance glanced dubiously at her. Nell had spent
three years in a traveling company of actors and sometimes had a tendency toward melodrama.

"There's no ghost haunting St. Giles," Temperance
replied firmly. The cold winter night was frightening
enough without the addition of specters.

"Oh, indeed, there is." Nell hoisted the sleeping babe

in her arms higher. "He wears a black mask and a harlequin's motley and carries a wicked sword."

Temperance frowned. "A harlequin's motley? That doesn't sound very ghostlike."

"It's ghostlike if he's the dead spirit of a harlequin player come back to haunt the living."

"For bad reviews?"

Nell sniffed. "*And* he's disfigured."

"How would anyone know that if he's masked?"

They were coming to a turn in the alley, and Temperance thought she saw light up ahead. She held her lantern high and gripped the ancient pistol in her other hand a little tighter. The weapon was heavy enough to make her arm ache. She could have brought a sack to carry it in, but that would've defeated its purpose as a deterrent. Though loaded, the pistol held but one shot, and to tell the truth, she was somewhat hazy on the actual operation of the weapon.

Still, the pistol looked dangerous, and Temperance was grateful for that. The night was black, the wind moaning eerily, bringing with it the smell of excrement and rotting offal. The sounds of St. Giles rose about them—voices raised in argument, moans and laughter, and now and again the odd, chilling scream. St. Giles was enough to send the most intrepid woman running for her life.

And that was without Nell's conversation.

"*Horribly* disfigured," Nell continued, ignoring Temperance's logic. "'Tis said his lips and eyelids are clean burned off, as if he died in a fire long ago. He seems to grin at you with his great yellow teeth as he comes to pull the guts from your belly."

Temperance wrinkled her nose. "Nell!"

"That's what they say," Nell said virtuously. "The ghost guts his victims and plays with their entrails before slipping away into the night."

Temperance shivered. "Why would he do that?"

"Envy," Nell said matter-of-factly. "He envies the living."

"Well, I don't believe in spirits in any case." Temperance took a breath as they turned the corner into a small, wretched courtyard. Two figures stood at the opposite end, but they scuttled away at their approach. Temperance let out her breath. "Lord, I hate being abroad at night."

Nell patted the infant's back. "Only a half mile more. Then we can put this wee one to bed and send for the wet nurse in the morning."

Temperance bit her lip as they ducked into another alley. "Do you think she'll live until morning?"

But Nell, usually quite free with her opinions, was silent. Temperance peered ahead and hurried her step. The baby looked to be only weeks old and had not yet made a sound since they'd recovered her from the arms of her dead mother. Normally a thriving infant was quite loud. Terrible to think that she and Nell might've made this dangerous outing for naught.

But then what choice had there been, really? When she'd received word at the Home for Unfortunate Infants and Foundling Children that a baby was in need of her help, it had still been light. She'd known from bitter experience that if they'd waited until morn to retrieve the child, it would either have expired in the night from lack of care or would've already been sold for a beggar's prop. She shuddered. The children bought by beggars were often made more pitiful to elicit sympathy from passersby.

An eye might be put out or a limb broken or twisted. No, she'd really had no choice. The baby couldn't wait until morning.

Still, she'd be very happy when they made it back to the home.

They were in a narrow passage now, the tall houses on either side leaning inward ominously. Nell was forced to walk behind Temperance or risk brushing the sides of the buildings. A scrawny cat snaked by, and then there was a shout very near.

Temperance's steps faltered.

"Someone's up ahead," Nell whispered hoarsely.

They could hear scuffling and then a sudden high scream.

Temperance swallowed. The alley had no side passages. They could either retreat or continue—and to retreat meant another twenty minutes added to their journey.

That decided her. The night was chilly, and the cold wasn't good for the babe.

"Stay close to me," she whispered to Nell.

"Like a flea on a dog," Nell muttered.

Temperance squared her shoulders and held the pistol firmly in front of her. Winter, her youngest brother, had said that one need only point it and shoot. That couldn't be too hard. The light from the lantern spilled before them as she entered another crooked courtyard. Here she stood still for just a second, her light illuminating the scene ahead like a pantomime on a stage.

A man lay on the ground, bleeding from the head. But that wasn't what froze her—blood and even death were common enough in St. Giles. No, what arrested her was the *second* man. He crouched over the first, his black cloak spread to either side of him like the wings of a great bird of prey. He held a long black walking stick, the end tipped with silver, echoing his hair, which was silver as well. It fell straight and long, glinting in the lantern's light. Though his face was mostly in darkness, his eyes glinted from under the brim of a black tricorne. Temperance could feel the weight of the stranger's stare. It was as if he physically touched her.

"Lord save and preserve us from evil," Nell murmured, for the first time sounding fearful. "Come away, ma'am. Swiftly!"

Thus urged, Temperance ran across the courtyard, her shoes clattering on the cobblestones. She darted into another passage and left the scene behind.

"Who was he, Nell?" she panted as they made their way through the stinking alley. "Do you know?"

The passage let out suddenly into a wider road, and Temperance relaxed a little, feeling safer without the walls pressing in.

Nell spat as if to clear a foul taste from her mouth.

Temperance looked at her curiously. "You sounded like you knew that man."

"Knew him, no," Nell replied. "But I've seen him about. That was Lord Caire. He's best left to himself."

"Why?"

Nell shook her head, pressing her lips firmly together. "I shouldn't be speaking about the likes of him to you at all, ma'am."

Temperance let that cryptic comment go. They were on a better street now—some of the shops had lanterns hanging by the doors, lit by the inhabitants within. Temperance turned one more corner onto Maiden Lane, and the foundling home came within sight. Like its neighbors, it was a tall brick building of cheap construction. The windows were few and very narrow, the doorway unmarked by any sign. In the fifteen precarious years of the foundling home's existence, there had never been a need to advertise.

Abandoned and orphaned children were all too common in St. Giles.

"Home safely," Temperance said as they reached the door. She set down the lantern on the worn stone step and took out the big iron key hanging by a cord at her waist. "I'm looking forward to a dish of hot tea."

"I'll put this wee one to bed," Nell said as they entered the dingy little hall. It was spotlessly clean, but that didn't hide the fallen plaster or the warped floorboards.

"Thank you." Temperance removed her cloak and was just hanging it on a peg when a tall male form appeared at the far doorway.

"Temperance."

She swallowed and turned. "Oh! Oh, Winter, I did not know you'd returned."

"Obviously," her younger brother said drily. He nodded to the maidservant. "A good eventide to you, Nell."

"Sir." Nell curtsied and looked nervously between brother and sister. "I'll just see to the, ah, children, shall I?"

And she fled upstairs, leaving Temperance to face Winter's disapproval alone.

Temperance squared her shoulders and moved past her brother. The foundling home was long and narrow, squeezed by the neighboring houses. There was one room off the small entryway. It was used for dining and, on occasion, receiving the home's infrequent important visitors. At the back of the house were the kitchens, which Temperance entered now. The children had all had their dinner promptly at five o'clock, but neither she nor her brother had eaten.

"I was just about to make some tea," she said as she went to stir the fire. Soot, the home's black cat, got up from his place in front of the hearth and stretched before padding off in search of mice. "There's a bit of beef left from yesterday and some new radishes I bought at market this morning."

Behind her Winter sighed. "Temperance."

She hurried to find the kettle. "The bread's a bit stale, but I can toast it if you like."

He was silent and she finally turned and faced the inevitable.

It was worse than she feared. Winter's long, thin face merely looked sad, which always made her feel terrible. She hated to disappoint him.

"It was still light when we set out," she said in a small voice.

He sighed again, taking off his round black hat and sitting at the kitchen table. "Could you not wait for my return, sister?"

Temperance looked at her brother. Winter was only five and twenty, but he bore himself with the air of a man twice his age. His countenance was lined with weariness, his wide shoulders slumped beneath his ill-fitting black coat, and his long limbs were much too thin. For the last five years, he had taught at the tiny daily school attached to the home.

On Papa's death last year, Winter's work had increased tremendously. Concord, their eldest brother, had taken over the family brewery. Asa, their next-eldest brother, had always been rather dismissive of the foundling home and had a mysterious business of his own. Both of their sisters, Verity, the eldest of the family, and Silence, the youngest, were married. That had left Winter to manage the foundling home. Even with her help—she'd worked at the home since the death of her husband nine years before—the task was overwhelming for one man. Temperance feared for her brother's well-being, but both the foundling home and the tiny day school had been founded by Papa. Winter felt it was his filial duty to keep the two charities alive.

If his health did not give out first.

She filled the teakettle from the water jar by the back door. "Had we waited, it would have been full dark with no assurance that the babe would still be there." She glanced at him as she placed the kettle over the fire. "Besides, have you not enough work to do?"

"If I lose my sister, think you that I'd be more free of work?"

Temperance looked away guiltily.

Her brother's voice softened. "And that discounts the lifelong sorrow I would feel had anything happened to you this night."

"Nell knew the mother of the baby—a girl of less than fifteen years." Temperance took out the bread and carved it into thin slices. "Besides, I carried the pistol."

"Hmm," Winter said behind her. "And had you been accosted, would you have used it?"

"Yes, of course," she said with flat certainty.

"And if the shot misfired?"

She wrinkled her nose. Their father had brought up all her brothers to debate a point finely, and that fact could be quite irritating at times.

She carried the bread slices to the fire to toast. "In any case, nothing did happen."

"*This* night." Winter sighed again. "Sister, you must promise me you'll not act so foolishly again."

"Mmm," Temperance mumbled, concentrating on the toast. "How was your day at the school?"

For a moment, she thought Winter wouldn't consent to her changing the subject. Then he said, "A good day, I think. The Samuels lad remembered his Latin lesson finally, and I did not have to punish any of the boys."

Temperance glanced at him with sympathy. She knew Winter hated to take a switch to a palm, let alone cane a boy's bottom. On the days that Winter had felt he must punish a boy, he came home in a black mood.

"I'm glad," she said simply.

He stirred in his chair. "I returned for luncheon, but you were not here."

Temperance took the toast from the fire and placed it on the table. "I must have been taking Mary Found to her new position. I think she'll do quite well there. Her mistress seemed very kind, and the woman took only five pounds as payment to apprentice Mary as her maid."

"God willing she'll actually teach the child something so we won't see Mary Found again."

Temperance poured the hot water into their small teapot and brought it to the table. "You sound cynical, brother."

Winter passed a hand over his brow. "Forgive me. Cynicism is a terrible vice. I shall try to correct my humor."

Temperance sat and silently served her brother, waiting. Something more than her late-night adventure was bothering him.

At last he said, "Mr. Wedge visited whilst I ate my luncheon."

Mr. Wedge was their landlord. Temperance paused, her hand on the teapot. "What did he say?"

"He'll give us only another two weeks, and then he'll have the foundling home forcibly vacated."

"Dear God."

Temperance stared at the little piece of beef on her plate. It was stringy and hard and from an obscure part of the cow, but she'd been looking forward to it. Now her appetite was suddenly gone. The foundling home's rent was in arrears—they hadn't been able to pay the full rent last month and nothing at all this month. Perhaps she shouldn't have bought the radishes, Temperance reflected morosely. But the children hadn't had anything but broth and bread for the last week.

"If only Sir Gilpin had remembered us in his will," she murmured.

Sir Stanley Gilpin had been Papa's good friend and the patron of the foundling home. A retired theater owner, he'd managed to make a fortune on the South Sea Company and had been wily enough to withdraw his funds before the notorious bubble burst. Sir Gilpin had been a generous patron while alive, but on his unexpected death six months before, the home had been left floundering. They'd limped along, using what money had been saved, but now they were in desperate straits.

"Sir Gilpin was an unusually generous man, it would seem," Winter replied. "I have not been able to find another gentleman so willing to fund a home for the infant poor."

Temperance poked at her beef. "What shall we do?"

"The Lord shall provide," Winter said, pushing aside his

half-eaten meal and rising. "And if he does not, well, then perhaps I can take on private students in the evenings."

"You already work too many hours," Temperance protested. "You hardly have time to sleep as it is."

Winter shrugged. "How can I live with myself if the innocents we protect are thrown into the street?"

Temperance looked down at her plate. She had no answer to that.

"Come." Her brother held out his hand and smiled.

Winter's smiles were so rare, so precious. When he smiled, his entire face lit as if from a flame within, and a dimple appeared on one cheek, making him look boyish, more his true age.

One couldn't help smiling back when Winter smiled, and Temperance did so as she laid her hand in his. "Where will we go?"

"Let us visit our charges," he said as he took a candle and led her to the stairs. "Have you ever noticed that they look quite angelic when asleep?"

Temperance laughed as they climbed the narrow wooden staircase to the next floor. There was a small hall here with three doors leading off it. They peered in the first as Winter held his candle high. Six tiny cots lined the walls of the room. The youngest of the foundlings slept here, two or three to a cot. Nell lay in an adult-sized bed by the door, already asleep.

Winter walked to the cot nearest Nell. Two babes lay there. The first was a boy, red-haired and pink-cheeked, sucking on his fist as he slept. The second child was half the size of the first, her cheeks pale and her eyes hollowed, even in sleep. Tiny whorls of fine black hair decorated her crown.

"This is the baby you rescued tonight?" Winter asked softly.

Temperance nodded. The little girl looked even more frail next to the thriving baby boy.

But Winter merely touched the baby's hand with a gentle finger. "How do you like the name Mary Hope?"

Temperance swallowed past the thickness in her throat. "'Tis very apt."

Winter nodded and, with a last caress for the tiny babe, left the room. The next door led to the boys' dormitory. Four beds held thirteen boys, all under the age of nine—the age when they were apprenticed out. The boys lay with limbs sprawled, faces flushed in sleep. Winter smiled and pulled a blanket over the three boys nearest the door, tucking in a leg that had escaped the bed.

Temperance sighed. "One would never think that they spent an hour at luncheon hunting for rats in the alley."

"Mmm," Winter answered as he closed the door softly behind them. "Small boys grow so swiftly to men."

"They do indeed." Temperance opened the last door—the one to the girls' dormitory—and a small face immediately popped off a pillow.

"Did you get 'er, ma'am?" Mary Whitsun whispered hoarsely.

She was the eldest of the girls in the foundling home, named for the Whitsunday morning nine years before when she'd been brought to the home as a child of three. Young though Mary Whitsun was, Temperance had to sometimes leave her in charge of the other children—as she'd had to tonight.

"Yes, Mary," Temperance whispered back. "Nell and I brought the babe home safely."

"I'm glad." Mary Whitsun yawned widely.

"You did well watching the children," Temperance whispered. "Now sleep. A new day will be here soon."

Mary Whitsun nodded sleepily and closed her eyes.

Winter picked up a candlestick from a little table by the door and led the way out of the girls' dormitory. "I shall take your kind advice, sister, and bid you good night."

He lit the candlestick from his own and gave it to Temperance.

"Sleep well," she replied. "I think I'll have one more cup of tea before retiring."

"Don't stay up too late," Winter said. He touched her cheek with a finger—much as he had the babe—and turned to mount the stairs.

Temperance watched him go, frowning at how slowly he moved up the stairs. It was past midnight, and he would rise again before five of the clock to read, write letters to prospective patrons, and prepare his school lessons for the day. He would lead the morning prayers at breakfast, hurry to his job as schoolmaster, work all morning before taking one hour for a meager luncheon, and then work again until after dark. In the evening, he heard the girls' lessons and read from the Bible to the older children. Yet, when she voiced her worries, Winter would merely raise an eyebrow and inquire who would do the work if not he?

Temperance shook her head. She should be to bed as well—her day started at six of the clock—but these moments by herself in the evening were precious. She'd sacrifice a half hour's sleep to sit alone with a cup of tea.

So she took her candle back downstairs. Out of habit, she checked to see that the front door was locked and barred. The wind whistled and shook the shutters as she made her way to the kitchen, and the back door rattled. She checked it as well and was relieved to see the door still barred. Temperance shivered, glad she was no longer outside on a night like this. She rinsed out the teapot and filled it again. To make a pot of tea with fresh leaves and only for herself was a terrible luxury. Soon she'd have to give this up as well, but tonight she'd enjoy her cup.

Off the kitchen was a tiny room. Its original purpose was forgotten, but it had a small fireplace, and Temperance had made it her own private sitting room. Inside was a stuffed chair, much battered but refurbished with a quilted blanket thrown over the back. A small table and a footstool were there as well—all she needed to sit by herself next to a warm fire.

Humming, Temperance placed her teapot and cup, a small dish of sugar, and the candlestick on an old wooden tray. Milk would have been nice, but what was left from this morning would go toward the children's breakfast on the morrow. As it was, the sugar was a shameful luxury. She looked at the small bowl, biting her lip. She really ought to put it back; she simply didn't deserve it. After a moment, she took the sugar dish off the tray, but the sacrifice brought her no feeling of wholesome goodness. Instead she was only weary. Temperance picked up the tray, and because both her hands were full, she backed into the door leading to her little sitting room.

Which was why she didn't notice until she turned that the sitting room was already occupied.

There, sprawled in her chair like a conjured demon, sat Lord Caire. His silver hair spilled over the shoulders of his black cape, a cocked hat lay on one knee, and his right hand caressed the end of his long ebony walking stick.

This close, she realized that his hair gave lie to his age. The lines about his startlingly blue eyes were few, his mouth and jaw firm. He couldn't be much older than five and thirty.

He inclined his head at her entrance and spoke, his voice deep and smooth and softly dangerous.

"Good evening, Mrs. Dews."

SHE STOOD WITH quiet confidence, this respectable woman who lived in the sewer that was St. Giles. Her eyes had widened at the sight of him, but she made no move to flee. Indeed, finding a strange man in her pathetic sitting room seemed not to frighten her at all.

Interesting.

"I am Lazarus Huntington, Lord Caire," he said.

"I know. What are you doing here?"

He tilted his head, studying her. She knew him, yet did not recoil in horror? Yes, she'd do quite well. "I've come to make a proposition to you, Mrs. Dews."

Still no sign of fear, though she eyed the doorway. "You've chosen the wrong lady, my lord. The night is late. Please leave my house."

No fear and no deference to his rank. An interesting woman indeed.

"My proposition is not, er, *illicit* in nature," he drawled. "In fact, it's quite respectable. Or nearly so."

She sighed and looked down at her tray, and then back up at him. "Would you like a cup of tea?"

He almost smiled. Tea? When had he last been offered something so very prosaic by a woman? He couldn't remember.

But he replied gravely enough. "Thank you, no."

She nodded. "Then if you don't mind?"

He waved a hand to indicate permission.

She set the tea tray on the wretched little table and sat on the padded footstool to pour herself a cup. He watched her. She was a monochromatic study. Her dress, bodice, hose, and shoes were all flat black. A fichu tucked in at her severe neckline, an apron, and a cap—no lace or ruffles—were all white. No color marred her aspect, making the lush red of her full lips all the more startling. She wore the clothes of a nun, yet had the mouth of a sybarite.

The contrast was fascinating—and arousing.

"You're a Puritan?" he asked.

Her beautiful mouth compressed. "No."

"Ah." He noted she did not say she was Church of England either. She probably belonged to one of the many obscure nonconformist sects, but then he was interested in her religious beliefs only as they impacted his own mission.

She took a sip of tea. "How do you know my name?"

He shrugged. "Mrs. Dews and her brother are well-known for their good deeds."

"Really?" Her tone was dry. "I was not aware we were so famous beyond the boundaries of St. Giles."

She might look demure, but there were teeth behind the prim expression. And she was quite right—he would never have heard of her had he not spent the last month stalking the shadows of St. Giles. Stalking fruitlessly, which was why he'd followed her home and sat before this miserable fire now.

"How did you get in?" she asked.

"I believe the back door was unlocked."

"No, it wasn't." Her brown eyes met his over her teacup. They were an odd light color, almost golden. "Why are you here, Lord Caire?"

"I wish to hire you, Mrs. Dews," he said softly.

She stiffened and set her teacup down on the tray. "No."

"You haven't heard the task for which I wish to hire you."

"It's past midnight, my lord, and I'm not inclined to games even during the day. Please leave or I shall be forced to call my brother."

He didn't move. "Not a husband?"

"I'm widowed, as I'm sure you already know." She turned to look into the fire, presenting a dismissive profile to him.

He stretched his legs in what room there was, his boots nearly in the fire. "You're quite correct—I do know. I also know that you and your brother have not paid the rent on this property in nearly two months."

She said nothing, merely sipping her tea.

"I'll pay handsomely for your time," he murmured.

She looked at him finally, and he saw a golden flame in those pale brown eyes. "You think all women can be bought?"

He rubbed his thumb across his chin, considering the question. "Yes, I do, though perhaps not strictly by money. And I do not limit it to women—all men can be bought in one form or another as well. The only trouble is in finding the applicable currency."

She simply stared at him with those odd eyes.

He dropped his hand, resting it on his knee. "You, for instance, Mrs. Dews. I would've thought your currency would be money for your foundling home, but perhaps I'm mistaken. Perhaps I've been fooled by your plain exterior, your reputation as a prim widow. Perhaps you would be better persuaded by influence or knowledge or even the pleasures of the flesh."

"You still haven't said what you want me for."

Though she hadn't moved, hadn't changed expression at all, her voice had a rough edge. He caught it only because he had years of experience at the chase. His nostrils flared involuntarily, as if the hunter within was trying to scent her. Which of his list had interested her?

"A guide." His eyelids drooped as he pretended to examine his fingernails. "Merely that." He watched her from under his brows and saw when that lush mouth pursed.

"A guide to what?"

"St. Giles."

"Why do you need a guide?"

Ah, this was where it got tricky. "I'm searching for…a certain person in St. Giles. I would like to interview some of the inhabitants, but I find my search confounded by my ignorance of the area and the people and by their reluctance to talk to me. Hence, a guide."

Her eyes had narrowed as she listened, her fingers tapping against the teacup. "Whom do you search for?"

He shook his head slowly. "Not unless you agree to be my guide."

"And that is all you want? A guide? Nothing else?"

He nodded, watching her.

She turned to look into the fire as if consulting it. For a moment, the only sound in the room was the snap of a piece of coal falling. He waited patiently, caressing the silver head of his cane.

Then she faced him fully. "You're right. Your money does not tempt me. It's a stopgap measure that would only delay our eventual eviction."

He cocked his head, watching as she carefully licked those lush lips, preparing her argument, no doubt. He felt the beat of the pulse beneath his skin, his body's response to her feminine vitality. "What do you want, then, Mrs. Dews?"

She met his gaze levelly, almost in challenge. "I want you to introduce me to the wealthy and titled people of London. I want you to help me find a new patron for our foundling home."

Lazarus kept his mouth firmly straight, but he felt a surge of triumph as the prim widow ran headlong into his talons.

"Done."